BENEATH
the
WATER

ALSO BY SARAH PAINTER

In the Light of What We See
The Garden of Magic
The Secrets of Ghosts
The Language of Spells

BENEATH

the

WATER

SARAH PAINTER

Text copyright © 2018 by Sarah Painter

Published by Lake Union Publishing, Seattle

www.apub.com

Amazon, the Amazon logo, and Lake Union Publishing are trademarks of Amazon.com, Inc., or its affiliates.

ISBN-13: 9781542047012
ISBN-10: 1542047013

Cover design by Emma Rogers

Printed in the United States of America

For Mum and Dad, with love and gratitude.

3rd October, 1847

My dearest Mary,

I have barely left your side and am already writing my first letter home – I can hear faither's words in my ears, telling me to 'haud on' and settle first, but my thoughts do not feel like true reflections until I have shared them with you. I do hope you are able to respond with haste and that you can tell me all that has occurred in my absence. I particularly wish to hear whether Flora D— was quite as green as she appeared. Some might think me wicked for thinking ill of such a wraith, but you know how well she tormented me for being both unlovely and likely to remain unloved. I can only hope that she is dining heartily upon her old opinion!

Your 'poorly wee Jessie' has managed a good match at last. I feel as though I have been tugging at the skirts of life, hoping to be asked to join the dance and now – happy day – my card is full. I know that you worry, but my only concern is that the folk at home understand the nature of our swift union. Mr Lockhart's readiness to marry stemmed from his ardent admiration and the pressure of his important work.

After all the excitement at home, the journey to Edinburgh felt very long and I still feel as though I am rattling in that coach. The causey stanes as we drew near – my dear! I thought my teeth might shake loose. Mr Lockhart laughed when I told him, but he patted my hand quite kindly. We are still rather strange with one another, but perhaps that is usual.

The weather was unseasonably bright and the house was shown in good aspect as we arrived. There are more trees than I imagined when I pictured Auld Reekie, and with the flaming red leaves set against the grey stone, my new home looked very fine indeed. Mr Lockhart made no exaggeration when he described his town house, it is both grand and large, with four stories and steps up to the front door bordered by shiny black railings. I confess I feel quite unworthy, but I hope I shall adjust in time. The high ceilings and wide stairs do not feel homely although that is not helped by the lack of furniture. Some rooms have shrouded items, as if some period of mourning is still in effect, while others are simply bare. It is cold, too, as my husband (see how I use the phrase – I am trying very hard to grow accustomed) prefers not to waste coal. Do not fret on my account, I believe there is plenty. Mr Lockhart is in great demand. Both with his work and with the men who wish to consult with him at every hour of the day and night. It is a far cry from our quiet wee village and I am frightened I shall let him down. I shall stop there afore I get maudlin.

I miss you and the family terribly and I'm still your wee Jinty in my heart. Please kiss faither for me.

Love always,

Mrs Jessie Lockhart

(Your wee Jinty)

CHAPTER ONE

We're all dying one minute at a time, it's just some of us are more aware of it. Stella Jackson placed her hand over her hammering heart and tried to slow her breathing. The familiar tightness in her chest increased. It became a band of iron which cinched her ribs smaller with every inhalation until she was taking shallow sips of air. She put one hand out, instinctively reaching to brace herself, relaxing her knees in case she fainted. Stella had done so many times before and knew it was better to crumple like a puppet with its strings cut, rather than topple like a tree.

It was his jacket. It was still hung there in the wardrobe and Stella had forgotten. She had not even been thinking about him when she opened the wardrobe door; hadn't thought about him in all the time since she'd woken up and dressed and had her morning coffee. That small miracle evaporated now, in the face of his navy-blue, mid-weight casual jacket. It was a velvet-like material and one of his favourites. She pinched the soft fabric between finger and thumb and wondered how he had been managing without it, whether he missed it at all.

Stella leaned against the wall and kicked the wardrobe door shut, hiding the jacket from view. It didn't help; the damage was already done. Ben's blue jacket. Ben. She closed her eyes and let her legs fold, her back sliding down the wall until she was sat on her bedroom floor.

Stella tipped her head back and let the tears come, wiping them monotonously with the sleeves of her woolly cardigan.

Her phone was buzzing. The screen was blurry but she registered that it was the agency. They would be calling with a job or to tell her that she was running late for one she'd forgotten about. Either option was distinctly unattractive, so she ignored it. She had always been so reliable, but the break-up had smashed everything into pieces, including her work ethic.

Once she could blink away the tears and see clearly, Stella looked through her emails, trying to summon the energy to reply to the increasingly concerned – and occasionally irritated – messages from her best friend, Caitlin. Or at the very least to distract herself from unhelpful looping thoughts. There was an email from her mum, too, wondering if she would like to visit on the weekend. There was mention of a roast lunch, a gentle countryside walk, and Stella tried to picture it, to conjure the comfort of home and have it fill the empty space which was gaping in her middle. Instead she found panic. It would be so easy to go home to Reading, to curl up in her old, familiar bedroom and slip into her old role. Poor little Stella. In an instant this dream of living a real life could be snuffed out.

Why had he left the jacket? Had he wanted, on some level, to leave a door open? A reason to contact her? He didn't seem to need excuses though, had been phoning and texting and emailing her every week since he left. Maybe, and Stella acknowledged that this was an unlikely, desperate thought, maybe he had wanted to leave a part of himself in their home. Maybe it meant that this was temporary, a nightmare from which she could wake up.

Stella pulled herself up from the carpet and went to the bathroom to splash water on her face. She avoided looking in the mirror. The big stone tiles, so carefully chosen, seemed to be moving inwards, compressing the space. She had tiled the walls and floor all in the same colour, aiming for chic minimalism, but it just increased the sense of being inside a box.

Downstairs, her second mug of coffee was on the low table in the living room, cold, and the television was playing, the sound muted. At once, Stella knew she couldn't stay in this house any longer. She had managed four months, had imagined that she had turned a corner, was on an even keel – and a million other trite phrases for the ability to get through the day without falling into a black hole – but the jacket had shattered that illusion. 'I am not okay,' Stella said to the table. The words came out very quietly, almost a whisper. It was like a promise. *I am not okay. I am not okay.*

Stella forced herself into motion. She made more coffee and cut up the apple that lay untouched on a plate, as she steeled herself to call the agency. She would see if she could get a placement for the rest of the week. She didn't like to think any further than that, but it was a start. Caitlin was right; she needed to keep to a routine, and work would help her to get back to normal. She tidied away the laundry first, folding and smoothing clothes until she could feel her breathing was even and deep. Or as deep as it ever got. The phone rang, making Stella jump, even though she knew it was probably a cold call about PPI or double-glazing. The display showed Ben's number and Stella's heart stuttered. She was powerless to resist. She could no more ignore his call than she could fly. She was unable to take her hand off the stove, no matter how much it hurt.

'Darling.' Ben's voice sent a bolt of longing from her toes to the top of her head. She closed her eyes, as if that would help.

'I'm running late,' Stella lied. 'Work.' She wondered if he was going to ask about his jacket and how freaked out she would be if he did. She'd always thought they were so in tune that they must have some kind of psychic link, but a demonstration of it would not be welcome now. It would only hurt more.

'This won't take a sec,' Ben said. 'I just need to check some figures with you. About the house.'

The house. Not 'our house'. Stella put her hand instinctively to her chest, but her heart wasn't racing.

'I still think you should keep it,' Ben said, oblivious. 'I don't like to think of you having to move. I could help you out with the finances if you could just tell me how much—'

'A change will do me good,' Stella said. She didn't want his guilt-money and she didn't want to talk about the mortgage, the final splitting of their entwined lives.

'But if it's just a matter of a few months, just until you get back on your feet. Or until you—'

Stella could sense the words 'meet someone else' lining up and she spoke quickly, interrupting him before he could get them out. 'I want to move. It's cool.' Cool? Where had that come from? Nothing about this was cool.

'I understand.' Ben was using a strangely careful voice. She missed him so much. Not the Ben she was speaking to at that moment – the new Ben, the one who spoke gently to her as if she might break at any moment, fly apart at the seams and smash ornaments – but the old Ben. The Ben who belonged with the jacket she had found in the wardrobe. The Ben who had loved her. The Ben who had wanted to build a life with her.

'I know this has been hard,' Ben was saying, 'but your mum says you're still planning on selling up and we both think you're being too hasty. I mean, it's a stressful business.'

He paused and Stella wondered when he had spoken to her mother. They used to talk all the time. She would hear him on the phone to her, relaying news about Stella's health, her latest check-up, how well she was doing. Stella had pretended to be annoyed, with a 'don't talk about me', but she had loved it. It had made her feel safe, cared for, adored.

When she didn't speak, Ben sighed. It was a 'you are being difficult' sigh. The sigh of a long-suffering man who was being reasonable. 'I just don't like to think of you having to go through all that upheaval. And you love that place, I know you do. I don't want you to make a rash decision and regret it later.'

Stella stared hard at the wallpaper. It had a beautiful abstract pattern reminiscent of a forest, and had cost an arm and two legs from Designers Guild. He was right, she did love the house, and she knew that Ben did, too. She couldn't help but think that was part of why he didn't want her to sell. He didn't want it to fall into a stranger's hands, even though he no longer wanted to live in it himself. 'You're being selfish,' Stella said, surprising herself. 'I need to move on. This isn't helping.'

'I understand,' Ben said quickly. 'You do whatever you think is best for you. I just want you to think about it. Promise me you'll think about it, take a bit more time.'

Stella had been standing too long. She tried not to picture somebody pouring liquid from a jug into her chest cavity, but it was difficult. She'd had too much practice. 'Okay,' she said, to finish the conversation. She ought to say goodbye and hang up, but she couldn't. A small part of her was waiting for Ben to say he'd changed his mind, made a mistake. That stupid small part of her which didn't appear capable of keeping up with current events.

'Right-oh,' he said instead. 'I'll let you get to work.'

Stella almost said she didn't have to go, forgetting that she'd already said that she did.

'Bye, bye, bye.' Ben always said 'bye' three times, very fast, when finishing a telephone conversation, and he hung up immediately afterwards, not waiting for the answering 'goodbye'.

Stella's strength was sapped. She sat on the sofa with her phone and tried not to think about how she ought to be in work. Just because she was grieving didn't mean she didn't need money. It was difficult to be motivated about a losing battle, though. Stella knew that she couldn't afford the mortgage even if she worked seven days a week, and that selling the house was another inevitable stage in this horrible process.

She read the latest email from Caitlin. *Do come up whenever you like. It would be so good to see you.* She and Rob had been inviting Stella to stay with them ever since the break-up and Stella had turned them down. First she'd been in denial, expecting Ben to change his mind. Then she hadn't been able to comprehend leaving what was familiar. Now Stella stared at the black characters on the lit screen and wondered. It would be ridiculous to go to Scotland. And Caitlin and Rob were probably only being polite. Caitlin had been in the role of caretaker their entire friendship, had probably breathed a big sigh of relief when Ben had taken Stella on and was now just offering out of habit, a sense of duty. Stella knew that wasn't really true – or not, at least, entirely true – but it burned nonetheless. *Poor Stella. Poor, delicate Stella.* And now, just when her physical heart had been fixed, her metaphorical one had been smashed to pieces instead.

She ought to stay, to bag up Ben's stuff and drop it at his flat like a grown-up. She ought to phone the agency and get work for the rest of the month. Go to her parents' house on the weekend and smile nicely and eat all of her lunch and laugh at her dad's awful jokes and reassure them that she was fine, fine, fine.

In one of her earliest memories, Stella is at the doctor's surgery. She is sitting on what feels like a very high bed. It's just the standard type, of course, but she is very small and the floor seems far away. Her legs dangle off the edge and she is frightened of toppling forward and falling and falling. Stella is stripped to the waist and ripping electrodes off her chest, as fast as the doctor can reattach them. Her hands are a blur, moving quickly to pull the hated things away, her terror overriding the innate sense of good behaviour.

That's what Stella remembered most: that she had been misbehaving. In that moment, she had been a wild thing.

It felt like that again, now. Stella's heart was racing, stuttering, but there was excitement mixed in with the fear. She felt a wildness. There weren't any electrodes to rip from her skin, but she could do the unexpected.

Stella moved before the feeling passed, knowing that if she waited she'd likely end up back in bed, the duvet pulled over her head.

It took less than an hour to reply to Caitlin's email and pack a bag. There was a line of ornaments on the retro G Plan sideboard and she took her favourite, her grandmother's green glass inkwell.

It was as if she didn't plan to come back.

CHAPTER TWO

It didn't seem possible, but the clouds actually got thicker and darker as Stella navigated the road towards Arisaig. Caitlin had given her detailed directions and warned her not to rely on satnav and to make sure she had a decent amount of petrol when she left Fort William, but she still felt ill-prepared.

When she was little, Stella had wanted very much to live in a Gothic fairy tale. Something with dark, enchanted woods and lakes filled with monsters and mermaids. A part of her had been expecting a little of that fantasy to come true in the Highlands, a part of her that had no doubt been seduced by novels and 'Visit Scotland' adverts. Instead, it was merely wet. She could barely see the road, let alone the scenery.

The rain continued as she crossed the River Lochy, and there were more cars and caravans than she had expected. Why the hell were people out in this weather? She was desperate, possibly experiencing some kind of psychological breakdown; what was their excuse? It seemed a ridiculously narrow road, too. Stella's knuckles were white from gripping the steering wheel after another lunatic overtook her car, but Caitlin had told her that, unbelievably, it used to be single-track only. She saw by the signs that she was approaching Glenfinnan with its famous Hogwarts Express viaduct, but it was too dingy to see anything; the clouds had closed around the day, as if shutting shop early.

When she finally saw the sign for Arisaig village, the cloudy blankness had merged into proper night-time dark and a howling wind had sprung up to join the party. Caitlin and Rob lived on the edge of the village, and Stella crawled along until she saw the turning Caitlin had described. Hedges and trees were just shapes, and when she switched off the headlights, Stella was plunged into an unreal blackness. The ground was soaked and she stood in a deep puddle the moment she stepped from the car.

Caitlin had warned Stella that she wouldn't be in to meet her upon arrival and that Stella should let herself in with the key under the mat.

'That's ridiculous, you can't leave your key outside your front door.'

Caitlin had laughed, the sound crackling in and out with the terrible mobile reception. 'You've been in London too long.'

Stella stumbled up the path to the cottage, cursing the pitiful glow from her phone and wishing she had a torch. The rain was still sheeting down and her hair was plastered to her skull within seconds.

She located the key and let herself into the house. The hall was tiny, with openings to the left and right and a steep flight of stairs facing the front door. Struggling against the wind, Stella slammed the door shut, and a coat hung on a small hook promptly fell onto the floor. To the right was a living room, a lamp on in one corner, and to the left a kitchen with a dining table pushed against the far wall.

Stella thought about making herself tea or sitting in the quiet rooms by herself, and decided she was too tired from the drive. She wanted to switch the light off on the day and close her ears to the howling wind.

When Stella woke up, it took a moment to realise where she was. The little room was unfamiliar, but the previous day's long drive, her arrival in the rain and the dark and eventual crashing in this comfortable bed came back in a rush. She was in Scotland. Ben had called yesterday and she'd flipped out and driven to Scotland. *Good grief.*

A door opened downstairs, and with it came the welcome smell of toast. Stella got dressed quickly, pulling on yesterday's clothes, which were crumpled and splattered with mud, and ventured onto the small landing. There were two other doors – one led to the bathroom that she'd used the night before and the other was ajar, revealing an empty double bed, the duvet pulled up neatly.

Downstairs, Caitlin was moving around the little kitchen with a manic energy Stella remembered well from university. She had shared a house with Caitlin and three other girls and Caitlin had always been the one to instigate cleaning sessions, new fitness regimes and long jolly walks on a Sunday. 'You're up!' Caitlin said, throwing a tea towel in the direction of the cooker. It hit the edge of the worktop next to the appliance and slid off onto the floor. Caitlin bounded across the small space and enfolded Stella in a hug. When Stella had waited for what felt like a polite amount of time, she dropped her arms and moved away only to be pulled back tighter by Caitlin.

After another moment, Caitlin released her from the embrace but held her at arm's length, apparently unwilling to let her go. 'How are you?' Caitlin had her head on one side, her face sympathetic and her hearty voice toned down to what would be normal volume for most people. 'Don't answer that! Stupid question.' Caitlin smacked herself theatrically on the forehead. 'Tea. You need tea, right?'

'Most definitely,' Stella said, perching on the metal bar stool in the corner of the tiny room. The padded top, encased in burgundy faux-leather wheezed in a decidedly rude manner as she put her weight on it.

'Brilliant, right?' Caitlin said. 'I died laughing. Trumping furniture.'

After a general catch-up with Caitlin – work was fine, Rob was fine, Caitlin was fine – Caitlin picked up her rucksack and sailed out the door, hurling apologies. 'Can't take a day at the moment, but make yourself at home. Help yourself to anything. I'll be back at five-ish and we can go to the pub.' She ran back for a last squeeze, solid in her layers of technical fleece and high-performance mountain gear. 'I'm so happy you came.'

The front door closed with a bang and Stella listened to Caitlin's footsteps on the path, the sound of the gate. She expected to hear a car start, but there was nothing. Perhaps Caitlin parked further down the street. Or maybe she walked to work. Stella realised how little she knew about her friend's day-to-day life and how long it had been since they'd lain in bed together, watching sitcoms and eating toast, avoiding their studies and talking about mutual friends, mutual plans.

Caitlin had left a list of instructions on the kitchen worktop which included how to operate the television remotes and the central heating. On top was a key for the front door and a pair of binoculars. At university, Caitlin would've used binoculars for one purpose only: trying to peek into the house across the street which was home to 'the hottest boy in Earth Sciences'.

After washing her face and adding a few layers to her outfit, Stella ventured outside. She took several deep breaths before setting off. There was a liquid fullness in her chest and she wondered whether she ought to make a check-up appointment once she got home. The word 'home' set off a fresh round of pain, so strong it made her dizzy. She didn't want to think about going back so she pushed the thought away. As surreal as her impulsive flit was, she couldn't imagine making the return journey. It was fine. She was here now, in this place, and she was going to explore. One step at a time, that was the key.

Caitlin and Rob's cottage was one of a row of three. Old buildings with modern additions like double-glazing and satellite dishes. The houses were long and low to the ground, like they were hugging the earth for security or had half risen up from beneath. They were covered in brown harling, the stone or brickwork completely hidden, and there were layers of thick white paint around the window openings. Stella did up the buttons of her cardigan and zipped up the fleece-lined raincoat she had just pulled on. Clearly, this was a place in which everyone and everything wore layers.

The ground was sodden from the rain in the night and the air was cool, but there was no longer a gale and the sky was light, with the promise of pale sunlight. Stella set off along the street in the direction of the village centre. It was further along the road than she'd expected, and all she could see was the occasional house or gate. The road sloped down and became narrower, and Stella had to step onto the grass verge, soaking her Converse, as cars passed. She was just beginning to think that a stroll had been a bad idea, when the road turned a corner and she saw the water. A break in the clouds meant that light was flung across it, turning the surface into a dark-grey and silver mottled mirror, an expanse of mercury glass. Clinging to the slope were the assorted houses of the village, and down near the edge of the water, across the curve of the loch, sat a large white building with several roof peaks and big windows.

Arisaig wasn't going to win any awards for size, but as the sun brightened, it suddenly looked precious and inviting. Then the clouds closed again and the landscape was pitched into gloom. It was a ridiculous place, Stella thought. Dual personality. But that fleeting glimpse of light on water had given an inkling of its charms.

At a T-junction, Stella hesitated. Having seen the village from above, she knew she must be heading down and towards the water, so she took the left-hand fork, following the road down a slope which became very steep, tipping Stella's feet forward in her trainers. The edges of the road closed in, thick with rhododendrons and birch, until the sky was just a narrow slice and the temperature dropped. The road twisted until Stella wasn't sure she was still headed in the right direction, and then, abruptly, the view opened wide.

Stella looked down onto the slated roof of a beautiful grey stone house. It was grand in size and style, with stepped gables and little turrets and several tall chimney stacks. Beyond it, the sea stretched out until it merged with the sky.

The road, which curved to the left past the house, was barred with a gate, and there was a small 'Private' sign. Stella wished she could go closer; the house looked both inviting and closed-off. She could imagine hiding in a place like that. If only she had the funds or the lineage. She turned back, taking the hill with small careful steps, until she reached the junction. Although the right-hand road had seemed to go in entirely the wrong direction, it soon turned and she found herself dropping down into Arisaig.

There were a few people in bright raincoats and walking boots milling around the entrance to a building called the Land, Sea and Isles Centre, but mainly Stella saw what she assumed to be locals. A couple of pensioners sitting on a bench looking out at the sea loch had a Thermos flask with a green tartan pattern and a small dog tucked halfway inside the woman's coat.

Stella paused at the lochside and tried to feel something. She was in a wild and beautiful place, she told herself. Having an adventure. There was an expanse of water and the islands of Eigg, Rùm and Skye in the distance. Stella could see that it was a good view, if you weren't all that interested in colour. A wind sprang up, finding its way under her collar, and she turned from the water and trudged back up the hill to the main road.

She passed a shop and, more to escape the drizzle which had begun than any sense of curiosity, ducked inside. The shop was split in two, a small bakery on one side and a general store on the other. The general store was stuffed with an unusual variety of items. Stella looked at the packaging for surgical tights and buttons – alongside parcel tape, cat food and apples – and felt as if she had stepped through a portal to a time that not even she truly remembered. The grocery counter was deserted, but after a few minutes, a woman came through from the bakery side and took up position by the register.

Stella thought about the contents of Caitlin's small fridge and felt she ought to contribute something. She'd arrived without gifts, not even a bottle of wine. She picked up butter from the chiller cabinet and began searching for jam.

'On holiday?' the woman said, in a not entirely friendly way.

'Visiting friends,' Stella said.

'In the village?'

'Yes,' Stella said, examining a locally made jar of bramble jelly.

There was a pause and Stella realised that the woman was waiting for her to elaborate, so she added, 'Caitlin and Rob Baird.'

'Oh, aye. I know the Bairds.' The woman smiled for the first time. 'I'm Marion. You should take a boat out to Eigg while you're here. My husband will give ye a good rate. Tell him you're a friend of Rob's.'

'Thanks,' Stella said. She had no intention of going out on that freezing grey expanse, had no idea why anybody would.

'Is there a hotel here? Other than the one by the loch?'

'There's one at Morar,' the woman said, frowning a little as if Stella had insulted her in some way. 'And the pub has rooms.'

'I passed a house,' Stella said, 'on my way in. It looked posh enough, I thought it might be—'

'That'll be Munro House.' Marion's frown deepened for a moment.

If it was a hotel, then Stella could wander in and have a look around. She didn't know why she'd felt so drawn to the place, but she had nothing but time, and it was a relief to feel the stirrings of curiosity.

'No.' The woman shook her head, her expression flat. 'Not for a while.'

'Okay.' Stella turned back to the shelf. She picked up an onion and chilli chutney along with the jam and went to the counter. There were bottles of booze lined up behind the till, mostly cheap brands of gin, vodka and whisky, but there were a couple of single malts. 'How much is the Ardbeg?'

'Forty-five,' Marion said, turning to get it down.

'Great,' Stella said, trying not to think of her bank balance.

'Nothing good ever happened there.' Marion was bagging Stella's purchases and she didn't look up.

'Sorry?'

'Munro House. It's a bad place.'

Teasing the gullible tourist. Nice. Stella forced a smile to show she was a good sport. 'Really? That sounds fun.'

Marion didn't smile back.

Back at the cottage, Stella washed up the breakfast dishes, swept the kitchen floor and tried to read a novel. After lunch she gave up on trying to act like a normal person and went back to bed for the afternoon. She told herself that she was still tired from the long drive the day before, but the truth was, she craved the magical switch-off of sleep. She set her alarm before crawling under the duvet, not wanting Caitlin to find her in bed. It would only make her worry and Stella was keenly aware that she was already a burden. Sleep came swiftly, bestowing the blessed release from thought and feeling that Stella craved.

'I'm back!' Caitlin yelled from the hallway. Stella opened her eyes, feeling just as weary, as if the three hours of sleep had been a hallucination. 'Are you ready to get out of here or do I have time for a cup of tea? I'm gasping.'

Stella found Caitlin in the kitchen, still with half of her outside layers on. She hit the switch on the kettle and got out a couple of mugs.

'Rob not back?' Caitlin said, flinging her scarf onto the counter and leaning against it.

Stella shook her head. 'I haven't seen him.'

'He said he might not bother coming home after work. He's got parents' evening at the school. We'll go on to the pub and I'll leave him a note.'

Stella's neck prickled at the thought of going out, even with Caitlin. She didn't want to meet anybody new, have to make small talk and smile. She felt cold inside, as the hollow space left by Ben yawned open.

'They're a nice bunch and the food is good. Not fancy, but good pub food, you know?'

When they got to the bar at the Arisaig Inn, Stella saw instantly what Caitlin meant. She meant the restaurant food of her childhood, not gastro stuff. Chicken and chips, gammon and pineapple, pie and mash, or fish, chips and mushy peas – all served on plates, not chopping boards or slates with the chips in a tiny replica fry basket. 'Don't get the salad,' Caitlin warned, needlessly. 'It's a bit old school. Coleslaw and iceberg.'

Stella was sitting on a cushioned bench near the massive stone hearth, complete with roaring fire. Her visions of having to speak to hundreds of friendly locals – Caitlin collected friends as easily as colds – hadn't come true, and now, with half a delicious nutty ale already in her system and the prospect of some deep-fried food, she felt more positive.

'I'll get the next round,' Stella said. 'Gin?' Caitlin had gone for a long drink, something clear with a slice of lemon.

'Lemonade,' Caitlin said. 'I'm driving.'

'We can walk,' Stella said, feeling guilty. 'It's no distance.'

'That's all right—' Caitlin began, but at that moment the door to the pub opened, letting in a blast of cold air along with loud male voices.

'Uh-oh. It's the boys,' Caitlin said, smiling.

Stella pretended she hadn't heard and continued her trajectory to the bar. She was buying some time, steeling herself for social interaction. It was an old habit, but as she waited to catch the attention of the barman, she imagined herself donning a cloak. Dark-blue velvet and edged with silver, it had a deep hood and hidden pockets and it made her feel safe and warm and strong. By the time she was back at the table, with a drink in each hand, she was ready to face the small crowd.

'Stella, this is Doug, Stewart and Bark.'

'Bark?' Stella asked the man with red hair cropped close to his skull and long pale eyelashes.

'Aye, short for Barclay.'

'Like the bank?'

'No.'

All right, then. Stella took a sip of her Laphroaig, concentrating on the smoke-and-engine-oil flavour, rather than the man who was now glaring at her.

'Stella is my pal from uni,' Caitlin was saying, the light accent she'd picked up since moving to Scotland with Rob becoming more pronounced.

'You staying for long?' the man Stella thought was Doug asked.

'Not sure,' Stella said. 'Things are a bit up in the air at the moment, life-wise.'

'Oh, aye. I ken what you mean,' Doug said. 'I was going to go to Stirling but I changed ma mind.'

'Were you going to study there?'

'Nah. There was a job, like. But then I stayed put. Still gonnae go one day.'

'Are there many jobs around here?' Stella asked, pretty sure she knew the answer. 'I'm thinking I might stay a while. I'll need to do something.'

The boys pulled faces, and Stewart said she'd be lucky.

'You're thinking of staying?' Caitlin said, her eyebrows raised.

'Maybe.' Stella shrugged. 'I'm not sure of my plans.' An image flashed into her mind. Her kitchen worktop with the rectangular white appointment card sitting on its oiled wooden surface. A tiny door into another reality.

The boys had started their own conversation, sensing that Stella and Caitlin might be having a private discussion.

'You can stay with us as long as you like,' Caitlin said. Stella had the urge to hug Caitlin. She was such a good friend. She had even managed to make the invitation sound genuine.

'I don't know what I'm doing, to be honest.' Stella put a hand on her arm. 'I'm a mess. I'll stay a few days and then decide. Don't worry, I won't intrude longer than that . . .'

'Munro is after a helper, mind,' Doug said, putting his pint glass onto the table and sitting down. 'Mairi went up and met him but he was needing someone good with computers.' Doug shook his head. 'Mairi's clever and all, but she cannae be doing with emails and spreadsheets and that stuff.'

'Ach, don't send her there, man,' Stewart said, sitting on the bench next to Stella, squishing against her. 'Especially not after that girl—'

'That wasn't in the house,' Caitlin said quickly, cutting him off.

'What are we talking about?' Stella said.

'At the big house,' Doug said. 'The superstar. Local boy made good, back from America.'

'Gracing us with his presence,' Stewart said.

'Except naebody's seen him,' Doug added.

'But he's looking for an office assistant?' Stella said. 'Which big house?'

'Mebbe. Unless he's found someone.' Bark shook his head. 'Bad family, mind. You don't want to get mixed up with him.'

'Gossip,' Caitlin said. 'You lot are a bunch of sweetie wives.'

'And I hear he's up to all sorts.' Doug made a significant face.

'Which house?' Stella said again.

'Munro House. Around the bay.'

Outside the pub, Stella was grateful that Caitlin had been on the soft drinks and could drive them back. It wasn't far to walk, but it was pitch-black and there was a freezing rain which stung her cheeks.

Caitlin linked her arm through Stella's. 'I'm so glad you're here.'

'Me too,' Stella said, although at that moment she would've preferred to be tucked up in her bed. She couldn't remember the last time she'd felt so cold. 'Are you sure Rob won't mind me staying?'

'Definitely. He's the one who said I should keep inviting you. Said we should drive down and kidnap you if you didn't take us up on the offer soon.'

Stella was thinking about her house in London. Their house. Her eyes were sore and tight with the effort not to cry. She shouldn't have had that third drink; it had weakened her.

She tried to distract herself on the short drive and had planned to turn down any further offers of social contact and get to bed as soon as was politely possible. The tiredness dragged every step until she felt barely able to get from the car to the cottage.

'Hello, hello.' Rob opened the door. 'I was wondering when you stop-outs would be back.'

Rob and Caitlin had met in the first year of university – the first week, in fact – and become a couple so quickly and completely that it was impossible to imagine them as separate entities. Caitlin-and-Rob. Rob-and-Caitlin.

Rob stepped forward and hugged Stella quickly, the hard stubble of his chin scraping her cheek, before turning to his wife. Caitlin and Rob had surprised exactly nobody when they'd tied the knot one year out of university in a sweet ceremony in Caitlin's home town. They had all been so excited and a little awkward, fidgeting with their fancy clothes and feeling like they were all playing at being grown-ups.

Stella had felt envious as well as happy; they had got married before attending weddings became the bane of everyone's summer, back when it was all fresh and new and eating canapés while wearing uncomfortable heels was still a novelty.

'Was it busy?'

'Not very,' Caitlin said. 'Usual crowd.'

Rob had hung up their coats and moved to the living room, firing questions. 'Tea? Coffee? Night cap?'

'Nothing for me, thanks,' Stella said, edging towards the door. 'I think I'll turn in.'

'Oh.' Caitlin looked disappointed. 'Could you wait just a sec?'

'Of course, you all right?'

'Hang on.' Caitlin tuned to Rob, who had a peculiar expression on his face. 'You do it. I can't say it.'

Stella had a premonition of what the happy couple were about to reveal and her insides shrank in readiness.

'I'm pregnant!' Caitlin was beaming and Rob slipped a proprietary arm around her shoulders.

'Wow! That's wonderful. Brilliant news. How exciting.' Stella's brain delivered the appropriate words. She made sure her face was turned from Rob as she hugged Caitlin, and then hid in Rob's shoulder when she hugged him, giving her time to work on an expression of delight.

'I still can't believe it,' Caitlin was saying. 'We only just started trying.'

'Well done,' Stella said. She realised she was looking at Rob, which made her think about his part in the proceedings. Not the mental image she wanted. Still, it distracted her from the urge to start sobbing.

'I wanted to tell you all evening. I thought you were going to guess when I wasn't drinking.' Caitlin was babbling with happiness. Her face was shining with pure joy and Stella felt her own feelings blacken, as if she were stuck on the other side of the coin. She formed a smile. Forced further words of congratulation and excitement and pulled her friend in for a longer hug, grateful to hide her face again.

Later, lying in bed with her eyes wide open, looking into the darkness, Stella tried to cry. She needed to mourn, she was pretty sure that the release of tears would make her feel better, but the oceans she had been holding in check all day had receded. Her eyes were dry as sand.

It was lovely news for Caitlin and Rob. They would be wonderful parents. Stella knew that their happiness and good fortune did not take away from hers, and at least she would get to be a fond auntie to their child. Even if she ran out of time to have one of her own.

Stella blinked in the darkness and wished, for the thousandth time, that she could speak to Ben. It was always at the end of the day that she missed him most. It felt strange not to be able to talk about Caitlin and Rob's announcement, this monumental shift in their friends' lives. And he would have understood, without her saying a word, how bittersweet the news was for Stella. She didn't want to remember how pleased she had been when she had been given the go-ahead by her cardiologist. Pregnancy put a strain on a healthy person's heart, and up until the valve replacement it had been out of the question. It felt as if a false hope had been dangled, cruelly.

Caitlin and Rob, in the bedroom down the hall, were no doubt lying entangled, talking over the day.

Stella did not want to feel jealous of her best friend, so she very carefully did not feel anything at all.

CHAPTER THREE

The next day, Caitlin left Rob lesson-planning and walked down through Arisaig village to look out at the water and show Stella the sights. 'There's a history place you'll like,' Caitlin said.

Stella had agreed to the walk, thinking that a blast of fresh air would help her lingering headache. She hadn't reckoned on the stinging hail and freezing wind though, and gladly followed Caitlin into the whitewashed building which housed the visitor centre.

Inside there were displays of text, maps and photographs, cases of artefacts, and a wall of windows which looked out on the bay and the boats moored in the calm waters of the sheltered sea loch. Caitlin picked up a pair of binoculars from the window ledge and Stella began reading the information boards. Her favourite activity as a child had been museum trips, and she had never had any doubt that, given the chance, she would study history. For a blissful year and a half, she had thrown herself into her degree, hoovering up the details of the Russian Revolution and the Age of Enlightenment, the Tudors and the Crimean War. Until it was all swept away.

Stella read about Arisaig's position as a place of shelter for a wide variety of people over the years, from Vikings to Bonnie Prince Charlie. The area had been used by the Special Operations Executive during World War Two to train field agents in commando techniques, with several private buildings requisitioned for the effort, including Rhubana Lodge and Munro House. Stella looked at the black-and-white photograph of the 'big house' and imagined how it must have felt to have your home taken away.

'They had only just rebuilt the place,' Caitlin said, pointing at a panel that described how a fire had consumed Munro House in 1931.

'I'm just closing now, sorry,' the kind-faced woman behind the till said on Stella's third walk around the centre.

'No problem,' Caitlin said.

Stella had drifted to a stand of pamphlets and books. She picked one up at random, conscious of the quiet village and deserted visitor centre.

'Thanks, dear,' the woman said, ringing up her purchase. 'You come far today?'

'I'm staying in the village,' Stella said.

'This is a good starter guide to the myths and legends,' the woman said, bagging the book.

There was a charity tin on the counter with the lifeboat symbol on it. Stella dropped a few coins into it. 'Must be busy . . .' she said. 'The lifeboat service.'

'Oh, aye. Lots of folk get into trouble. Kayakers mostly.'

'What about bigger boats? Ships and things?'

The woman nodded. 'It happens.'

'Are there a lot of wrecks out there, do you think? It looks so peaceful.'

'Hundreds,' she said calmly. 'Once you get out into the sound itself and between the islands. There's a board over there about the 1853 *Annie Jane* tragedy. Terrible business.' She spoke with sorrow, as if it had happened last month, not over one hundred and sixty years ago.

Stella had read the board, but she obediently followed the woman's finger and reread it. Over three hundred souls lost, many of them women and children. The ship had been packed with emigrants, heading to Quebec for work. They had been looking for a new life, but instead they had ended up at the bottom of the sea, miles deep in the cold and the dark.

Stella went to sleep with a nightcap of single malt and the book of folklore. There were a disturbing number of bad omens, from phantom clipper ships out at sea to long-haired women next to the water's edge. Every single one spoke of sorrow and tragedy either in the past or still to come.

She awoke to the quiet of an empty house. Caitlin and Rob had gone grocery shopping in Fort William, and had left a note on the kitchen table. Back in London, Stella had been finding it impossible to sleep later than four or five in the morning, but she had been soundly unconscious for twelve hours. Perhaps it was the Highland air. Or the whisky.

She emailed her mother back, turning down the lunch invitation and mentioning oh-so-casually that she was visiting Caitlin. The reply pinged back almost immediately but the tone was neutral. *Have a lovely time, darling. Speak soon.* Stella filled in the invisible words of concern, the questions about how she had travelled so far, whether she was over-tired, how she was coping. Or perhaps they weren't there, only existing in Stella's imagination. She was so finely tuned to her parents' feelings, and so used to their caution, that she could no longer separate their true voices from the ones she heard in her own mind. She tapped out a quick reply: *Feeling much better, think the change of scenery is doing me good.* Lies, but she didn't want them to worry. They had been through enough, after all.

She had a shower in the small bathroom and then drove to Mallaig to look at where the boats left for the islands. Caitlin had mentioned that there was an outdoor gear shop and, sick of shivering in her leather jacket, Stella was determined to make use of it.

After stocking up on a hat, gloves, waterproof boots and a technical raincoat with warm lining which instantly became the most expensive item of clothing she had ever owned, Stella wandered the harbour, and looked at the steel grey of the water and tried not to think too hard about what she was doing. Ben was far away and that helped. There was a kind of magic in the physical distance, and a relief in the knowledge that he wasn't about to pop round, letting himself into the house with the key he refused to give back. 'It's my house, too,' he had said when she had asked him for it. Offended.

The next day Stella didn't even leave the cottage. She sat on the sofa, wrapped in a duvet, and watched television shows about people buying houses in the country or selling antiques, and counted down the hours until Caitlin and Rob came home, filling the house with laughter and warmth.

On the fifth morning, Stella braved the cold and walked around the village. She sat on one of the benches looking out to sea and nodded to the elderly couple with their Thermos. She called into every open business and loitered by the tourist information board. She stared at the simplified map and its large red dot marked with the words 'You are here' as if it contained a significant truth. By the time Caitlin came back from a day clearing a footpath in the Glen Beasdale reserve, Stella had decided that it was time she went back to London. The momentum which had brought her to Scotland had drained away, and she felt as numb and empty as she had before.

At dinner, Caitlin was uncharacteristically quiet.

'You okay?' Stella said, holding out the salad bowl.

'Fine,' Caitlin smiled, but she still looked worried.

'Do you feel ill?' Stella stood up. 'Do you want some water? Is it morning sickness?'

Rob leaned back in his chair, unconcerned. 'Lovely lasagne. Thanks, babe.' He was still wearing his work outfit of a neatly pressed polo shirt tucked firmly into smart trousers, and it made Stella feel oddly shy, as if he were an entirely different person from the goatee-wearing student she remembered.

'I'm past that, thank Christ.' Caitlin rested her hand on the tiny curve of her stomach. 'And the bloody tiredness. That was the worst.'

Now that Stella knew, she could see Caitlin's pregnancy bump. She didn't know why she hadn't noticed right away. Too wrapped up in herself, probably. Selfish. She took a deep breath, ready to tell them that she was going to head back down south on the weekend.

'You may as well tell her, babe,' Rob said, leaning over and running a finger down Caitlin's cheek. 'Get it over with.'

Ice ran down Stella's back and panicked thoughts flickered through her mind. Ben had been in an accident? Someone was sick? 'Tell me what?'

'Don't be mad, okay?'

'I won't,' Stella said automatically, still waiting for the axe to fall.

'I emailed about that job,' Caitlin said. 'On your behalf.'

'What?'

'The job at the big house. With Jamie Munro.'

'The one that Doug was talking about?' Stella said, confused. 'In the pub?'

'Aye,' Rob said. 'Doug's Mairi went up for it a couple of weeks back, but he's needing someone with computer skills. I told Caitlin she ought to recommend you.'

'You've got an interview tomorrow,' Caitlin said, clearly trying not to smile as she spoke, but failing.

Stella was surprised, but it felt second-hand. Everything was still so muted, like she was swimming underwater and real life was going on above her on the surface. There was a spark of relief, too, that Caitlin hadn't been hiding truly bad news. She realised that Caitlin was waiting for her to speak. 'Didn't it seem a bit odd, me not applying myself?'

'Well' – Caitlin looked at her empty plate, embarrassed – 'I set up an email and pretended to be you. Don't be mad.'

'I . . .' Stella began and then fell silent. She ought to be furious. Old Stella would have been. Old Stella would have told Caitlin off for treating her like a special case, an invalid, a pathetic victim. Instead she just felt relief that she had something concrete to do in the morning, something that would put off decision-making for another day.

'I didn't think you would do it,' Caitlin was saying, 'and if we didn't move fast then someone else will get the job, there aren't many around here, you know, and it's bound to be decent money.'

'Unless he's as tight as his father,' Rob said.

Caitlin shot Rob a look and carried on. 'I know it was a cheek and I'm sorry, but we really felt like you needed help.'

'This could be really good for you,' Rob said. 'Give you something else to focus on.'

'And you'd said how much you liked it here. We thought you might want to stay a while.' Caitlin put out a hand. 'Say something. Please.'

'It's fine,' Stella said. 'I'll go.' She managed a weak 'thank you' and they finished their meal, carefully not talking about it.

When Stella hugged Caitlin and said goodnight, she knew that Caitlin was avoiding her eye. Stella knew she should make more of an effort to show that she wasn't angry, or to say something more enthusiastic about the job interview, but fighting the strange numbness took all of her energy. It took everything she had to appear halfway normal. She would go to the interview in the interests of friendship, to prove to Caitlin that she wasn't cross with her. Then, on the weekend or early the following week, she would drive back to her life.

The next day, once Rob and Caitlin had left for work, Stella spent a couple of hours preparing for her meeting at the big house. She might be in the middle of some kind of breakdown, but old habits die hard and she wasn't about to walk into an interview without doing her homework. Besides, with the sun pouring through the cottage windows and a blessed lack of rain, the prospect of getting to stay in Arisaig for a while longer took on an attractive glow.

Jamie Munro's website was slick and well stocked with information. To his credit, he appeared to give out a lot of content for free, with in-depth articles, interviews and videos. Stella read the biography, studied his list of *New York Times* bestselling books, and then watched a video of an interview with the man himself. He was smiling and relaxed, charming the interviewer and the live audience with a performance she associated more with actors or television hosts. 'It's about refining the human experience. I take the things that interest me, more often than not, things that we all struggle with, like weight or fitness or learning or work, and then I dissect the process so that I can improve it. There are so many small changes we can make that make a substantial difference to our performance, our energy levels and our happiness.'

'It's interesting you mention happiness – that's not something that you have covered in your books so far, I don't think . . .'

'I think it's a by-product of reaching your peak performance, but you're right, Jared, it's not something I have exclusively looked at, yet. Perhaps I should.'

'Maybe your next bestseller will be *The Happiness Hack*?'

'Oh, I like that. Maybe. Although I'm already deep in research for my next title, *Living Well Forever*.'

Stella clicked the button to stop the video. It was dated June of the previous year, and the 'Latest News' page said that the book was 'coming soon'. A quick Google search revealed a short news piece which suggested Jamie's book was delayed by work commitments, and it had a quote from his literary agent saying that 'good enough' wasn't in Jamie Munro's vocabulary and that the fans would be 'rewarded for their patience with something spectacular'.

The day stayed bright and dry, so Stella decided to walk to her job interview. There had been hardly any traffic on the route, so she felt it was safe enough. At the T-junction she took the left-hand fork to the estate and, abruptly, the wind dropped and she could hear birdsong.

The road descended sharply after a blind bend, and the trees parted to reveal an imposing stone building and, beyond it, the sea. The house sprawled around an inner courtyard. Stella could see through an archway, large enough for a Land Rover, that there was at least one car parked inside and it looked decidedly expensive. The leaves had mostly turned and the view was filled with shades of orange, brown and yellow, which looked bright against the grey stone of the big house and the grey-purple of the roof tiles.

Stella told herself not to be overawed. It was a very nice house. A very large house, certainly, but that did not mean that the man she was about to meet was any better than she was. Stella was determined to grow into a strong woman, the kind who was calm but outspoken, but she mostly felt like an uncertain girl, tugging on the skirts of life and asking to be allowed to join in. She didn't know if this was because of her sheltered upbringing, or whether most people felt the same way inside.

Stella searched in vain for an entryphone or something to indicate the main entrance. She walked through the archway, hoping she wasn't about to be shot for trespassing – there were far too many shotguns in this part of the world for her comfort – and into the gravelled courtyard. Steps led up to a grand entrance with a heavy wooden door which was wide open, revealing a tiled vestibule and a closed inner door. A tremendous barking came from somewhere in the house, and Stella steeled herself to be jumped on. Ben's parents had a rescue greyhound and it never failed to greet Stella by putting its paws onto her chest and licking her face. It was disgusting, but nothing Mr and Mrs Dawson did could stop him.

A single rowan tree stood in the middle of the courtyard and the wind sprang up, shaking the branches and blowing a flurry of leaves like a sudden, red-and-orange snowstorm.

The door opened and a woman with grey hair and a rosy complexion frowned at her. 'Can I help you?' She spoke in a tone that suggested this was unlikely.

Stella peeled away a stray orange leaf which had stuck to her cheek, and tried to look capable. 'I have an appointment with Mr Munro. At ten.'

The woman nodded. 'You'd better come in, then. He's in his bath at the minute.'

Stella didn't know how to respond to that piece of information, so she said nothing.

The woman turned her head and said something in a firm voice to the unseen dogs, who fell instantly silent. Stella followed the woman up the steps and into a wide hallway. There were oil paintings of seascapes and lochs and mountains, and an old oriental runner in red and gold. The house smelled of wood and neroli and wax polish, and classical music was playing somewhere in the house. A cello concerto, Stella thought, maybe Elgar.

'You can wait in here.' The woman gestured to a closed door. She was wearing a padded navy gilet and warm-looking trousers, and close-up Stella could see that her hair was actually a mix of white, silver-grey and pewter and rather beautiful. She wore it swept back off her make-up-free face. It wasn't much warmer inside the house than it had been outside, and Stella took her coat off with reluctance. She had borrowed a shift dress from Caitlin and it was a bit of a tight fit. She hoped the long grey cardigan she had put over the top was keeping her decent.

'Thank you . . .' Stella said, leaving a pause at the end of the sentence for the woman to fill in her name, but she had already turned away. Stella watched her retreating back for a moment before opening the door.

If the hallway had been exactly what Stella had expected from a house of this size and age, this room was less so. She wondered if she had even been directed into the right place, as it was full of packing boxes and dust sheets. A large cardboard box was on its side, open with foil packets spilling out, and there was a rack of what looked like torture devices pushed in front of a beautiful carved-oak fireplace. There was a single chair. Modern moulded plastic and uncomfortable-looking. The sort of chair which had a woman's name like Alexis and cost more than a small car.

A door slammed above and there was a thundering of footsteps. It was so loud and energetic that Stella expected a troop out on manoeuvres, and not one single man bounding into the room, droplets shaking from long wet hair and a deeply carved frown. 'Am I late? Sorry.' He stuck his hand out. 'I'm Jamie.'

'Stella,' she said, taking the proffered hand. It was surprisingly cool.

'Who?' He dropped her hand like he'd been burned.

The expression on his face was unnerving and it made Stella stutter over her words. 'I thought I was here for an interview,' she managed.

'How the hell did you find me?' His voice was low and furious. 'Was it Magnus?'

'I'm sorry?' Stella took an instinctive step back. He stood there, running a hand through his sopping-wet, reddish hair and scowling in her direction. 'How did you get in?'

'A lady let me in,' Stella managed. 'I didn't catch her name.'

He turned, his mouth open as if ready to shout, when a different look came across his face. It was like watching the sun rise. 'Ah. Hang on. Did you say Stella?'

Stella nodded.

'You're here about the job,' he said.

'Yes,' Stella said. 'I'm here for an interview. I thought you said ten.'

'Screen reader said you were Sarah. Or I misheard it. I was working out.'

There was an awkward pause.

Stella was pretty sure she didn't want to work for this man, that she couldn't deal with his flakiness and nervous energy. She felt exhausted by him.

'I'm really sorry. Can we start again?' He held his hand out. 'I'm Jamie Munro.'

He smiled. It was a good smile, and Stella thought it had probably been getting him out of awkward situations for a long, long time.

She ignored the hand. One of the few advantages to having her life implode was that she no longer felt the need to waste time on doomed pursuits. 'The purpose of a job interview is for both candidate and employer to decide if they are a good match. I don't believe that's the case, so I won't waste any more of your time,' she said.

Stella walked to the door before she could ruin the effect by bursting into tears.

'Wait,' Jamie said. 'Won't you at least give me a chance to make a better impression?'

He looked amused. As if she were a puppy who had done a trick. She felt a twist of anger in her chest and the answering tightness. On the other hand, she needed a job and they weren't exactly abundant in this part of the world. Arisaig was wet and cold, but there was something about it, something that meant she wasn't ready to leave. Not yet.

'Would you like a tour?' Jamie was saying. 'I can show you around, explain what I need help with, and you can tell me if it's something you think you'd like to do.'

He was being charming now. He'd switched to that mode as easily as breathing.

'All right,' Stella said. At least she'd seen the real man first.

If she hadn't, she might have found him attractive.

'And I can ask you questions as we walk, get to know you. It's better if we don't sit. Sitting is killing us all.'

'So I've read,' Stella said. 'I'm pretty sure breathing is killing us, too.'

'What do you mean?'

We're all dying. One breath at a time. 'No point worrying about it,' Stella said. 'The alternative is rubbish.'

He gave her a strange look. It made Stella feel less like a clever puppy and more like one that had just widdled on the carpet. He started to speak but stopped abruptly, took a visible breath and started again. 'As you can see in here, I haven't unpacked properly, yet. So I need help with that.' He walked out of the room and Stella followed, curious despite the almost-certainty that Jamie Munro was rude and self-centred.

The hallway that Stella had already seen stretched the length of the building and was studded with doors, mostly closed. The end of the hallway opened into a large dining room with a polished table, big enough to seat ten people with room to spare. A gigantic antique cabinet with glass doors was filled with delicate patterned china and shining silverware. It was like something from a stately home. 'I don't use this room,' he said. 'I don't use half of the rooms. Probably more.'

'It's a beautiful house,' Stella said, giving credit where it was due. The windows in the dining room held views of the land tumbling down to the ocean. The grey-blue of the water, merged with the silvery sky and the dark shapes of the islands, Muck and Eigg, and, in the distance, Rùm. Stella would've liked to stay looking at the view for longer, but Jamie had already disappeared through yet another doorway. This one led to the kitchen. Stella didn't know if this had been the original site of the kitchen, but it had certainly been refitted. It was modern and industrial-looking, with a stainless-steel island and a rack hung with pots and pans. The cooker was enormous, with several burners, and there was a fridge that a small family could make into a comfortable home.

'In here, you'll need to find your way around my routine,' Jamie was saying. He kept speaking as if he'd already offered her the job and she had accepted. Stella didn't think it was a done deal, just that it was his style. More charm. More confidence. 'I eat the same things at the same time every day.' He gestured to the shelves in the fridge. There were lots of labelled plastic containers and a drawer full of dark green salad. 'I drink rocket fuel in the mornings, and after two o'clock I switch to this.' He picked up a plastic beaker with a lid. It was filled with something the colour of urine.

The charm offensive was wearing. 'You want me to prepare your food?'

'No. Not at all. I just need you to know my nutrition routine and my meds. I shouldn't need any help, but it's just in case. And you'll be in charge of ordering supplies so it's a good idea to be familiar with the products and to have the background so you know why these things are so important.'

The word 'meds' stabbed Stella and she felt a shimmer of sympathy. Being sick wasn't fun, and if Jamie Munro was dealing with some long-term condition alongside his hectic schedule, it might explain some of the curious specifics of his routine. She didn't want to be interested, didn't want to feel sympathy, but she immediately began guessing. Diabetes? Epilepsy?

After the kitchen, Jamie showed Stella the garden, from which you could see the tennis court. 'You'd be welcome to use that whenever I'm not.' And an outbuilding which was filled with weights and gym equipment. Back in the main house, Jamie hesitated outside a closed door. 'This is my office. It's got a desk for you but I don't want to show you this space unless you're going to take the job. It's private.'

'Fair enough,' Stella said.

'Privacy is very important to me,' he said. His voice was light but his expression intense. 'Discretion is probably the number one trait that I require in my team. Are you discreet?'

The question seemed to come suddenly; after all the talking Jamie had been doing, he'd barely asked her anything about her work experience or background.

'Very,' she said.

He nodded, probably waiting for her to elaborate, but Stella's mind had gone blank. How did you convince somebody you were trustworthy with words? A few phrases popped into her mind but they felt second-hand. Stella worried that anything she said would sound as if she were trying too hard to convince him.

After a moment, in which Jamie Munro appeared to be staring into her very soul, he turned away from the office door. 'Every team member signs an NDA. Nothing that goes on in this house is to be revealed to anybody outside this house.'

Stella was looking around, trying to soak up a few details of the beautiful interior before she was ejected. When she looked back, Jamie was looking at her expectantly.

'Yes,' she said.

'Non-disclosure agreement. It's legally binding. Think official secrets for private business.'

'I know,' Stella said.

She waited for him to say something else.

He dipped his head. 'So, what do you reckon?'

'Sorry?'

Jamie smiled a little. Not a smarmy smile or a particularly confident one. Stella would lay money that he'd practised it in front of a mirror, but it was very effective nonetheless. 'Do you think you could put up with me?' Then he named a starting salary which exceeded her best-paying temp job to date. 'I know that sounds generous, but it reflects the demanding nature of the job. I know that I'm quite intense.' Here he gave a small, self-deprecating laugh. 'Obsessive, really, and I think it's only fair to properly compensate my team. Also, there will be some out-of-hours work. If you need to communicate with people in other time zones, for example. I don't mind if you want to work flexitime in those instances or to claim overtime, whichever you like.'

'Don't you want to ask me questions about my experience? Software packages I've used . . .' Stella waved a hand, unable to believe that anything good could be this easy.

'I read your CV,' he said, appearing mystified. 'It's a waste of time to get you to rehash it.'

Stella opened her mouth and then closed it again.

'Besides, you're a friend of Rob Baird. He'll vouch for you, no doubt.'

'Rob?'

Jamie shrugged. 'Everyone knows everyone in a place like this. He used to come to Hogmanay here with his family. Everyone in the village did.' Jamie smiled, but she could tell he was already keen to move on to the next item on his list for the day. He was practically bouncing on the balls of his feet. 'So, what do you reckon? Give it a go?'

'Yes,' Stella said, before her brain could argue.

CHAPTER FOUR

When Stella arrived for her first day, Jamie Munro didn't waste time on polite chitchat.

'This way.' He strode along the hall and into the dining room. Neat piles of paper were laid out on the shiny surface of the table, presided over by an enormous pair of stag's antlers jutting out from the wall. 'Contract, NDA, bank information.' Munro stabbed a finger. 'It's no problem if you want to take the contract away and have it checked by your lawyer, but the NDA has to be signed right now. Is that going to be an issue?'

'No.'

'Good.'

He pulled the chair out and Stella sat down, dropping her handbag onto the floor. She hadn't even taken her coat off but there was a sense of urgency. Munro stayed behind the chair, looming over her as she bowed her head over the paper. She read the NDA as quickly as she could, glad that it was a single page, and then signed using the fountain pen provided. The language was clear enough; it prevented her from speaking or writing about anything which occurred within Munro estate or anything she discussed with her new boss, regardless of the location of their conversation. There were another two copies to sign and date, and then she felt the air in the room change.

Jamie gave her a tight smile. 'Now I can show you around properly.'

Stella could understand why Jamie kept his office private. It wasn't that the room was embarrassingly messy or that the warnings from the locals about ungodly goings-on were founded, but it was distinctive. Jamie Munro might not have finished unpacking the rest of the house, but this room had clearly been his priority. There were large whiteboards on one wall, covered in writing in different colours. A standing desk with an exercise mat and a balance ball stood in the middle of the room with a television screen on the wall opposite.

There were books everywhere, stacked on every available surface, including the floor. Another desk, with a complicated-looking ergonomic chair, was against the far wall. In stark contrast to the modern equipment, there was a deep bay window with velvet curtains and a large fireplace with a carved wooden surround. Lined up along the mantelpiece was an assortment of what looked like antique scientific equipment, including a set of glass flasks. Stella wanted to step forward and examine the strange collection – her love of history was still sparking underneath its winter coat of office work and life trouble – but she forced herself to look away, not wanting to appear nosy.

'Through here,' Jamie said, opening a door to an adjoining room. 'It's a bit small.'

It was hard to say what the room had been in the past – an under-butler's snug? A gun room? Now, it was a square space, with eau-de-Nil walls and a couple of gently moulting antique armchairs. Marooned in the middle of the carpet was a landline telephone on a charger stand, the cord snaking into a newly installed point on the wall. 'Your first job will be to get a laptop,' Jamie said, running his hand through his hair. 'Or a desktop. I don't care, whichever you prefer. And some furniture. I recommend an adjustable standing desk and a balance ball but it's personal preference. In the meantime, feel free to grab whatever table and chair look like they might be the right height. Take regular breaks, though.'

Stella waited for a break in his flow. 'Haven't you had an assistant before?'

'Loads. Back in San Francisco. And when I was in London. Not here, though.'

Stella asked the obvious question. 'Why not keep your existing assistant? If they didn't want to move, I'm sure they could work remotely. Skype and email and all that.'

'Oh, I've kept him on. Guy's great. You'll meet him at some point. But I need somebody physically here. Skype isn't secure, for one thing. Hacking is a real issue.'

Stella forced herself not to smile. To hear Jamie talk, you would have thought he was an international spy, not writing a diet book.

'Besides,' Jamie said. 'You should always employ local. It's one of the rules somewhere like this. Shop local, employ local. The economy is in the toilet, so it's the very least I can do.'

Stella felt a stab of guilt alongside a grudging respect for his attitude. 'I'm not local. I'm a visitor.'

'Local enough for my conscience.' Jamie darted back into his office and came back with an iPad. 'You can use this to order stuff.'

He scribbled a figure onto a piece of paper and gave her a credit card. 'That's your budget. Don't skimp on the hardware.'

Stella felt like she ought to sit down. She stared at the number but it remained the same.

'I'm sorry about last week,' he said abruptly.

'What?' Stella was still considering the number on the piece of paper. What did he expect her to purchase with that? A 3D printer? A flight simulator?

'I was coming to the end of a water fast. Bit grumpy. And my cognitive function wasn't at its peak.'

Stella wanted to ask why he'd been fasting but stopped herself. Could be for a medical procedure, something private he didn't want to discuss. She had enough experience of invasive questions about her own health to know how wearing they could be.

'There's something I wanted to ask you. It might sound a bit weird, but if it bothers you then it's a good sign that this isn't going to work out and I'd rather not waste time.'

Stella forced herself to look at her new boss directly. She wanted to show that she wasn't easily shocked, while hoping that he wasn't going to say something too wild. She had only been in the house for a short time and she already knew she wanted to stay. For a while, at least.

'I want to extend my ice baths, try for longer times. That comes with an increased risk so I need a buddy.'

'Like with diving?'

'Yes,' he said, looking delighted with the analogy. His face transformed when he was pleased, like a glimpse of gold buried in dark earth. 'You don't have to watch or be in the room or anything, but I'm videoing the sessions and I need you to watch them after for any problematic episodes. Loss of consciousness, specifically. This could happen for a couple of seconds and I wouldn't necessarily know about it. I want you review the footage.'

'You might pass out? In the bath?' Stella pushed down her sudden anxiety. She wanted to add that she had done a first-aid course, but didn't think her certificate was up-to-date anymore.

'It's very unlikely, but it is possible. Especially as I intend to take longer sessions. I'll let you know when I'm going in and you set your watch or something. I'll call to you through the door when I'm getting out after the agreed time, and if I don't, you check on me.'

'In the bathroom?'

'Door will be unlocked. I won't be naked.' He ran a hand through his hair. 'Fuck. It does sound weird. I swear this is not harassment.'

'The thought hadn't crossed my mind,' Stella said. He wouldn't be in much of a state to harass her after ten minutes in a bath full of ice.

Even if she were the kind of woman men felt inclined to leer at. Which she wasn't.

'Great. Is that okay with you? It would be a big help. I could ask Esmé but she has enough to do.'

'May I ask a question?'

'Of course.'

'Why do you want to stay in the bath for longer? I thought you believed in the minimum effective dose in all things?'

'You've been doing your homework.' He turned to the iPad and brought up a graph. 'Three minutes is MED for fat reduction, but I read a study by Gabriel Hernandez which suggested that cell regeneration could be triggered at the five-minute mark. I thought it was worth testing.'

'Fair enough. It will have to be one hell of a benefit to get me into one, though.'

He straightened up and looked her directly in the eye. 'People always say things like that. They call me crazy, but I think they're the mad ones. No offence.'

'None taken.' Stella fought the urge to step back, to look away. He really was unnervingly intense.

'I mean, we get one shot here, right? Why not optimise your life? Why not be as fit and as healthy and as sharp for as long as possible?'

Stella opened her mouth to reply but Jamie was already moving on to the next thing.

'And then there are people like James Young Simpson. He was this Edinburgh doctor in the nineteenth century and he was thirty-six when he discovered the anaesthetic properties of chloroform, and revolutionised surgery and childbirth. If I'm going to do something important, I have to push my limits.' Jamie suddenly seemed to notice that he was pacing the floor. He stopped and pulled a goofy smile, which was unlike any expression Stella had seen from him so far. 'Sorry. I go on. Just really enthusiastic about this stuff.'

It was kind of nice to meet someone so passionate, Stella thought when he had left her with his tablet to order her equipment. Not restful, but definitely interesting.

Stella was replying to emails using Jamie Munro's detailed response guide when the telephone rang. She answered it with a chirpy 'Jamie Munro's office', enjoying the familiar routine of work, the feeling of being useful.

'And who might you be?' The voice was deep and American. She thought East Coast, but wouldn't have put money on it.

'I'm Stella, Mr Munro's temporary assistant.' Stella didn't know why she'd said 'temporary' – she wouldn't usually. There was something about the caller's manner which made her want to apologise.

'A new one. Okay. You need to get him for me. It's urgent.'

'Mr Munro isn't available at the moment, I'm afraid,' Stella said. Jamie had instructed her that he was going to meditate and shouldn't be disturbed. 'May I take a message?'

'Stella, sweetheart. I'm his agent. Nathan Schwartz. I'm on the list.'

'Sorry?'

'You know, like at a club? Or the entrance to the VIP lounge. Or waiting on the phone to speak to my client. My name's on the list and you wave me through.'

'He's really not available right now,' Stella said, trying to project light amusement rather than irritation. 'I can take a message for you, though.'

'Oh, you're good,' the agent said, sounding delighted. 'Well done. You're like a big black bouncer. Or a white guy with no neck and a tattoo. I can see why he hired you.'

'Thank you,' Stella said. 'But I'm still not disturbing him.'

'He's there, then? Is he working? Please tell me he's writing.'

'Was there a message, Mr Schwartz?'

There was a barking sound which Stella decided must be laughter. 'I like you. Get him to call me later with an update. I want to know

46

where he is with the book. If he doesn't call me, you call me. I need that update.' He lowered his voice. 'Between us girls, he's blown through his last three deadlines and the publisher is getting kinda antsy. They'll put up with a lotta shit, but he's not untouchable. Gotta remember that.'

Stella looked at the phone for a moment after she pressed the button to end the call. She hadn't really believed there were people like that in the world. She pictured Nathan Schwartz leaning back in his chair, chomping on a cigar and terrorising his staff.

At the end of the day, as Stella was putting on the technical raincoat and mentally preparing herself for the wet walk back up the hill, Jamie emerged from his office. His hair and T-shirt were both wet with sweat and he had a length of cord in one hand. 'Is it five already?'

'Half past,' Stella said. 'Did you want me to stay later?'

He shook his head and sat on the arm of one of the chairs. 'Did you walk?'

'Yes.' Stella zipped up her coat. She had just realised that she hadn't thought about Ben all day.

'And you're staying with the Bairds? For how long?'

Jamie was staring straight at her with unnerving intensity, not breaking eye contact. His right knee was bouncing up and down in something she would have called a nervous tic in a person less obviously confident. 'Sorry,' he was saying. 'None of my business, I know. It's just there are houses on the estate. Empty ones. If you want, you can stay in one. Pick one, I don't care.'

He was so full of energy, it was hard to remember that he was unwell. 'You have empty houses, just lying around.' Stella gave him a long look.

'My parents did them up as holiday rentals. I ran them like that, through an agency, while I've been away, but I didn't want strangers around now that I'm here full-time. I want peace and quiet.'

Stella wanted to laugh. How much space did one man need? How much peace? 'Rent?'

He waved a hand. 'Don't worry about it.'

'That's insane,' Stella said. 'Not that I'm not grateful, but you could make a fortune with this place. In the summer, at any rate.'

'Maybe next year,' he said. 'I just have to finish this book. I can't split my focus right now.'

'But—' Stella began. This was too much and far too good to be true.

'You know I hired you to make my life easier, right?' His smile had vanished and his relaxed tone was replaced with something flatter, formal. 'That doesn't include giving me a hard time over my estate. It's my property and I can do what I like.'

'I'm just trying to help,' Stella said. 'And I don't want you to think I'm taking advantage of your good nature.'

'According to most people, I don't have one.'

'Well they clearly don't know about your attitude to staff benefits,' Stella said.

He smiled then, looking relaxed for a few microseconds before jumping up in a sudden movement that made Stella take a reflexive step back.

'Do you want to choose one, then?'

'I'll think about it,' Stella said. 'Thank you.'

That evening at Caitlin and Rob's, Stella got the third degree.

'So, what's he like, then? The great Jamie Munro.' Rob was smiling as he unscrewed the top from a bottle of red wine, but there was no good humour in his voice.

Stella thought about the non-disclosure agreement; it left her with precious few details she could divulge.

'You know him, don't you?' she said instead. 'From way back.'

'Do you, Rob?' Caitlin removed her head from the cupboard where she had been locating a gigantic saucepan with two handles. 'You never said.'

'Not know him. Not really.' Rob shrugged. 'Everyone around here knows *of* him, though. Him and his posh family.' He filled Stella's glass and then his own. 'So, is he as nuts as everybody says? What mad things does he have you doing?'

Stella lifted her wine glass before lying through her teeth. 'Just the usual. Same as every other admin job I've ever had.'

Rob shook his head. 'Now that I don't believe. He is looking for the Holy Grail, is he not? How to live forever—'

'He said you could vouch for me,' Stella said, trying to shift the conversation. 'He remembers your family.'

Rob's shoulders went up a notch and he took a big swig from his glass. 'God, I need this. You won't believe what that little shite Shane Watson did today.'

'Didn't you go to parties at the Munro house?' Stella didn't know why she couldn't leave it alone. Rob clearly didn't remember. Or he didn't want to discuss it.

'Mebbe,' Rob said, looking away. 'When I was really wee.'

'Ceilidhs?' Caitlin said, straightening up. 'I bet you were adorable in a kilt.'

'Naturally,' Rob said, smiling properly now as he looked at his wife.

'Do you think you'll stay?' Caitlin said, turning to Stella. 'Was it all right?'

'It was mostly good.' Stella took the pan from Caitlin and set it on the hob. She didn't know how to encompass the excitement and uncertainty of the place. 'He offered me somewhere to stay, too. Rent-free.'

'Oh, aye?' Rob raised an eyebrow, his expression black. 'What does he want in return for that, then?'

'Nothing,' Stella said, unsettled by Rob's sneering tone. He had always been protective, but this tension seemed out of proportion. 'He did say there might be some unusual hours, but that I could take the time off. Flexi. And I get overtime payments.'

'Well that sounds brilliant,' Caitlin said, seemingly oblivious. 'If I didn't love my job I'd be jealous.'

Caitlin had always been a hardy, outdoors type, and she had landed a job as an estate worker with Scottish Natural Heritage. She was hoping it would lead to a nature-reserve warden position in the fullness of time.

Stella opened her mouth to ask about Caitlin's day, hoping to switch the focus from Jamie Munro, but Rob had other ideas.

'Don't let him take advantage,' Rob said. He was gripping the stem of his wine glass in his fist, as if an invisible force was trying to take it away from him. 'Lord of the bloody manor.'

'He's too distracted to take advantage,' Stella said. 'Workaholic type.'

'You don't have to move.' Caitlin looked worried. 'Don't feel obliged to take the accommodation, you can stay with us as long as you like.'

'Thank you,' Stella said. 'I'm not sure whether to take it or not. I mean, I wanted a change, and it's only temporary so I'm not locked in—'

'The contract's temp?'

'Yeah,' Stella said. 'But I mean this is just temporary.' She waved her hand, indicating everything around them. 'I'm just having a break from reality. Then I'll go home and work out what to do with my life.'

'Perfect,' Caitlin said, visibly relaxing.

Later, when Caitlin had gone up to bed and Stella was washing the wine glasses, Rob stretched out his long legs and said, 'So, what did you really think of Munro?'

'What do you mean?'

He tilted his head. 'I know you, Stells. I know that look you get when you're weighing everything up. You're not sure, are you?'

'It's too soon to be sure,' Stella said. She put a glass on the draining rack. 'And you know me, I'm cautious.'

Rob made a noise halfway between amusement and agreement.

'There's nothing wrong with that,' Stella said, glancing over her shoulder for a moment. His eyes were warm and she was suddenly aware of the smallness of the room.

'I know,' he said. 'I just think you should stretch your wings while you're here. Live a little.'

'I'll take the cottage,' Stella said. 'If that's what you mean.'

'Thank you.' Rob's voice was low and quiet and it seemed to make their conversation more intimate.

Stella shrugged, raising her voice as she ran the water to rinse the sink. 'It's rent-free and it will give me an awesome commute.'

'We need you to leave,' Rob said, and Stella was glad she was facing away from him. 'I mean, it's great to have you. To see you. But with everything that's going on. You know, the baby. And this place is tiny.'

'No problem,' Stella said. Rob had always been very straightforward. When she had first met him at university she had thought him blunt to the point of rudeness, but he was a good match for Caitlin, who wasn't exactly the queen of tact herself.

'And you're better off out of here. Caitlin gets up about a hundred times every night already. God knows what she'll be like later on.'

Stella forced a smile.

'It will be much quieter if you stay in your own place, and I know how important it is that you get your rest.'

Stella tried not to resent Rob for speaking as if she were still an invalid. Caitlin had been Stella's best and only friend when she began university, and her social circle had steadily refused to widen. She'd lived at home with her parents and had to miss half her lectures due to exhaustion, so it had been difficult to make much progress in that direction. When Rob and Caitlin had become an item, Rob had adopted Stella entirely: carrying her books, emailing notes from missed classes, and looking out for her every bit as much as Caitlin. The kindness that had been so welcome before was like acid to her now, but that wasn't Rob's fault.

Stella conjured a smile for Rob and then escaped upstairs to the privacy of her room. It couldn't be any clearer: Rob and Caitlin were a unit. The kind of unit that Stella had wanted to be a part of with Ben. She crawled into bed and pulled the covers over her head, intensely grateful that tomorrow she would be spending the day with a misfit stranger. Grateful that she would be out of the cottage and distracted from the thing she wanted most in the world and could no longer have.

CHAPTER FIVE

Stella chose the smallest of the houses on the estate. It was next to the tennis court, right at the bottom of the formal gardens, and had two bedrooms, one master with a double bed and a smaller twin room. From the window in her bedroom she could see the terraces leading up to the main house, its frontage facing the water, as if the house itself were enjoying the view.

The kitchen window of the cottage looked out on the rough road which curved around the side of the estate from the main house, while both the master bedroom and small living room looked out to the sea.

It was such a relief to be in her own space again. Alone. Looking from the windows at the deserted view, she felt gratitude to Rob for giving her the push. This was a real adventure now.

Better yet, the cottage was entirely devoid of memories and utterly impersonal. She loved the plain dishes in the cupboard, the hotel-style white bed linen, and the plain brown leather sofa and small television. It was all so clearly temporary. It was a transitional space, her own little cocoon from which she would emerge, renewed.

In Stella's experience, there were two ways people went when they had a better-than-average chance of dying young: either hedonistic denial or intense practicality. She thought both reactions were perfectly reasonable, but was incapable of altering the camp into which she fell.

Stella was painfully aware that a little cottage and office job would not be most people's idea of high adventure, but most people hadn't spent their teenage years doing schoolwork in bed, so she didn't think they had any right to judge.

Stella looked out of the window and wondered about putting on her layers of clothes and going down to the shore. She had never walked on a beach at night and the idea was alluring. But it was dark and she might trip. It would be more sensible to walk it during the daytime first, to get familiar with the route. And she would need a head torch. Instead, she unpacked her few possessions and ate a sandwich before retiring early to get a good night's sleep.

Her practical streak kept her safe, but it couldn't stop her from dreaming about Ben. Or prevent the waves of fresh pain buffeting her as if he had left her only yesterday, not four months ago.

In her dream, Stella is in her favourite café in Camden. She knows she is dreaming but Ben is sitting opposite her and she remembers that this really happened. She tries to wake up, doesn't want to relive the scene. Dream Ben lingers, pouring his coffee with the sunlight picking out the blond in his hair. She isn't strong enough to push him out.

'What are you thinking?' Ben asks, and Stella looks past his face to focus on the door of the café. She could get up and leave. She could walk out of this place and just keep going. She could start all over again, but she knows she doesn't have the time. Her heart is a ticking clock.

He takes her hand. 'We're such a good team.'

He's right, too. Which is frustrating. And Stella wants to make a life with him. Worse still, she doesn't think she can make one on her own. The ticking sound is deafening and Stella looks around, can't believe that other people can't hear it.

'What's stopping you?' Ben leans forward. 'Tell me. Maybe we can solve it.'

'I want children,' she says, knowing it will end the conversation. End the relationship, too. She thought she would feel like crying but she doesn't. Stella is cold and smooth all over, like stone.

He doesn't hesitate. 'We can do that.'

Stella realises that he's known all along that it would come to this and that he's already thought it through, made the calculation. Anger surges. If he's known, why didn't he bring it up? All of the misery and the soul-searching and the worry. If he'd known that she was going to force this issue, before even she knew, why didn't he put her out of her misery? Stella knows the answer, but she doesn't let the thought form.

'We would make beautiful babies,' he says.

His face is perfect. She never tires of looking at it. His voice is soft and earnest and, in that moment, she can believe that he wants children. That he wants them with her. She is kidding herself and knows that she is doing so, but her desire is greater. 'We would.' Stella feels the smile on her face.

'Let's get married, too,' he says. 'Make it official.'

'Are you proposing?'

'Shall I get onto one knee?'

'Yes, please,' Stella says. And then she wakes up.

Stella spent the morning working through more of Jamie's backlog of emails, dutifully filing the ones from Nathan Schwartz as 'Urgent'. She refused to think about her dream, filing Ben along with the emails in a folder marked 'Later'.

At lunchtime, Stella walked into the kitchen, hoping there would be bread and cheese so she could make a toastie. Jamie had mentioned food being included but not whether it would consist entirely of the vegetables she had seen in the fridge.

The room looked different to the day before, as if a secret doorway had been opened by the signing of the NDA, revealing a fundamentally different place. Lined up along the worktop were jars and bottles, tubs and pill packets. A few medical-looking gadgets in the standard beige-plastic hue sat in the middle, next to sealed packets of testing strips. The only sign that Jamie was still in residence was the row of empty glasses on the side of the sink, grass-coloured slime dried to the sides. At once Stella felt the strangeness of her situation. What was she doing here? How did she end up in this man's kitchen and how long was she going to borrow this life?

'There you are,' Esmé said, as if Stella had been hiding. 'Mr Munro asked me to give you this.' Esmé passed her a keyring with a large brass key and a couple of Yale types, and a piece of paper with four digits printed in the middle. 'Those are for the house, in case you need access when we're out. We're never both out at the same time so you won't need them. And that's the code for the lock on the shed. You won't need that, either.'

'Okay. Thanks.'

'Don't lose your keys. Don't lend your keys.'

'I won't,' Stella said, wondering how she had managed to piss this woman off already.

'No guests in the house.'

'Right—'

'And I don't know whether Mr Munro mentioned this, but no guests in the cottage, either. Treat it as an extension of this house. It is not your private domain and you have no rights to it whatsoever. If you do not vacate the premises immediately whenever you are told to do so, we will bring the full force of the law down upon you. Do you understand?'

'Perfectly,' Stella said. 'Have you had problems with tenants before?'

'You are not a tenant,' Esmé said darkly. 'You are a visitor.'

'Jamie says I'm part of the team,' Stella couldn't resist saying, sick of the woman's curt tone. Gratifyingly, Esmé's rosy cheeks went one shade darker.

'Mr Munro is not himself right now. He's not thinking clearly.'

Stella hesitated. Jamie didn't look unwell. His skin was a healthy colour, not pale or yellow-tinged, although he did have shadows underneath his eyes. Stella smothered her automatic alarm. When she had been little, she had been kept away from people with colds, sore throats, flu – which, given how often kids got snotty, had meant a great deal of alone time. Things were different now, she reminded herself. She was fine. She needn't be afraid.

'What are these?' Stella gestured to the gadgets.

'You'll have to ask Jamie about that,' Esmé said. 'It's up to him what he tells you.'

'Not if it will affect me directly,' Stella said. If Jamie Munro had something contagious, threatening, she needed to know. She had to be able to do a risk assessment.

Esmé gazed at her in silence for a few uncomfortable moments and then turned away. 'Oh,' she said, turning back like Columbo, ready to deliver her killer blow. 'Don't try to pet the dogs. They'll have your hand off.'

Jamie remained cloistered in his office for hours at a time, and now that Stella's laptop had arrived via courier, she was similarly enclosed in the second office. She left the door open so that if Jamie wanted her, he could simply yell through. She could hear him pacing the room, and sometimes a rhythmic thudding, as if he were throwing a ball against the wall or punching something.

Jamie emailed a list of tasks, which included viewing the videos of his ice baths. She was to log that they had been independently reviewed in the spreadsheet, and to note any changes in behaviour or consciousness. Stella clicked on one of the videos at random. She recognised the grey-and-white colour scheme of the main bathroom. The claw-foot tub was rendered in glorious HD, and when Jamie spoke, his voice was clear. 'Eight a.m., morning ice bath twenty-seven,' he said from behind the camera. The image zoomed in on the bath, showing it three-quarters full of water and ice. Then it zoomed back and Jamie appeared in a towelling dressing gown, holding a bucket. He showed it to the camera, before adding it to the bath. The sound of ice cubes splashing into the water was surprisingly loud.

Stella felt herself shivering in empathy as Jamie disrobed and climbed into the bath. She felt like a voyeur and couldn't help noticing the view of Jamie as he got into the bath, wearing just snug trunks. His broad back, the muscles in his shoulders, the lines along his thighs. She knew she ought to look away, but instead she had the urge to press rewind and watch him again.

There was a small noise as he got into the bath, an involuntary 'oh' that was barely audible. Then he did something Stella hadn't been expecting: he sunk beneath the surface, submerging his entire head, even his nose disappearing beneath the icy water. Stella was light-headed and she realised she was holding her own breath. She had expected him to sit up in the bath for a moment or two, like one of those charity people sitting in a bath of baked beans. She glanced at the clock, wondering how long it was safe for him to stay like that. Which was ridiculous. The video was a recording. She knew Jamie was all right. She could hear him moving around in the room next door. Finally, he broke the surface, sitting up and wiping water from his eyes with one hand, holding on to the side of the tub with the other. He stood up and climbed out of the bath, grabbing his robe. Then he sat on a chair and clipped something to his finger. She leaned towards the screen instinctively, trying to work out what it was for.

'Pulse oximeter.'

Stella hadn't heard Jamie walk in and she jumped slightly.

'I take it before and after every bath. And my blood so that I can test for DHEA, testosterone, and cholesterol and triglyceride levels, too.'

'Have you come to any conclusions yet?' Stella looked back at the screen, where the recorded Jamie was taking a pinprick of blood from his thumb. She hoped she wasn't blushing.

'A few. It's too early, though. I need more time.'

'Don't you have enough for the book?' Stella said, aware of another irate email from Nathan Schwartz.

'Oh, I've got loads of stuff. More than enough, really. It's just I keep thinking of something else. And then I think, *What if I'm just about to find out something big?* and I put off finishing again.'

'You could always publish a follow-up. It doesn't all have to go into this one.'

Stella wasn't sure if Jamie had heard her; he was watching the video on her screen with a small frown. 'It's not ready.'

'The deadline is—' she began.

'I know,' he said sharply. 'You don't have to remind me.'

Stella bit back a retort, watching the rest of the video with dedicated concentration and updating the spreadsheet with the results.

'Day fifteen, done,' the more pleasant, on-screen Jamie said, and the video cut out.

'I'm sorry,' Jamie said. 'I just can't think about the deadline. I'd rather the book was late than rubbish.'

'I understand,' Stella said. 'It's your name on the cover.'

'I don't want to release a rehash. I want to provide something genuinely useful.'

'I know,' Stella said, looking at him now. 'Really, I get it.'

'And it's not just a book anymore. I don't want to just write a new book.'

Stella nodded, although he had lost her.

'I want to do real research. I want to make a difference, like James Young Simpson or Alexander Fleming. People think that's all ancient history, but it's not. We benefit every day from the leaps made by those people.'

'I'm agreeing with you,' Stella said. She pointed at herself. 'Look. I'm nodding my head. I agree it's important. It's interesting.'

'People think everything big has been discovered already, but that's not true. One person can still make an impact. Can you imagine, knowing that your life is going to affect thousands of people down through the generations. Don't you want to be part of something big?'

'Maybe. Not medical stuff, though. I've had enough of that for one lifetime, thank you very much.' Stella felt that she was grateful and that ought to be enough. She didn't want to think about the procedures which had saved her life, or put herself in any situation that required a check-up. She knew that the heart-lung machine, which had been invented in the 1950s, was the only reason she was alive. Without it, the surgeons wouldn't have had the time to complete the tricky procedure. That piece of information was enough; she didn't want to think about the operation any more than that. With an effort of will, Stella resisted the urge to put her hand to her chest, to feel her heart thudding away.

'What do you mean?'

Stella looked away. 'What is this?' She picked up a contraption which appeared to be two smooth pieces of metal held together with springs.

'Grip strengthener. You're changing the subject.' He moved closer and took the device from her, slipping it into his palm and squeezing.

'Why do you need a strong grip?' Stella said.

He sighed as if she were being obtuse, which she was. 'Why won't you talk to me?'

'I understand why you think research is important, but I don't understand why you feel compelled to experiment on yourself, especially considering . . . I mean, why not donate money to a research programme? I don't agree with your method so it seems more polite to stop talking.'

'That's not a reason not to debate. That's exactly the opposite. What do you mean, *especially considering*? Considering what?'

'Well, what does your doctor think about all this?'

Jamie grinned. 'She thinks I'm nuts.'

'Well, then,' Stella said. He was still smiling and maybe it was that momentary transformation that made the words fly from Stella's mouth. 'What do you have?' The question, one Stella and her fellow patients had asked each other all the time – the sick kid version of 'what are you planning to study at uni?' – suddenly sounded very bold. 'Sorry,' she began, but Jamie's brows were drawn down.

'What have you heard?' His voice was low and urgent. Furious.

'Nothing.' Stella took an involuntary step back.

'I don't understand.' He shook his head, one sharp movement like he was trying to clear it. 'Why do you think—'

'All the medical supplies. Those machines in the kitchen . . .'

'I use them to monitor my blood cholesterol, triglycerides, sugar and lactate. I haven't got anything,' he said. 'I'm optimising my health, not trying to cure anything specific.'

'You don't need to do any of it?'

'I do if I want to make advances.' The frown was back.

Stella put a hand to her chest and felt her heartbeat. Her mind was reeling. He chose all of this. He chose needles and physical therapy and drugs. Why would anyone *choose* all of that?

'You don't agree with my methods?'

Stella took a breath before she spoke. 'You are very tiring.' She forced a lightness into her tone, determined not to reveal her feelings. 'Do you never just let something go?'

'Not when I'm interested,' Jamie said. He was watching her intently and there was a part of Stella that was flattered. It was nice to be so completely in somebody's beam of attention. She could see why people were lining up to be interviewed for his books and research. It wasn't just the publicity, they were flattered by the intensity of his listening skills. What they didn't know is that he would move on as quickly as snapping his fingers. Stella had no desire to be a ten-minute diversion, a footnote in his research.

He narrowed his eyes. 'I will find out, Stella Jackson. I don't give up.'

'I'm not that interesting,' Stella said. 'I promise.'

He tilted his head. 'There, you are mistaken.'

～

Esmé pushed the door open, her arms filled with a large brown box. She scowled at Jamie. 'Nathan has sent a UPS delivery. Again. It upsets the dogs, you know. They hate that brown van, and I can't work out why.'

'Thank you.' Jamie bounded over and took the box, putting it on the table and leaning in to kiss Esmé on the cheek. 'I know he's a pain. You're a saint.'

'None of that,' Esmé said, her cheeks pink.

'Why do you put up with him?' Stella asked once Esmé had left the room. She assumed that Jamie would be able to get a new agent if he wanted. He was successful enough, after all.

'We've been friends for years,' Jamie said, opening the box with a penknife. He began pulling out packages of coffee and a bottle of amber-coloured liquid.

'Whisky?'

'Cinnamon liqueur,' Jamie said. 'Made in Palo Alto. It's really good with tequila.'

'We have coffee and booze here, or does he not know that?'

'He's trying to remind me of San Francisco, of what he thinks I'm missing. He thinks if I go back, I'll stop getting distracted and turn the book in.' Jamie glanced at Stella. 'He's a good guy.'

Stella opened her mouth to say something rude, then shut it again.

'I know,' Jamie said. 'He hides it well. But he's loyal and that's not something you just throw away.'

Stella thought about Ben. She'd been loyal to him but that hadn't been enough.

CHAPTER SIX

1st November, 1847

My dearest Mary,

I do not care for it here and wish to come home. There are evil spirits in this house and no amount of fine food or cheerful faces can erase that fact or make me forget it.

Two nights ago, a knocking awoke me in the small hours. It was the door to the rear of the house, the one which leads to the scullery and backstairs, and a mob of low men made a tremendous noise, wrestling a heavy burden which they dropped on more than one occasion. They were all the worse for some drink, I believe, and did not have the wit to keep themselves quiet. I was very frightened and believed we were being invaded by some picky-fingered nicht walkers. By the time I kent they were delivering a package, I was frozen with fear to my spot at the turn in the stair, and there I stayed, praying that I would make it through the ordeal unmolested.

Mary, I cannot speak of what they brought into the house. It is most ungodly and the souls of us all are in peril.

Please send the money for my passage home. I cannot stay here. I must not stay here.

Your loving sister,

Jessie

By Friday night, Stella was ready for some company. She arranged to meet Caitlin and Rob at the pub in the village, but when she got there the whole group was there, enthusiastically drinking. Rob seemed to have started early, though.

'Celebrating the weekend,' Caitlin said apologetically.

Rob was tipping the remains of a bag of crisps into his mouth, but most of it ended up down the front of his T-shirt. 'More cheesy ones,' he said, stabbing a finger at Doug.

'They're all out,' Doug said. 'I already told you.'

'That's because you bastards ate the lot.' Rob spoke into his shirt, dabbing at the crumbs with a finger shining with spit.

Caitlin nudged Rob. 'You need to get home before one of the parents sees you.'

'How's the lord of the manor?' Rob fixed his red eyes upon Stella.

'Great,' Stella said. She tried to move Rob's pint away from him, but he held on to it with a fierce grip.

'I bet he has you doing all kinds of weird things,' Rob said, his words slurring.

Stella hadn't seen him so drunk since an ill-advised pub crawl during their second year at university. She had seen him tipsy plenty of times, of course, but that night he had been so drunk he had even tried to kiss Stella while she was helping him to the last stop of the night. Caitlin had been in the group ahead of them, thank goodness, and hadn't witnessed the ungainly grapple which had ensued. Stella had planned to demand an apology once Rob was sober, but the sight of his suffering the following day and his clear amnesia of all events post pint number six had blunted the urge.

The belligerent set to his face brought it all back and she tried to move seats. Rob stuck out a hand and grabbed her arm, hauling her close. His fingers dug painfully into her flesh. 'Devil worship?'

'What?' Stella leaned away. 'Let go, Rob. That hurts.'

'Why does Jamie fucking Munro get everything handed to him on a plate?' Rob addressed the entire pub, his voice carrying over the chatter as one arm made a sweeping gesture. 'Answer. He made a deal with the devil.'

'Oh Jesus, man,' Stewart said. 'You are in a bad way the night.' He had been about to join their table but spun on his heel and went to join another group.

'Come on, mister. Time for bed.' Caitlin prised Rob's fingers from Stella's arm, mouthing 'sorry'.

'Need a hand?' Doug put his hands underneath Rob's armpits and lifted. Rob was not especially small but he shot upwards with amazing ease. Being a postman was obviously more of a workout than Stella realised.

'Thank you,' Caitlin said. 'Stella?'

It took the three of them to encourage Rob outside. Once they had folded him into the passenger seat of the car, Doug went back inside.

Stella opened the rear door, but Caitlin put a hand on her arm, in the same place Rob had gripped. 'No, you stay.'

'Are you sure?' Stella was torn between the desire to stay away from drunk Rob, and friendship duty. Rob was pressed against the window, his eyes shut. If he went to sleep like that, Stella wasn't sure Caitlin would be able to get him into the house.

'No sense in ruining your night, too,' Caitlin said. 'He'll be embarrassed when he sobers up.' She pulled a face, the light from the pub windows illuminating her odd expression.

Stella wanted to ask if he did this often, but was worried it would sound judgemental.

'He's just had a bad day,' Caitlin said, as if reading Stella's thoughts. 'He Skyped with his mum earlier and that wound him up. I don't know why.'

'Skyped?' Stella had assumed that Rob's family lived nearby, that their proximity would have been one of the reasons Rob and Caitlin moved to this part of the world.

'Yeah.' Caitlin turned to check on Rob. 'You know how it is with parents.'

Turning back to the pub, Stella was surprised by how comfortable she felt walking in.

'You didn't want a lift, then?' Doug said. 'I thought we'd lost you for the night.'

'Not now,' Stella said, checking to see if there were any crisps left in the open packets. 'It's still early.'

'You deserve some time off,' Doug said approvingly. 'You work too hard.'

'How on earth do you know that?' Stella was amused by his earnest expression.

'You're that type,' he said sagely.

Stella licked salt and vinegar from her fingers while she contemplated this. She had never thought of herself as especially hardworking. Conscientious, yes. She always did what needed to be done and had been praised by her temporary managers at any number of the office jobs she'd taken, even offered permanent contracts over and over again, but she'd never felt she'd worked especially hard. 'I like working,' she said, and realised as she spoke that it was the truth. She liked being efficient and helpful. It was true that her position as Jamie's assistant seemed mostly an exercise in formulating lists of things he then refused to deal with or discuss, but she had certainly worked in more soul-destroying places. And besides, she wasn't beaten yet. On Monday she would confront Jamie about the situation with his book deadline. After all, what did she have left to lose?

'You're unusual. Most folk can't wait for the weekend.'

'It's all about balance.' Stella knew that she sounded like Jamie now, but she couldn't stop herself. She had been going through the backlog of articles and podcasts on his website, trying to get to know the business, and the sheer strength of his conviction was compelling. Or website Jamie, anyway. Real-life Jamie was more complicated: arrogant and brusque one moment, and then endearingly genuine and enthusiastic the next.

'Is that right?' Doug was smiling. He lifted his pint and the small shot of whisky next to it. 'Like a drink in each hand?'

Stella nodded, but her mood had dipped. She had always felt she was too mutable, too quick to alter her own opinions. Like soft wax pressed into the mould of whoever she happened to be with. When she had first got together with Ben, Caitlin had jokingly pointed out that Stella had stopped wearing long hippyish skirts and swapped them for skinny jeans and heels practically overnight. Stella had straightened her back. That was just growing up, leaving university and no longer dressing like a lefty student.

She pushed the thought aside and focused on Doug, getting him to tell her about his worst delivery mishaps.

'And then there was the time I dropped a parcel in a puddle and it soaked the paper. The insides were coming out as I handed it over to the wee wifie at the door.'

'Was she angry?'

'Nuh.' Doug shook his head. 'Mortified, more like. It was the biggest dildo you can imagine. Not even in plastic packaging. More like it was a personal gift.' He paused for effect. 'Or a loaner.'

'Ew!' Stella obliged him with a dramatic expression of disgust.

'Are you talking about that sex toy again?' Stewart was carrying a bowl of sticky toffee pudding and ice cream, which he put down on the table next to his mug of tea. 'You're obsessed, man.'

'Haunted, more like,' Doug said, the light glinting off his spectacles. He took a long pull of his pint. 'Anyway, just cheering up the lassie, here. She's needin' a laugh.'

'That Munro bastard giving you a hard time, hen?'

'He's very nice,' Stella said. 'To me, anyway. But I know you don't like him. Nobody round here seems to, I get that loud and clear.'

'It's no his fault,' Stewart said. 'His father was a right bastard and it's hard to get round that. Especially when he doesn't mix. Naebody has anything to go on so they go on the bad memories, if you ken what I mean.'

'I do,' Stella said. 'Did you know the family, then?'

'Oh, aye. He was in my primary until he went away to school.'

Stella had seen the local kids in their dark green sweatshirts, running around the playground. 'They didn't always send him private, then?'

'It's a question of logistics. If you want your kid to go to school nearby when they're wee, you've got Morar Primary and that's about it.'

In most rural places you had limited choices, Stella knew that, but it was definitely more extreme in this area. The roads were vastly improved, as everyone kept saying, but it still took much longer to drive from place to place than you thought possible. Ten miles was not 'nipping', and twenty could take an hour and a half if you got stuck behind a tractor or a line of caravans. And that was before you factored in the weather. She had already begun to look longingly at the four-wheel drives.

'Did you go to the house for Hogmanay?'

'Aye, most years,' Doug said. 'You didnae, eh, Stu?'

'My dad had a falling-out with Mr Munro.' Stewart shook his head cheerfully.

'Tell her,' Doug said. He nudged Stella. 'This is brilliant.'

'Dad decked Munro.'

Stella waited for elaboration, but that seemed to be it. Stewart put a loaded spoonful of pudding into his mouth.

'He was all for getting the polis at the time, but he never did,' Doug said.

Stewart swallowed with some difficulty and added: 'Didn't want that kind of attention. Guilty conscience.'

'Why did your dad hit Jamie's dad?'

Stewart looked at her as if she were simple. 'Because he was beating on Jamie's mum.'

'Oh God.' Stella's hand went to her mouth. 'That's awful.'

'He had a temper. Especially when he'd had a few.' Stewart was scraping his bowl now, carefully getting every trace of the cream. 'It was ironic that Dad was angry about it. Except when you ken how much he likes a fight. Any excuse.'

Doug was draining his pint glass and now he stood up. 'Another one?'

'I'm okay, thanks.' Stella was still working on hers.

'I'm set.' Stewart nodded at his tea.

The bar had filled up and Doug joined the scrum, chatting easily to those around him. He seemed to know everyone, which, in a place like this, was entirely possible.

'Jamie's mum wasn't very nice, but she didn't deserve that.'

'No,' Stella said. 'Was he often violent?'

Stewart held out his hand and tipped it from side to side. 'Hard to say. Mostly it was words, I think. He expected her to do anything he said, anything he wanted, but she would pick Jamie up from school in dark glasses.'

'Shades?'

'In winter, aye.' He gave her a meaningful look.

'Did no one report it?'

'No point. She'd deny it. He'd deny it.' Stewart shrugged. 'And it wasn't like now. You didn't talk about this kind of thing. You dealt with it quietly and in the family or with the locals.'

'If it was dealt with at all,' Stella said.

'Aye.' Stewart picked up his spoon as if forgetting that he'd finished, then put it down again.

'Did he hurt Jamie?' Stella was trying not to picture a young skinny Jamie, cowering in a dark corner, frightened and alone, but the image was there nonetheless.

Stewart shrugged. 'Mebbe. Kid was probably happy to go away to school.'

'When was that?'

'I don't know. Primary five?' Seeing her expression, he added, 'That's about eight or nine.'

'Were you friends?'

Stewart looked surprised. 'Of course. You don't really have a choice when there's twenty kids in the entire school.'

'Oh, right.' Stella felt stupid. There had been more than that in each class of her primary school.

'But he left. People do, right enough. There aren't any jobs around here so it's hard to stay, but somehow we think worse of them anyway.'

'For deserting the village?' Stella asked.

Stewart smiled. 'Quitters. Exactly.'

'And now he's back. And with a ton of money,' Stella said.

'He always had money, that was another thing. It goes deep. Those that own the land and those who scrape a living from it.'

'It's not his fault, though, surely . . .'

'I'm not having a go,' Stewart said. 'I've got nothing against him. He's done well, and good for him. At least he's been working, not just spending Daddy's money.'

'Lot of people don't call it work,' Stella said, 'but it is.'

'Just jealousy, if you ask me.' Stewart drank some tea. 'That lot would give their right arm to sit around writing books for a fat payout. Give their left arm to go to California, too.'

Doug arrived back with his fresh pint, and conversation moved on to football and Doug and Mairi's plans for their dining room. 'We're knocking through,' he said proudly. 'We'll have a dinner when it's all done. You'll have to come.'

'Doug's curries are amazing,' Stewart said, warming to the new subject with endearing enthusiasm. 'He makes them from scratch.'

When the bell rang for last orders, Doug got a final dram and Stewart ordered a hot chocolate with whipped cream and marshmallows. 'He always gets that,' Doug said. 'It's his version of a night cap.'

Stewart offered Stella a lift home and she took it, grateful that Stewart didn't drink.

It was pitch-black, and the rain of earlier had transformed into freezing sleet which was hurled horizontally. Stella zipped up her leather jacket and pulled her new hat down over her ears. There was a blanket on the passenger seat of the car, and she put it over her legs while she waited for the car heater to warm up.

Stewart was concentrating on the road and Stella admired his profile, wondering why he didn't have a girlfriend. Or boyfriend. She opened her mouth to ask him, alcohol loosening her tongue, when he said, 'You know I said it was ironic that my dad had been so angry with Mr Munro.'

It took Stella a second to remember. 'You said he liked a fight.'

'Usually he stuck with folk he could win against. Me. My mum. But when he was really drunk, he'd have a go with anyone.'

'I'm sorry,' Stella said, hating how useless and small those words were.

'He's dead now,' Stewart said. 'Good riddance.' The phrase had the ring of putting on a brave face, tough talk to hide pain, but Stewart flashed her a reassuring smile.

Stella couldn't help but smile back. Stewart was one of those people it felt good to be around.

71

The car ate up the slope from the village to the main road, and Stewart took the sharp turning back down the hill to Munro House. The high-voltage security lights came on as they approached, and Stewart turned the car carefully in the courtyard before stopping.

'Thanks so much,' Stella said, relinquishing the blanket.

'No problem, doll.'

She put her hand on the door handle and Stewart said, 'Watch out for him, ay.' It wasn't a question; it was the strange reflexive addition of the vowel sound on the end of the sentence that so many Scots seemed to use.

'Honestly, don't worry about me. He's really nice. Nothing like his father.' Stella got out of the car and went to shut the door.

'Blood will out,' Stewart said so quietly Stella wasn't sure she'd heard him right.

'What?' she said, leaning down.

'Bye, then.' Stewart held up a hand in salute and Stella obediently closed the door so that he could drive away.

After her Friday night in the pub, Stella felt like being alone. Caitlin had issued an open invitation, but Stella was overwhelmed by change and knew she had reached the end of her reserves. She had always tired easily, and had wondered if this delicacy was part of her condition or purely psychosomatic. After a quiet weekend, in which she slept a great deal and avoided switching on her mobile phone on the off chance it would get a signal and somebody – her parents, Ben, Caitlin – would manage to get through, Stella felt her energy returning.

She drove to Mallaig to stock up on groceries and bought several paperbacks in the lifeboat charity shop, including a pristine copy of Jamie's first hit, *Your Best Body*. She passed the lifeboat station just as the bright orange boat was launching, the water churning in its wake as it sped out to the open water. There was a man with a Co-op shopping bag who had stopped to watch, shading his eyes with one hand. 'Is there an emergency?' Stella asked, feeling the worry in the pit of her stomach.

'Naw, hen. Just a practice drill, like.'

Stella stayed away from the main house, not wanting to encroach on Jamie's territory or risk him changing his mind about her free lodging, and she didn't see him at all. She caught sight of Esmé though, striding through the woodland which edged the property, and again as she crossed the beach, with the two dogs jumping in and out of the sea with abandon. Stella slept a great deal and went out for walks, taking big gulps of the chilly air like it was medicine.

On Monday, Stella got to work in the room she had seen on her interview tour. She ignored the odd exercise equipment and concentrated on the cardboard boxes. There were vitamin supplements she had never heard of and a hefty box of protein bars. Stella moved a good number to the kitchen and then sealed the box with tape and wrote the name of the bars on the outside in black marker. The next few boxes had other vitamin supplements and protein powder, and there was an unmarked plastic tub which housed a block of dried matter. It looked organic, like grass, and Stella's first thought was that Jamie was doing some very unstealthy drug-smuggling. It didn't smell of marijuana, though, more of something fermented and spiced. Exotic.

Jamie chose that moment to put his head around the door. He looked momentarily bemused and Stella wondered if he had forgotten about hiring her. For a horrible moment, she thought it was going to be a rerun of her interview. Then he smiled and held a hand up in greeting.

'Where do you want this?'

'Oh, you found my tea. Brilliant.' He wandered away, holding onto the block with one hand and a grip strengthener, which he was squeezing, in the other. He was talking all the while into a headset microphone, either having a very one-sided conversation or dictating.

A moment later he popped his head back around the door. He no longer looked relaxed and his voice was tense. 'You haven't been in there, have you?' He pointed across the hall to one of the many doors.

Stella shook her head. If it hadn't been on the tour, she hadn't been inside, figuring that was a decent rule for this weird domestic–work environment.

'Good,' Jamie said. 'Leave it.'

Spoken like she was a dog nosing something unmentionable on the pavement. Charming.

Stella worked her way through the boxes of supplies, making a note of substances and amounts in a spreadsheet. She estimated usage where possible and put alerts into her phone for reordering. Then she moved into the kitchen, partly to familiarise herself and partly because she was ready for coffee. Esmé was next to the Aga mixing something in a large bowl. 'Apple and oat muffins,' she said. 'There's soup for lunch if you want it.'

'Thank you,' Stella said. 'I didn't expect to get fed. I can make my own food. Not that I'm not grateful.' Stella stopped speaking with a massive effort. There was something about Esmé which made her intensely nervous.

Esmé didn't respond, so Stella took her coffee and returned to work.

It was almost half past four and Stella was thinking about shutting down her computer. She had started early that morning and worked her hours, but part of her didn't want to go back to the little cottage too soon, as she was worried that if she had too much time on her hands, she might weaken and call Ben.

'Can you stay a little longer?' Jamie appeared in the doorway just as Stella was putting on her jacket.

'No problem,' Stella said, relieved.

'I'm going for a bath. Going to try for ten minutes. Can you time me?'

In the kitchen, Jamie filled three buckets with ice and gave one to Stella. 'Are you okay with that?' He seemed so self-obsessed that these moments of concern for her well-being were like tiny, heart-warming bullets. If she wasn't careful, she knew she could build the idea of a good man where there wasn't one. Her track record in assessing personality wasn't exactly encouraging.

He carried the other two and led the way to the main bathroom.

'I'll wait outside the door,' Stella said, unnecessarily, backing out of the room. She set the timer function on her phone. 'Shout through when you get in.'

'You'll probably hear me splashing,' Jamie said.

Stella slid down the wall to sit on the floor next to the closed door. She heard the final bucket of ice being sloshed into the water and then a stifled gasp as Jamie got in. 'Never gets easier,' he called, embarrassment in his voice.

'I'm timing you,' Stella called back.

After a minute or so of silence, Jamie spoke, his voice carrying surprisingly well. 'So, how are you getting on? Has Esmé been feeding you? Help yourself to anything you like in the kitchen.'

Stella thought of the muffins that had been delicious warm from the oven. So good she had had two. 'Do you not mind having food like that in the house? Isn't it harder to stick to your special diets?'

A splashing noise came from inside and Stella looked at the timer. Only three minutes so far.

'My official line is "no", but yeah. Sometimes. But I want the data more so I have to do it.'

Jamie's voice sounded weird and his teeth were chattering, but it was quite nice to speak to him this way. With a wall between them and no intense eye contact, Jamie seemed more manageable. Definitely less alarming. 'Why has it got to be you?'

'I would never ask anybody else to be a guinea pig. That would be unethical. I'm happy to experiment on myself, I choose to do this, but

I would never ask anyone else to take the risk. I'm dipping down now,' Jamie said. 'I'll count to sixty and then tell you when I'm back up.'

'Okay.' Stella checked the time and waited, counting silently as well as watching the timer, determined not to make a mistake. She was so used to being cautious on her own behalf, worrying about somebody else was almost pleasurable.

'Up!'

'Okay!' Stella called back. 'Five more minutes?'

'Right.'

Stella had seen Esmé cross the back garden, dogs in tow, so she felt fairly safe yelling out her name through the door. She wondered how to introduce the question 'why does your housekeeper hate me?'. She decided to ease into the subject.

'Has Esmé worked here for long?'

'Esmé is family,' Jamie said. 'She was looking after this place before I was even born.'

Stella congratulated herself on her tact. Complaining about Esmé's manner would clearly not have been a good idea.

'One minute to go,' Stella said after a silence. 'How do you feel?'

'Alive,' Jamie said, his voice strained.

Stella kept her eyes on the timer, counting down the seconds. Right on time, she heard water sloshing and a muffled bang as Jamie got out of the bath. 'I'm on dry land,' he said, sounding relieved. There was something else in his voice, too, something which stabbed Stella through her core. She felt as if she had glimpsed the hard price of Jamie's obsessive intensity.

He came out of the bathroom, wrapped in a thick towelling dressing gown. She tried not to be self-conscious, but it was strange to be in such close, domestic proximity with a new boss. He rubbed a towel over his hair and thanked her for timing his bath, sounding weirdly stiff and formal, as if he was also noticing the oddness of the situation.

'I saw you unpacked. Thanks.'

'No problem.' Stella turned to leave, but Jamie hadn't finished.

He looked uncomfortable for a second. 'There's more, I'm afraid. I haven't really done much with the house since getting back.'

'Do you want rooms opened up?' Stella pulled her phone from her pocket, ready to add it to the to-do list.

He shook his head. 'No. I just want to get my stuff organised. I wasn't expecting to stay this long and then I had some more shipped but I haven't had a chance to—'

'No problem,' Stella said again. She made a note.

'I thought Esmé would, but I think she's been busy.'

'This place is too much for one person,' Stella said. 'Don't you have a cleaner and a gardener and all that?'

'There were people employed for that when I got here. They did the turnaround cleaning and laundry for the cottages, too, but I didn't want strangers around the place so I let them go.'

'Well, it's too much for Esmé,' Stella said.

He nodded. 'Good thing you're here now, then.'

Stella remembered her resolution. It was time to take her new boss in hand. 'I've sorted out the urgent emails, did you want me to forward them to you?'

'God, no,' Jamie said. 'You just deal with them. If you don't know how, just leave them and I'll get to them later.'

'Your agent called again,' Stella said, determined to make headway. 'He really wants to speak to you—'

'He wants to tell me off, more like.' Jamie smiled, not looking worried about this prospect.

Stella gave up. 'I started early this morning so I'm going to finish now, if that's okay? Going for a walk in the last of the light.'

'Of course, no worries.' Jamie already seemed distracted, probably planning his next activity.

Stella was halfway down the main stairs when he called. 'Be careful along the shore. The rocks can be slippy.'

CHAPTER SEVEN

21st November, 1847

My dearest Mary,

Thank you for your letter and for your wise counsel. You always know how to soothe my mind and I am grateful for it. Please do not be concerned. I have grown accustomed to my new situation. Even the night visitors are less troubling to me now. Mr Lockhart has explained their great significance and I am no longer afraid. Mr Lockhart says that to be afraid of ghouls is to spit in the face of science.

To show you how fearless I have become, let me tell you about yesterday evening. It was long after supper and I was in my nightclothes. There was a great commotion on the backstairs, with a thumping noise and loud voices. I crept out of my room and saw that the cargo had slipped from the group and fallen down the steps. The mouth of the sack had fallen open and I beheld something pale and fleshy protruding. I did not linger. I was not unduly frightened, but the odour during these times is truly unbearable.

There. You see! I am calm and almost unbearably modern! Mr Lockhart bade me meet a body and said that I would never now imagine ghosts or the supernatural. He is most wise, as I could never now mistake one for the other.

Truly, it is a privilege to witness at close quarters the genius of Mr Lockhart. The bell rings day and night with people who wish to consult with him. Matters of medicine, naturally, but other subjects, too. He is known for his wise and learned ways and the quality of conversation in his secret meetings. Yes! I said 'secret' and they must be the worst-kept of all time. The parlour is more often filled with gentlemen from the Royal College than with patients, and Maggie, the maid who sees to the fire in that room, told me a little of their conversation. Many of the words were unfamiliar, but I love to hear nonetheless. It is thrilling to be near so great a man. You can feel the intellectualism in the air, it is woven into the rugs, and seems to leak from the walls and furniture.

It has awakened a thirst in me, but one I must conceal. Mr Lockhart does not like to see a lady reading, save the Holy Bible. Still, I cannot help but think it would be wonderful to understand these things.

Please do not be shocked. And do not tell Mother and Father. They would only worry and I have caused them enough concern for three lifetimes already. Instead, I beg that you send me more news. You said that things were 'much as usual' but I wish you to write every detail of your day that I might imagine myself with you. Did you finish hemming the muslins in good time? How is dear Callum – I trust the wretched cough has cleared?

Your loving Jessie

Stella took the rutted track which led, through two gates with both 'Private' and 'Keep closed' signs, to a marsh. She stepped from tussock to tussock, avoiding the areas with reeds until she found a worn path to follow. It had seemed like a relatively mild day when she started out, and she had left the technical raincoat in the cottage, but now the breeze was cutting straight through her leather jacket. There was a clarity and cleanliness to the air, though, which made Stella feel more alive than she could remember. She took in great lungfuls, feeling her chest expand, grow strong. At once, she could understand why they used to build hospitals and sanatoriums on coastlines, why 'a change of air' was said to do you good. Never mind writing another bestseller, if Jamie could bottle the Highland air he could sell it to Londoners.

She climbed the stile and crossed the scrappy dunes to the shoreline, walking along the pebbled beach. It was deserted. Eerily so, like something from an apocalyptic film. Jamie had said that hikers and fishers crossed the beach as they traversed the coast, but the only other way to access this part of the bay was the one she had just taken. Her pocket was buzzing and it took a moment for Stella to realise it was her phone. The signal was so patchy that she was already out of the habit of checking it, although she kept it fully charged in case of emergency. She looked now, and saw multiple texts from Ben. She put it back in her pocket without reading them and looked out at the sea, the islands like giant creatures, and, in the distance to her left, the snow-capped mountains. She walked around the curve of the bay and scrambled over rocks which spilled out from under the cliff. She passed a wilted bouquet of flowers and wondered if they had been washed up or left purposely. Perhaps it was a local tradition, something to make wishes come true or to appease the bad spirits.

A massive slab of yellowish stone was begging to be climbed and she did, enjoying the stretch in her muscles, the slight exertion. At the top, there was a surprisingly flat surface, like a seat had been deliberately worn away by the sea and the weather, and Stella sat on her jacket and watched the waves roll into shore.

When she couldn't resist the urge any longer, she read Ben's messages. Quickly, like ripping off a plaster.

Need to talk to you about the house. I have a plan. Call me! X

Why won't you speak to me? Please, let's talk. It's important. X

Where are you? House is empty (you left curtains open but I have closed). I am really worried. Should I call police?! Xx

Seriously, Stella. What is going on? Are you still angry with me? Where are you? I NEED to speak to you. Xx

ARE YOU OKAY? CALL ME.

Stella read the messages several times, waiting to feel something. There was a little trickle of guilt. Almost automatic. And a small sense of pleasure at Ben's concern. It was nice to have his attention. Stella looked out at the waves, strands of hair escaping from her ponytail and flicking across her face. *I'm not very nice*, Stella thought. *I shouldn't be pleased that he's worried.*

The feelings were very small, though. Blessedly so. After weeks of drowning in the break-up, of taking gulps of misery and longing and pulling them down deep into her lungs and stomach, she felt light and empty. Almost free.

The sea was silver and black and, in the distance, the back of Eigg rose from the water, long and low, like a giant creature. An Sgùrr, the distinctive mound of volcanic rock at one end, only added to the illusion and Stella narrowed her eyes, imagining what ancient travellers must have seen as they navigated by boat, their senses playing with the shapes thrown by the waves and the strange Highland light.

A small part of her mind refused to be distracted by the landscape. It was still running the Stella and Ben show. Ben and Stella. As joined at the hip as the golden couple, Rob and Caitlin. After that first night, Ben had called around at Stella's shared house the next day and asked if she fancied a triple bill at the cinema. It was a celebration of Rodriguez's work and, truth be told, Stella fell asleep during the middle film, but she had never felt so comfortable with a man before. It was as if they had known each other in a past life. Their instant connection, with the sharing of likes and dislikes, opinions and humour, was intoxicating. Stella felt as if she had been walking around as half a person and now the rest had been returned.

They talked all the time, and when they weren't talking, sometimes they just sat with their foreheads resting together and stared into each other's eyes. Stella had never told anybody that, as it sounded like the worst cliché of romance, worse even than red roses and an engagement ring in a glass of champagne, but it was the truth. They had created a place between them. Her safe place. No matter what else was going on, no matter how frightened she felt, she could lean into Ben and feel her heart slowing down until it beat with his, steady and true.

The tears were pouring now, stinging with the cold air that whipped in from the sea. Stella was glad. She knew that she had poked the wound intentionally, as if she had been frightened by her calm reaction to reading Ben's texts. No matter how bad the misery of the past few months had been, it was familiar. This light and airy feeling of freedom was terrifying and new. The wind coming off the sea had blown her wide open, and a part of Stella wanted nothing more than to sink back beneath the waves of her grief.

The next day, after a late lunch break in which she ate a sandwich in the deserted kitchen, Stella decided to take Jamie at his word when he said he wanted his things organised. She checked for stray boxes in all of the rooms, and discovered several which were entirely devoid of furniture, and another that was filled with white dust sheets. They lay over the lumpy shapes of furniture like shrouds. Stella closed the door with relief.

She moved every cardboard box, every piece of equipment, suitcase and unopened jiffy bag into one room – a place that had probably been a breakfast room as it had a smaller, less grand version of the polished table in the dining room. A row of taxidermy watched from a sideboard the size of a small boat while Stella unpacked and catalogued. She moved the unopened mail to a newly emptied packing box in her office.

Whenever she felt her breath grow shallow and her muscles begin to burn with the exertion, she repeated her mantra – *You are fine, you are fine, you are fine* – and resisted the urge to take unnecessary breaks. She wanted to get stronger and knew the only way was to push herself, however terrifying she found it. The problem, Stella reflected as she hoisted a box on top of another, was that she had been ill for so much of her life that she had no real reference for what was 'good' and 'healthy' tiredness, and what was a dangerous symptom. Her consultant had said that normal exercise was completely fine, but Stella had spent much of her childhood lying down, unable to breathe, and so these days she had absolutely no idea what 'normal' felt like.

Needing a break from the black shining eyes of the largest piece of taxidermy – an otter, unnaturally twisted and holding a fish in its claws, Stella poured herself a decaf coffee and took it into the deserted dining room. It had, in her opinion, the best view, and was quite a pleasant room if you avoided looking at the sharp tips of the antlers threatening an invisible foe.

The late afternoon sky was glowing, turning opal in places behind the clouds. Stella wiped condensation from the old sash window, to get a better look at the odd light. Frost glistened on the grass and trees, turning the garden into something magical for a moment. A small bird of prey, maybe a sparrowhawk, landed on the wall which separated the old vegetable garden from the lawn.

Something flashed and Stella blinked. She thought it was a security light, over by the hedge at the left-hand side of the garden. But it had only shone for a moment, so perhaps someone was using a torch. It flashed again and she realised that the setting sun was catching something reflective. The flash came again, and she saw that it was from the middle of the hedge, at the gap for a low gate. There was something black and circular wedged in the side of the foliage. Squinting into the shadows and letting her eyes adjust, Stella saw the object move. It was a cylinder and there was something bulky and dark behind it. Then, a movement and a pale oval appeared and disappeared. A face.

It was a person with a camera. A long telephoto lens and they were stood on the boundary of the garden. Which meant they were on the track that led alongside the house and was private property. The photographer had come through the gates with their forbidding signs, which meant they were knowingly breaking the law. Stella felt a thrill of fear. As an inveterate rule-follower, she had a visceral reaction to the chaos that breaking them implied.

And if a person was willing to ignore a sign, what else were they willing to do?

Stella knew that the sensible option was to call the police and hope that they got there in time to catch the photographer in situ. But she also knew that Jamie wouldn't thank her for bringing more people and attention to his home. She stepped away from the window so that she could no longer be seen, and messaged Jamie.

The reply pinged back. *Stay put. No police. Act natural.*

As she'd expected.

Stella resumed her position, drinking her coffee and gazing out at the garden, acting as though nothing was amiss. Her skin tingled as if aware of being watched. Stella imagined the photographer behind the camera, wondered what they were thinking as they watched her sip her coffee. She knew Jamie didn't want her to alert the illicit photographer that they had been caught, but then it occurred to her to wonder why.

A second later she saw Jamie moving stealthily along the side of the hedge, shielded from the view of where she had seen the flash of light. Seeing him at this distance, moving with quiet purpose and with his solid, muscular figure, he looked almost dangerous. For a second, Stella could see why everybody kept warning her away. He was going to confront the intruder. At once Stella felt a spurt of fear, saw images of punches thrown, the glint of light on a knife blade. Ridiculous. She was letting her overactive danger-reaction lead again, but her heart was pounding nonetheless. Stella put her palm to her chest as she scanned the hedge for another flash of light, a sign that the photographer was still there.

The camera seemed to have gone. Or it had been a figment of her imagination. Or Jamie had caught some skinny boy with an iPhone and was beating the crap out of him. There was an intensity to Jamie's wish for privacy that bordered on the pathological. Stella continued to scan the garden, paralysed by indecision about what else to do.

After ten minutes, Stella began to really worry. She went to the back door and dithered for a few minutes, wondering whether to get a torch and go out into the gathering dark to look for Jamie. Unable to decide, she stood on the threshold with the door wide open, listening. It was eerily quiet, with just the rustling of wind in the trees.

Another ten minutes crept by, and Stella had just decided that she would go and find Esmé in her private quarters, ask the housekeeper for advice, when Jamie banged through the door and pulled his boots off. He was sweaty and dishevelled and smelled of the cold outside. Stella felt her heart hammering as she trailed him down the hall and into the sitting room. She balled up a fist against her ribs. 'What happened? Are you all right?'

Jamie was scowling and there were dark-green stains on his clothes and scrapes on his hands and forearms. 'Couldn't find the bastard.' He was vibrating with anger.

'Must have scared them off,' Stella said, not sure she believed him. 'That's good.'

'Not good.' He spat the words as if she were an idiot. 'I wanted to get the pictures first.'

'They can't use them though, surely.' Stella struggled to keep her voice calm. She was not going to be cowed by the great Jamie Munro in a bad mood. Even if that was a frightening sight. 'Not if they were breaking the law to take them.'

'Maybe not in a newspaper, but online,' Jamie said. 'Anonymous blog. Cowardly fucking bastards.'

'You could still get the police to investigate if that happens, though.'

He sat down on the nearest chair and tipped his head back as if searching the ceiling for answers, his face still tense.

'Or get a lawyer to have it taken down.'

There was a short silence, and Stella watched the muscles in Jamie's jaw working as he visibly struggled with his frustration. His voice was quieter now, and he no longer looked as if he were about to punch something. 'That all takes time, and a load of people will already have seen them, downloaded them. Once information is online it's impossible to take it back.'

'Maybe they won't post them,' Stella said, trying not to sound as if she was clutching at straws. 'Maybe they're for personal use only.' Too late, she realised that 'creepy stalker' wasn't much of a step up.

Jamie looked cheered, though. He stopped studying the ceiling and fixed onto her. 'Mebbe,' he said. Then: 'Sorry I snapped. Just tense.'

'I know,' Stella said. 'You want to feel safe here.'

He looked shocked, and Stella mentally slapped herself on the forehead. Why had she used such an emotive word? He was going to think she was cracked. What was wrong with 'value your privacy'?

'What do you mean?' Jamie was on his feet, advancing.

'Safe from the media – all that outside intrusion, distraction.' Stella waved a hand in what she hoped was an airy manner. 'You know.'

Jamie stopped and nodded. 'That's what Arisaig means. In Gaelic.'

'Sorry?'

'Safe place.' Then he changed direction. 'I'm pumped. Gonnae lift some weights, use the energy.'

'I'm going to eat my own weight in buttered toast,' Stella said.

'You know, carbohydrate addiction is a real thing,' Jamie said as he headed for the door.

'I know,' Stella said. 'And it's the most delicious and satisfying of all the addictions.'

'Not quite all,' Jamie said. Then he blushed, something Stella wouldn't have thought possible, and left to lift ridiculous weights for five minutes.

That night, Jamie didn't leave his office until past one. Stella wasn't intending to monitor his patterns, wasn't consciously waiting for him to go to bed before she left for the day, but she felt uneasy, her adrenaline still running. She had channelled it into work, becoming engrossed in updating a spreadsheet and replying to the raft of emails that had come through when America jumped online.

He poked his head around the door. He no longer looked half-crazed, and Stella felt the tension she wasn't aware she had been holding loosen. 'Are you still working?'

'I lost track of time,' Stella said, not entirely honestly. There had been a small part of her that had not wanted to walk outside in the dark.

A flicker of a thought that suggested the photographer would be lying there on the path, beaten bloody. She felt guilty as she remembered how unsettled Jamie had been. Just because he valued his privacy and was physically strong didn't mean he was violent.

'Bloody hell,' he said, smiling. 'You're as bad as me. Make sure you come in late tomorrow. Or take the day off.'

'Night,' she said as he closed the door.

It opened again immediately and he said. 'Did you want me to walk you down to the cottage? I didn't think about it earlier, sorry.'

'That's okay.' The last thing Stella wanted was to be a burden. Or for him to think she was weak. She switched off her computer and stood. 'I'll go now.'

'You could just sleep in one of the spare rooms tonight, if you like,' Jamie said. 'I've locked up the house already.'

Tiredness hit and Stella thought about walking down the quiet track to the empty cottage, imagined the darkness pressing in and the sounds of the night. The stranger with the camera could still be hanging around, too. Unlikely, but possible. She weighed the risks and said, 'Thank you, I am a bit tired.'

Lying in the unfamiliar bedroom, Stella tried to pretend she wasn't listening for Jamie's tread on the stairs, but she couldn't deny it when, at five past three, she felt relieved to hear him walk along the landing past her door. He was a grown man and perfectly capable of looking after himself, but she couldn't help reliving the evening. He had been genuinely upset and the crack in his usual armour was arresting. Her own heart still stuttered, ready for fight or flight. She uncurled her fingers, trying to relax, but she replayed Jamie's words and heard the panicked tone of his voice. The contrast between his easy-going, in-control persona and the fear she had glimpsed was oddly seductive. Stella had spent so many years as the 'poorly girl', and the past four months in a fog of misery and loss, that it was refreshing to worry about somebody else for a change.

Poorly girl. The phrase ran around Stella's mind and she knew that sleep was a long way off. By the time she had left childhood and truly grasped that her 'weak health' wasn't going to magically go away with a letter from Hogwarts, Stella was well versed in her own little calculations. First, she wanted to become a teenager. She didn't want to die before she had hit puberty and found out what it was like to have breasts. She wanted to wear make-up and have a first kiss and go see her favourite band play live. When all that happened and she found herself post-GCSEs and still breathing, she shifted her plans, looking forward to university but never, ever, planning too far; never hoping for too much.

Lying in the bedroom at Munro House, Stella stared into the darkness and tried to stop crying. She ground her knuckles into her breastbone, a reflexive movement from childhood that she had never been able to shake. She was lucky, she reminded herself. So very lucky.

CHAPTER EIGHT

15th February, 1848

Dearest Mary,

Please forgive me for not writing sooner. I have been ill and had not the strength to sit up with a writing desk. I asked Mr Lockhart to send a message, but he said I should not worry you needlessly as I was clearly getting better every hour. I did not feel it, I admit, but he was quite right! Here I am, sitting up in bed and feeling well enough to endanger the bed sheets with my ink. It was an indecent illness and I will not dwell upon it, suffice to say that I ate something that did not agree with me.

Mr Lockhart was most attentive. It was almost agreeable to be unwell, the attention he lavished upon me. He sat up holding my hand all the first night. At least I believe he did so, as he was always there when I awoke. He wrote everything down in his little book, too, so I felt quite important. He usually only puts his valued work down in that book.

Another fortunate aspect to the unpleasant sickness was the effect it had on my husband's spirits. He had been terribly miserable, his mood both foul and black. He lost the university chair to J. Y. Simpson and had been brooding on it for days. He was so black you would have thought there had been a death in the family. Now he seems quite recovered. The light is back in his eyes and he held my hand this morning before he went to work and called me his 'dear dove'.

Now that I am well I wish to go riding again. Mr Lockhart has promised a trip home to Haddington once the weather grows warm. I do hope that I stay well this time. You know that I try not to curse my delicate health, but I do miss you so, Mary. Now we are both respectable married ladies (how peculiar it still feels to count myself in the same station) and you are very busy with the children and the house, but I like to dream of hours riding faither's horses as we once did. Do you remember the trip to Aberlady bay? I think of it often. The salt-edged air was so clean and cold, it felt like a medicine, and the sea was made of a thousand silver points of light. When we took the horses into the surf and the waves caught our feet, we laughed and laughed and the wind took every sound. See how I tug at your heartstrings!

I will stop writing now before my scribble becomes entirely unreadable, but I just have the strength to beg that you urge dear Callum to take up the offer sent by Mr Lockhart. I was speaking to Mrs Baxter, a most canny woman, and extolling the fine shoes made by your husband and she has promised to order a pair. I confess my plan is entirely selfish – if Callum gains custom in Edinburgh, perhaps he will bring the coach to deliver orders and I shall see your fair brown eyes and calm face.

Your poorly wee Jessie

Stella was dreaming that she was in the cool grey bathroom at Munro House. The giant claw-footed tub was filled with ice but her skin felt as if it were on fire. She opened her mouth to tell Jamie that she didn't like it and suddenly he was there, watching her as if she were a specimen in a laboratory. 'Four more minutes,' dream-Jamie said, his mouth barely moving.

Stella tried to scream, but she couldn't make a sound, couldn't move. Dream-Jamie leaned down from his great height and put his hands on her shoulders. Then he pushed until she slipped beneath the water, his face blurred now. Her lungs were filling with liquid and she couldn't breathe; Stella felt the familiar sensation of drowning and she panicked, while part of her brain, the part that was aware that this was a dream, told her to wake up, told her that the ringing in her ears was not real, that this was just a—

There was a ringing sound. It was loud and it was real. Stella opened her eyes and realised that it was an unfamiliar doorbell ringing. A moment later she grasped that she was in the cottage on the estate and that somebody was at the door. She pulled on her dressing gown and went downstairs. She expected either Jamie or Esmé, so was surprised to find Doug on the doorstep. He was wearing a bright-red fleece and long shorts. 'Sorry,' he said. 'Didn't mean to wake you.'

'No worries,' Stella said, pulling her gown tighter. 'Is everything all right?'

'That's my line,' Doug said, smiling.

'I'm sorry?'

'Rob asked me to check on you,' Doug explained. 'Make sure you were getting on fine.'

'Oh,' Stella said. She glanced behind her, trying to work out what to do. 'I would invite you in, but I'm not supposed to have visitors. If Jamie sees you here—'

'I'm the postie,' Doug said easily. 'Official business, like.'

Stella looked back up the track and saw the red van parked behind the gate. She half expected to see Jamie or Esmé storming down the lane, shouting about privacy.

'So you're all right, then?' Doug dipped his head a little. 'I can tell Rob to stop fussing?'

'Yes,' Stella said. 'I'm fine.'

'Good, then.' Doug turned to leave. 'Just let me know if you're needing anything.'

'I'm fine,' Stella said, again. The air was cold on her legs, reminding her of the chilled water of her dream. She felt her teeth begin to chatter and she clenched her jaw.

'Right, then.' Doug started back up the path. He raised a hand in farewell and Stella closed the door, catching sight of a figure at the back of the house as she did so. It was Esmé. She was stood very still, watching. Stella could just make out the pinkish oval of her face but not her expression.

༺

Stella was walking back from the kitchen with her third coffee of the day when she heard the dogs barking. She stopped, listening for a doorbell or knock, something that would have set them off. Although not overly fond of large, noisy canines, she was not particularly alarmed, either. Esmé had them under good control and, however bad-tempered she appeared at times, Stella didn't believe Esmé would set the dogs upon her.

The barking continued, however, and there was no sound of Esmé's brisk but reassuring commands. Unnerved, Stella slowed her pace. The barking was louder and there was a manic edge to it that made her worry they were trapped somewhere in the house, or in trouble. If she ignored them, that would not help relations with Esmé, but they might attack her in their fury and fright. She straightened her shoulders and opened the door.

Jamie was lying on the floor with the black Labrador on top of him. It looked like they were cuddling and, opening her huge jaws, the Lab uncurled a pink tongue and licked Jamie's face. The collie was leaping around and around this calm and affectionate tableau as if on amphetamines, barking manically. At the sound of the door, he turned and bounded over to Stella, teeth snapping. Jamie sat up, dislodging the Lab. 'Angus! Lie down!'

The collie dropped to the floor. Instantly, he went from snarling beast to alert hound, his head on his paws and his eyes trained on Stella.

'Sorry about that,' Jamie said, clambering to his feet. 'Angus is the guard dog.' He patted the Labrador affectionately. 'Good thing, too, since Tabitha here is such a softy. She would just invite a stranger in, wouldn't you, darling?'

'Esmé told me to be wary,' Stella said, trying to explain her expression of horror and the fact that she wasn't petting the dogs.

'Oh, she's just teasing. She always says that to visitors, just to put the wind up them.'

'Right.' Stella took a step backwards and Angus lifted a lip, a low growl rising from his throat.

'Angus!' Jamie said sharply and the growl stopped. He frowned at the dog. 'Angus, this is Stella. Be nice.'

Tabitha was nosing forward, but Jamie held her back. 'Do you like dogs?'

'I haven't known very many,' Stella said diplomatically. She was trying not to be frightened, but Angus was still watching her like a hawk with a mouse. He looked like he wanted to take a juicy bite from her leg.

'These two are crazy, but they're good dogs. They won't hurt you, I promise.' Jamie smiled. 'Angus! Treat!' The collie rolled over and stuck his legs straight into the air, holding the pose with his tongue lolling out. It looked both comical and faintly obscene.

'Good boy,' Jamie said, and the dog sprang back, sitting in front of Jamie, his tail brushing the floor with an enthusiastic wag. Jamie took something from his pocket and gave it to Angus.

'You should carry some of these,' Jamie said. 'The way to a dog's heart is definitely through its stomach. Don't give them every time they obey, though. Expect obedience as a matter of course; reward sporadically.'

Stella was distracted by Tabitha, who had evidently decided she was friendly and was now trying to nose her way between Stella's legs. Stella clamped them together and pushed Tabitha's nose away from her crotch. 'No, thank you,' she said.

'See,' Jamie said, 'she likes you.'

Stella looked at him to see if he was laughing at her, but he seemed sincere.

'Tabitha can be shy, so that's a great honour.'

Stella shoved Tabitha's nose a little harder, twisting her body away to dislodge the dog, who seemed determined to get acquainted with a very specific part of her anatomy. At the same time, she vowed to make friends with the dogs. She recognised a gauntlet when it had been smacked in her face, and she was damned if she was going to let Esmé win. Stella had dealt with many territorial managers over the last few years and she knew how to play their games.

The sky had changed again and the view from the kitchen window showed the dark ridges of the mountains in the distance, looking moody and forbidding, while the sea was made of a thousand silver points of light. Stella surprised herself by wishing she was outside, stomping over the pebbles of the bay, climbing the jagged slabs of rock, picking through the ancient woodland dripping with moss. She had never thought of herself as being an outdoorsy type, but then she had never had much opportunity.

Of course, the out-of-character urge was probably prompted by the claustrophobic atmosphere of Munro House. The forbidden doorways, the shrouded furniture and the sense that she was spinning her wheels.

Stella trailed back to her office, determined to make headway with her assigned job. Within a few weeks of every temp job she'd ever held, she had been called 'the best assistant I've ever had', and she had no intention of breaking her streak. Jamie Munro might be a bit more unusual than the corporate-types she was used to handling, but she liked a challenge. Jamie's door was shut and all was quiet, and Stella sat in her own office, in front of her space-age computer.

A notification pinged. *Update. Now.* Nathan Schwartz was, thankfully, not on the telephone, but he was using his second-favourite method of communication: the instant messaging on Skype.

Working, Stella typed.

On what?

Stella looked at the white space and the flashing cursor for a few moments. She knew from past experience that he wouldn't stop asking and, if dissatisfied with the answer, would call and shout. *I will check for you*, she typed and stood up, stretching her arms above her head.

Jamie was in his office at his standing desk. A heavy volume was open, the pages filled with brightly coloured slips of paper and a yellow legal pad next to it.

'Sorry to interrupt,' Stella said.

Jamie smiled when he looked up. 'No problem. What do you need?'

'Nathan wants an update.'

'Deflect him,' Jamie said and looked back at the page. She was dismissed.

Back in her own small room, Stella looked at the beautiful wallpaper to centre herself, grateful it was a calming colour, and went back to the blinking cursor. After a moment she typed *Research* and clicked to close the conversation.

Later that afternoon, she knocked on the door to his office and went in, ready to offer coffee and to make Jamie answer the string of urgent questions she had collated from his messages. Jamie was surrounded by open archive boxes and piles of books, and he was staring with his trademark intensity at an unfolded paper map.

'Nathan wants me to stop you doing this,' Stella said. She tapped the top of one of the archive boxes. 'He says you've gotten obsessed with things in the past and that I must remind you of your more pressing business concerns.'

Jamie looked up from the map. 'Did you know it used to take three hours to travel from Arisaig to Fort William by coach? We could be in Barcelona in that time.'

'Did you hear me?' Stella was channelling cheerful and efficient with all her might. She had no idea what was going on in her head but she knew she wanted to keep this job. And Nathan had made it clear that he would do everything in his power to get rid of her if she didn't get some results.

'Nathan's worried. I heard.'

'What shall I tell him?'

Jamie waved a hand. 'Anything you like. Tell him I'm working on the book.'

'You're the boss,' Stella said, keeping her tone neutral. It was a balancing act. She didn't know how much influence Nathan had over Jamie, and everything she had heard about the Munro family suggested that Jamie wouldn't think twice about sacking her if she annoyed him.

Jamie glanced up. 'You think I'm obsessing?'

Stella couldn't stop a smile from escaping as she looked at the avalanche of history books, maps and papers. 'I think you can spend your time however you choose.'

'Genetics are important. The more we understand about our health, the more we discover is encoded from birth. Passed down through the generations.'

'Makes it difficult to fight against, though,' Stella said, thinking of Jamie's book. *It's All Genetic So You're Fucked* didn't seem like a very motivational title.

'Not at all.' Jamie stood up and began pacing the room, stretching his arms above his head and doing weird little knee bends every so often. 'We know there are certain genes which switch on certain conditions, but then there are ones which just indicate an increased likelihood. Like, I've been mapped and I've got the Parkinson's gene. Knowing that means I can make better choices about certain therapies and lifestyle changes. The more detailed and individual the information, the more specific and tailored our healthcare can be.'

'I suppose,' Stella said. 'Don't you think it might be nicer not to know, though? If you've got an increased risk of something horrible.' She kept her face carefully averted, to make sure he couldn't read anything in it.

'If I'm going to discover something really useful about extending a healthy life, then I need to look to the past.'

'Is that what the new book is about?' Stella said, trying to get him back on track.

'*Living Well Forever*,' Jamie said. 'That's the working title.'

Stella thought she was doing a good job of keeping a neutral expression, but she must have been mistaken, as Jamie laughed. 'Don't look like that, Miss Sceptical. You're supposed to be on my team.'

'I am,' Stella said, smiling supportively for all she was worth. 'It's a very catchy title.'

His face clouded. 'It's not a gimmick. People said the last book was a gimmick—'

'So, is it actually possible to extend our lifespan?' Stella asked quickly.

'They did studies in the 1930s with rats, which showed that severely limiting their calorie intake resulted in the rats living for forty per cent longer.'

'Forty per cent is a lot.'

'The research wasn't really followed at the time, probably halted by the war like so many other things, but it's been taken up again recently.'

'Is that why you've been fasting?'

'Yeah, partly. But there could be answers in our genetics, too,' Jamie said. 'It's not about finding out what illnesses might come along, it's about how to optimise the system we've inherited.'

'And that's what you're doing here?' Stella waved a hand to encompass the papers, maps and photographs. 'Investigating your genetics.'

He smiled ruefully. 'Not really. I started out that way, but now I'm just fascinated. I mean, I never wanted to be anything like my father, but it turns out his father was a scientist. That's cool. And now I think his dad, my great-grandfather, might have had similar interests. It makes me think about genetic memory. What if my family is just programmed to experiment? Isn't that interesting?'

'I prefer to think I have free will,' Stella said. 'The word "programmed" makes me feel squeamish.'

He stopped pacing for a moment. 'That's a good point. How much free will do we have if so much is written in our code?' He darted to the desk and scribbled in his notebook. 'I don't want to see behaviour that way, either. But I do like the feeling that I'm carrying on a tradition. Maybe I could even finish some research that one of my ancestors began. I want to do something meaningful with my life, not just exist. And this' – he swept an arm out over the laden table – 'feels like a signpost.'

'Fair enough,' Stella said, although she wasn't sure she meant it. It seemed as if he was picking the bits from the theory that he liked the sound of and ignoring the rest. She had never expected to do anything meaningful with her life. She had hoped to have children and to be a good mother and for that to be her legacy. Other than that, she hoped to be good. Not to worry her parents or friends too much. To love and be loved. And to enjoy the time she had as much as possible. That wasn't always easy, though. Life was too complicated for enjoyment a great deal of the time.

'I just want to get this out of the way. I feel like I have to, I don't know—' He broke off for a moment and then took a deep breath. 'I feel like I need to do something really important, really good. I've got so much to make up for. I know what people say about my family . . .'

Stella kept her expression neutral.

'I can't do anything about my dad, but if my ancestors advanced medical science, then that's something to be proud of. I just feel like I need the boost, and then I'll be able to concentrate on the final draft of the book.'

'It's written, then,' Stella said, latching on to the one part of Jamie's garbled speech which had anything to do with her task as his assistant. If there was a readable draft, perhaps Jamie would let her send that to Nathan and the man could stop phoning her every day and shouting.

'Oh, yeah,' Jamie said, his gaze back on the map. He reached for one of the journals.

'Can I send it to Nathan? Give him something to read so that he knows the final is really on its way?'

'Hmm?'

'The first draft,' Stella tried again. 'Can I send it to Nathan?'

Jamie shook his head. 'It's not ready.' He got up. 'Time for my bath, though. Are you free?'

'Sure,' Stella said. She liked the way he phrased that, as if she weren't just a lackey. He might be difficult, but the man had class.

Esmé walked into the kitchen just as Stella was feeding Tabitha a piece of cold chicken from her sandwich. Rather than look guilty or apologise, Stella decided that Esmé's grumpiness would be best met by strength. She forced herself to meet the older woman's laser-like gaze. 'Isn't she a darling?'

To her surprise, and relief, Esmé laughed.

'There's tea in the pot,' Stella said.

'Thank you.' Esmé moved around her, patting Tabitha on the head as she passed.

When they both had fresh mugs of tea and Stella had finished her sandwich, she pushed her plate away and caught Esmé watching her, her expression unreadable. 'What?'

'What brought you to Arisaig?'

Stella thought about lying or being evasive but there was something about Esmé which demanded directness.

'I had my heart broken and I realised I had to make a change. I sort of ran away from my life.'

Esmé nodded as if this were perfectly reasonable. 'Why here, though?'

'Old friends. I came to visit them and then wanted to stay.' Tabitha's heavy head was lying on her leg, her eyes rolled up to gaze at her with adoration, or possibly a silent request for more chicken.

'You've done this before?'

'Running away? Never.' Stella wondered if that was why Esmé seemed so mistrustful, some sense of flightiness. 'I'm very reliable. Usually. I've been temping for years and I was in between contracts. It was a good time to make an escape, as it turns out.'

'Down!' Esmé turned and shouted, making Stella jump. A sheepish-looking Angus dropped to the floor. Tabitha sighed. A moment later, a noxious smell wafted around the table.

'Oh, Tabitha,' Esmé said. 'Sorry about that. She always does that when I shout.'

Stella resisted the urge to say that Tabitha must be permanently walking around in a fart-tastic miasma.

A moment later, Esmé said, 'Temping, eh?'

'Personal assistant, office manager, that kind of thing,' Stella said.

'I don't like the sound of that,' Esmé said, pursing her lips.

Stella was about to ask what she could possibly have against secretarial work, when Esmé added, 'Changing jobs, moving around. I wouldn't like that at all.'

'I get bored easily,' Stella said. 'Once I've sorted out systems so that things run smoothly, it's not enough of a challenge.' She didn't add that she had also hoped to be at home with a baby in the near future.

'So what will you do when you get bored with Jamie?'

'I can't imagine that happening.' Stella spoke without thinking first, and then wanted to pull the words back.

Esmé just nodded, though. 'He's a live wire.' She drained her mug and stood up. 'Well, I can't sit around here blethering all morning.' At the door, she whistled and Tabitha raced to her side, leaving a cold patch on Stella's leg where her head had been and a damp circle of drool.

'Who are your old friends?' Esmé said, turning back for a moment.

'Rob and Caitlin Baird.'

Esmé froze, her hand above Tabitha's head mid-pat. Then she nodded and said, 'I ken Rob Baird all right,' in a perfectly even tone.

As another Friday night rolled around, Stella decided to go into the village for an early drink. She had started work at five in the morning for a Skype session with Jamie's marketing manager in Japan, so she shut down her computer at four and walked into Arisaig.

It was good to get off the estate. Stella would never have believed that a place so big could feel cramped, but it was nice to see different faces and to sit on a slightly sticky chair in the bar and watch the world go by. Unfortunately, the wind was blowing rain horizontally and there weren't many folk out strolling, but there were plenty of people in the pub, and sooner or later Stella guessed one of them would speak to her. It was like that around here. Whereas you could sit in a pub in London and cry into your beer and no one would so much as offer you a handkerchief.

After a couple of quick chats about the weather with people passing her table to find their own seats, a man with a red nose, and a pint of beer in one hand and a whisky in the other, shuffled across the bar and took the seat opposite. 'All right, hen?'

Stella nodded and smiled. Of course it had to be the local drunk.

'I ken yer up at the big hoose,' he said, slurring more than a little. Up-close, the man was younger than she'd expected. Maybe only in his forties, although it was hard to tell.

'That's right,' Stella said. She wasn't surprised. A few weeks had taught her there were no secrets in Arisaig. Probably no secrets in all of Scotland.

'Nice lassie like you,' he said, shaking his head sorrowfully. It was theatrically done and Stella had the impression that he was enjoying himself, putting on a show for the gullible incomer.

'I like it,' Stella said. 'It's beautiful around here,' she added, hoping to get him onside. The terminally drunk could turn in a moment; that was a common truth wherever you lived.

As if on cue, he leaned forwards, an intense look in his eye. 'I'm no messing with you, gurlie. There are things you wouldn't believe.'

A spray of spittle accompanied his words and Stella leaned back a little.

'He'll make you help with his experiments.' He put clumsy air quotes around the word 'experiments'. 'The last one is deid.'

'The last one?'

'Girl from Mallaig. She fell on the rocks and hit her head.'

'How awful,' Stella said, feeling her stomach swoop in sympathy.

'At least, that's what he said. That's what he tol the polis.'

'Why don't you think it's the truth?'

'He's just like his father,' he said, trailing off. 'Jus like him.' He shook his head. 'I was there, ye ken. I saw him.'

'You saw Jamie do what?'

'Naw. Not the bairn. His da. I saw him back in the day. He had his hand up her skirt and I don't think she was too pleased about it, like.'

Stella sensed a darkness opening up and she was both intrigued and disgusted. And a bit disappointed in her own interest. Another couple of weeks here and she'd be a gossip, too. She tried to bring the conversation back to focus on the present day. 'The police would've investigated. If a girl died.'

'Jamie's da would bang anything that moved,' he said, clearly unwilling to leave his pet subject. 'Naebody wanted their daughters working up at the hoose. Not unless they knew karate or something.'

'That's a very serious accusation.'

He sat back, eyes twinkling with inappropriate amusement. 'Oh, aye. And who is gonnae sue me? He's deid, hen. You can't slander a dead man.'

'Can't you?'

'Not unless their relatives get funny about it. Then it gets iffy.' He held a hand out and waggled it. 'Twenty years on *The Post*.'

'The Post?'

'Newspaper. You remember those,' he said, suddenly sounding sober. 'Before we had the wonders of the Internet.'

'You were a journalist?'

'I didn't get in this state from being a choirboy.' He gestured to himself, taking in the grubby clothes, sweat stains spreading on his shirt, and the patchily shaved jaw. 'I was going to get a good story on him, but it never came together. Couldn't get the sources. Naebody would speak ill of him.'

'That hasn't been my experience,' Stella said.

'Aye,' he nodded, acknowledging the truth of this. 'But naebody would speak on the record, like.'

'Didn't you think that might be a sign?'

'Of what?'

'His innocence.'

He laughed for so long and with so much wheezing and coughing that Stella began to worry he was going to make himself sick. Finally, wiping his eyes, he managed to say, 'You'd never use that word if you'd met him.'

'Nobody seems to like Mr Munro, I get that, but why is everyone so hard on Jamie? He hardly saw his parents, as far as I can tell.'

'Boarding school.' He nodded. 'Still. Like faither like son.'

'Nonsense,' Stella said. 'He's a perfectly nice man and he's done nothing wrong.'

Okay, so 'nice' wasn't really the word, but still.

'Oh, dearie me,' the man said. 'It's like that, is it? You want to watch yourself. And ask him about Ellie MacDonald.'

Stella pushed the words aside. She didn't believe the drunk, journalist or not. Who knew how competent he'd been at his job? And as for his accusation of Jamie's father, who knew how reliable his memory was for things which had happened when he was a teenager? Perhaps he'd been an alcoholic even then; maybe he'd been out of his head the whole time.

She couldn't stop herself from googling the name Ellie MacDonald when she got home, though. Sure enough, a tragic accident had occurred on the shore by Munro House a few months earlier. A nineteen-year-old girl had slipped on the rocks and fallen badly, cracking her head and dying later in hospital. Stella felt a chill in her stomach. The byline for the story was for a Shona McQueen. Not her friend from the pub, then.

The story was reported in the local paper, too, and Stella felt sick as she realised something; Caitlin and Rob must have known about Ellie MacDonald and had chosen not to tell her. Stella felt sure that it would have been to protect her from unnecessary worry, but Caitlin knew Stella's attitude to risk. How could Caitlin have kept information like this secret? And what else might Caitlin have decided not to tell her? Without consciously agreeing to it, Stella typed in *James Munro*. Jamie's Wikipedia entry was first on the list, followed by his own website, that of his publisher, and a raft of interview links, but the second page of hits mentioned his father.

There had been a boating accident. Ten years ago, when Jamie was just twenty and away at university. The bodies were never recovered. The story was illustrated with a picture of James and Helen Munro and another of their boat. Given she knew absolutely nothing about boats, it looked expensive. Further down the page was a small headshot of Jamie – a school picture, judging from the style. The article didn't quote Jamie, but Stella knew that he would have had journalists asking him how he felt. She felt a rush of sympathy and understanding; Jamie's need for privacy and his aversion to the press had no doubt started early.

There was another piece, published a couple of months later, titled MUNRO TRAGEDY SHROUDED IN MYSTERY. It rehashed the – scant – details of the original news story and then speculated as to the reason Helen Munro had accompanied her partner that day. *Friends close to Mrs Munro reveal that she hated the water and never made use of the family yacht.* Along the bottom were links to related articles, one titled HIDDEN TREASURE. That seemed insensitive, but Stella clicked on it anyway. It was a piece about the number of shipwrecks in the waters around the Small Isles, Eigg and Rùm, which sat just off the coast from Arisaig. Galleons containing ancient gold, U-boats from World War Two, fishing vessels and canoes – the seabed was littered, apparently. And the bodies of the drowned. All those sailors and passengers, their bodies sinking below the surface, never to be seen again.

CHAPTER NINE

3rd March, 1848

My dearest Mary,

Thank you for your letter and the picture of wee Angus. You are silly to say that you dashed it off, as I simply cannot believe that to be so. It is quite a darling sketch and you have captured his likeness very well.

I am sorry we did not get to Haddington on the first, as promised. Mr Lockhart had a flurry of patients and could not spare the time for a trip. It was selfish of me to ask for it when I know perfectly well how busy he is with his work. I know you will understand and not judge too harshly. It must be similar when Callum is rushed at his workshop. Speaking of which, I was very sorry to hear of the disaster with the tacket-mackers. The Provost must understand that if the tackets cannot be found, then your dear Callum cannot finish his boots. I remember Provost Urquhart as being a reasonable fellow but perhaps the matter to which you alluded has soured his nature of late. Wives must comfort their guid men, not add to their woes!

On a brighter note, I write to you in great excitement. I have finally found my feet here in the city and have been invited to no less than four engagements this week alone. Great store is set by the tea circuit and, just as in dear Haddington, there is a hierarchy. You know how Mrs Gillies would serve dainty wheat bread to some folk and neeps and tatties to others? Well, it is just the same in Edinburgh society. Mr Lockhart is very pleased because I have been invited to dine with Lady Anstruther on Thursday. He wants me to take my place in society and it is a reflection of his reputation as a doctor. He says I am to listen carefully if the talk should turn to medical matters and, if it is at all appropriate, I should mention the way he cured Lady Bailie's sister from puerperal fever when he was visiting Newburgh.

I was so naive. I believed that doctors simply sat back and waited for their customers to seek them out (old Dr McInnes was always busier than he seemed to like) but Mr Lockhart says that is only any use if you don't much care about the quality of your patients. To become a physician to those of breeding you must cultivate a reputation and that is what he intends to do.

I quite understand. Mary, the coal situation is not quite as bonny as I had first assumed. He is not thrifty entirely from a moral standpoint. The downstairs rooms are warm and sumptuous, but the rest of the house is bare and cold. And Mary, I made an awful mistake in asking for some cloth for a new dress. He grew quite wild. He soon calmed when I reminded him of my visiting duties and all was well. He said that I must be presentable for Lady Anstruther and has ordered a bolt of silk.

Do write to me soon and pass on my love and good wishes to the family – with an extra kiss for wee Angus.

Your loving Jessie

On the following Saturday, Stella picked Caitlin up and drove to Fort William. Having packed a suitcase for a few days only, she had begun to think longingly of her wardrobe and felt the need to buy some clothes and toiletries. After a solid couple of hours of retail therapy, including an hour in Mothercare looking at impossibly sweet sleepsuits and tiny vests with poppers, they stopped at an Italian café for coffee and millefeuille. And two large glasses of cold milk for Caitlin, who was craving the stuff.

They talked about how Caitlin was coping with her job. 'I thought the early months were the worst with the tiredness, but it's getting harder. I can't lift stuff and that's a major issue,' Caitlin said, chasing the last of her milk with her straw. 'I'm really down to wildlife counts and paperwork. Everyone is being really nice about it, but I feel bad. It's not like we're overstaffed.'

Stella made sympathetic noises as she attacked her cake, the fork slicing through layers of delicate pastry and soft crème pâtissière. She wondered what Jamie would be enjoying for his Saturday-afternoon treat. A handful of almonds and goji berries, perhaps.

'I always said I wouldn't take much maternity leave,' Caitlin said, 'but now I'm not even sure I want to go back at all after the baby arrives.'

'You're tired at the moment,' Stella said. 'Who knows how you'll feel later?'

'Yeah, I'm going to be so well rested when I've got a tiny baby screaming at me all night.' Caitlin was smiling but her voice was flat.

'Is everything all right?'

Caitlin picked up her second glass of milk and then put it down again. 'It's just the unknown. And I'm on a temporary contract. I'll have to reapply, assuming there's even still funding for my position. And temp work means my maternity benefit isn't amazing.'

'Does Rob get paternity leave?'

'Yeah, some. But he won't be able to take the unpaid stuff or we won't be able to pay the mortgage.' She drained her milk. 'At least he has the long holidays.'

Stella was finding her cake too sweet. Her throat closed and she put her fork down, pushing her plate away. 'Can you manage on his salary? If you don't get a new contract with the countryside council people?'

'Scottish Natural Heritage? I don't know.' Caitlin shook her head. 'But I think we're going to have to.'

'Babies don't cost much to start with,' Stella said. She had run the figures for her and Ben, back when she had been in full planning mode.

Caitlin gave her a look. 'Did you see the price of those prams?'

'I'll buy you a pram,' Stella said. 'Baby gift.'

Caitlin laughed. 'Thanks. Rob's mum is getting the pram. And my folks are springing for the cot. I've already been given a Moses basket and a metric ton of clothes.'

'There you are, then.' Stella pushed her plate across to Caitlin. 'Eat up.'

Caitlin scooped up a forkful of cake and then put it down. 'I thought I was going to have more help. I mean, we came here to start a family. Rob wanted them to grow up where he did, and with his mum being on her own, I know he's always felt responsible for her. It's just . . .'

'You miss your parents?'

'Yeah.' Caitlin pushed the plate away. 'And now Rob's mum has buggered off, anyway. She moved to Lewis a few months ago. Totally out of the blue.'

'Why?'

Caitlin's eyes slid to the left. 'Family stuff. I've been reading your boss's book.'

Stella accepted the change of subject. Caitlin had never been a big one for heart-to-hearts. 'Which one? I picked up the body one in the charity shop.'

'No, the one about working efficiently. It doesn't really apply to my job, unfortunately. There's only one way to count butterflies or build a path.'

Stella thought that Jamie would probably have an answer to that. He had an answer for everything.

'So what's he like?'

'Intense,' Stella said. 'You should ask Rob, though. He must have known him at primary school. Before Jamie went to boarding school, anyway.'

'Bladder alert,' Caitlin said, getting up. 'I swear this baby must be bigger than they think.'

While Caitlin was in the bathroom, Stella pulled Jamie's paperback from her bag and continued reading. It wasn't exactly enjoyable, but she had always taken pride in being knowledgeable about the companies she worked for, even if she was only temporary. In Stella's mind, nothing lasted forever and a temporary contract was no excuse to half-arse things.

Only a fool does more than is necessary. It's a waste of time and energy. Why exercise for hours every week when fifteen minutes of large-muscle high-intensity workout will give you the same or better results?

Stella looked up from the chapter which advocated two-minute sessions of deep squats or pull-ups ninety minutes before and immediately after every meal. High-intensity workouts were all the rage now, but Jamie must have been one of the first to advocate the technique. Caitlin was making her way back to their table, another glass of milk in hand.

'Couldn't resist,' she said, sitting down.

Once Caitlin was settled in her seat, Stella was ready to rant. 'It's like he's never met anybody with anything less than a perfect body. Not everyone can do deep squats.' Stella had tried, in fact, and had fallen over on the fifth one, her thigh muscles quivering. 'The way he talks, it's like anything less than perfect – the best, most optimised peak performance – is a failure. And who decides what peak performance is, anyway? Loads of athletes have health problems. Not to mention it's not exactly a balanced way of life.'

'You might be taking this a bit personally,' Caitlin said, clearly amused.

'Why do you say that?' Stella held up the book. 'This says it's going to help, but it just makes people feel bad. We're all imperfect, all of us, and drinking kale juice isn't going to change that fact.' The feelings of insecurity – of inferiority – that she had been suppressing bubbled up. Stella could understand why people gave Jamie Munro such a hard time; he made them feel bad about themselves. Next to his self-discipline and productivity and fitness, everyone else was a slob.

'Well, you have had to overcome health problems—' Caitlin began.

'I haven't overcome anything.' Stella held up a hand to stop Caitlin from continuing. 'You know I hate that phrase. You don't overcome chronic illness, you survive it. You live with it. You keep on keeping on. It's not a battle you can win through the force of your will.'

Caitlin had her hands up. 'I know, I know. Sorry.'

As quickly as the anger had come, it had gone again. 'No, I'm sorry.' Stella looked around, hoping that her voice hadn't carried. The other patrons seemed unconcerned and their table was reasonably isolated, thank goodness. 'I didn't mean to get ranty. I just hate the language people use. As if someone who dies from an illness didn't try as hard not to as a person who doesn't. I'm not brave or strong because I'm still alive, I'm just lucky.'

Caitlin put a hand on her arm. 'I understand what you're saying. And I know how much you hate all that.' She smiled widely, raising her glass of milk in salute. 'I still think you're brave.'

'I don't feel very brave,' Stella said. She tried to keep her voice light, to disguise the swooping feeling in her stomach.

'How do you mean?'

'I don't know what I'm doing. I don't know what I want. I know I don't want to go home yet, but I don't know about Munro House, either. There's a weird vibe and Jamie is—' She broke off. She had been going to say 'split personality' but wasn't sure if that would contravene the NDA.

'Weird vibe?' Caitlin leaned forward.

Stella shook her head. 'It's probably me, projecting. I'm still really unsettled. Nothing feels safe anymore. Not since Ben left.'

'That makes sense. You need time to adjust.'

Stella went back to the book and read out a few more choice nuggets, trying to make Caitlin laugh. It went on to suggest inversion therapy to expand the spaces between the vertebrae, and high doses of a vitamin supplement she had never heard of. The disclaimer I AM NOT A DOCTOR SO PLEASE CONSULT YOUR PHYSICIAN appeared at the front of the book and regularly throughout.

Caitlin moved her chair around to Stella's side of the table and looked over her shoulder at the page. 'How many times do you reckon he's been sued?'

'Lots, probably.'

She nudged Stella's arm. 'What's the new book about, then?'

'You know I can't tell you,' Stella said.

'Not even a hint?' Caitlin said.

'Why are you so interested? I thought you thought he was a quack.'

'Gossip, though. I bet he's a character. Rob keeps asking if I've met him yet. I think he wants you to introduce us.'

'Jamie's not very sociable,' Stella said. 'Why is Rob so worried, anyway? He sent Doug to check up on me.'

'Oh, you know he's always been like that. Overprotective. He'll make a brilliant father.'

Stella knew she was going to sound daft and Caitlin would laugh like a drain, but she couldn't stop herself from asking: 'Do you think I should be worried?'

Caitlin didn't laugh. She looked concerned, which was worse. 'Are you all right?' She put a hand on Stella's arm. 'Are you sleeping?'

'I know how it sounds,' Stella said. She weighed the words carefully in her mind before speaking, wondering how Caitlin would react. 'I was reading about Ellie MacDonald.'

'Oh God, yeah,' Caitlin spoke after a slight hesitation. 'That was tragic.'

'You knew?' Stella tried to keep her tone even.

'Everyone knows everything around here, you've seen what it's like.' Caitlin pulled a face. 'Rob always says I've got to be on my best behaviour, 'cause nobody will let you forget—' She broke off, seeing something in Stella's expression. 'It was an accident. Just bad luck.'

'I know,' Stella said, and she steered the conversation back to prams.

Stella had thought that she felt better after talking to Caitlin, but back at work at Munro House on Monday, she felt the strange tension return. She had been trying to get Jamie to look at the daily digest of messages, to sign some forms from the US tax authority, and deal with several other small things she could not sort out without his help. He waved her away, eyes fixed on a battered old notebook.

The man was impossible.

Stella marched out of the office, slamming the door behind her. She kept up the pace along the wide hallway and through the formal dining room.

She was so angry, suddenly, that she could hardly see where she was going. She knew it probably wasn't Jamie's offhand manner which was causing her fury, just the all-too-familiar sense of inertia. Stella wanted to take control of her life, but it felt as if every attempt to steer her own destiny was thwarted. She felt as if she was being continually pushed around – by her health, other people, her boss . . . It took a moment after she had stormed into the kitchen and opened the fridge before she realised that the room wasn't empty.

Esmé put down the white package she was carrying and began opening it. The scent of raw meat hit Stella and she turned back to the fridge, staring at the contents as if they would give her the answers she needed.

Why was Jamie so hard to reach and deliberately evasive? And why didn't she just leave him to it? Get the hell out of this backwater. Go home.

'He wasn't always like this,' Esmé said.

Stella was so surprised to hear her speak, her anger disappeared completely. She grabbed a bottle of milk and closed the fridge.

'He was such a sweet wee boy.'

Esmé's voice was soft and, since she wasn't scowling at Stella, she looked quite pleasant.

'Tea?' Stella said, reaching for the kettle.

'I'll do that.' Esmé reached across and plucked the kettle from Stella's grasp.

'Why won't you let me help?'

'You have a job and it's not in here. Got to set boundaries or people will walk all over you.'

'I'm not trying to walk over you.'

Esmé made a short barking noise which might have been a laugh if she was the laughing sort. 'Not me. People will walk over you. You're paid to do one job, you shouldn't take on any more. That boy' – she pointed at the doorway as if Jamie were stood there – 'will take and take and he won't notice that there's nothing left.'

'I thought you said he was a sweet boy?' Stella didn't understand the change in Esmé, why she was suddenly speaking to her like an ally, not an enemy.

'He was,' Esmé said. 'He still is at times. But he's like his father. He's only got eyes for his own wants. You have to look after yourself with folk like that or they'll drag you right along with them.'

'Maybe I want to be dragged,' Stella said. 'It beats doing nothing, and God knows I need the distraction.' Stella realised the truth of the words; she was angry with Jamie for obstructing her job as his assistant because she craved the distraction of work, of feeling needed and useful and efficient.

Esmé swirled water in the teapot to warm it, then tipped it out. 'Just mind yeself. If you're staying, you're gonnae have to learn to handle Jamie.'

'I thought you wanted me to leave?'

'Aye, well . . .' Esmé measured leaves into the pot and poured on boiling water. Stella waited for her to elaborate, but she just busied herself with the cups and saucers. Finally, Esmé said, 'I've asked around and you haven't been blabbing. Credit where it's due.'

'Of course not,' Stella said.

Esmé shrugged. 'People are always looking to take advantage of this family, one way or another.'

'I'm not taking advantage. Jamie hired me to do a job. I don't know why, though,' Stella said. 'He won't look at any of his correspondence. He asked for a daily report, but I know he doesn't read them. What's the point?'

'He's taking a break, and mebbe it's about time.'

'I see that, but why bother with an assistant? Why not just ignore the lot? Or leave his team in America to do it.'

Esmé shrugged. She pushed a cup and saucer in Stella's direction and then turned away to start preparing dinner.

'Please let me do something in here. Anything.' Stella wanted to peel a big pile of spuds or whip some cream. Something tangible.

Esmé made a shooing gesture. 'You're in my way. Go and see what Jamie wants.'

'I might shout at him,' Stella said, aware that she was not her usual calm self. A tight coil of suppressed anger buried deep inside her body felt ready to unravel.

Stella knew it had been there for months, that Jamie Munro was not the real cause, but that knowledge didn't make the anger disappear.

'Shouting is fine,' Esmé said. 'Do you both the world of good. Just don't throw anything irreplaceable. Take some plain dishes if you think you'll want to smash something for effect.'

'I don't do things for effect,' Stella said. 'It's not a performance.'

Esmé smiled at her. 'The dishes will be just as broken either way. Take his tea if you've a spare hand.'

'He can fetch his own,' Stella said, and went to find Jamie.

Stella was prepared to argue with Jamie about her role and the way he was ignoring both the administration of his business and the writing of his new book, so she was as surprised as he was when the words 'who is Ellie MacDonald?' popped out instead.

Jamie was preparing to do a powerlifting session, and stopped putting on his gloves to look at her. 'She worked here for a couple of days.'

Stella was taken aback at his readiness to admit it. 'You said you hadn't had an assistant before. Here. You lied.'

He looked away. 'I didn't lie. She wasn't my assistant.'

'That's not what Doug said.' Stella had decided that she wasn't going to tell Jamie about the journalist. Retired or not, she had the feeling that mentioning a member of the press talking about his family would throw the conversation off-track immediately. Or that he might fire her instantly for speaking to the man.

'And who is Doug?'

'Postman. Drinks at the Arisaig Inn. You'd know, if you left your ivory tower once in a while.'

He moved closer to the barbell, bending his knees and elbows a few times as if to warm up. 'And you think he would know better than me what Ellie MacDonald was hired to do?'

'Well . . .' Stella felt she was losing control of the conversation. 'You didn't tell me she'd died.'

'I didn't think it was relevant. I don't think it's relevant now.'

'She died here, two months before I came for an interview. I think that's relevant.'

'Why?' He looked genuinely confused. 'She had an accident. Not even in the house. Down on the rocks around the bay. Where I told you to be careful.'

'You should have told me why.'

Jamie stopped stretching and looked at her as if she had grown an extra head. 'So that you could be frightened? It was bad luck. A freak accident. If she hadn't fallen in that particular way then it wouldn't have been so serious. I fell on the rocks when I was fifteen, broke a rib.'

'Then maybe they should be cordoned off,' Stella said, still angry but not so sure what to do with it.

'Oh, you're not one of those, are you? Health and safety notices everywhere, pointing out the bleeding obvious. Ban bungee jumping and skydiving and skiing, just in case someone gets an ouchie.'

'I don't call dead an "ouchie". Don't be such a dick.'

The word hung between them in the ensuing silence.

Stella couldn't believe she had been so unprofessional, said something so unacceptable. At the same time, she didn't care. He *was* being a dick. She waited for the axe to fall. Instant dismissal?

Instead, he smiled widely. 'When you reach the point in a discussion when the other person just starts throwing insults, you know you've won.' He bent his knees and gripped the heavy barbell, panting as he lifted it a short distance then put it back. Stella had seen him do this routine before. He lifted maybe ten times, only a short distance each time, but the weight was so heavy that he was sweating and red by the end.

'Aren't those supposed to go over your head?'

He didn't answer until he'd put the weight down again, then said, 'Only if you want to show off. If you want to be effective, this works.'

Stella waited until he'd finished his lifts, trying to hold on to her anger.

'I hired Ellie to help Esmé with the house. Cleaning and that kind of thing. She's been living here alone for years and I kind of felt like I was intruding, or mebbe interrupting her routine. And I didn't want her to go to extra trouble just because I was here, but you can't tell Esmé what to do. I wanted her to be able to carry on as she was before or take a break completely. Whatever she wanted. She deserves that.' He put one arm across his body, stretching. 'It didn't really work out. Ellie was only here for a couple of days before Esmé told me she wasn't suitable. It was supposed to be a one-month trial, but I told her she could head home and I'd pay her anyway. She went for a walk instead.' He looked down. 'I did worry that she was more upset than she seemed. Mebbe that's why she wasn't paying proper attention on the rocks, but she seemed all right. I swear, she was chuffed about getting full pay and she seemed kind of relieved. I don't think Esmé had been very easy . . .'

Stella felt the last of her anger drain away. He hadn't lied to her about Ellie, not really. Not mentioning was not the same thing. And whatever Doug or anybody else said, he didn't seem like a bad person. Annoying, yes. Occasionally smug, definitely, but not evil. Remembering the way he was spoken about in the village softened her mood further.

'I didn't like hearing about Ellie from someone else,' she said. 'I wish you'd told me.'

He grabbed a towel and rubbed his face and neck. When his face was visible again, it was serious. 'I understand. Sorry about that.'

'I'll leave you in peace.' Stella turned to go.

'It's not cursed, if that's what's worrying you.'

Stella wanted to laugh but her throat was suddenly dry. 'Cursed?'

'This place. I know there's a rumour. It's been going on for so long now that it's become folklore. Some idiotic bastard put it in his book of local tales and that didn't help. Newspapers picked up on it and started calling it "house of tragedy", which made the whole thing worse.'

'I've heard a few things,' Stella said, deciding to be honest. 'In the village.'

Jamie pulled a wry smile. 'I'll bet. But I don't want you to worry—'

'I don't think this house is cursed,' Stella said quickly. 'I just don't like being in the dark. I like to have all the facts and then I can make informed decisions.'

'Absolutely,' Jamie said. 'I'm exactly the same. I'm sorry.'

'All right, then. Is there anything else I should know?'

'About local gossip?'

'About anything.'

'I'm glad you're here,' Jamie said. 'I think this arrangement is working out very well.'

Stella felt the heat travel up to her cheeks, and a feeling not unlike happiness. 'Thank you.'

CHAPTER TEN

24th March, 1848

My dearest Mary,

Thank you for your letter and the pressed violet. My only wish is that you cover several pages rather than just one. I know that I am being greedy, but every message from you is a shining light and I hunger for every detail of home. I am so glad that wee Angus has recovered from his fever. I know you were feart, although you did not say so; it was written between every line. Please give him a kiss from his loving aunt and tell him that he must abide by your wishes and not play in the river until the weather has truly warmed.

It is so frustrating to be a new wife and considered young and silly. Ladies will not speak of certain matters in my presence and they quickly change the subject when I arrive. I know this is true, as I waited outside the door to the salon at my last visit and I heard Lady Anstruther ask Mrs Fraser whether she had heard of the new instrument Mr Simpson had devised and how it allowed him to listen 'most accurately to the shape of the—' I did not catch the last part of the sentence, and then I was no longer alone and had no choice but to enter the room whereupon the conversation was swiftly turned to Lady Anstruther's fine headdress. It was beautiful, a circlet holding her long dark hair and festooned with wild brambles. Not pretend branches, but real brambles gathered from a bush. The other ladies thought this ingenious beyond the telling but I could only think of how it would be looked down upon in our dear Haddington, where artificial flowers are held in high esteem. Now I think on it, though, why the fakery should be preferred over the natural, I do not know.

I am trying to be a good wife but it is not always simple. Mr Lockhart is changeable in his moods and desires and I do not seem to please him often. I am trying, though, and will continue to do so. I must remember the pressure he feels and try to alleviate his discomfort in whichever way I can. A good wife soothes her husband and is a good companion. I miss you, Mary, and wish you were here to advise me.

Your loving Jessie

Stella had been feeling under the weather all day after fighting with Jamie. She told herself that she was just handling her client, the way she always did, but her heart told her otherwise. She cared. And she had been properly angry, not playacting. She hadn't been lying to Esmé, but she had been lying to Jamie. No matter how silly or fanciful, she was a little bit worried about all that had gone on in Munro House – in her bleaker moments it felt as if the house could be cursed. There was something about the big lonely house and the stretch of grey water. Knowing that a girl had slipped on the rocks and died, just weeks before she arrived, did nothing to ease her foreboding.

But she didn't want to leave, either. Her whole being was rooted to the place.

Stella felt her breath coming in small, hard-won sips, and considered cancelling her dinner date with Caitlin and Rob. People tended to think of heart problems causing pain in the chest, but it actually felt as if the problem was in your lungs. Stella's breath got shallow, then it became impossible to take in even a tiny bit of air, nothing going in or out until her head began to swim with the lack of oxygen and her entire body went weak. Then there was the ringing in her ears, the sense of drowning on dry land.

She picked up her mobile, still debating whether to ask for a rain check, when the sight of the message on the display stopped her cold. *Out of service.* She looked around for a landline, even though she had been staying in the cottage for a couple of weeks and hadn't seen one. Why would there be a landline for a holiday cottage, after all? *Because the mobile reception out here is awful and it's basic safety.* Well, there was that, but most people weren't as cautious, perhaps. *Most people don't have a higher-than-normal chance of a medical emergency*, a small voice at the back of Stella's mind added. She felt her chest tighten in response and she sat on the small sofa, taking deep slow breaths, reassuring herself that she still could.

After a few minutes, she put on her walking boots, hat and raincoat and set out. She kept checking her mobile phone, trying to find out the point at which it would work, and hoping that it wasn't too far from her new bolthole. She passed the big house with no signal, but pushed her worry to one side. Something to think about another time.

The small hill which led up from the Munro estate and then down again into the village seemed to have grown in size since she last walked it, and halfway up the slope Stella was seriously considering going back for her car, red wine be damned. Her chest was tight and she could feel her pulse in her head, never a good sign. She slipped a hand into her jacket pocket and closed her fingers around the little pill box with her emergency beta blockers, standing still for a few moments and struggling to pull more air into her lungs.

After a while, she felt strong enough to carry on, and walked the rest of the slope in tiny, slow steps, stopping frequently.

The curtains were shut at Caitlin's cottage, but light was shining through the material, casting a cheerful glow onto the frosty ground outside.

Stella could feel herself folding down, and she leaned against the door for a few moments, hoping that the buzzing in her muscles would subside. When she realised that she wasn't getting better, she knocked anyway, figuring that a sit-down in the warm was preferable to collapsing on the frozen doorstep.

Caitlin opened the door mercifully quickly. Her welcoming smile disappearing in an instant. 'Crap, you look terrible.'

Stella wanted to say something sarcastic but she didn't have the breath.

Caitlin took Stella's arm and helped her into the house, shutting the front door. Stella couldn't speak and the buzzing sensation had turned to full numbness in her fingers, toes and lips. Her vision had narrowed to a tunnel and she felt herself slump.

'Help us,' Caitlin said when Rob appeared in the hallway. He was there in an instant, hands lifting and carrying and Stella was in a chair. She wanted to put her head down low to get some blood back to her brain but slumping forward would compress her lungs, so she leaned back instead. The ceiling had a stain on it and she concentrated on that and took small sips of oxygen, waiting for the black edges of her vision to recede.

'What happened?' Rob's face was uncomfortably close. She could see the enlarged pores around his nose. 'Did he do this?'

'No,' Stella managed, not sure who or what Rob was talking about.

'I'm calling an ambulance,' Caitlin said, her mobile in her hand.

'No,' Stella said, reaching for her. 'Please don't.'

'Doctor, then. Someone,' Rob said. He was spitting a little as he spoke. 'If something's happened you have to tell us. It can't go on—'

Stella closed her eyes, her head was swimming but it was already better now that she was sitting down. 'I'm fine.'

Her breathing was getting easier. 'Pills.' She drew the box from her jacket, but her fingers weren't cooperating and it fell onto the floor.

Rob got a glass of water while Caitlin stooped awkwardly to retrieve it. She opened the clicky lid. 'How many?'

Stella held up one finger and then swallowed the tablet. After a few more minutes she was able to speak. 'Sorry to freak you out. I'm fine. Just overdid it.'

'He's working you too hard?' Caitlin was frowning. 'Or did he upset you?'

'It's not Jamie,' Stella said.

'It's supposed to be a desk job,' Caitlin said. 'Quiet.' She had her hands on her hips and she looked ready to storm Munro House and drag Jamie out by one earlobe.

'It's not his fault.'

'How often do you have to take those?' Rob said, eyeing the bottle of pills.

'It varies,' Stella said, her hand on her chest, feeling her heartbeat, which was still hammering away. 'Not that often.'

'I thought you were all better. After your last op—'

'Mostly.' Stella was willing her heart to slow. Blood was still pounding in her ears, making it difficult to think. It was like being at the bottom of an ocean, the pressure on her eardrums and nose and eyes. Her whole body shuddering with the runaway train in her chest. Sometimes she felt her heart was a weak, fluttering bird, and other times it seemed powerful enough to break her apart.

'Tell us what happened,' Rob said, and he was still too close. His face seemed weirdly magnified and his flushed skin made him look more angry than concerned. Stella had always thought of Rob as gentle

125

and mild to the point of weakness. 'We can't help if we don't know,' he was saying. 'If he—'

Caitlin shot him a 'shut up' look and Rob walked out of the room, muttering about getting a glass of water.

'You want me to call someone?' Caitlin said once they were on their own. 'Your parents?'

'No. Definitely not.' Stella was feeling better already. The pill had worked its magic. 'And if they call here, don't you dare tell them.'

'They have a right to know. If you're not well—'

'You know what they have a right to?' Stella managed. 'Peace of mind.'

'But—'

'No.' Stella put all the force she could muster into the word, then repeated it again for good measure. 'No.'

'Okay.' Caitlin had her hands up.

'Do you know the only thing you can do when you have put your parents through hell? The very least you can do for the rest of your natural-born life?' Stella knew she was shouting, but she couldn't stop. The lack of breath made it a wheezy, quiet sort of shout, which just made her sound more unhinged. 'The least you can do is not. Fucking. Worry them. Again.' Her breath had gone again and her head was thumping. A band of pain cinched around her temples and forehead. Stella leaned back and closed her eyes.

She heard Rob and Caitlin speaking quietly, Caitlin having joined him in the hallway. Fair enough. Stella knew she had probably shown too much emotion, shocked them. Caitlin was always super-sensible. Not one for emotional displays.

She felt a touch on her arm and opened her eyes. Caitlin passed her a mug of tea. 'Sorry,' Stella said. 'I'm fine. Really.'

'I trust you,' Caitlin said. 'Rob is still all for calling the doctor, but I won't let him if you don't want one.'

'Thank you,' Stella said. She wrapped her fingers around the warmth of the mug. She couldn't stop thinking about Ben and the first time she'd had a turn in front of him. He'd been so calm. He had looked after her, but he hadn't fussed. He hadn't suggested calling her mum and dad, hadn't pressed her to go to the doctor. She had liked the way he'd trusted her, trusted that she would be fine. It made her feel strong. Now she wondered if it had been such a good sign. That was one of the hardest things about the break-up – she kept on going over old events and conversations, looking for the signs she must have missed. Seeing everything in a different light, as if his final act of leaving her changed everything which had gone before. It made her feel as if she'd lost the last six years as well as her future.

'Will you do one thing for me, though?' Caitlin said. 'Will you have a check-up?'

'All right,' Stella said, although she didn't mean it. 'You know I'm fine now. This isn't like at university. That was the valve playing up, and now they've replaced that, I'm good as new.'

'Still,' Caitlin said. 'Just to be safe.'

Having filed the day's correspondence and curated a short digest of the most important-seeming items, Stella closed the email application and stretched her arms above her head, feeling her shoulders crack.

She could hear Jamie's pacing next door, the now-familiar tread as he walked the carpet, muttering into his digital voice recorder. She went in and found him red-eyed.

'What's wrong?'

He stopped moving. 'Nothing.'

'Shall I send you the digest through, or not bother?'

He smiled. 'You don't have to bother with that anymore. I think we've established that I'm not going to look at them.'

'I'll just keep hold of it, then,' Stella said. 'For now. You might change your mind.'

He shook his head. 'I just can't seem to get worked up about my email anymore.' He rubbed his arms as if they were aching, then said, 'My grandfather rebuilt this place, you know. After the fire burned the original building.'

'I read about that,' Stella said. 'That's why the interior is 1930s and the building 1800s.' Stepping through the door of Munro House gave a peculiar jolting sensation, as the outside was solid, grey, Scottish baronial architecture and the inside full of sensuous art-deco curves.

'He'd just completed it and was going to move back in when it got requisitioned for the war effort. Imagine that, years of his life rebuilding a home for his family and then having it taken away again.'

'Must have been hard. Where did he stay?'

'I don't know. Somewhere in the village, I guess.' He darted across the room to his overflowing desk and began searching through the piles of paper and books. 'There's a picture here somewhere. Just before my dad was born. He was a late baby. My grandmother was well over forty when he arrived.'

Stella realised something. Jamie was late for his ice bath. He was never late for his ice bath. She asked him and he spun around, blinking hard. 'Christ. Yes. Let's go.'

Looking straight into his face, Stella thought he actually didn't look well. 'How did you sleep?'

'I didn't,' Jamie said. 'Don't fuss, I'll nap later. Mebbe.'

She put a hand on his forehead. It was hot. 'You've got a temperature. Bed. Now.'

'No, I need to do my ice bath. After I find that picture, I want to show you—'

'I'll look for it later. But you're not doing your bath. If you're ill, it will affect your results. You can't.' Stella knew that appealing to common sense wouldn't work and so she went straight for the scientific method instead.

'Fuck.'

'Come on. Upstairs.'

'I just want to go through this stuff.' He waved a hand. 'I need to know what I've got.'

'I can do that,' Stella said. 'You go to bed for a few hours. Get some sleep.'

She followed him upstairs and into his bedroom. It was a big room, with tall windows that looked out to the sea. The giant wooden bed was made with expensive-looking grey linen with a small geometric pattern, which looked less out-of-place in the art-deco room than she would have expected.

Jamie stumbled as he walked around the room and Stella realised that he probably hadn't eaten, either. 'Shall I bring you some food?'

He shook his head. 'Fasting day.'

Stella straightened. 'I think we just established that you are ill. That means all experimentation is off today.'

'It'll put me back, I'll have to start the fasting pattern again.'

'So be it,' Stella said. 'You can't do this when you are ill.'

He paused, looking at her. 'You're my employee, you know. You can't tell me—'

'I'm your assistant. I'm here to make your life run smoothly, and that includes stopping you from turning a cold into something serious like pneumonia. You push your body when it's weak and you risk knocking out months of productivity, not just one day. You know this, but you're not thinking straight.'

His face darkened, and for a horrible moment Stella thought he was going to banish her from the house, but then his shoulders slumped. 'I'm sorry. You're right.'

'Get into bed, I'll be back in a minute.'

Stella went downstairs and washed her hands thoroughly. No sense in risking catching the flu herself. Then she made scrambled eggs and buttered toast. She put a glass of orange juice on the tray and a pint glass of water with two paracetamol on the side.

Jamie had obediently got into bed and was sitting up against some pillows. Ignoring the weird intimacy of seeing him that way, Stella put the tray on his lap and said, 'No arguments.'

Later that day, Esmé came in from walking the dogs, bringing the smell of fresh air and seawater. Glad to have something to say to the woman, Stella passed on an update on Jamie.

'He's in bed?' Esmé patted Tabitha's head absently as she spoke.

'Asleep,' Stella said, feeling absurdly proud of her nursing skills. 'And he ate some toast.'

'Well I'll be damned.'

Stella tried not to look too pleased.

Esmé turned away to fill the kettle. With her back facing Stella, she said, 'You ought to stay up here.'

'What?'

'There's a decent en-suite upstairs. I've aired it out.'

'You think I should move into the house?'

'No sense in heating the cottage when we've plenty of space up here.'

'Right,' Stella said, more happy than she wanted to show. She felt as if she had just passed a test.

It didn't take long to pack her stuff and carry it up the track to the house. The sky was pale-blue above the purple-grey roof, and the green of the trees seemed brighter than usual. Even the brown dirt of the track looked rich and pleasant. The house looked as imposing as ever, but now there was something homely about it, too. Just being familiar with the interior and no longer being in dread fear of the dogs made a big difference.

Esmé showed her to her new bedroom. It had pale china-blue walls, a solid mahogany chest of drawers, and a dressing table with a big oval mirror. There was a blue-and-white bedspread which matched the curtains. Angus had bounded up the stairs ahead of them and was now running in delighted circles around the room.

He jumped on the bed and Esmé shouted at him to get down.

'I don't mind,' Stella said.

'You will at four o'clock in the morning,' Esmé said.

Stella put her green inkwell on the dressing table so that the light from the window lit it, and the bubbles trapped in the glass sparkled iridescent. She unpacked in her new room and made sure that Jamie drank plenty of fluids. When she checked on him later in the day, he was sound asleep, burrowed underneath a duvet and extra blanket. His forehead was damp with sweat and it wasn't cold in the room, so Stella took the blanket off the bed and crept out without waking him.

By the evening, he was awake and up again, but he agreed not to do any work and to sit at the kitchen table and eat some soup.

CHAPTER ELEVEN

12th April, 1848

My dearest Mary,

I am sorry for the terrible delay in my reply. I know that you will be quite cross with me but I beg your forgiveness. I am certain you no longer need the recipe for the biscuits but I have enclosed it in case.

Mr Lockhart said that he would send word but when I did not hear from you I was not sure it had reached Haddington. I have been unwell and, in truth, asleep for the best part of the last two weeks. I do not remember much at all but Mr Lockhart has been most attentive. It is one of the advantages of being the wife of a medical man, I have received the best care that money can buy. Truly, nothing has been too much for him and I have had all manner of tinctures and pills and the most modern treatments.

Do send me your news as soon as you can. I miss you terribly but cannot say when we shall meet. Mr Lockhart says that homesickness is a symptom of my continuing weakness after the fever. I dare not mention it again in case he resumes my treatment.

Your loving Jessie

P.S. I had the cook list the recipe and I wrote it down for you and the girls. Looking at it with fresh eyes I can see that I did not make a fine script and I blame the blasted sickness. I was still feeling a wee bit shoogly, as our dear mother would have termed my condition. Where I have written 'arrowroot' I made a smudge but it ought to read 'one tablespoon'.

The next day, Jamie was back to his usual self. Stella found him drinking one of his green smoothies in the kitchen, chatting with Esmé, and he was clear-eyed and his skin was a healthy colour again.

It was the first thing Stella had seen that was a true advert for his regime. Stella expected him to get straight back to his ice bath routine, but he buried himself in his family research instead.

Stella dragged herself to the computer, ready to go through emails and summarise them in reports Jamie wasn't going to look at. She had done plenty of seemingly meaningless tasks in her years of temping, but had never felt so disappointed. For a few days at the start, she had really thought that this job would be different.

The door was ajar and Jamie knocked lightly, pushing it open at the same time. 'Sorry to interrupt,' he said.

'No problem.' Stella turned and gave him her professional smile. She didn't want him to feel odd about her putting him to bed the day before. She imagined he would be all prickly and hyper-manly today to make up for her seeing him show weakness. He surprised her by producing a cup of coffee and a plate with a slice of carrot cake. 'Thank you for your help,' he said. 'Nursing a grumpy bastard with a cold is above and beyond.'

Stella took the cake and the mug. 'You weren't that grumpy.'

He hesitated, looking unsure.

'What?'

'Would you help me with my research?' He gestured behind, indicating his office. 'I have so much stuff. I got more boxes down from the attic and there's the books and the archive from the local history library and that's not even starting on the online resources.'

Stella could almost hear Nathan's voice, telling her that she had to get Jamie back on track, steer him away from his family research and back onto his book.

As if Jamie could hear Nathan, too, he added, 'I do want to make the next book truly useful. If fasting or using cold therapy can help people stay mentally sharp for longer, then I think that's worth pursuing. I think it's valuable. But the other lines of research I was looking at, I don't know anymore . . .' He glanced out of the window. 'Since being back here, it all feels very far away. And now Google has started the California Life Company, and others – people who always called me crazy – are funding research, it just doesn't feel as necessary that I do it.'

'You liked being a lone wolf.'

'I guess. A bit. I liked being a voice of dissent, going against the status quo. And it felt important to do that because so few were. I mean, we discovered that restricting calorie intake extended the lifespan of rats back in the 1930s. I feel like more should have been done, but it was seen as a crank project. Now it's becoming mainstream.' He shrugged. 'I mean, Google . . . you know?'

Stella nodded.

'And being here just really makes me think about family. I know I shouldn't be focusing on the ancestry stuff. I do know that. But I can't stop.'

'It's your life,' Stella said. 'Why not follow your passion? It's an approach which has served you well in the past.'

He looked her straight in the eye. 'It's not what you signed up for,' he said.

'I'd love to help,' she said, and enjoyed the warmth of his smile.

Jamie was clearly still not up to his usual speed and he hadn't even opened all of the boxes. Stella grabbed a notebook and pen and began listing the contents of each, replacing everything where she had found it and taping the list to the top of the box. A bit of order was just what she needed to calm her mind.

Despite the absorbing routine, it was still strange to be working alongside Jamie. They moved around each other in the room, which had seemed a good size before but had been shrunk by the boxes and their recent intimacy. Working in someone's home was always tricky and the key was strict boundaries, but now that she had seen Jamie unwell and, worse, tucked up in his bed, she couldn't stop herself from stealing little glances at him while he wasn't looking, storing images. The lines of his shoulders. The colour of his eyelashes.

The last box that Stella opened contained letters. Neatly bundled and tied with faded ribbon. She looked at the first one, pencil poised to note down a couple of details for filing and move on, but instead she found herself unfolding the thin sheet of paper and reading to the end.

'Who is Jessie?'

Jamie looked up. 'No idea.'

'Grandmother? No, wait. This is too early. Great-great-great-grandmother?'

He shrugged and Stella went back to the letter. It was written to a Mary and the return address, in careful script, said Mrs Jessie Lockhart.

'The surname is Lockhart.'

Jamie shook his head. 'Doesn't ring a bell. I've been reading about my grandfather and his dad. They were both James Munro. Family tradition. Although my great-grandfather went by Jack, according to this stuff.'

Stella made a note on a piece of paper and refolded the letter. Most of the bundle appeared to be loose sheets, although there were some envelopes. She made a note about the stamps. Stella knew nothing about these things, but thought that well-preserved, Victorian-era stamps might be worth something to someone. Worth checking for insurance purposes, anyway.

'Are you all right?'

Stella realised that she was still staring at that first letter. The script hadn't been easy to read at first, but it was beautiful. The sloped writing and the occasional ink spot which brought to life the humanity of the item. Stella had been handling old books and photographs and newspaper clippings and handwritten notes for the last half an hour, but now, in that moment, she knew that she was holding something which had been created by a young woman one hundred and seventy years ago. She felt as if she had time-travelled, the physical paper which existed both then and now, a tangible link to the past. 'What are causey stanes?'

Jamie blinked. 'Cobblestones.'

'Scots?'

Jamie nodded. 'Are you sure you're all right?'

Stella forced herself to move, to refold the soft paper and replace its fellows. She did not want to put the bundle of letters back in the box. 'Do you mind if I read these?'

Jamie had already looked away and become engrossed in a leather ledger, which looked like an accounts book. He glanced up. 'Sure.'

Stella finished her work, the box of letters sitting on the corner of her desk like a promise. Every so often she allowed herself to take the top one and unfold it, feeling its softness under her fingertips and lifting it to inhale the delicious scent of old paper.

She couldn't explain why they gave her strength, but she suddenly felt a rush of energy. She wanted to get away from the house to phone Ben, but she didn't trust her mobile reception not to cut out in the middle of the call or for her resolve not to disappear if she waited for too long. After a moment's deliberation, she waited until Jamie was doing his upside-down spine therapy, and then took the cordless handset to the furthest room from his inversion rig.

'It's me,' she said when Ben answered.

'About bloody time,' Ben said. 'I've been worried sick.'

'Yeah. Sorry.' Stella didn't know why she was apologising. He had no right to be worried about her. She was no longer his concern.

He took an audible breath and when he spoke next, his voice was more gentle. 'Where are you?'

'Scotland,' Stella said.

A beat. 'Holiday?'

'Not really,' Stella said. 'Listen. I called to tell you something.'

'It's not good to leave the house empty for so long. I stayed there last night, just so that anybody watching would see that it's still occupied.'

Stella was momentarily derailed by the thought of Ben inside her home. Had he slept in her bed? Their bed? She swallowed the sudden urge to throw up and tried to get her thoughts back on track. It didn't matter. She had rung to tell him that it didn't matter.

'It looked like you left in a hurry, you've hardly got any of your clothes,' Ben was saying. 'You can understand why I was so worried. I know I've no right to that—'

'It's nothing to do with you . . . what I do now. You don't need to worry about me and I don't need to worry about you worrying.'

'It's not that simple, though, is it?'

Stella looked out of the window. A rabbit was on the lawn and, a moment later, there was a terrific barking and one of the dogs ran out to try to catch it.

'Stella?'

'The files for the mortgage stuff are in the cupboard in the dining room.' Stella had used the table in there as her home office. Sitting with her laptop and receipts to reconcile their bank account, write the occasional cheque, make transfers and set up direct debits. Phone for the best prices on electricity and gas and insurance, and for quotes on rendering or plumbing or whatever the money pit of a house required next. Ben had loved the house, did love the house, but Stella had been its mother. The one who wiped its nose and made sure it had dinner money.

'You need the password and code to log into the joint bank account. The code is on a card in that file and I can give you the password now if you have a pen. I didn't want to email it.'

'I think I just need the mortgage details, account number and all that. Then I can phone them and find out—'

'Yes, but you're going to need a new mortgage. We can't keep the same account if you're going to buy me out. And you'll need details of outgoings and all that for the application. Go into the joint account and you'll find them all under direct debits. It's the easiest way as they're all in one place. You can print off that page.'

'Right, got it. Okay.'

'I don't know exactly how this works, but I'm sure either our old mortgage company or whoever you go with will be able to talk you through it. Just keep me up to date. Email is fine.'

'You're being very efficient,' Ben said.

It was an old insult. Ben had always said she was being efficient when he was teasing her about not enjoying herself more, not fully engaging with the place they were visiting, or when he wanted to suggest that her organisation skills were more a curse than a blessing.

'And thank Christ for that,' Stella said. 'I assume you want to get this sorted sooner rather than later, and I know I don't want to pay a half-share on a house I'm not living in for any longer than I have to.'

There was a small pause. 'You're not coming back, then?'

'Not to the house, no. It's all yours.'

'Thank you,' Ben said.

'It has nothing to do with you,' Stella said, and it was only half a lie.

❧

The next day, Stella was working through the emails to Jamie's website, marvelling at the range of correspondence he received from fans. Among the kind and complimentary messages were tales of courage and hope and triumph which warmed the heart. Sprinkled throughout, however, were some truly horrifying messages from some very angry people. Death threats. Suggestions for sexual practices that were anatomically impossible. Obscene pictures. Religious diatribes that ended with a graphic description of the tortures which awaited Jamie in hell. Stella had set up a filter to catch the majority of the nasty stuff and put it into a specially created 'whackjob' folder, but she still felt it important to check that something genuine and non-insane hadn't been missed. Plus, every so often a death threat would be so carefully worded that it bypassed the filter and Stella only discovered halfway through the message that she was reading a reasoned argument as to the how and why Jamie was going to be poisoned in his sleep or killed in a car 'accident'.

After an hour or so of this job, Stella felt her attention straying to the bundle of letters from Jessie Lockhart. They were enthralling and she had wanted to devour them in one sitting, but luckily the handwriting was difficult to decipher to her modern eyes and that had helped Stella to ration them out. She took one now, as a treat for dealing with the unpleasant emails.

I have been unwell and, in truth, asleep for the best part of the last two weeks . . . Truly, nothing has been too much for him and I have had all manner of tinctures and pills and the most modern treatments.

'Tinctures.' Stella said the word out loud. There was an old-fashioned ring to it which was oddly comforting but, Stella knew, the reality was not. Medical man or not, James Lockhart was treating his wife with the limited resources of the day, and Stella felt a gut-wrenching, instinctual sisterhood with 'poorly wee Jessie'. She tried to imagine what her outcome would have been, if she and Jessie swapped places. It was a pointless exercise; she wouldn't have survived babyhood.

'Do you know what this is?' Jamie walked into the room and held out an envelope.

'No,' Stella said, her mind back on death threats. 'Let me see.'

The envelope was A5, white, and had *Jamie Munro* written on the front in familiar handwriting. It was Caitlin's, Stella thought. Mystified, she opened the envelope.

'Don't,' Jamie said. 'It might be anthrax.'

'I doubt it,' Stella said.

Jamie plucked the folded sheet of paper before she could read it. 'Who is Caitlin?'

'Caitlin Baird. The friend I was staying with before I came here.' Stella's mind was scrambling – why would Caitlin write to Jamie? Had she misaddressed the envelope? Was it some weird Scottish tradition?

'Oh, yeah. Right.' Jamie was reading the letter, a crease between his eyes.

'What is it?'

His expression was blank. 'She says you are ill.'

Stella felt herself blush. 'That's not—'

'Stella Jackson has a heart condition which makes her heart beat erratically. She had an episode on Monday and refused medical treatment. I am worried about her and was hoping you could persuade her to go for a check-up. She promised me that she would, but I know her. She won't.'

'Bloody hell,' Stella said.

'You don't want to go to the hospital?'

'No.' Stella shook her head. 'I really, really don't. I have had enough of hospitals to last me a lifetime.'

'Fair enough,' Jamie said. 'It's none of my business.' He dropped the letter into the wastepaper bin and went back to his office.

Stella waited for the relief to wash over her and it did, but it was shallow and not nearly as comforting as she'd expected.

That evening, Stella was working late. She had taken time off in the afternoon and walked with the dogs through the woods, Angus running circles around almost every tree and barking at squirrels, leaves and dirt. Having Skyped with Jamie's accountancy firm in San Francisco, an entirely pointless meeting as far as she could tell, but something they seemed to feel they needed, Stella began shutting her applications down. The sound of rotor blades made her head jerk up.

'Jamie?' Stella found his office empty. Through the big window in the dining room, she saw a black helicopter on the lower lawn, its blades slowing. Coming up the steps at the side of the garden was a man she didn't recognise, deep in conversation with Jamie. She stepped away from the window and hovered, uncertain as to what to do, where to go. Finally, she went into the kitchen and filled the kettle. Tea. The answer to every question.

The men walked into the kitchen, bringing the smell of fresh air and diesel with them. 'Stella, this is my pal, Alek Brzezicki.'

'Nice to meet you.' Stella took the enormous hand that was being offered by Alek. He was well over six foot and towered over Jamie. She guessed he must be one of the 'world-class' athletes Jamie was always talking about when studying performance and health. His shoulders seemed too wide for the doorway and his skin glowed in a way which suggested ice baths, morning runs and green smoothies. If it wasn't for the height difference, he and Jamie could have been brothers.

Stella felt even softer and more knackered than usual next to these two visions of vitality. 'Shall we get started?' Alek said. 'I need to get back tonight. Sorry.'

'That's okay,' Jamie said. 'Thanks for coming, man.'

'Do you need me for anything?' Stella wondered if they would ask Esmé to cook them dinner or whether they would just dig into a protein bar or huff some oxygen from the canister Jamie kept in his exercise room.

Jamie didn't look at her, his attention on his guest. 'Do you want refreshments?'

'No, let's get started.' Alek smiled at Stella. 'Just a quick check-up. Nothing to worry about, I promise.'

'What?'

'You said you didn't want to go to hospital and I respect that,' Jamie said. He wasn't looking directly at her and Stella realised that he was worried about her reaction. 'Alek is a cardiologist.'

Stella stopped herself from saying 'what?' again. 'I'm fine,' she said instead.

'That's good,' Alek said enthusiastically. 'I'll just take a few readings and be out of your hair.'

Without exactly agreeing, Stella found herself in one of the many spare bedrooms, with Alek unravelling the wires of his portable EKG machine.

'So, you're in private practice, I assume. Are all your clients like Jamie?' It seemed politer than asking why he wasn't a film star. He had the cheekbones for it.

Alek shook his head. 'Nope. St Barts. Jamie's a friend.'

'He's not paying you?'

'Oh, I charge him, all right. But I wouldn't have come up here on three hours' notice for a patient who says they are perfectly well and who doesn't want to see a doctor, unless he was a mate.'

Stella realised that the best way to get this over with as quickly as possible was to cooperate. She reeled off her diagnosis, the corrective surgery she had undergone as a child, the valve replacement four years ago and her current maintenance regime.

'When did you last see your own doctor?'

'Every year, as recommended.'

Alek tilted his head. 'Is that a fact?'

'I might have missed the last one.' Or two.

Alek's expression didn't alter. 'Bisoprolol? It works well for you?'

'I hardly ever need it,' Stella said. She unbuttoned her shirt and let Alek attach the electrodes on her chest.

There was silence for a few moments while the machine did its thing. Stella found a spot on the wall opposite and concentrated on that. She had always hated the EKG, even though it didn't hurt. The mapping of her heartbeat, the sense of a test she might fail. The old machines used to spew out a long piece of paper, her heart beat drawn in jaggy lines of ink. Now, like everything else, it was a digital image. Stella preferred the screen version. It was easier to distance from herself, somehow.

'I would like to take some blood, if I may?' Alek was getting out a kit with syringes, needles and empty vials.

Stella hated needles. She wanted to say no. He couldn't make her, after all, but the thought of Jamie downstairs, pacing and worried – worried enough to fly a doctor to Scotland just to check her over – stopped her. 'I need to lie down,' Stella said, moving her feet onto the bed. 'I have a tendency to faint.'

'Good to know.'

Stella didn't watch the preparations or the needle going in. She looked at a watercolour seascape and asked Alek questions about how he had met Jamie. Another boarding school connection. Stella thought about her school, the sprawling comprehensive in St Albans, and tried to recall the names of her friends. She was in touch with a fair number on Facebook, but only a couple in real life, and she wasn't close enough to any of them to fly them to Scotland for a favour.

'All done,' Alek said.

'You're not going to make me do a stress test?' Stella said, relieved.

He shook his beautiful head. 'Not unless you want me to.'

'No. I'm completely fine.' She really was, and all of this actually made her feel like a fake. All those years of medical attention that she had most definitely needed and now this high-class appointment to tell her what she already knew.

Alek was studying her scars with a professional gaze. She lifted the band of her bra so that he could see the most recent. They had gone in underneath her breast to give her the most discreet scar possible. It seemed like an unnecessary courtesy – she still had the gigantic one going down the middle, after all, but she appreciated the kindness. He nodded. 'Neat job and it's healed well. Any post-op problems?'

'Nope,' Stella said. 'Good as new.'

'And it was a weakened valve, not picked up during your original surgery?'

'Not present,' Stella corrected. 'My cardiologist said it was weakened through the growth period while they were still getting my arrhythmia under control.'

He nodded. 'You shouldn't have any more issues, then. Congratulations.'

'I'm very lucky,' Stella said.

He tilted his head. 'Any other symptoms post-op? Anxiety? Depression? Low mood?'

'About being cured?' Stella attempted a smile. 'What kind of person doesn't feel happy about getting their life back?'

He didn't answer and Stella found herself going over her words, looking for an unintended meaning or something she hadn't meant to reveal.

'In my line of work, I have seen every reaction possible to both good news and bad. All I can tell you is that the human heart is unpredictable.'

Stella concentrated on doing up her shirt, unable to meet his eye.

'You don't have to feel guilty if you're not ecstatic. You've been through a lot.'

Stella finished with her shirt. She wanted to say 'I'm fine' but the words wouldn't come.

'It will take a few days for the results. I'll call you. But I don't want you to worry. Your EKG looks good and it sounds as if your medication controls your symptoms just fine. Are there any side effects?'

'Dry mouth, sometimes,' Stella said, 'but I take them so infrequently it's not an issue.'

'Anything else you're concerned about? Do you have any questions about your heart or anything else?'

Stella's throat closed up from the simple kindness of the question. She shook her head. 'Thank you. No.'

He smiled. 'Shall I tell the worrier to stop worrying, then?'

'Yes, please,' Stella said.

He packed away his equipment, telling Stella about the holiday to Cuba he was taking at the end of the month.

'Will it get better or will it get worse?'

Alek switched topics with ease. 'No way to tell,' he said. 'It might just stay the same.'

'And I might live a long time.' Stella kept her voice perfectly flat. She didn't want to seem hopeful. Didn't want to make his job any worse than it already was.

'Absolutely.'

'Or I might not?'

'There is a statistical increase in the likelihood of heart attack, but it isn't large. There is also a possibility that your arrhythmia will get worse and, if that happens, there are surgical options as well as other medicines available. It's not likely, though. You would be very unlucky indeed to have another valve issue.'

'If it gets worse does that increase the likelihood of heart attack?'

'Yes.'

None of this was news, but hearing it again, even from someone who looked as if they ought to play a doctor on television, made it seem more real than ever. Stella realised that there had been a small part of her which had hoped that a fancy, private-practice doctor might have a different answer for her. 'And I have a statistical likelihood of a decreased lifespan?'

'That's not the way to look at it,' Alek said. 'You were born with a terrible prognosis, grew up with a bad prognosis, but now you are here. Healthy. And with an excellent prognosis. It really is cause for celebration.'

He left the room first and Stella finished sorting out her shirt. She put her shoes back on and waited a few minutes before going downstairs. This was why she avoided check-ups. They forced her to think about things which she preferred to keep buried.

Alek and Jamie were in the kitchen, talking about Cuba. Stella paused outside the door for a moment, and then went to her own room. She propped herself up on the bed with lots of pillows and read a book.

An hour or so later, Stella heard the rotor blades start up. She went to the window and watched the helicopter leave. When Jamie knocked on her door, she was ready to be angry with him, ready to shout at his overbearing, egotistical personality and his thoughtless, controlling behaviour.

The figure that stood in her doorway, ducking his head and looking worried, wasn't quite the Jamie Munro of her imagination. He looked uncertain. 'You want dinner? Esmé is roasting a chicken.'

Stella realised that she was starving. 'Yes, please.'

CHAPTER TWELVE

21st April, 1848

My dearest Mary,

I hope this letter finds you well. It is such a relief to sit at the writing desk with the pen in my hand, knowing that my scratchings will be seen by your beloved eyes and understood by that quick brain you have possessed always. I have no one to confide in here and, truthfully, being a wife is a more lonely occupation than I had imagined. Do you ever have such feelings, Mary? Or is it disrespectful to form such a question? I hope that you won't take offence – you know how deeply I esteem your dear Callum and that I consider him the finest brother.

James Young Simpson was in The Times newspaper today, and although we only take The Scotsman, Mr Watson showed the wretched thing to my husband and he has been in a state of great fury ever since. I ordered the cook to make his favourite dish for supper, pigeon pudding, but it did not soothe him in the slightest.

I wish I had not seen the paper, but once I began reading I was powerless to stop. It spoke at length on the wisdom of Dr Simpson and his supposed advancement of obstetrics and anaesthesia. Mary, it was so toadying in tone as to make one quite ill. Everybody loves that man to distraction, and it is as if he can do no wrong, it is such a trial for my own husband. My Mr Lockhart is but a few minutes late for the onset of a lady's pains and she screeches like a banshee.

I am sorry to report that visage has a lot more to do with our feelings than we might like. Everyone likes Simpson's round and smiling face, while Mr Lockhart has a serious, rather thin aspect. I suggested that he might smile more and he held my hand over a candle until I cried and agreed that smiling was for fools.

Mr Lockhart still has a great many visitors and his parlour, where the patients wait, is always full, but he is still dissatisfied. It is the quality of the patient which vexes him. He longs for the Lady Anstruthers of the town, but has to make do with drapers and pharmacists. The latter paid in laudanum which Mr Lockhart let me sample. It was a most pleasant effect but I felt woolly-headed and stupid the next day. I didn't care for that, but Mr Lockhart has prescribed a regimen. He asks me lots of questions and writes down the answers in his book. It's the closest we have ever been, I believe, and he is hoping to prove that laudanum is superior to chloroform. He says it is far safer than pursuing a new substance and that his experiments are for the greater good of the poor suffering surgical patients and the ladies crying out when they birth their babies, but I believe he wishes to humiliate Simpson. To usurp his position and take it for his own.

His friends urge him on and encourage these flights. I took the back stairs and passed the drawing room where they were drinking whisky after dinner and I could hear Mr Campbell, who has the biggest booming voice, telling Mr Lockhart that his patients did not appreciate his genius and that he ought to close his doors to all except the worthy. 'You must be firm,' he shouted, 'and turn away the lower classes before the higher ranks will cross your threshold.' I wanted to open the door and tell that man that he was talking nonsense. Mr Simpson saw patients at the Edinburgh Infirmary, and on the same day he was appointed physician to the queen, he attended to a fishwife in the ferry. Besides which, how will we live if Mr Lockhart turns away his patients?

Your loving Jessie

P.S. My last question was not an idle one and I crave your answer. However improper it may be, I seek your counsel.

Stella passed Jamie's office and called a cheery 'hello' to the closed door, knowing that he probably would not hear her. He would likely have his headphones in, meditating or listening to an audiobook or going through documents via the speech reader while he did his morning stretches, the lunatic. She felt herself smile at the thought and quickly wiped it from her face. She was not going to become charmed by the crazed man-child. Absolutely not.

The kitchen smelled of amazing coffee and Esmé was nowhere to be seen. Stella poured a generous cup of caffeine and considered breakfast.

Jamie hadn't eaten yet, so there was no lingering odour of black beans or tuna fish to offend her nostrils. No carbohydrates either, though. Esmé had clearly been overruled, as the bread bin was empty and the cake tin had one small piece of fruit loaf. Stella didn't want to be the one to finish it so she picked an apple from the fruit bowl and turned to go to her office, eager to open the archive box which had been couriered from the library, when she saw a figure in the doorway and jumped, slopping hot coffee over the side of her mug.

'Sorry, didn't mean to startle you.'

Stella recognised the voice immediately but it took her a beat to reconcile it with the physical presence.

She had imagined Nathan in great detail after countless phone calls. In her mind, he was big as a bear and had a cigar gripped between his teeth. He wore an enormous coat and had slicked-back hair, grey at the temples, and a perma-tan.

The real-life version turned out to be barely taller than she was, and as thin and youthful-looking as a teenage boy. He had light-brown hair, which was artfully tousled, and wide brown eyes like a deer.

'You're here. When did you arrive?' Stella said, still trying to adjust her mental picture to cope with reality.

'Last night. Or the day before. Or tomorrow. Jetlag's a bitch.' He was openly appraising her as he spoke, his gaze travelling up and down, a small smile on his lips. 'Lovely welcome makes up for it, though. Do you always look this good first thing in the morning?'

'Would you like some coffee?' Stella injected as much professional detachment into her tone as was humanly possible, but Nathan's smile just widened.

'That accent is adorable. Not as cute as Jamie's, of course, but he's the star.'

'Leave me out of it,' Jamie said, pushing the door open and heading straight for the fridge.

'I'll leave you to your beans,' Stella said. She hoped Nathan would move out of the way but he didn't, forcing her to turn to one side and sidle past.

᠁

Stella hid in her office and worked on her research while Jamie took Nathan out for a walk around the estate. Stella hoped he would step into a puddle or two. Maybe fall into the burn. She had so been looking forward to her morning, to the opportunity to dive into the bundle of letters, but her concentration was off. The Victorian scrawl seemed utterly impenetrable.

> My dearest Mary,
> I do not care for it here and wish to come home. There
> are evil spirits in this house . . .

And then there was another indecipherable squiggle. The next bit that Stella could read sounded more alarmed than ever, and Stella felt her heart rate increase in sympathy. The pen scratchings themselves appeared panicked and wild.

> Mary, I cannot speak of what they brought into the
> house. It is most ungodly and the souls of us all are
> in peril.

'There you are. Hiding.' Nathan had pushed open her door and was leaning against the frame.

'I'm not hiding, I'm working,' Stella said. Her dislike for the man was not improved by familiarity.

'I need you.' He turned and left, clicking his fingers.

Stella didn't get up.

A few seconds later, he was back. 'I don't think you understand how this works. This' – he clicked his fingers – 'means you follow.'

'I work for Mr Munro, not you,' Stella said. Years of temporary work in a variety of offices and with a glittering range of managerial styles had left her with very definite rules of engagement. 'I have never responded to somebody clicking their fingers and I don't intend to start.'

Nathan looked delighted. 'You are adorable, you know that, right?'

Stella opened her mouth to respond but Nathan just barrelled on. 'I gotta talk to you, though. And if you have his best interests at heart, and I know that you do, you'll listen to me. Come on, I prefer to walk and talk. Gotta get my cardio in. Don't want to drop dead at thirty-five.'

Stella picked up her jacket and walked out ahead of Nathan. She wasn't going to follow him, but if he cared to walk with her, she'd hear him out. She pulled on her boots by the back door in double-quick time and headed outside.

He caught up with her on the path which led from the back door next to the old pantry and the wash house. Stella was buttoning her coat against the ever-present wind when he took her arm, tucking her hand in the crook of his elbow like an old-time gentleman. Stella pulled away, quickening her pace. 'I'm waiting,' she said, trying to hide being flustered behind clipped words.

'For what?'

'An explanation of your behaviour and attitude. Failing that, a brief description of what you're doing here and what you want from me.'

'I need you onside,' he said, as if it were obvious. 'Jamie's obsessive, you may have noticed, and is much worse when he's writing. He trusts you and so I need you to handle him for me at this difficult time.'

'Why is it a difficult time? It's just a deadline.'

'You don't understand.'

Stella waited for him to explain.

He opened his mouth, but then swore loudly, instead of anything more illuminating. His foot was up to the calf in mud, a deep rut which had been hidden underneath a covering of wet orange leaves. 'Oh, dear,' Stella said. 'Your shoes are ruined.'

'Bloody country. I hate Scotland.'

'Do you not have mud in America?'

'Not in New York.'

'Poor you,' Stella said sweetly. 'I love the mud. And the rain.'

He narrowed his eyes at her. 'Why are you obstructing me? We both want the same thing.'

'Do we?'

'For Jamie to finish his book and have another awesome success and to make another boatload of cash and to buy you something pretty to say thank you. Or are you hoping for more than that?'

'I'm not hoping for anything of the kind. I'm just doing the job Mr Munro pays me to do.'

'I could have you fired, you know.'

'I doubt it,' Stella said, with no idea if she was right. She didn't particularly care one way or the other.

'He listens to me. You think he trusts you and he does, within reason, but he hardly knows you. We've been friends for years and years.'

'How nice,' Stella said. 'Good luck finding a replacement.' The most wonderful thing about being dumped by the love of her life and leaving her home and moving in with a complete stranger was that she found she no longer cared about anything very much. She felt invincible in lack of emotion. Bring. It. On.

'You know he went off the deep end last year? You must have read about it in the papers?'

'No,' Stella said.

'Oh, come on,' he said, wiping his shoe ineffectually on a patch of grass.

'I don't read gossip. Hadn't even heard of Jamie Munro before I got this job.'

'Of course not.' Nathan curled his lip. 'You'll be well above the rest of the poor schmucks with their gossip rags and reality TV.'

'Don't be offended, it's just not my area of interest.'

'Well . . .' Nathan looked around as if checking for listeners hiding among the trees. He lowered his voice. 'He had a breakdown. Couldn't leave the apartment. Agoraphobia. Panic attacks. Depression. You name it, he had it.'

Stella bit down on the urge to say 'nonsense', not believing for a second that Nathan was telling the truth. Jamie Munro had the strongest mind and discipline of anybody she had ever met.

'Now, I'm only telling you this so that you understand the situation fully. If he doesn't release a manuscript to me in the next week, he's going to miss his slot in the publishing schedule. Then Christ knows when it'll come out. The publicity I've got lined up, the television slots, the promotions, it'll all go to hell. And the book will flop and then I don't know—' He broke off, passing a hand across his eyes as if overcome with emotion.

Stella was impressed by his acting skills. The man would clearly go above and beyond for his fifteen per cent. She steeled herself not to get dragged in, though. Nathan was a master manipulator, she had no doubt. After a moment, he looked at her and Stella had to dig her fingernails into her palm in order to stay strong and not reach out a comforting arm. He looked genuinely upset. 'I don't know what he'd do.'

Despite her best intentions, Stella felt a trickle of sympathy. 'I'll talk to him. I'll see how things are going and get an update on the book. I won't push him, though. That's not my job.'

Nathan went quiet for a few minutes, and Stella thought the conversation was over. She increased her pace, taking the path through the woods which led in a winding circle around the promontory. There were still a few autumn leaves on the ground, but they were black with rain and rot, and the bare branches of the trees creaked in the wind. The air smelled of wood and salt.

She could hear Nathan following as the path narrowed, and when she stopped to get her breath and to let him pass her if he wished, he stopped, too, and began digging in his pocket. He produced a lighter and a packet of cigarettes. 'Do you mind?'

She shook her head. There was a bird calling plaintively from a nearby tree, and a gleam of sunlight lit the edges of the clouds. Stella took one of her deep breaths. Not because she felt unwell but because she could and because it felt so good.

'I just don't think this is the healthiest place for him to be,' Nathan said, blowing out a plume of smoke.

'I disagree,' Stella said. 'The fresh air is magical.'

'I don't mean the entire country,' Nathan said, irritated. 'Although—'

'What do you mean?' Stella stuck her hands in her pockets and looked at him directly.

'We're friends, now, right?' Nathan said, taking a deep pull on his cigarette. 'Whatever you might think, I haven't come here to be a pain in the ass. I think we can both agree that Jamie has lost the juice for *Living Well Forever*.'

'That's for him to—'

Nathan ignored her. 'And while I would prefer he worked on the contracted book, I am also his friend. I would rather he played hooky with you than he spend any more time buried in those musty old papers. Turning over the past isn't doing him any good. We should all look forward, not backward, but that is especially true for Jamie.'

'Why?'

Nathan glanced at Stella, as if trying to work out how much to say. 'How much do you know about Jamie's childhood?'

'I know he spent a lot of it away at school.'

'And thank God for that,' Nathan said. 'Some people shouldn't have children.'

Stella swallowed.

'What I don't understand is what he's doing here. If he's going to have a breakdown or a holiday' – Nathan put the word in air quotes – 'why do it here? It's classic self-sabotage. He needs to go back to his shrink.'

'Why do you say that?'

Nathan finished his cigarette, grinding it out with his shoe. 'We met at boarding school, you know. I spent my last two years at Merchiston's, and Jamie was always really quiet before every holiday. Most boys wore their metaphorical shields to school, but you could sense Jamie putting his on before he went home.'

'Were his parents that bad?'

Nathan shrugged. 'He never said.'

'And then they died.'

'Exactly.'

Stella couldn't settle to work for the rest of the afternoon. Nathan being in the house made her jumpy and she could understand why Jamie had wanted to isolate himself. It was easier to concentrate when you knew you were alone, that there were no surprises lurking behind doors.

She went outside to walk around the gardens, hoping that more of that amazing air would calm her mind and that she would be able to power through the day's emails afterwards. Esmé was on the lower lawn, throwing a ball for the dogs using a plastic contraption which flung it further.

She nodded as Stella approached.

'Is he staying long?'

'I wouldn't know,' Esmé said, and Stella liked the way she didn't pretend not to know who they were talking about. It made her feel accepted in some small way.

She sought to consolidate the connection. 'He wants me to put pressure on Jamie to finish the book.'

Esmé glanced at her. 'You must do what you think is best.'

'I think he should leave.'

'That's up to Jamie,' Esmé said.

'I don't know why he puts up with him. Isn't there something we can do?'

'Nathan is an old friend,' Esmé said, not looking at Stella.

'That's what Jamie said, but he's not a friend, it's business.'

'They were friends first,' Esmé said. 'And you can't interfere.'

Stella felt herself told off.

Esmé's expression was grim and she threw the ball for the dogs with more force than seemed necessary.

'Right, then,' Stella said. 'None of my business.'

'Just do your job,' Esmé said.

Stella tried to do exactly that. She pushed aside Nathan's warnings and settled down in an armchair to read another of Jessie Lockhart's letters. She kept a notepad and pen by her side, so that she could take notes, but found herself falling into the world of nineteenth-century Edinburgh, as if into a dream. It reminded her of the escape of reading when she was a child, and the long hours in hospital waiting rooms she had transformed through the pages of a book.

> 11th June, 1848
>
> My dearest Mary,
>
> I have very little time for letter writing today and will have to send this poor excuse. It is very poor indeed, especially after your fine description of faither's birthday dinner, but all I can do is promise to send a better

effort next time. The house is in a state of uproar as Mr Lockhart bade our housekeeper dismiss our remaining scullery maid. He said the parlour maid (who is a quite lovely girl and very hardworking) must make do and divide her labour, and the cook (who is not at all lovely) is in a fearsome temper.

Meanwhile, my Mr Lockhart remains utterly blind to the domestic chaos as he has discovered a new fancy. Worse still, his faithful patients sit in the parlour, their faces drawn with heavy lines of pain and fear and they wait and wait and wait – longer than ever.

Mr Lockhart's latest 'grand idea' is the publication of pamphlets. I don't know how popular they are in dear Haddington, but here in the city they are quite the thing. Seemingly, Mr Lockhart is always in the middle of writing one. He says that J. Y. Simpson is the same and, as ever, he seeks to emulate the man. He brought me a sheet from his travels yesterday. It is called 'Woman's Rights' and I cannot help but feel my husband is dissatisfied and seeks to instruct me. The poem begins 'The right to be a comforter, when other comforts fail' and ends with 'The right to comfort man on earth, and smooth his path to Heaven.'

I am trying to be a comfort, Mary. I truly am.

Your loving Jessie

The light had died and the small window was a black mirror, throwing back images from the room and hiding the outside world. The lamp she had clicked on an hour earlier to illuminate her chair was an oasis in the gloom. Stella stretched, feeling the bones in her neck protest, while her mind still belonged to Jessie Lockhart. Jessie's desire to be a good wife, to help her husband, leaped from the page and straight into Stella's heart. It was as if Jessie had written the words in an email just that morning, not countless decades ago.

They made Stella confront something in herself; she had always liked being helpful, but there was something about Jamie Munro that made that urge much stronger. She wanted to be a comfort, as Jessie put it. Which was worrying. Stella thought that she had escaped her old life, but perhaps she was just trying to recreate it here, with Jamie Munro in the role of Ben?

She shook herself from this unpleasant thought and went to Jamie's office to check for more correspondence from Jessie Lockhart. Jamie wasn't there, and Stella was grateful not to have to see him at that moment. She checked the neat lists taped to the top of each box, looking for mention of private correspondence, letters, or the name 'Lockhart'.

There were drifts of paper and books all over the office and Stella suddenly saw the room as Nathan might, the outward manifestation of a disordered mind. Jamie was like a one-man cyclone and Stella automatically began shepherding some of the mess.

'Don't touch anything in here,' Jamie said, walking in to find her in the process of moving one stack of books from his chair to the table.

His sharp tone made Stella waspish in return. Her earlier thoughts didn't help, and she felt the rush of blood to her cheeks. Either irritation or embarrassment or something else. 'You store your reading material on your chair? Where do you sit?'

'I try not to. Sitting is killing us all.'

Stella was saved from answering by the sound of the landline. Jamie never answered it so she was surprised when he reached across the desk and picked up the handset. She moved towards the door to her office, giving him privacy, but then she heard her name.

'Stella? Did she give you this number?'

She turned to see Jamie frowning at her with full force as he listened to whoever was on the telephone. She shook her head to indicate that she hadn't given Jamie's home number to anybody. Which she had not. Caitlin had requested it for emergencies but Stella had fobbed her off by saying that she would give it to her later.

'Hold on, I will see if she is free.' He covered the receiver with his hand. 'Ben Dawson.'

Stella shook her head, sudden panic shooting through her body. Not here. Not now.

'Hi, Ben,' Jamie spoke into the phone, not taking his eyes off Stella. 'She just stepped out. Can I take a message?'

When he had finished the call, Stella started to say 'thank you', but Jamie was already speaking. Low and quiet and absolutely furious. 'What part of "discreet" did you not understand? My privacy is the most important thing to me. If I can't trust you not to hand out my home phone number—'

'I didn't,' Stella said. 'I swear to you.'

Jamie paused, evidently seeing something in her face. 'Then how the hell—'

'I have not given your number or any other information about you to a single person.' Stella hesitated, then corrected herself. 'Barring the sanctioned information you have allowed for replying to certain correspondence and to your agent.' She felt the sudden urge to cry and widened her eyes, willing the tears to stay put. It was irritating how that response could mark you out as weak or unprofessional when it had absolutely nothing to do with the sharpness of your mind or your ability to do your job and was only a physical reaction.

'Who is he, then?' Jamie crossed his arms. 'Ben Dawson.'

'A friend,' Stella said.

'And you told him you were working for me?'

Stella shook her head. She hadn't given Ben Jamie's name, hadn't told him anything about her job. She was about to say so when a thought hit her. She had telephoned from Jamie's landline. 'He usually texts me. Maybe he rang Caitlin, he has her number.'

'You think she told him?'

'No.' Stella took a deep breath. 'I rang him and I was worried about the reception cutting out so I used the landline. I didn't withhold the number. I forgot to dial 141.'

'For fuck's sake, Stella,' Jamie said.

'Sorry,' Stella said.

Jamie didn't say anything else, was already distracted by something on his computer screen. Stella left the room, adrenaline coursing through her body. He really was unbelievably rude at times. Too much time on his own. Too much money. At least that answered one question: she definitely wasn't trying to replace Ben with Jamie Munro. The man was insufferable.

CHAPTER THIRTEEN

28th July, 1848

My dearest Mary,

I have the most astounding news. I am going to have a baby! I know this is probably not so shocking to you and is quite the natural order, but I had begun to worry that it would never happen. I was concerned that I was too infirm and sickly. My breath does not always come easily and although I have followed all of your good advice, it still often feels as if I have been laced too tightly and for too long. Mr Lockhart had grown quite impatient at my barren nature and I was concerned that he was disappointed and that he might even regret our union. But, Mary, I am wi' bairn! My own wee one. My happiness is almost complete. To make it so, I would just need you with me. Mr Lockhart says that you will be able to come and stay with us, if you wish, once the babe is safely born. He says that the excitement will be too much for me before. I hope you understand. Curse my delicate health!

Do write soon. Please give my love to all the family with an extra kiss for yourself.

Jessie

Stella folded the letter carefully and stared out of the window, not seeing anything. Another pregnancy. It was borderline insane to be envious of a woman who had lived and died years ago, a woman she didn't know. Along with the needle prick of envy, Stella felt happy for Jessie, and that was a relief. She didn't want to be a bitter person. She put a hand to her chest, felt her heart beating and wondered about Jessie's 'delicate health'. It had been a concern of her own and she had got as far as making an appointment with her consultant to discuss possible complications of her hoped-for pregnancy. An appointment that she then cancelled when Ben left, the questions still unanswered. The last thing she had been told was that 'normal activities' were unlikely to cause her any problems, but whether pregnancy and birth were counted in that category she hadn't thought to ask at the time, or possibly she hadn't broached it as she didn't care to hear a doctor say it might not be a good idea.

Later that evening, Stella could hear voices coming from the living room. Jamie was sitting on the sofa with a glass of wine and laughing in a way Stella had never heard. Free and big and almost uncontrolled. Nathan was in the middle of some riff, waving his arms around and playing to his audience. She paused in the doorway, uncertain whether to intrude.

Jamie saw her and straightened up. 'Have a drink with us!'

'Yeah, do,' Nathan said, sounding less sincere.

Jamie was already up and pouring a glass of wine. Stella took it, vowing to herself to sip slowly and leave as soon as humanly possible. Jamie put his hand on her arm, drawing her to the sofa. Stella stepped away and took one of the armchairs instead. Nathan watched her as she did, a smile that was most definitely more of a smirk on his lips.

'What's a girl like you doing in a place like this?'

'Working,' Stella said crisply. 'As you know.'

'I meant this place,' he waved at the window. 'The ass-end of nowhere. I mean, he's got to be here. Family ties. I can see that, but why you?'

He emphasised the last two words, making it sound like a larger question. More like *why do you exist, what is the point of you?* than an innocent query on location.

'I have friends in the village,' Stella said. 'Rob and Caitlin Baird.'

Jamie nodded. 'I know Rob Baird. His family used to be invited to the godawful Hogmanay Dad always put on.'

'Oh, Christ. Hogmanay.' Nathan pulled a face.

'What have you got against New Year's Eve?' Stella said. She didn't know what it was about Nathan that made her argumentative, but he made her want to stake her place, prove herself in some way.

'Hogmanay is a much bigger deal in Scotland than Christmas,' Jamie said. 'Turn of the year, light in the darkness, all that.'

'Auld Lang Syne.' Nathan raised his glass.

'Aye. Lang may yer lum reek,' Jamie said, smiling. Then he drank, too.

Stella was wondering if this new, relaxed-looking Jamie was entirely down to the alcohol, or whether he had turned some kind of corner, when the door opened and Esmé appeared with a tray.

'I didn't know you had company,' she said, lips pursed. 'There's fruit cake.'

'That's all right,' Jamie said. 'We're on the booze now.'

'Fruit cake would be lovely,' Stella said, standing up to help with the tray. Anything to soak up the alcohol. Her head seemed to swim very quickly in this house, like the air was intoxicating.

'You look radiant tonight, Mrs C,' Nathan said. 'Going somewhere special?'

Esmé was wearing a silky blouse with her customary trousers and jacket, and her hair looked neater than usual. 'What I do in my own time is none of your concern,' Esmé said, walking out with the empty tray.

Nathan waited a beat for the door to close and then turned to Jamie, his mouth opening. Whatever smart remark he had planned stayed unsaid as a crash in the hallway made them all jump.

Jamie was first into the hall and Stella's view of Esmé on the floor was partially obscured by his broad back. 'What is it?' Nathan said but Stella couldn't answer. Everything slowed as she got down on the floor. 'Esmé! Esmé, can you hear me?' Jamie was on the other side. Esmé was very still, but when Stella leaned down she felt breath on her cheek and saw a slight rise of her chest. Her silk blouse had fallen open at the neck and Stella rearranged it, feeling awkward for doing so but knowing that a woman as proud as Esmé would not want any hint of her underwear on display. 'Jesus wept,' Jamie muttered. He placed two fingers on his housekeeper's neck and looked at his enormous watch.

Nathan had his mobile out and was swearing at it. 'Landline,' Stella said, rising for the phone. Her head swam and the edges of her vision went dark. *Not now*, Stella prayed, and reached out a hand to steady herself. Nathan was down the corridor and at the telephone table before she had taken two steps. Stella took a few deep breaths and then sank carefully back down at Esmé's side. She held the hand that Jamie wasn't using to take her pulse, and kept up a stream of inane reassurance, hoping that Esmé could hear her.

'They're sending a chopper,' Nathan said, joining them.

'Good,' Jamie said. He hadn't looked away from Esmé, and now he leaned close and said, 'Hear that? You're getting the mountain rescue. They'll be here in a minute. Just hold on.'

Esmé's eyes fluttered and for a moment Stella thought she might look around and ask what all the fuss was about, but she didn't. Her eyes did open though, showing yellowed whites.

'It's okay,' Stella said. 'You're okay. You fainted.'

Esmé seemed to be trying to focus, and her mouth moved as if she were going to speak, but then just a terrifying, slurred mumble came out, along with some spittle.

'Help her sit up,' Jamie said.

'No,' Stella said. 'She fell, and she might have hurt her back or her neck. We can't move her.'

Esmé was still making sounds, but they were clearer now. 'Tabitha.'

'Get Tabitha,' Jamie said, and Nathan obediently left.

It didn't seem possible that someone as solid and steady as Esmé could be ill, but then she wasn't a young woman. 'Does she take medication?'

'What?' Jamie glanced up. 'I don't know. I don't think so.'

Esmé was struggling to move, trying to sit up.

Jamie glanced helplessly at Stella. 'Stay still,' he said. 'You need to stay lying down. Do you take any medicine? We need to know.'

'Tabitha,' Esmé said.

'I'll check her room. They might need to know.' Stella was glad to have something to do, to be in motion.

Esmé's room was neat and smelled like Esmé. A mixture of allspice and fresh air with the faintest floral undertone. There was a pot of rose-scented face cream on top of the chest of drawers and a pile of library books on the table by the bed. Stella didn't want to invade Esmé's privacy but she had no choice. The small drawer in the bedside table held a handkerchief, reading glasses and a small address book. There was a brown plastic tub with a white printed label, but it just held ibuprofen. Standard strength. She pocketed it anyway.

There was nothing on any of the surfaces, and a quick look in the chest of drawers revealed neatly folded clothes.

As Stella had assumed, Esmé appeared to be supremely healthy. Stella tried not to think of horrible things like brain tumours or heart attacks or strokes, all of which could fly out of the clear blue sky. She hadn't seemed to be having a heart attack but then the symptoms for women were different. Women were less likely to clutch their chest or complain of pain down one arm; they often had backache, shortness of breath or nausea instead.

Back in the hall, Jamie was still kneeling next to Esmé, talking quietly. He looked up as Stella approached. 'She's cold.'

'I'll get a blanket,' Stella said, turning on her heel.

'And a pillow for her head,' Jamie called.

Stella ran up the stairs and into her bedroom. She had seen folded blankets on the top shelf of the wardrobe and she grabbed them both. She forced herself to descend the stairs carefully, knowing that around seven hundred people died every year through falling on steps.

Back downstairs, Stella handed the blankets to Jamie. 'I don't know whether we should lift her head onto a pillow,' she said. She wished she knew more about the specific statistics for neck injuries.

Jamie had already taken off his lightweight jumper and folded it underneath Esmé's head. 'You're fine,' he was saying quietly. 'The paramedics are on their way.'

'I feel sick,' Esmé mumbled, turning her head to one side.

'Is that bad?' Jamie said, looking helplessly up at Stella.

'I'll get a basin,' Stella said.

As she crossed the front hall towards the kitchen she heard a *whump, whump* sound. She went into the dining room and looked at the back garden. On the lowest lawn, the large rectangle of tended grass before the wild stretch of marsh and scrub which acted as a buffer between the garden and the beach, was an orange helicopter with two uniformed figures already running towards the house. Stella went to the nearest door and opened it wide. 'This way.' Her voice was lost in the sound of the helicopter; the blades were still turning, slowing down.

The paramedics followed, carrying professional-looking bags and a folding stretcher. Stella led them to Esmé, who had her eyes closed again. The sharp smell of vomit overlaid the usual scent of floor polish and there was a pool of viscous brown fluid on the floor.

'They're here,' Jamie said to Esmé, moving back to give the paramedics access.

Within moments, their bulky bags were open and an air of brisk efficiency surrounded the scene. Esmé wasn't moving and her skin was waxy and pale, but the grown-ups had arrived. Jamie, Nathan and Stella stood back, relieved to be sidelined. 'Can you go with her?' Jamie said. 'There will only be room in the helicopter for one, maybe not even that.'

'No problem,' Stella said automatically. It wasn't until she was being strapped into the back of the aircraft that she realised how odd this was. This wasn't a job for the hired staff, this was Jamie's place. Esmé was the only family he had left and he was down on the ground, looking up as the helicopter lifted, his hand shading his eyes and his expression unreadable. Stella didn't know where to look on the short flight. Esmé was still and had a mask over her face. One of the paramedics was leaning over her, adjusting things, speaking to her and generally doing useful and life-saving things. Stella reached out and touched the hand nearest, squeezing Esmé's fingers and then just holding them loosely. Occasionally she thought she felt Esmé squeeze back but she wasn't sure if she was imagining it.

At the hospital, Stella was shut out of the room while they got to work. After what felt like a day, but was less than an hour, she was moved to a ward and Stella was allowed to see her. Esmé's eyes were open but Stella wasn't sure if she was actually awake. She didn't move her head for a few minutes, and then her eyes swivelled slowly and her mouth pulled up a little as if she was trying to smile or speak. 'You're in the hospital,' Stella said. 'But everything is okay. You're going to be fine. They're looking after you.' In the absence of actual information, Stella didn't know what else to say. Also, she had the feeling you were supposed to be encouraging in situations like this. Esmé nodded and closed her eyes. Just when Stella thought she was asleep she murmured, 'Tell Jamie.' Stella waited for the rest of the instruction, but after five minutes all was quiet. Just Esmé's uneven breath and the sounds of the hospital.

Out in the corridor, Stella used her mobile to phone the landline at Arisaig. She didn't realise she was angry until Jamie answered the phone and her words came out clipped and business-like. 'I thought you might like an update,' she began. 'They are working on the theory that she took too much of a heart medication.'

'Is she all right, though?'

'They seem to think she'll make a full recovery.'

'Thank Christ,' Jamie said, the emotion in his voice making Stella soften a little. But then the fury came back, stronger than before. 'You should be here,' she said.

There was a pause. 'I know,' Jamie said. 'I want to be. How long do you think before they'll let you bring her home?'

'I don't know,' Stella said. 'You should come in. You're the one listed as her next of kin. Nathan can look after the dogs.'

'He's gone to Glasgow,' Jamie said. 'There's a sister in Inverness. They're not close. I might have a number for her somewhere. Do you think I should let her know?'

'Do whatever you think,' Stella said, suddenly desperate to get away from the conversation. These were not her people; this was not her problem. She didn't understand why Jamie hadn't come to the hospital with Esmé, and was trying to ignore the sharp stab of disappointment at his behaviour.

'Anything she needs,' Jamie was saying. 'Use the company credit card. If she needs care at home, I can get a private nurse.'

'Anything as long as it doesn't stop you working, right?' The words were out without prior consultation with Stella's brain.

'It's not like that,' Jamie said, sounding anguished.

'Uh-huh,' Stella said. 'I'll keep you posted.' She hung up before she could say anything she regretted and stood for a moment, feeling her hands shaking.

Esmé was sitting up when Stella went back into the room. Her skin tone still matched the pillowcase, but she was properly awake. 'The doctor said I had a funny turn,' she said. 'I don't remember.'

'You fainted, I think,' Stella said. 'Passed out. You didn't wake up so we called the ambulance.' It sounded so simple put like that. No sense of the horror at seeing Esmé on the floor, the deep fear that she wouldn't wake up.

Esmé nodded. 'Were we having cake?'

'You had just brought some in.'

'To the boys,' Esmé said. 'I remember. That horrid little runt.'

Stella was no fan of Nathan, but Esmé's tone of disgust surprised her. Esmé was usually so circumspect. Of course, she might not be entirely in her right mind. 'How are you feeling?'

'Like I fell over and something drove over me.' Her eyes widened. 'How are the dogs?'

'They're fine.' Stella smiled. 'They miss you, of course, but Jamie is looking after them.'

'He gets distracted,' Esmé said. 'He might forget—'

'I'm on the case, too,' Stella said. 'Don't worry. Is there anything I can get for you?'

'Is Jamie here?' Esmé looked past Stella, as if he might be hiding behind her.

'Not yet,' Stella said, feeling supremely awkward.

Esmé's mouth set into a straight line but she looked resigned rather than upset. 'He won't come out here.'

'Would you like to speak to him on the telephone?'

'I think I'll take a nap,' Esmé said, closing her eyes. 'Can you see yourself out?'

Stella hovered for a moment, watching Esmé's face for signs of pain. She had been dismissed, though, so she left, closing the door behind her and heading to the front desk. 'Is there someone who can talk to me about Esmé?'

'Are you family?'

'I'm her family's employee,' Stella said. 'I'm supposed to relay the information.'

'Family only,' the nurse said.

Stella went downstairs and got a terrible cup of coffee in the small café.

Back up in the ward, Esmé had been joined by an old dear who was snoring loudly in the bed closest to the window. The other two beds were still blessedly unoccupied. The curtains were pulled around Esmé's bed and there was a doctor looking at her chart when Stella returned.

'Ah, your mother's awake now,' he said unnecessarily.

'She's not—' Stella began but Esmé cut across her.

'What happened, then? And is it going to happen again?'

'I shouldn't think so,' the doctor said. He glanced at Stella before saying: 'Is there a chance you took too many of your tablets?'

'What sort of tablets?' Stella asked. 'Ibuprofen?'

'I don't take medicine. There's nothing wrong with me.' Esmé waved a hand around to indicate the bed, the room. 'Usually.'

'You like to stay healthy? Do you take multivitamins?'

'You think she took an overdose of something?' Stella said, turning to the doctor. She tried to keep her voice low, but without whispering it was impossible to stop Esmé's bat ears from hearing.

'Accidental,' the doctor said quickly, glancing at Esmé. 'Most likely vitamin A. It's more common than you think. Especially in people who are—'

Esmé glared at him and he broke off whatever he was going to say.

'Finish that sentence,' Esmé said sweetly, ice in her eyes. 'Don't mind me. But I didn't down a bottle of tablets.'

The doctor straightened up. 'I apologise, Mrs Collins.'

'So, is she all right?' Stella said. 'And shouldn't we be sure about this vitamin thing? Have you ruled out everything else?'

'We've done a thorough check and there's no sign of stroke or heart attack,' the doctor said. 'And the symptoms are consistent with hypervitaminosis. The blood test will confirm, but that won't be back until tomorrow morning at the earliest.'

'But if she didn't take them, then how—'

'I don't know,' the doctor said. 'But right now, your mother needs to rest. This isn't likely helping her at the moment.' He cut his eyes bedwards and Stella took the hint.

'I'll let you sleep,' Stella said. She didn't know if she ought to hug Esmé or kiss her on the cheek, but both seemed impossible. She sat on the bed for a moment and patted her arm. 'I'm going to pop home and then I'll come back. Is there anything you need?'

'Stay there. Sleep in your own bed,' Esmé said. 'Come back in the morning if you like, but you don't need to come sooner.'

'Are you sure?'

'Completely,' Esmé said. 'We both need to rest.' Her eyes suddenly widened. 'The dogs.'

'Don't worry, I'll look after them.'

'Jamie can do that,' Esmé said, and Stella tried not to feel hurt. 'But thank you. They like you. Especially Tabitha.'

'I'm sorry about Jamie,' Stella said, suddenly angry. 'He should be here.'

'Don't be too hard on him.' Esmé sounded tired. 'He's got his own cross to bear.'

'It's not right,' Stella began, but Esmé silenced her with a hard look.

'Don't talk about things you don't know about. Jamie's like a son to me.' Esmé closed her eyes, the conversation clearly over.

⁓

Stella followed the doctor out and tugged his sleeve before he could scoot off to another patient. 'Is there anything else?'

'Sorry?'

Stella inclined her head to indicate the ward in which Esmé was hopefully falling asleep. 'What's her prognosis? Will there be long-term effects?'

'Liver damage is the main concern and we'll know more when the blood work comes back.'

Stella nodded. 'Okay. Thank you.'

'Your mother is a fighter, try not to worry.'

Stella forced a smile around the sudden urge to belt the doctor. 'Thank you,' she said. 'I'll be back in the morning. Call me if there's any change.'

'Of course,' he said, already hurrying away.

Stella stood in the foyer of the hospital and called a taxi. The driver chatted all the way back along the dark and twisting road, and Stella found herself longing for London and a driver who played obnoxious radio too loudly but who didn't require any kind of response. Here, Stella knew that the man driving the taxi would probably turn out to be Caitlin's next-door neighbour or a cousin of Esmé's. By the time she got back to the house, her eyelids were closing. She didn't want to see Jamie but knew she had to give him an update. He was in his office, of course, tapping at his keyboard. He stood up when she walked in and his face made some of her anger flee. His healthy colour had been replaced by milk-white. 'How is she?'

'Awake,' Stella said. She leaned against the wall for support. Exhausted but not wanting to sit down. She needed to get this over with and go to bed. Close her eyes and sleep for a hundred years. 'She's fine in herself. Didn't seem to be in any pain. They think she might have accidentally taken too many vitamins or something. Blood test will be back tomorrow.'

'Tomorrow? Bloody hell.' He shook his head. 'Did you tell them I'd pay for private treatment?'

'I think that's just how long they take. At the lab.'

Stella felt as if she were swaying. She could feel the solid wall at her back, but still felt as though she were tipping forward. Her chest wasn't tight so she knew it was just tiredness and the after-effects of the adrenaline. She began to say that she was going to bed, but her vision went dark and she wasn't sure if the words came out.

'Stella?'

She opened her eyes. The ceiling was directly above and, much closer, Jamie's face. She could see stubble poking through his skin and purple shadows under his eyes. His lips were moving but she could only hear a ringing sound. She wanted to ask if it was a fire alarm, had the vague feeling they ought to be running somewhere.

'Bloody hell.' The words came through as the alarm receded and became a quiet ringing in her ears. Tinnitus. 'You've got to stop doing that,' Jamie said.

'Tired,' Stella said. 'Just tired.'

'Right-o.' He stood up and Stella felt cold. Jamie stretched above her like a giant redwood. That was an image she would keep to herself. It would give him ideas, otherwise.

He crouched down a moment later and put one arm around her shoulders. His other hand moved under her body and Stella jerked fully awake. 'You don't have to lift—'

And she was up. She wrapped her arms around his neck instinctively. He carried her across the room and down the hall.

'You don't have to—' she began again.

'Humour me,' Jamie said. He wasn't looking at her, was concentrating on navigating a doorway without bashing her legs or elbow, but she saw a smile tug at the corner of his mouth.

'You can't carry me all the way upstairs.' The truth was that the exhaustion had swept over her like the returning tide, and her voice didn't sound right to her own ears. It was as if she were speaking underwater.

She let her eyes close, but felt the motion shift as Jamie took the stairs and heard his breathing deepen with the exertion.

'You're not sleeping alone,' Jamie said. 'I need to keep an eye on you.'

Stella realised that they were in his bedroom a moment before he put her onto the king-size bed.

'Don't worry, clean sheets.' Jamie turned and began gathering clothes and toiletries from around the room. 'I'll sleep next door so that I can check on you.'

'You don't need to,' Stella said. 'I'm completely fine. Just knackered.'

'You fainted.'

'I most certainly did not.'

'You say potato—'

'You should visit Esmé. She says you're like a son to her.'

His expression softened. 'She must have been doped-up to get that soppy.'

'It's not funny. People will say you're heartless.' Stella wanted to say that she thought he was pretty heartless, but the man had just carried her to her bed like a knight in shining armour and was looking at her with an expression of such sweet concern it stopped her breath.

'I don't care what people say,' he said, sounding sad rather than defiant.

'But you care about Esmé.'

'Of course I do.'

'Then why? I don't understand,' Stella couldn't stop a gigantic yawn from escaping, even though it undercut her argument somewhat.

'You. Sleep.'

When Stella opened her eyes, the light looked wrong. It was too light to be before nine and before she looked at the clock she knew she had slept late. 'Bugger.' It was almost half past eleven. Stella launched out of bed and showered as quickly as she could before going to find Jamie.

He was in his office, hair wet from his ice bath, a tall glass of green sludge next to his keyboard. He finished a couple of clicks before looking up. 'Do you feel better?'

'Much,' Stella said. 'Poor Esmé, though. Alone this morning, I should have—'

'Jenny's there. Well' – he glanced at the time – 'she'll be away, now. Morning visiting finishes at eleven fifteen. Afternoon starts at two.'

'Jenny?'

'Friend of Esmé's. One of many. They'll have a rota fixed up by now. Someone's already been by to fetch some more of her stuff and to drop off a casserole.'

'For us? Why?'

'Because Esmé would want us looked after.'

'I hope you told them I am more than capable—'

'Let them help,' he said, looking back at his screen. 'People want to keep busy.'

Stella took a second, adjusting her view of him as heartless. It was possible he was sticking to his routine, working as normal, because he had to in order to keep it together.

But still. Esmé was the only family he had left. All the reading and research he was happy to do on his flesh and blood, but now that Esmé was in need he was sitting in his office with the door shut. Stella went back up to Jamie's bedroom and began packing him an overnight bag. She channelled her anger into action, hauling out clothes from drawers and toiletries from the cabinet in the en-suite.

Jamie stood in the doorway, looking confused. 'What are you doing?'

'You need to go to the hospital.'

'I told you . . .' Jamie looked at the floor. 'I can't leave the estate.'

'Nonsense,' Stella said.

'I have anxiety,' he said after a moment of silence. The words seemed dragged from inside, unwillingly. 'Panic attacks. Imagine that. Superman has panic attacks. If the press find out they'll have a fucking party.' Jamie looked away from her, at the window.

'Nobody needs to find out,' Stella said. She wanted to say something about how they might feel terrible to him but, from the outside, people probably couldn't tell.

He shook his head. 'They were happening all the time in San Francisco. Nathan knew about them and it was only a matter of time. Felt like it, anyway. And when I got back here I had one in the village shop. Was just buying some milk and I freaked out completely. I don't have them at home, though. I haven't had a single one on the estate.'

Stella didn't know if it was years of dealing with her own wayward heart, but she still didn't see why this would stop Jamie from visiting Esmé. She faced him, looking straight into his eyes. 'So you might have a panic attack. So what?'

'You don't understand. They make you feel like you're dying.'

'I understand perfectly. You are frightened that you might have a panic attack if you leave the estate, and I'm telling you that it doesn't matter. You might have one and you might not. If you have one it will be horrible and frightening, but it will not kill you. And once it's over you can still visit Esmé.'

He looked at her. 'It's not that simple.'

'It really is,' Stella said. 'Anything else is your anxiety lying to you.'

'They make me feel weak. Like I'm dying.'

'They lie,' Stella said.

'I'm not making it up, it's a real condition.'

'I know that,' Stella said. 'And it's bloody awful. You have my full sympathy, but what you have is an illness. It's not your fault and it's not weakness and it's nothing to be ashamed of, but at the same time you are letting it stop you from doing something you have to do. If you had a broken leg, you'd take some extra painkillers and get someone to drive you and, if necessary, push you in a wheelchair, but you'd still visit Esmé. Just because you have an illness doesn't mean it has to change who you are, and I don't think you're the kind of man who would leave his own kin lying alone in a hospital bed.' Stella knew she had her hands on her hips and that her tone was far too strident for a paid employee but she did not care. He could fire her later. After he'd visited Esmé. 'Or am I wrong about you?'

Jamie stared at her for moment. Then he said, 'No.'

'Right, then. Shoes and coat, let's go.'

'You'll make a wonderful mother one day,' he said, smiling a little.

The words were like being stabbed and Stella turned to hide her face. 'Do you have medication you want to take before we go?' Staying with the practicalities. 'I don't know if you have diazepam or anything?'

'I have some, but I don't take it.'

'Put one in your pocket just in case. You won't need it, but it will make you feel better to know it's there. It's like insurance.'

'How do you know so much about this stuff?' Jamie tilted his head. 'Have you—'

'No.' Stella shook her head. 'Not anxiety.'

Jamie looked as if he was going to ask something else, so Stella headed to the boot room to locate their coats and to the kitchen to fill a couple of bottles of water.

The roads were icy so Stella was very happy to borrow Jamie's four-by-four. It was far shinier and more expensive than any vehicle she'd driven previously, and the inside had a theme of leather and chrome. Stella hauled herself into the comfortable seat and spent a happy few minutes adjusting the position and enjoying the seat-warming facility.

'I don't know about this,' Jamie said. 'I've got way too much to do today.'

'If you say you are "too busy", it's a sign that your life is not well organised and that you have lost sight of your main priorities.' Stella knew he was having a bad day and that she shouldn't enjoy quoting his book at him, but she couldn't help herself.

'I suppose you think that's hilarious,' Jamie said after a moment.

'Little bit,' Stella agreed, as she concentrated on navigating the steep slope. It was as icy as she expected, but the car's four-wheel drive and excellent tyres made light work of the treacherous surface. The turning onto the main road was uneventful and Stella let herself relax a little as they headed towards Fort William. Jamie's hands were bunched into fists, his knuckles bright white.

'How long have you lived here?' Stella asked, trying to distract him.

'Since I was born. I went away to school when I was nine, though.'

'You were home for holidays though, I assume?'

'Quite a few of them, yeah.'

'I can't imagine going away at such a young age. Did you mind?'

'Hated it.' Jamie was staring out of the windscreen with a fixed expression of horror, but Stella didn't know if that was down to her questions or an incoming panic attack.

'Do you want me to stop for a bit?'

He rolled his shoulders. 'No. It's okay. I'm all right. Just getting used to it.' He glanced at Stella. 'And don't take this the wrong way, but I don't like being driven, either.'

'By a woman?' Stella said, ready to despise him.

'By anyone. Control thing.'

'Fair enough,' Stella said. She was exactly the same. Trust issues, Ben had said. 'Did school get better?'

'I got used to it.'

He didn't say anything for a few minutes and Stella thought the subject was closed.

She was just taking a sharp bend in the road when Jamie said, 'It was better than being here, anyway. It was away from my dad.'

'I'm sorry,' Stella said. 'What was he like?'

'Obsessive. Often angry.' Jamie's voice was even. 'I used to think it was me, that I brought out the worst in him, but now I think he was frustrated. He drank too much and wasted a lot of his time on different pursuits. He did biochemistry at university and then went into business. He made plenty of money, but I think he wanted to do something remarkable.'

'That sounds familiar.'

'I'm nothing like him,' Jamie said quickly. 'Nothing.'

The sky was a blanket of white, streaked with pale yellow and silvery lilac. It was so pretty and still that it looked like a painted backdrop. The bare trees stood out starkly against the sky and the snow-covered hills, defining the landscape. 'It's so beautiful,' Stella began to say, but the back wheels of the car were sliding as she took yet another tight bend in the road. She resisted the urge to correct the slide or hit the brake, turning the wheel with the car's direction instead.

A silver car was approaching on the other side but Stella got the BMW under control and back on the right side of the road before it reached them. Everything seemed to have happened in a leisurely few minutes, but as normal time came back Stella realised it had been very quick. 'Are you all right?' She glanced at Jamie who was white-faced, his lips pale and thin.

'Yeah. Fuck.' He blew out a rush of air. 'Well done.'

'Thanks.'

'I would have messed that up,' Jamie said. 'I would have skidded, probably crashed. Out of practice driving in these conditions.'

'I took a course,' Stella said, both embarrassed and pleased by his admiration. 'Advanced driving. Taught by a terrifying ex-special forces guy.' She could feel him watching her and, after a minute, said, 'What?'

'Why did you do the course? Not that I'm not grateful for your hidden talents.'

Stella weighed up how honest to be, then she thought, *Sod it*. Although she no longer wanted her stay at Munro House to be temporary, Jamie had made no mention of making her position permanent. In the big scheme of things, it probably didn't matter. 'I don't like taking risks,' Stella said. 'Driving with just the standard training seemed like an unacceptable risk. People with the advanced driving certificate are twenty-five per cent less likely to be in a road traffic incident.'

'How did I get so lucky?'

'Pardon?' Stella took another tricky bend, accelerating out of it and up the slope.

'To find you. I love your logic.'

Stella knew that he meant that he had been lucky to find her as an assistant, an employee, but a warm glow still settled in her stomach. 'I think you'll remember, I found you.'

He grinned. 'And you never let me get away with anything. I love it.'

Stella wondered just how many 'yes men' Jamie was used to. It made sense of Nathan. He might be a pain in the arse, but he was honest with Jamie, in his own way.

'I used to love driving these roads,' Jamie said, looking out of the window. 'There's nowhere quite like it.'

'Not around London there isn't, that's for damn sure.'

'Is that why you moved up here? For the scenery?'

'Not exactly,' Stella said. 'I needed to get away and Caitlin kept inviting me. Once I got here I felt like I was meant to come, though. I don't believe in fate and I'm not superstitious, but it was a really strong feeling. That's why I decided to try to hang around.'

'Gut feelings are always worth paying attention to,' Jamie said. 'There have been studies which have shown our first decisions are often our best.'

'I thought we carried a load of biases which made our gut reactions or guesses suspect.'

'Yeah, we have a ton of biases which can make some of our thought processes and assumptions flawed, but the studies on our first reactions, the things we think in the very first moments that we don't even realise we're thinking . . . those tend to be pretty reliable. They're separate to the rational mind. But there was solid work done on split-second decisions being the best and the amount of information we take in about our surroundings that we're not even aware of.'

'Like spotting the tiger hiding in the bushes and feeling alert and afraid before we even know why.' Stella said.

'Exactly. It's survival stuff. On the most basic level, if your instincts are shit you wouldn't be here. Biologically speaking you would've been weeded out of the gene pool long ago.'

'The world has changed so much so quickly, though. It makes you wonder what survival traits we haven't honed yet.'

'Is your risk aversion because of your heart condition?'

Stella kept her eyes firmly on the road. She didn't intend not to answer but she couldn't form the words and then the pause had gone on too long, become a silence.

'You don't want to talk about it,' Jamie said, after a while.

'Not while I'm driving,' Stella said. She could feel her heart fluttering in her chest, her pulse quickening. She punched the button on the steering wheel to turn on the radio.

CHAPTER FOURTEEN

23rd September, 1848

My dearest Mary,

I have the most marvellous news; I have been accepted at last! I even heard from Mrs Goode that Lady Anstruther had taken to calling me 'the rose of Haddington'. The ladies all have special names for one another so I take that as high praise indeed, although I fear it might have the edge of unkindness as my cheeks are whiter than ever and even a sharp pinch brings 'roses' for a moment and no more.

However, what do I care? Now that my ankles have swollen to twice their usual size and I have a most disturbing waddle, the other ladies speak to me more freely and that is a blessing. There is a code, of course, so that only ladies who have become mothers already speak of certain matters, but I feel as if I have been allowed to loiter in the doorway of the club, at least.

Lady Anstruther was speaking highly of Mr James Young Simpson. Apparently ladies from all over Europe are flocking to Edinburgh for his care. Mr Lockhart had indeed spoke to me of this phenomenon, saying that we were fortunate to live in such times. It will be good for all physicians, it is true, as the reputation of our fine city spreads throughout the English-speaking world. I am quoting my husband, here. He has a very fine turn of phrase. It makes you feel quite invigorated, as if almost anything is possible if only one could reach out and take it.

Lady Anstruther became quite animated as she described a special instrument which Mr Simpson had developed. It is for use when a lady is having difficulty and apparently it seizes the baby about the ears and means it can be pulled – quite safely and undamaged. I feel faint at the thought, but Mr Lockhart was very pleased when I related the conversation. So many husbands want nothing at all to do with female concerns, I am very lucky.

I received dear Annie's note and while I shall respond in kind, I must relay my physical affection through your arms. Hold her too tightly until she wishes to wriggle free so that she can know how deeply she lives in my heart. On the matter which you alluded to regarding Annie's music lessons, I quite agree with you and think you should proceed.

I have only a few minutes before I must dress for dinner but I wished to thank you for advising me as to the efficacy of ginger tea. It was most welcome and I have found it to be a great relief to the cursed sickness. Kiss faither for me.

Your loving Jessie

Jamie had been in the dining room with the police officer for half an hour. Stella had been in once to offer coffee, and when both men said 'no thanks' she had hung around in the kitchen, trying to stay occupied and not to think too much about what was going on in the room next door. Stella still couldn't believe that Nathan had simply left when it had happened, but there was part of her that was relieved. She could imagine him ruffling feathers with the local police, making everything worse.

She heard the door open and voices in the hall. A couple of minutes later, Jamie walked into the kitchen and headed straight for the fridge. He stood in front of it for a minute before closing the door and sitting at the table.

'Can I get you something?' Stella said, hating how pale and tired he looked.

'They found way too much vitamin A in her blood. It caused the dizziness and fainting. It can cause pressure on the brain and liver damage.' He looked sick.

'Oh Christ.' Stella thought of the plastic tubs of pills, the bottles of liquid supplements, the powders, all lined up on the kitchen counter, and the boxes of the stuff stacked in the weights room.

'But she wouldn't have taken any,' Jamie said. His eyes were hollow with fatigue and he rubbed a hand over his face. 'No chance.'

Stella couldn't think of a nice way of phrasing the next thought that popped into her mind, so she just asked it quickly. 'Had you mixed some into a smoothie? Or your coffee? Something she might have had without realising—'

'Definitely not. And she wouldn't drink one of my concoctions, anyway. Calls them "marsh water". Besides, it was acute toxicity, which means she must have had a huge dose in a short space of time. It doesn't make any sense.'

'I know,' Stella said. 'But what could cause that? Maybe the vitamins interacted with something else she had taken.'

Jamie shook his head. 'I don't know what. She hardly ever even took paracetamol. As far as I know, anyway. And it's not like I have anything stronger just lying about. I'm not an idiot.'

Stella resisted the urge to put her hand in her pocket, feel the emergency tablet she kept in a special case. She had already checked her supply. As far as she could tell there were no pills missing, although she didn't keep an exact count so she wouldn't be able to swear on it in court. *Court. Fuck.*

'Could anybody want to hurt her?' Stella held up her hands. 'I know that sounds crazy, but I can't help thinking—'

'The police asked that and the answer is no. Esmé is as popular around here as I am unpopular. At least she always was. I haven't been out much, so—'

'I haven't heard a bad word said about her,' Stella said. 'And people seem to be lining up to give me their opinions.'

'Well, that's good. And they say bad stuff is usually family, right? And she doesn't have any left around here.'

'Except for you,' Stella said.

Jamie smiled. 'That's true.' Then his smile disappeared. 'No wonder the police want to speak to me again.'

Stella didn't know what to say, but Jamie summoned up another grim smile. 'It's all right. I haven't done anything wrong so I've got nothing to worry about.'

Without discussing it, Jamie and Stella fell back into their research routine. Stella had catalogued the contents of the boxes and was immersed in reading Jessie's letters. Sometimes it was difficult to decipher the handwriting and the pen scratches seemed to dance in front of her eyes; other times entire passages would reveal themselves as easily as a waking dream. It was comforting to sit in the big armchair near the window with Tabitha's head on her lap and a letter in her hand and, although she felt vaguely guilty for thinking it when Esmé was still unwell, she wasn't sure if she had ever felt more at home in a place and time.

Her childhood had been overshadowed by hospitals and worry. Her parents had done their best and she had plenty of good memories, too, but when she thought of growing up she thought of fear and tests and the sense that she had no control over what happened to her or her own body.

University had been thrilling and terrifying at the same time. The freedom going hand in hand with the sense that she might crash to earth at any moment. After graduating she had tried so hard to make a safe and stable life. But she had always felt anxious and out-of-step, always rushing to the next thing, always trying to plan out the best way of using the little time she had available. As if her life were a test that she had to pass.

Listening to the clock ticking on the mantelpiece and watching the sky change from the arched window, Stella felt her heart slow and steady in her chest. When she checked her emails on her phone and saw one from Ben, she hit 'delete' without even opening it.

Once it passed five, Stella went to visit Caitlin and Rob. She knew that the news about Esmé would have already travelled around the village and that they might be worried. The anger that she had felt over Caitlin shopping her to Jamie had been overlaid by recent events and, although she tried to summon a bit of outrage as she walked to the cottage, it felt faded and unreal.

Caitlin opened the door and immediately pulled Stella in for a quick hug.

'I guess you heard,' Stella said, the last of her anger disappearing in the face of Caitlin's obvious distress.

Caitlin pulled back to look into her eyes. 'Are you all right?'

'Fine,' Stella said, touched by her concern.

They went through to the kitchen and sat down.

'I wasn't sure if you were speaking to me,' Caitlin said, looking at the table.

'I wasn't thrilled about the note you sent,' Stella said. 'But I understand that you were worried about me. You don't have to be, though. I'm sorry you saw what you saw, but it's nothing new. And I really am fine.'

'Did you go to the doctor?' Caitlin raised one eyebrow, hamming up her quizzical expression to soften the question.

'Jamie brought one to the house.' Stella couldn't stop smiling at the memory. It was undeniably fancy.

Caitlin didn't seem as impressed as Stella expected. In fact she was distracted, jumpy. 'Are you leaving?'

Stella lost her smile. 'Jamie? No.'

'But you're not going to stay there? You can come back to us, you know. Any time.' Caitlin was shredding a tissue as she spoke, white flakes floating over the table.

'Why wouldn't I stay?'

'Esmé's in hospital. Something in that house made her ill.'

'She's on the mend,' Stella said, feeling defensive. 'She'll be home soon.'

'I heard she's going to stay with a friend in Edinburgh.'

News really did travel in Arisaig. 'Oh,' Stella said. 'Well, that's good. She deserves a rest.' She didn't want to admit it, but the thought gave her a thrill. Alone with Jamie. And he'd need her help even more. It made her job more secure. Not that she'd wish ill on Esmé, of course. Not for a moment.

'But what if she was poisoned?' Caitlin put a hand on Stella's arm. 'It's not safe there.'

'Oh, come on. It was just an accident. Who would want to poison Esmé?'

Caitlin looked down. 'Maybe it was an accident. Maybe they were after Jamie.'

Stella was alarmed by the sincerity in Caitlin's voice. There was the sound of a key scraping and then the front door opening.

'Stella's here!' Caitlin yelled, sounding urgent. 'We're in the kitchen.'

Stella was momentarily surprised, then realised that Caitlin had been warning him that she had company. Maybe he had a habit of disrobing in the hallway or something.

'I'm sorry,' Caitlin said urgently, quietly. 'Please come back here to stay. Or go home. You still have your house.'

'I feel more at home here than I have in years,' Stella said, trying to reassure Caitlin.

She shook her head. 'It's not safe—' Caitlin broke off as Rob entered the kitchen.

'Hello, girls,' Rob said, kissing Caitlin on the top of the head and smiling at Stella. 'Who fancies the pub?'

After a good meal in the bar of the hotel and a pint of beer, Stella decided to head home. It was pitch-black and cold and was only going to get worse. 'Stay for one more,' Caitlin said, leaning back in her chair and rubbing her stomach. 'We've hardly seen you.'

'Aye,' Rob said. 'Or are you too good for us now you're settled in the big hoose?'

He was smiling as he spoke, but Stella felt a stab of guilt. Had she been neglecting them? Rob had been keen for her to give them space, but she had been busy. She forced herself to smile back. 'I was always too good for you, Rob, you know that.' It was meant to be a joke, the kind of thing they had used to say to each other all the time, but somehow it fell flat. Rob's expression went dark and Caitlin raised her eyebrows at Stella as if to say, *What are you talking about?*

'Have you spoken to the polis?' Rob said abruptly. 'About Esmé.'

'I answered their questions,' Stella said.

'Did they ask about the MacDonald girl? Ellie?'

Stella's head jerked up. 'He had nothing to do with that.'

'That's not what I heard,' Rob said. His eyes were narrowed. 'Another "accident" up at the big hoose and they still haven't arrested him. And you wonder why we don't trust the polis. One set of rules for the Munros and another for the rest of us.'

'Ellie MacDonald slipped on the rocks. And Esmé must have taken too many multivitamins or eaten too much liver pâté or something. Bad luck.' Stella could hear panic in her voice and she took a breath.

'It was Munro, I bet. Doing some stupid experiment on his own staff. Nae morals.'

Stella wanted to laugh at the thought of Esmé taking part in one of Jamie's 'hair-brained' trials, but then she remembered that she was really sick and the urge disappeared.

'Nobody can talk Esmé into doing anything she doesn't want,' Stella said. 'She's not exactly a pushover.'

'Blind when it comes to him, though,' Rob said. 'You'll see.'

On the walk home, her torch beam illuminating the road ahead, Stella turned her thoughts to Caitlin's agitation. She hadn't brought up her fears in the pub in front of Rob, but that was probably because she didn't want to add to his paranoia about Jamie. The police had spoken to everybody and then things had gone quiet. If they thought Esmé had been deliberately poisoned, something else would be happening. Esmé must have developed a taste for Jamie's health drinks, not realising that she could not have more than one a day. Or perhaps she had taken a load of the supplements to try to get rid of a cold or something. People didn't always act rationally. Especially if Esmé had been ill; even something like a bladder infection could affect your judgement. Stella remembered how loopy she had felt when she had a bad bout of cystitis.

Stella let herself into the main house and took off her boots and coat. Sitting on the bench to unlace them, she was eye level with the shoe rack opposite. There were wellingtons in different sizes and Esmé's walking boots, and on the bottom rack a few pairs of much smaller shoes. Presumably they had belonged to Jamie as a child. A thought that she had been pushing away, trying not to be judgemental, veered up. What kind of people sent their only son away to school? If she ever got to be a mother, she would never do such a thing. Although, perhaps Jamie's mother was protecting him. If even half of the rumours about the curse of the Munro family and his father's personality were true, then Jamie had been better off at boarding school.

The next morning, the house felt very empty without Esmé, and the dogs were subdued. Jamie seemed determined to show Stella his bad side, as if wilfully confirming the terrible things people had been saying in the pub the night before. *Well*, Stella thought, *not 'people' so much as 'Rob'*.

Jamie barely spoke to her in the kitchen, sticking to the absolute essentials as they moved around each other. She left him mixing his protein shake and wondered if he was hung over.

Now, he appeared from his office. 'Can you scan these?' He was holding out a sheaf of papers.

'No problem,' Stella said, expecting him to place them on her desk. Instead, he stood behind her, waiting.

'Just a minute.' Stella was emailing her mum. It was the usual message, cut-and-paste that all was well, and she just had to type her name.

'I'm fine. No problems.' He was reading over her shoulder. 'What's that supposed to mean?'

'What?' Stella pressed 'send' and turned to give him her attention. 'You shouldn't read people's private correspondence. It's rude.'

'If it's about me then I think I will.' Jamie's bad mood had boiled over and his expression was dark. 'What do you mean "no problems"? What problems were you expecting? And you signed an NDA, you're not supposed to be talking about—'

'I'm not,' Stella said, her amusement at his prickly response transforming into anger. 'And if you have so little faith in my professionalism, I don't know why you hired me.'

Jamie took a visible breath. The deep crease between his eyebrows smoothed. 'That wasn't about me, was it?'

'Not everything is, you'd be amazed to discover,' Stella said. Although she realised with a stab of fear that there was something about Jamie that made her distinctly unprofessional. He got under her skin, made her speak in a way she would never – had never – spoken to an employer before. Luckily, he didn't seem to mind, and the last of his frown disappeared and was replaced with a small smile.

Stella turned back to her screen, but Jamie didn't leave. 'Why wouldn't you be fine? Is this your heart thing?'

'When I went away to university I promised I would keep in touch every day, let them know I was all right. So they wouldn't worry.'

'You've contacted them every day since you were eighteen?'

'It doesn't take long and it makes them feel better.'

'But you're okay?'

'I'm fine,' Stella said. 'Especially now. I got worse again at uni, had to drop out in my second year, but since the valve op I'm better than fine. I'm brand new.'

'So why the daily digest?'

Stella turned back to him, weighing up her answer. It was habit, mainly, she supposed. And it would feel like tempting fate. If she said *hey, I'm well now, I'll just phone on Sundays like a normal person*, fate might swoop down and crush her for her hubris. Well, she wasn't going to tell Jamie that. That wasn't rational. 'It isn't difficult and I don't want to make them worry.'

'But maybe it does. Make them worry, and you. It keeps your condition front and centre in their minds, stops them from moving on.'

Stella's mouth went dry. She hadn't considered that, was so used to it being front and centre, whether she wanted it to be or not.

'Sorry,' Jamie said. 'None of my business.'

'That's okay,' Stella said. 'You make a valid point.' What she didn't add was that she had spent her whole life waiting for the other shoe to drop and she didn't know any other way to live.

'I just found this.' He leaned down and opened the web browser, typing rapidly. A basic-looking blog appeared on the screen with the title MUNRO FRAUD. Stella glanced at Jamie. 'You shouldn't google your own name, you know.'

'I know,' he said. 'Look.'

There were only a couple of posts on the blog, both dated within the last week. The first had a picture of the house at night, the windows lit up and, in one, Stella just visible. 'Bloody hell,' Stella said. 'Our mystery photographer.'

'Contact my lawyer, please,' Jamie said. 'See what he has to say.'

After Jamie had left, Stella read the entries. They were light on fact and heavy on speculation.

Jamie Munro is known for his dangerous self-experimentation, but in the light of recent events, it must be assumed that he has extended these reckless activities to others, to the detriment of their health. Local girl Ellie MacDonald died in mysterious circumstances just a few months ago and the Munro's long-serving housekeeper was recently rushed to hospital and has not yet returned. Could she be the latest victim of the notorious Munro Curse?

As if matching Jamie's bad mood, the sunlight disappeared. Stella pulled on her coat and stomped around the grounds, releasing her pent-up energy and giving the dogs some exercise at the same time. 'He's a grumpy bastard, isn't he, Tabs?' She stroked the dog's silky head and tried to laugh away the hurt. She didn't want to care, but the wanting made no difference.

Without warning, the sky turned black and freezing drops of rain began hurling down, stinging Stella's skin. She called Angus and Tabitha and ran back to the house, all three of them drenched and frightened by the sudden wildness. Stella dried the dogs with the old towels Esmé kept in the boot room and gave them each one of the tooth-friendly treats from the bag in the kitchen. Angus lay down happily in his bed, chewing contentedly, but Tabitha stuck to Stella's side, shadowing her so closely she kept almost pushing her over.

The storm raged all afternoon and Stella couldn't settle to work. She avoided Jamie's office and watched from one of the upstairs windows as lightning flashed across the sky and the sea churned and roiled like the opening to hell. She kept stroking Tabitha and telling her that everything was all right, but Stella had never felt the remoteness of their location so keenly.

As the sea boiled and the rain lashed horizontally across the landscape, Stella could easily imagine some mythical beast rising from the depths and she hoped the lifeboat at Mallaig hadn't been called into service. No human should be outside at that moment, let alone on the water.

It wasn't late, but the early dark and freezing air made it feel that way. Stella ate a couple of rounds of cheese on toast and made herself a second mug of tea to chase it down. She washed some red grapes and put them in a bowl to take upstairs to balance out the protein-and-carb dinner. Jamie was in his exercise room, probably hanging from his inversion bar like a bat.

Stella said goodnight and closeted herself in her bedroom. It was already familiar and comforting and Stella was perfectly happy pottering around and then getting into bed early to read.

Stella was sitting up in bed, reading through the bundle of letters, when the lights went out. The curtains were drawn tightly against the cold and the darkness was absolute. She reached out and felt on the bedside table for the small torch Jamie had given her. With its light, she located her jumper and put it on over her vest top, and then wondered whether she ought to go and see if something needed to be done, or sit tight in her warm bedclothes and wait it out. The air in the room was cooling rapidly.

There was a knock at her door and she said, 'Come in.'

A glow sliced into the room and Jamie put his head around the door frame. 'Just a power cut. Nothing to worry about.'

'I'm fine,' Stella said and then wondered why she had.

Jamie stepped into the room. He had a lantern in one hand and it lit the room impressively. 'It might stay off for a wee while. I'll light the Aga, make sure the place doesn't get too cold. I can bring a gas heater up here if you like?'

'No, it's okay. I'll just wrap up,' Stella said. 'Do you need help with anything?'

He shook his head. 'That's above and beyond. I'll just light the fire and head back to bed.'

His gaze fell upon the pile of letters. 'Were you working?'

'Just reading,' Stella said.

He looked uncomfortable, and for a horrible moment Stella thought he was going to say that she'd crossed a line, that by reading out-of-hours she was somehow violating his privacy.

'Am I that bad?'

'What do you mean?'

'As a boss,' he said, walking closer and frowning at the letters. 'This stuff isn't urgent. I probably won't even use it in the book—'

'Oh no,' Stella said, relieved. 'I'm not reading it for you. For work. I'm just interested. I've gotten quite fond of Jessie. She's expecting, now, and I want to see what she has.'

'She's pregnant?'

'Yes.' Stella waved the letter she'd been reading. 'I guess she and her husband were closer than it seemed.'

'You're really into this, aren't you?' He shook his head. 'Seriously, Stella. How did I get so lucky?'

He looked into her eyes, and there was a moment. A spark of connection. Stella felt her chest tighten and she forced herself to breathe out. *If you don't breathe out, you can't breathe in.* That's one of the first things you learn. It came out a bit noisier than she had planned and Jamie moved forward in concern. 'You all right?'

Stella gulped some air before answering. 'Fine.'

'I'm sorry I've been a bit tense recently.'

'You've had a lot on your mind,' Stella said.

'I shouldn't take it out on other people. My dad—' He stopped, looking down. 'He did that.'

'Esmé is going to be all right,' Stella said. 'She'll be home before you know it.'

He put the lantern down on the floor and pulled matches from his pocket. There was a candle in a holder on the dressing table, something which Stella had seen as purely decorative until this moment, when Jamie carried it over to her bedside table. Then he lit the pillar candles that were in the old fireplace. Finally, he took a small box from his pocket and showed it to Stella. 'Head torch. The strap comes out here.' He pulled an elastic from the back until it extended, then let it go with a snap. 'Switch is on the side. Use this if you go walkabout so that you've got your hands free.'

'Thank you,' Stella said.

'No problem.' Jamie hesitated as if he was going to say something else, but then he just smiled and left, closing the door gently behind him.

Stella looked at the door for a moment, seeing his figure as if he was still stood there. Solid and reassuring, smiling at her as if he cared, looking as if he saw her. Spots danced in front of her eyes, mixing with the flickering shadows, and Stella realised that she wasn't breathing again.

◦◦◦

The power came on by lunchtime the next day and Stella went around blowing out candles and switching on lights before sitting down in front of the welcome glow of her computer screen. The wind had calmed a little, but the rain was still lashing down and the sky so thick with black cloud that it looked like evening, not midday. By three o'clock it was full-dark and Stella went back around the house, closing the curtains.

'I just heard from Nathan,' Jamie said, finding Stella yanking some recalcitrant drapery in the dining room.

'Oh, right,' Stella said, not looking at him.

'He's still in Glasgow. Doesn't think he'll make it back until the weekend.'

'Doesn't he have work?'

Jamie smiled. 'Nathan can work anywhere. He's probably talent-spotting as we speak.'

Not for the first time, Stella wanted to ask why Jamie worked with Nathan, why he felt so loyal. Instead, she peered out at the slice of gloomy garden still visible through the curtains. 'How many miles of cloud does it take to make it this dark at this time?'

'Sun would be setting soon, anyway.' Jamie joined her at the big bay window.

'I don't know how you stand it,' Stella said.

'I don't all that well. Hence, California.'

'Oh, right, yes. God, you must miss it.'

'Not at all, actually,' Jamie said. 'It's good to be back. I can't believe how much I like being here, to be honest.'

Stella twitched the curtains into place, closing the gap so that she didn't have to see the rain blattering at the glass. 'It's such a shame. It's so beautiful around here when it's not pissing down.'

'Maybe it's even more beautiful because it's fleeting,' Jamie said. 'And it makes you work a bit for it.'

'I suppose. And if Scotland had glorious weather, it would be instantly overcrowded. Everyone would live here.'

'There is that,' he said. 'It's actually a government secret. We keep it cold to keep the English out. Joke,' he added quickly. 'I've nothing against the English.'

'Well, some of us are all right,' she said, deadpan.

He laughed and Stella tried not to feel too pleased. Jamie smiled a lot, part of his charm-boy routine, but he didn't laugh often. He sounded really young when he did and his face just creased up completely, lines around his eyes folding like origami. When he laughed, she wanted to make him do it again.

CHAPTER FIFTEEN

9th October, 1848

My dearest Mary,

I write this to you while my husband is out of the house and in the strictest confidence. Please do not tell faither or any other person as I cannot risk word reaching Edinburgh, however unlikely that may seem. I am perfectly well but I feel the need to unburden myself and there is nobody here I can speak with candidly.

Mr Lockhart has been vexed of late and last night he became most agitated. He claimed that I did not care for him at all and that I was plotting with my society friends to keep patients from his door. It was not helped by our dinner guests who had been speaking with animation about dear Simmy – which is the name some of them use for Mr Simpson. They moved from his kindly manner and sonsie face to the enormous fun enjoyed at mealtime. Mr Laing said that Simmy had been rolling about on the floor with his children and they had all laughed until they felt sick. Mrs Laing had tried the famous chloroform and become so silly that she had begun impressions of farmyard animals, much to Mr Laing's amusement. Apparently Mrs Laing has never seen a coo as she made a noise like a dog and flapped her arms like a bird.

I told Mr Lockhart that nobody could expect that of him as he did not have children, but that one day he would be able to frolic with the dear one we are expecting. It did not calm him in the way I hoped and he even spoke of bringing a child in from elsewhere and demanded to know if you had an unwanted child, perhaps, waiting in the wings to be brought onto our stage. When I told him that I did not know of any unwanted children, he said that I should 'wait until there was a death in the family'. And that 'if a man is lost, there are hungry mouths to feed and children become surplus. And if a mother is lost their babe may be moved to another pair of arms for safe-keeping.' It was a warning, Mary. He must increase his business before this bairn arrives or I do not know what he will do. If I could turn the hands of the clock forward, produce a strapping five- or six-year-old for Mr Lockhart, I would, but alas that is impossible.

Mary, I need your counsel. What should I do? I talk of his services and pass on every little compliment I can think of but it does not seem to help. I do not feel it is my place, nor that I make an especially compelling hawker. However, I feel I have no other choice. I have agreed to try.

Your loving Jessie

'I'm extending my ice bath today,' Jamie said.

Stella looked up from the spreadsheet. Jamie's ice bath experiment had run for the full thirty days and she assumed he would be stopping them, not making them worse. 'Why?'

'I have been thinking about the benefits of a slow heart rate.'

Just the word sent Stella's hand fluttering to her chest.

'You've seen the results,' he said, gesturing to the screen. 'Resting heart rate is consistently ten bpm slower after the bath than before. Even taken after the physical movement of getting out. I've been concentrating on the ketones in my blood, but I want to repeat the experiment with a focus on heart rate. I'll take a resting pulse every twenty minutes for the first two hours after the ice, and then every hour for the following six.'

'What are you hoping to see?'

'A good scientist never hopes to find a particular result. It increases bias,' Jamie said. 'But I'm hoping to find a sustained improvement in my resting heart rate.'

Stella helped Jamie carry the buckets of ice up the stairs, while continuing to voice her concern. 'You already had extended it, remember? There are health risks involved. You told me that—'

'It'll be fine,' Jamie said. 'And you're my safety.'

'You know I'm not medically trained.'

'I'm not stupid,' Jamie said. 'I bought one of these.' He put the ice in the bathroom and disappeared down the hall, into his bedroom, coming back with a small case of dark-green moulded plastic. 'Defibrillator. Just in case.'

'You're not funny,' Stella said, a split second before she realised that he wasn't joking and had just handed her a life-saving piece of equipment. He headed into the bathroom and shut the door.

'Take a look at it,' Jamie called from inside the bathroom. 'There are instructions inside, but it's pretty straightforward. They're designed so that anyone can use them.'

'Thanks,' Stella muttered. She opened the case and was confronted by the alarming sight of two chest patches, attached to the machine with wires. More reassuring were the clear instructions on the inside of the lid. There were only three steps and the chest patches were colour-coded to make sure you put them on the correct places on the body.

Every part of Stella's being was telling her that this was a bad idea. More strongly still that it was something she wanted no part of. A spurt of anger that Jamie would hand her such an object, knowing her medical history. His obsessions were blinding him. In that moment, Stella knew that she was not going to be like Jessie Lockhart. Jamie held the keys to her current domestic arrangement, but he was not her husband and this was not the Victorian era.

Stella pushed open the door. Jamie had already stripped and was stood next to the tub in a pair of swimming shorts and nothing else. It was a diverting sight, but Stella pulled her gaze to the floor and said, 'I'm not letting you do this.'

'What are you talking about?' Jamie said. Then, irritation in his voice: 'You can look at me, you know.'

Stella risked a glance and saw that he had wrapped a towel around his waist. He was still very naked, though. She had seen this body on the videos, of course, but now it was close to her and suddenly very real. 'This isn't safe,' she said. 'You're stressed out. The blog, Esmé, your deadline. It's affecting your judgement.'

'I appreciate your concern—'

'No.' Stella took a step forward, willing him to take her seriously. 'If you get into that bath I will dial 999.'

'Don't be ridiculous.' Jamie was obviously struggling to stay calm. 'You're overreacting.'

'You think you're superhuman, but you're not.'

'I'm being careful,' Jamie said. He was pale, his skin waxy underneath a day's stubble, and Stella could see the stress in the way he was standing. 'This stuff is bringing real results. Data that could lead to an actual breakthrough down the line. Imagine if we could cure Alzheimer's? Imagine if we didn't have to lose cognitive function as we age?'

'It's not down to you. You're not a doctor or a scientist—'

'Which means I'm not bound by the same restrictions. Just because things have been done a certain way for a while, doesn't mean they've always been done that way or should be done that way. It wasn't long ago that laypeople were making important discoveries, things which changed our understanding of the world.'

'Please don't mention Einstein.' Stella tried a smile. 'I know he worked for the patent office.'

'Well he did. And Alexander Graham Bell worked as a teacher. Imagine if they had decided to leave science and engineering to the professionals.'

'I'm not saying individuals can't make contributions, I'm not saying that you can't. I just want you to recognise your limitations. To enlist help.'

'I've got an MD on the payroll.' Jamie bent to pick up the last bucket of ice and emptied it into the bath with a clatter.

'Yeah, but you pay his bills.' Stella touched his arm. 'You can't trust the people you pay. They've got a vested interest. You need to go to hospital and get checked out by someone who isn't relying on you for income.'

'I'm paying you and it doesn't seem to stop you telling me I'm being an eejit.'

'I don't think I said eejit.'

'You're thinking it though.'

Stella smiled. 'Only a little.' She waited for him to smile back, for the tension in the room to be released, but the strange light was back in his eyes.

'People are often afraid of the road less taken. It's always hard for the visionaries, the trailblazers. People always think they're nut jobs. Until they get results, of course, and then everyone says they're a genius. You should have heard the hassle I got over my diet book.'

'You still get hassle over that,' Stella said. 'I read your emails, don't forget.'

'Aye.' Jamie looked momentarily taken aback, as if he had forgotten who he was speaking to. 'So you know, better than most. You're damned if you do and damned if you don't, so I'd rather do.'

'I'm not trying to curb your genius.' Stella forced herself not to use sarcastic air quotes. 'I'm trying to stop you hurting yourself.'

'Just because you're too frightened to live your life doesn't mean I need to join you.'

Stella felt as if he'd slapped her. 'We're not talking about me. And I'm not frightened,' she said stiffly. 'I live.'

'Aye, right,' Jamie said, his accent coming out more strongly now. 'You're hiding away here and avoiding phone calls from your boyfriend because you're so full of fucking life.'

'He's not my boyfriend,' Stella said. 'He's my ex.'

Jamie hesitated. 'Well. The point still stands. You're so afraid to take risks you're stuck. What are you going to do with your life? When are you going to start making choices for yourself? You only live once, you know.'

'I'm aware,' Stella said. She focused on a spot just above Jamie's left shoulder, smoothing her features to offer a blank expression. 'Are we done here?'

'Ah, fuck,' Jamie said, rubbing his neck. 'I'm sorry. I shouldn't have said that.'

'My personal life is none of your business. But I'm not leaving until you abandon this project.'

'That is not your call,' Jamie said, angry again. 'If you don't wish to act as my safety, I certainly cannot make you, but you are not authorised to make a judgement on my work. As you said yourself, you are not medically trained, you don't have the professional experience.'

Stella recognised this type of bombast. Any moment now, Jamie was going to turn into every other egotistical manager she had worked for. Any moment now he was going to tell her she was *just an assistant*.

'You don't get to tell me what I can and cannot do in my work. That is beyond your remit.'

This last word was enunciated so clearly, the final 't' sound was almost spat.

Stella fought the urge to run away. She put her hand to her chest in the familiar, reassuring place. Her heart was a little fast, but nothing serious. 'Listen to me,' she said. 'I am not trying to undermine your work; I am trying to help you. You have been working on your ancestral research, looking into your family tree. You said yourself that you had lost the taste for your experimentation. This' – Stella motioned to the bath – 'seems like a sudden departure. You haven't prepared for it properly.'

'I bought a defibrillator,' Jamie said. 'That's preparation.'

'Exactly,' Stella said. 'You prepared for something terrible to happen, something dangerous. That must tell you something.'

'That I'm being sensibly cautious,' Jamie replied.

'Or that you know, deep down, that this is dangerous.'

'Life is risk. You can't have greatness without taking chances.'

'Fine,' Stella said. Her heart was racing, and she forced herself to take a couple of long slow breaths. 'I will do it for you.'

'What?'

Stella took off her woolly cardigan and dropped it onto the floor. 'I'll take the bath. You can time me.'

'No,' Jamie said, looking horrified.

'Why?'

'You know why.'

'What is life without risk?' Stella said.

'That's not what I meant,' Jamie began. 'I didn't mean you should—'

'You just told me it was perfectly safe,' Stella said. She slipped off her shoes and bent to take off her socks.

'No!' Jamie's hands were on her shoulders, pulling her upright. He was very close and Stella had the urge to laugh. She was arguing in a bathroom with her half-naked boss. Nobody could accuse her of not trying new things.

Jamie, however, seemed oblivious. 'I'm happy to try things on myself, but I won't put anybody else through them. You know that. You know that about me.'

'I do,' Stella said. 'But can't you see that you are horrified at the thought, because you know it's a bad idea?'

He dropped his hands from her shoulders. 'Why are you obstructing me? You're supposed to help. You're my assistant, you're supposed to make things easier for me.'

'Fire me, if you must,' Stella said. 'But I'm not leaving until I'm sure you are safe. And if you proceed' – she gestured to the bath – 'I will call an ambulance.'

'Have it your way.' Jamie twisted away and bent over the bath. For a moment she thought he was going to test her assertion and get in, but instead he yanked the plug out and then moved past her and out of the room.

For the rest of the day, Stella avoided being in the same room as Jamie, while keeping tabs on his activities. She buried herself in Jessie Lockhart's letters again, looking for confirmation that she had done the right thing. Any moment she expected Jamie to walk in and tell her she had to leave. He could give her one month's pay and send her packing. That was the truth of it.

The phone rang at eight the next morning, echoing in the hall and setting the dogs barking. Stella ran to pick it up, worried that it would be Ben again. She wasn't worried that Jamie would be grumpy, but she was worried that he would get curious, and she wasn't ready to face his laser-focused questioning.

'Stella? It's Caitlin.'

Stella glanced down the empty hall. 'How did you get this number?'

'Your mobile was out of service,' Caitlin said, which wasn't an answer. 'Can you come round this morning?'

'Now?' Stella glanced at her watch.

'It's important,' Caitlin said.

'Are you okay?' Stella felt a spurt of fear. 'Is the baby all right?'

'Everything is fine,' Caitlin said. 'I would just rather talk to you in person. I could come to you—'

'No,' Stella interrupted. 'I'll come to you. See you in five.'

She grabbed a coat and bag and went to her car. It was only as she pulled up outside that she wondered why Caitlin wasn't at work.

'What's wrong?' Stella said as soon as Caitlin opened the door. 'Are you sick?'

Caitlin looked surprised. 'No, I told you. I'm fine.'

'Why aren't you at work?'

Caitlin moved down the narrow hallway, leaving room for Stella to come inside and slip off her boots.

'Short contracts, I told you.'

'I didn't realise it was ending so soon.'

Caitlin pulled a face. 'I was hoping they would keep me on for a bit longer, but . . .' She shrugged. 'I'm not exactly an asset right now.'

'But equal opportunities. They can't do that.'

'Zero-hours temp contract,' Caitlin said. 'They can do whatever the hell they like.'

'I'm so sorry,' Stella said, feeling like crap. She had been so wrapped up in Jamie and Munro House and Jessie Lockhart that she hadn't been paying attention to her friends. Of course, if Jamie decided to kick her out, she would have a whole lot more time on her hands. 'Is Rob all right?'

Caitlin looked over her shoulder, startled. 'Why do you ask?'

'Just the stress. I mean, one income . . .'

Caitlin shrugged and seemed about to brush off the comment with her trademark bulletproof manner, but then her face crumpled a little. 'Rob is freaking out. His dad left when he was a teenager and it was a real struggle financially. I know he's scared of not being able to provide for this one.' Caitlin looked down at her stomach.

Stella reached out a hand, but Caitlin had already turned away.

Stella followed Caitlin into the kitchen and sat in her usual place, trying to work out what to say to reassure Caitlin about money. She was keenly aware that she was not in the same position and never had been. Stella's family had always been comfortable and she had grown up knowing that, whatever else might be difficult in her life, there was always a financial safety net beneath her.

Caitlin had scales, a sieve and a bag of flour on the worktop. She took sugar from a shelf and, not looking at Stella, said, 'Ben rang.'

Stella realised that she had hardly thought of Ben since he'd called at the house. She hadn't checked her old email account or her mobile for texts, either. Didn't bother to switch it on these days.

'He says you're not answering your phone,' Caitlin said. 'I don't blame you,' she added, moving around the room, fetching ingredients, still not looking at Stella.

The unease she had felt on the phone doubled. Stella could almost sense the other shoe, just waiting to drop.

'I need a clean break,' Stella said, wondering why Ben wanted to speak to her. She had told him what he needed in order to sort out the mortgage. He could have the house, move in with a new partner, do whatever he wanted. Stella waited for the pain and sense of loss to crush her, but it didn't. There was just a wave of sadness, cool and gentle.

Caitlin nodded. 'Fair enough.'

There was a short silence as Caitlin got eggs from the fridge, then filled the kettle, flipping the switch. When Stella couldn't stand it anymore, she said, 'What?'

'Nothing,' Caitlin said quickly. 'It's just . . . well, he sounded really worried when he rang here.'

'I don't know why.'

'I want a muffin,' Caitlin said, changing direction and getting a large bowl out from one of the cabinets. She caught Stella's eye and patted her bump. 'It's a craving.'

Stella smiled. 'Got to give the baby what it wants.'

'Exactly,' Caitlin said, but she didn't return the smile. 'He said he wants to talk to you. And I think he's worried about the house being left empty for so long. Security.'

'Yeah, he said all that when we spoke last week.' Stella still expected the memory to hurt, but she felt too distracted by Caitlin's pale complexion and obvious anxiety. She got up and joined Caitlin at the worktop. 'Is there anything I can do?' Stella wondered if she should offer Caitlin a loan. She didn't want to offend her or make things weird between them, but she was living rent-free and being paid a good salary; she could help a little.

'I think he wants to hear from you,' Caitlin began cracking eggs into a glass bowl.

'Not him. You. Is there anything I can do about the job thing? If you need money—'

'No!' Caitlin almost shouted, finally looking at Stella with wide, unhappy eyes.

'Sorry, sorry.' Stella reached out a hand to pat Caitlin on the arm.

'No, I'm sorry.' Caitlin turned away, her cheeks flushed. 'Honestly. We're fine.'

Stella began to help with the baking, putting the bowl onto the scales and sifting flour.

'It's a fair point, I suppose,' Caitlin said. 'You and he own a house together. You should probably speak.'

Stella stopped sifting and looked at her. Caitlin was concentrating on chopping chocolate and didn't look up. There was tension in her face. 'What did he ask you to do?' Ben could talk anybody into anything. She always said he ought to have been a salesman.

Caitlin glanced across. Sighed. 'Just to talk to you. See if I could get you to go home. I didn't say I'd do that, but I said I'd pass on the message. And check that you were all right.'

'I'm great,' Stella said. She smiled to reassure Caitlin but realised that it was true and that the smile was real. 'I feel much better here. Must be the air.'

They both looked to the window, where the rain was lashing against the glass.

Ben would be going out of his mind, Stella knew. To ring Caitlin, to ask for help. He was fiercely autonomous and that wouldn't have been easy. Stella wished she could read it as a sign he had changed his mind, but she knew he had not. She wasn't so certain she wanted him to change his mind, either.

Caitlin was still looking at her with an uneasy expression. 'I don't know whether to say this or not. You are doing so much better . . .'

Stella went cold. Here it came. 'Just tell me.'

'I think he's having second thoughts.'

Whatever Stella had expected Caitlin to say, it wasn't that. 'What?'

'You two need to talk. He can tell you what he means better than me. I'm worried I'm going to put my foot in it, say the wrong thing and mess things up.'

'You can't mess things up between me and Ben. That ship has sailed. Trust me.'

'He said—' Caitlin began.

'I don't care,' Stella said. 'I don't want to know.'

Caitlin nodded and resumed stirring. Once the cases were filled with mixture and the muffins were in the oven, filling the room with a sweet smell and welcome warmth, Caitlin returned to the subject. 'What happened with you guys, anyway?'

Stella realised that she still hadn't told Caitlin, her best friend. In the beginning it had all been too raw and, after a while, she'd been in the habit of not discussing it. She had never been a big sharer, anyway, and it was easier not to spell it out. Now Stella realised she had been almost superstitious; if she didn't say the words out loud then maybe they would no longer be true. She squared her shoulders, and then, after all this time of avoiding them, found that the words slipped out easily. 'He fell in love with someone else.'

'Christ. I'm sorry.' Caitlin pulled a sympathetic face. She opened a cupboard and pulled out a bottle of single malt.

'Is it not a bit early?'

'A nip will chase the cold.'

'It's medicinal, then.' Stella took the bottle and splashed a little into her empty mug. Without thinking, she said, 'Slàinte', the Gaelic version of 'cheers' that Jamie always used.

Caitlin raised an eyebrow. 'My, we have gone native, haven't we?'

'Her name is Laura.' Stella addressed the words to her glass, focusing on the delicious amber liquid.

'Maybe it's just a passing thing.'

'Ben told me he loves her. He's not cruel, he wouldn't have said that if he wasn't sure.' She had started so she would finish. If Stella could get the words out now, then perhaps she would never have to say them again. 'He says he loves me but that he's not "in love" with me. Couldn't even be bloody original in his break-up speech.'

'I'm sorry,' Caitlin said.

'He said he didn't love me the way I thought he loved me, but he was wrong. I didn't think he loved me in the usual way, I always knew he didn't have huge passion for me, but I thought we had an agreement. That's why I feel so fucking stupid. I wasted all that time and it turns out we didn't have the agreement.' Stella was surprised to find that she was still angry. She thought that had burned out by now.

'What agreement? I'm sorry,' Caitlin said. 'I'm lost. Do you mean the engagement?'

'I should have got it in writing.' Stella smiled and could feel it brittle on her face, like a china mask. She forced it wider, to show Caitlin that she was fine. That she might sound a bit strange and wobbly but that she wasn't a victim. She was still strong. She took a steadying breath. 'He didn't want to have children. Definitely not yet, and possibly not ever, but he knew I did. We had an agreement that we would do up the house, and I would pay the mortgage while he finished his training. Then we would get married and try for a baby.' Stella forced a laugh. 'Stupid thing is, he met Laura on his bloody course. Fucking irony.'

'I'm really sorry,' Caitlin said. 'Is it really serious between them? I mean, are they living together?'

'I haven't asked,' Stella said. 'I didn't want to know. I was hoping he would change his mind, realise what he was throwing away. And, now . . .' She stopped, shrugging. 'I honestly don't know how I feel now.'

There was a pause, and Stella could almost see Caitlin trying to work out how to respond. After a moment she settled on: 'How long has it been going on?'

Stella couldn't answer. She had wondered the same thing, whether Ben and Laura had been having an affair and for how long. She had dissected every moment of the past year, looking for clues, trying to work out what she had missed. She drank her whisky, enjoying the burn as it went down her throat and the instant warm glow.

'Why is he so keen to get you back now, then?' Caitlin put a hand up to her mouth. 'Sorry. That came out a bit too blunt, even for me.'

Stella smiled, suddenly glad of Caitlin's straight-talking. It was a relief to be able to speak to someone who wasn't easily shocked. Or who would be honestly and openly shocked, not pretend they felt nothing and then stew quietly or speak behind your back.

'Money, I would guess,' Stella said. 'He's realised that he can't afford the mortgage on our house. Truth is, we were struggling on just my salary and even though he qualifies next year, he won't be earning much to start with. I kept having to borrow cash from my parents. He didn't always pay that much attention to the finance side of things and I don't think he realised just how much I'd been subbing him. Or how much Mum and Dad had, anyway.'

'Maybe it's not the money, maybe he's realised that he made a mistake. About his feelings. Maybe it was a bit of excitement, a mini-panic because of the commitment of the engagement. Maybe it's something he just had to get out of his system before you guys got married.'

Stella reached out and squeezed Caitlin's hand, grateful for her friend's attempt. 'We hardly ever had sex, you know. Even in the beginning. That should have been a warning sign, but I put it down to a low drive. Or I thought that mine was abnormally large or something. I mean, nobody really talks about that stuff. Not about not doing it, anyway.' Stella looked down. 'I think I knew from the beginning but I didn't admit it. That's on me. I chose to be with him anyway. I thought that everything else we had was enough. Everyone says that you can't build a relationship on sex and that that side of things goes off the boil once you're married.'

Caitlin shook her head. 'I always thought you two had the perfect relationship.'

'We did,' Stella said. 'In a way, it really was. We got on so well. We loved each other so much.'

'I know,' Caitlin said. 'It was almost painful to be around you two sometimes.'

Stella wasn't sure what to say to that. Caitlin and Rob were the golden couple, always had been. 'Are you and Rob okay?'

Caitlin looked down. 'We're fine. It's just life, you know. You get busy and you hardly see each other and then you're picking up their dirty socks and you can't quite remember why you ever thought it was a good idea.'

'It must be hard. I know you're tired at the moment.' Stella carefully didn't use the word 'hormonal'.

'Yeah,' Caitlin said. 'And it's this time of year. We all go a bit stir-crazy. I mean, I'm lucky that I'm outdoors so much.'

Stella privately didn't agree that it was 'lucky'. Still, it was true that Caitlin had always been the hardy, physical type. She had loved hill-walking and rowing at university, had surprised exactly nobody when she got a job as an estate worker after her course in Environmental Science, rather than staying on to do her masters.

'I mean, I was. With work.' Caitlin's mouth twisted. 'And it's so dark all the time.'

'And cold.'

'I don't mind the cold. I can't wait for it to get colder, to be honest. Get rid of this bloody wet.' Caitlin wrapped her hands around her mug of tea. 'People go a bit funny over winter, though. The house seems smaller than usual and moods get low. Rob will be happier after the solstice. Anyway, that's enough of that. I'm not complaining to you.'

Stella tried not to be hurt by her tone. She didn't want Caitlin to see her as 'poor delicate Stella' or 'poor broken Stella' or 'poor rejected Stella with the messed-up life and no fucking idea what she's doing', but she couldn't really blame her. 'Complain all you like,' Stella said. 'That's medicinal, too.'

Caitlin managed a watery smile. 'You're a good friend.'

'The best,' Stella said. 'And I'm not running back down south, so anything you need . . . Anything.' She clinked her glass against Caitlin's mug and threw back the last of the whisky.

❧

Back at Munro House, Stella sat in her office and tried to work. She checked her mobile and, sure enough, there were several missed calls from Ben. The first message he had left just said: 'Please call me.' The second was the same, but with a big, hitching breath after, as if Ben was trying not to cry. That wasn't like him. The third said: 'I've made a huge mistake—' Stella pressed the disconnect button before listening to the rest.

The whisky that she had drunk with Caitlin had worn off and she had already eaten the second chocolate muffin Caitlin had given her 'for the road'. Stella thought about taking the dogs for a walk but instead she sat on the bed and pulled the blanket up, paralysed by indecision. The Stella of three months ago would have been in the car and driving south. She had wanted so very much to hear Ben say those words, had dreamed of it. For the first while after Ben told her that he had fallen for Laura, she had wished for it so hard that she had hardly been able to think of anything else. But she hadn't been entirely open with Caitlin.

There was one more truth that she hadn't been able to say out loud. A rectangle of white card which had changed everything.

There was no excuse, really. You shouldn't open another person's correspondence, and if you did it was snooping and you deserved everything you got. Nobody would feel the slightest compassion for Stella, she was well aware. But she had seen the NHS logo on the brown envelope and panicked. Now that she had finally escaped from under her own sword of Damocles, here it was again, aiming for its new target. She felt the punch in her stomach. *Not Ben*, she'd thought. *Please, not Ben.* Stella didn't want to die, but she'd had plenty of time to think about the possibility. Now that she had her own life back, it seemed the height of cruelty to snatch Ben from her. She tried to stop the litany of terrors, but they advanced across her mind. Cancer. Brain tumour. Heart disease. Tropical parasite acquired on his gap year.

The paper of the envelope was already torn. Stella couldn't exactly recall the moment she slipped her finger into the gap at the edge of the gummed flap, but she remembered the paper ripping, giving way.

Inside was a single white rectangle. An appointment card. She checked the hospital department. Not oncology. Thank God. Not cardiology. Not tropical disease or neurology. There was no time for relief, though, as her brain was trying to process something else. Pure shock that made everything go blinding white for a moment.

Printed in impersonal black type underneath Ben's name was the date and time for two appointments at the Urology outpatient clinic. The first, a pre-op appointment at 11.15 a.m. on Tuesday 3 October, and the second for a vasectomy under local anaesthetic for the week after.

Stella had fallen asleep on the bed and she didn't wake up until almost six. She still felt tired and it reminded her of the exhausted numbness of those early months after the split. She splashed water onto her face, trying to wake herself up from that unwelcome state, and went downstairs. Stella planned to have scrambled egg on toast followed by a family pack of crisps, with a glass of orange juice for the vitamin C. Jamie was usually running outside or dangling upside down at this time in the evening, so she was surprised to find him in the kitchen.

She steeled herself for the guillotine to fall, for Jamie to tell her to pack her stuff and get out. The man was rich enough to pay for an assistant who would obey his every command, who wouldn't obstruct him or tell him when he was acting irrationally. She wondered if he would give her a good reference and whether she would be able to get another job in the area or whether she would have to go back to London.

'Join me,' Jamie said, indicating the cooker. 'I'm making plenty.' He had a striped tea towel draped over one shoulder and a pair of tongs in one hand. She had never seen him look more domestic, more normal.

It was unsettling.

The pan sizzled invitingly as he placed the steak onto it. 'You can dress the salad.'

Stella wasn't a big fan of being ordered around in the kitchen, or anywhere for that matter, but the man was about to feed her and that made up for a lot. She washed her hands at the giant butler's sink and tried not to notice how close they were to each other. It seemed safer to move to the other side of the table in the middle of the room.

'How do you like your steak? I'm having medium.'

'Medium is fine,' Stella said, relieved that he wasn't going to try to get her to eat the stuff rare. She poured the oil mixture onto the leaves and moved them around with her hands. Some foodie people could be annoyingly evangelical. They made it their mission to make you try the disgusting things in life like squishy seafood, and you could never shake the feeling that they were secretly playing a practical joke.

'I've got some Shiraz open, but the Malbec is good, too.' Jamie nodded over his shoulder at the bottles of wine on the worktop. 'Do you want to open the Malbec, then you've got a choice?'

'Sure,' Stella said. She knew from experience that it was easiest to agree with Jamie, especially over food and drink. Besides, drawing attention to the fact that they were just two people and they didn't need to open two bottles of wine seemed unnecessarily parsimonious. Stella didn't know if it was that Jamie was naturally generous or whether it came from being wealthy.

She poured two balloon-shaped glasses with a small amount of Shiraz and passed one to Jamie. 'Thank Christ you eat something other than beans.'

He grinned. 'It's somewhat difficult to get a beautiful woman to have dinner with you if you're offering eggs and beans with a kale smoothie.'

'Where are the chips, though?' Stella said, only half teasing. 'Got to have chips with steak. I'm pretty sure it's the law.'

'No carbs,' Jamie said, smiling. 'Carbs are poison.'

'Except for the ones in the wine, presumably,' Stella said, keeping her voice light.

'Well, there's alcohol, too, and that's a poison. I like to think they battle and cancel each other out.'

'For someone who prides themselves on rational thinking, that is a truly crap argument.'

'But it means I get to drink wine,' Jamie said.

Stella raised her glass. 'I'll drink to that.'

'Plus,' he said, pulling an apologetic face, 'there is a compound in red wine called resveratrol which has been shown to extend the life of yeast cells. It's been used in studies on mice with positive results, which might account for the French paradox.'

'The French paradox?'

'Yeah, you know. The way they eat a rich diet while maintaining a low incidence of heart disease.'

Once the steak was cooked, Jamie put it onto a wooden board and sliced it across the grain, plating it up with the dressed salad. It was delicious, but Stella couldn't help but think that some crusty bread or a few chips would make the whole thing perfect. 'Do you really not have bread, ever?'

'Once a week, I eat whatever I want. Loaf of bread and butter, a chocolate gateau, ice cream, crisps, anything. I couldn't stick to it the rest of the time if I didn't.'

'Makes sense,' Stella said, adjusting to this new information. 'I had thought it was pretty impossible.'

'Well, it's still not always easy, but the results are so good.'

'So, was it a weight thing that got you started?'

'Fitness,' Jamie said, mock-offended. Then, in his normal voice, he said, 'I wasn't overweight but I was pretty soft. I had a bit of a belly.'

Stella sucked in her own stomach automatically and then let it go again. What was the point? She did not have an athletic figure and restricting her breathing wasn't going to change that. 'Did that bother you?'

Jamie pulled a face. 'I know it sounds shallow and I'm not supposed to care, but it did. And then I got results really quickly and it encouraged me to stick with it.'

'And improve it,' Stella said, smiling.

'Exactly. Test it. Refine it. Package it for others to follow.'

'The standard Jamie Munro drill.'

They chatted over the food, Jamie telling Stella about a phone call he'd had with Esmé. She was doing well in Edinburgh and was going to stay another week. 'She misses the dogs, but I think she's enjoying the break. It's good, she deserves one.'

After, they took their wine glasses and the open bottle to the living room. The room was cosy in the lamplight and the glow from the wood burner. The curtains were still wide open, showing the moon reflecting on the sea and creating shadows in the gardens which sloped away from the window. Stella looked out at the view for a while, sipping the delicious wine and trying not to get carried away. Jamie had finally chosen some music and was sitting on the sofa, one leg bent with his ankle resting on his other knee. Even sitting he seemed to radiate energy. One hand was tapping in time to the rhythm of the music and he was staring at her openly, his expression a challenge.

'What?' Stella said, crossing the room to sit on the sofa. Near, but not too close. She put her back against the arm of the seat and sat cross-legged, facing him.

'I've been thinking about you a lot.' He took a sip of wine. 'And not in a professional capacity.'

Stella opened her mouth to reply, but couldn't think of anything to say except 'oh', so she shut it again and drank instead.

'I was wondering whether it was mutual at all? It's completely fine if it isn't, of course,' he said quickly. 'And I don't want to make you uncomfortable. Please say if you want me to stop talking. Or just hold your hand up and I'll change the subject. We can talk about the database or segmenting the mailing list or Nathan or gardening.'

Stella smiled. 'It's fine. I don't mind.'

'You don't mind that I like you?'

'No,' Stella felt the blush run up her neck and over her face. She lifted her wine glass to her lips, hoping to hide her embarrassment.

'Okay, then.' Jamie uncrossed his leg.

'It's just—'

'You don't feel the same,' he said quickly. 'That's fine. Forget I said anything.' He pulled a face. 'Please.'

'Not that,' Stella said. 'I thought you were going to fire me. Because of yesterday.'

Jamie put his glass down and leaned forward, his arms resting on his knees. 'You were right.'

'I was over the line.' He looked her square in the face and Stella felt the connection between them. The intensity she had felt the very first time she had met him.

'What were you saying about not feeling professional?'

He smiled. 'Come over here.'

Stella couldn't speak. Somehow she managed to untangle her legs and make it to a standing position. She stood in front of Jamie, who was sitting up straight, then realised she was still gripping her wine glass.

She turned and put it onto the low wooden coffee table and, as she turned back, felt his hand low on her waist, caressing her hip and then, when she faced him, tugging her closer.

'Is this a good idea?'

'Definitely,' Jamie said. His pupils were dilated in the dim light and they no longer looked blue or green, just black. He looked like the devil he had been painted as by the villagers and he pulled her onto his lap, arranging her thighs in quick, matter-of-fact motions so that she was suddenly, shockingly astride him, far too much of her body pressing against far too much of his.

Then he kissed her, igniting all of Stella's nerves at once so that she thought she was going to explode. His hand on the back of her head, knotting her hair and tugging gently, tipping her face down to his, and Stella couldn't think when she had last been touched like this. With desire. With raw need.

She put her hands on his chest, feeling the muscles there, and then ran her palms over the hardness of his shoulders and arms. If anyone had asked her, she would've said that gym-muscles did nothing for her, that she preferred the slim aesthetic of Ben, but she found her body didn't seem to agree. Some primal part of her brain appeared to have woken up and was tingling at the thought of being crushed by this solid slab of human being. Pleasantly crushed. Deliciously crushed. Every part of his body pressing into hers.

When his fingers found the edge of her silk top and began to lift it, reality came crashing back. She stopped kissing him and leaned back a little. 'There's something I should warn you about.'

He smiled at her, looking happier and more relaxed than she'd ever seen him. It seemed a shame to spoil the mood, but Stella remembered the look of surprise on Ben's face when they had first got naked and she had no desire to relive her past mistakes. 'I have a big scar on my chest. It's not that bad but I didn't want you to be surprised.'

Stella had trained herself not to say 'a nasty surprise'. She knew she had nothing to be sorry for, that many people had far worse, that appearances weren't the most important thing and that she was still attractive enough despite it. She had trained herself not to sound pitying and needy and pathetic. She had told herself it was a badge of survival, something to be proud of. She had told herself that so often that she believed it. She had told herself so often that she could barely recall the tone of disgust when a school friend had pointed out the worm on her body when she had been changing into gym clothes at primary school.

He straightened up, looking fascinated. That was both pleasing and worrying. She didn't want to be anyone's fetish.

'It's right across my chest,' Stella said, touching the material of her top. She traced the line from her sternum, down between her breasts. 'They didn't think I was going to survive, so aesthetics weren't top priority.'

She took his hand and put it on her side, where there was a deep pit. 'And this is where they put a shunt in.' She shivered as his fingers explored the dip and ridges, the puckered skin. It still had the strange nervy feeling and she stretched away.

'Sorry,' Jamie said, moving his hand. 'Does it hurt?'

She shook her head. 'Just feels weird.'

'Is this why you get out of breath?'

'I'm not out of breath,' Stella said. 'You're not that good a kisser.'

He grinned and kissed her until she felt dizzy, until he had thoroughly vanquished her lie. His hand slid up under her top, skimming over her skin and the material of her bra. She wondered if it bothered him. He was obsessed with perfection. His last girlfriend was probably a model or an actress or a fitness instructor. A body builder.

She pushed the thought out of her head. He was kissing her. *Because I happen to be here*, a treacherous voice supplied.

'What?' Jamie wasn't kissing her anymore, he was peering up at her, a tiny frown between his brows.

'Nothing.' Stella forced a smile.

'Do you want to stop?'

'Do you?'

'No,' he said quickly. He moved his hands away though, deliberately. 'Are you having second thoughts?'

'I always have second thoughts,' Stella said. 'About everything. This? This qualifies for third and fourth thoughts, too.' Well, that was the mood well and truly broken. Stella extricated herself from his lap, suddenly embarrassed. 'I'd better go.'

He didn't try to stop her. As Stella walked from the room, she could feel him watching her, the back of her neck prickling and her legs wobbly.

She walked up the main staircase and to her bedroom, closing the door and leaning against it for a moment. What was she thinking? You didn't get romantic with your colleagues and you never, ever got romantic with your boss. That was just common sense.

The words were true, but the feeling underneath said something different. Jamie was different. This job was different.

Christ. Stella closed her eyes. What if things went wrong between them and she had to leave? Her heart clutched at the thought of leaving Munro House. Did tonight already count as 'gone wrong', though? Perhaps if she just acted completely normal in the morning and they never, ever spoke of it. That could work.

Stella changed into pyjamas. Her cutest cotton set with the camisole-style top in broderie anglaise. When she realised that she had her hand on the door handle and was about to go wandering the house in the hope of bumping into Jamie and picking up where they'd left off, she marched herself to the sink in the corner and brushed her teeth. Then she got into the cold bed and tried not to think.

An hour later and the red wine buzz had drained away and Stella was wide-eyed and staring into the dark. She wondered whether Jamie was asleep. She had heard his footsteps on the stairs and had hoped that he would knock on her door. She had strained to hear his bedroom door open and shut, but it was too far down the corridor and he was too light on his feet. Surprisingly light for such a solidly built person. So many things were surprising about Jamie.

She could picture him, lying in his bed, maybe curled on one side, the way he had slept when he was ill. Every part of her yearned to go and get into the bed beside him. She kept replaying the scene downstairs, the way his lips and hands had felt, the way they had fitted together. Why hadn't he stopped her from leaving? Why hadn't he knocked on her door? A cold thought crept out from the back of her mind. Maybe it was Ben all over again. She just wasn't the kind of woman men lost their minds over.

He's just not that into you, Stella thought, disgusted with her own neediness, and turned over to try to sleep.

Another twenty minutes crawled by, and then Stella sat up and switched on her bedside light. There was another reason Jamie might not have stopped her from leaving: he knew he was her boss and he didn't want to put pressure on her. Stella tried to dismiss it with a cynical *he's been in America for ages, he's probably paranoid I'll sue him*, trying to get her old distance back, but it didn't work. Jamie was a good man, she could feel it in her bones.

He's a good man who might not want you. Kissing you probably did nothing for him. The small cruel voices were back, but Stella ignored them and threw back the covers. It was freezing out of bed and she pulled on a big woolly cardigan over her nightwear and went out into the hall. The light was on and she walked to the end, stopping outside Jamie's bedroom and putting her hand on her chest to feel her heart pounding. She raised a hand to knock and the door opened. Jamie was wearing a T-shirt and joggers, as if he were about to go for a midnight run.

'I thought I heard you,' he said.

'You were listening?' Stella said, hoping that was true.

He smiled, and opened the door wider. 'Would you like to come in?'

'Yes,' Stella said. 'Very much.'

CHAPTER SIXTEEN

28th October, 1848
My dearest Mary,
I write to you to ask that you visit. I do not know whether this letter will get to you as I am unable to leave the house at present and must rely upon our housemaid to deliver it to the post. I do not know whether she is naturally slapdash or whether she is acting upon another instruction. Regardless, I have not received word from you or faither and must assume that my letters are not being delivered. Or that I have been forsaken by you all. No. I shall not believe that. Not until the very last.

Please please come to Queen Street. Just to see your face would be balm enough, I feel. My time is very close, now, and I waddle like a matron. It is a good thing that I still have a lady's maid. I have no idea how the poor folk manage to dress themselves. Perhaps they sleep in their day clothes?

Although Mr Lockhart is very capable, he has urged me to seek advice from J. Y. Simpson. I could not believe it when he first broached the subject. Just to hear that man's name spring from my husband's lips was most shocking. He usually flies into a rage should anybody else use the name. He says that he believes the baby is lying in the wrong way for birth and that it wouldn't be proper for him to administer to his own wife. This, you may remember, is after months of treatment both before I was with child and since. He had no compunctions then, nor every day when he takes a little sample of blood. Oh, how I hate that ritual. I know that I should not complain and that I am fortunate to be under such careful watch, but I cannot abide the needle.

Mr Lockhart wrote the note for Mr Simpson, naturally, but I had to sign my name at the bottom. He said that Simpson cannot resist the plea from a lady in need and that is why he ended up in obstetrics. While many of the doctors sneer at that field, Mr Lockhart believes it is an area ripe for advancement. In that, he and Mr Simpson are in perfect agreement. Having heard so many stories over the last year, both in the parlour and from my maid, I cannot help but agree. Why must ladies suffer so much torment when bringing new life into the world? The minister says that it is God's will and that our suffering is penance for Eve's sins, but I say that my God is too kind to punish us all so harshly. I do not say it out loud, you need not fear.

I believe that J.Y.S. will attend to me at home, if he concedes to assist in my confinement. I wish it were not so. I would dearly love to leave this house, even if for such a terrifying purpose. The walls oppress and the days grow longer and longer. I have stitched a layette and am working on a sampler but my fingers shake and I cannot make as neat stitches as I used to. I grow afraid, too. Not of the birth, although I cannot say I am anticipating it with pleasure, but of motherhood. How will I care for an infant, guide and teach a child, while I am so weak?

Jessie

The next morning, Stella opened her eyes to discover that she was not in her own bed in her house with the duck-egg-and-silver wallpaper she had spent three weeks choosing, but she wasn't in the blue bedroom in Munro House, either. She was in Jamie's bedroom. In his bed. And, yes, if she turned her head to one side, there was the man himself. His eyes closed and breathing deep and even. She watched him for a moment, memorising his features and wondering how things could have changed so completely between them in one night. Of course, Stella thought as she rolled onto her back and stretched, it had been quite a night. She had probably had less than two hours' sleep, but she felt fantastic.

'Good morning.' Jamie's eyes were open now.

'Good morning,' Stella said, happiness rushing through her body.

Jamie propped himself up on one elbow, looking down with a sleepy smile that was just for her. 'How are you?'

Stella thought for a moment, determined to be honest in this new relationship. Then she said: 'Excellent.'

After leaving Jamie so that she could shower and have a carbohydrate-heavy breakfast, Stella went down to the office to do some online shopping for books and clothes; the essentials.

Jamie appeared almost as soon as she had switched on the computer. 'I was thinking about tackling the attic properly this morning. You game?'

'Sure,' Stella said. 'Is there anything in particular you're hoping to find?'

'Not really,' he said. 'It's just an excuse to get you into a dark enclosed space.'

'Well you don't need a ruse for that,' Stella said, smiling. He caught her for a kiss and then went in search of a head torch. Once he had them both kitted out, he opened a door which Stella had assumed hid a cupboard but actually revealed a very narrow set of wooden stairs.

The torches turned out not to be necessary, as the attic was well lit and roomier than Stella had expected. In fact, the attic was a series of interconnected rooms, matching the grand proportions of the house below. You could stand easily in the middle of the floored space; in a smaller house, it would have been instantly converted into a spare room. Of course, the Munros had no need of extra space. She could see the tension in Jamie's shoulders as he looked around, and she thought about asking him if he really wanted to go poking about. Ancient history was one thing, but he might find out stuff about his parents or grandparents he would prefer not to know.

'When did you last come up here?' she said instead, knowing that Jamie was focused on answers and that, no matter what had happened between them, it was his house. His history.

'Never,' he said. 'Off-limits when I was a kid. And I was very obedient.' His mouth twisted a little and Stella's heart ached for him. She had looked at the photographs of Jamie's father and heard the stories and none of it made her feel sad that the man was no longer in residence.

The attic smelled clean and dry, with just the faintest edge of rotting cardboard from the packing boxes. There was a lot of paper and cardboard – packaging for household items going back to the forties, and Stella began moving it from on top of every box, crate and piece of furniture, and stacking it in a pile. 'Granddad was very thrifty,' Jamie said, smiling, joining in with the task. 'If a kettle or something broke, he wanted to be able to return it so he kept all the original packaging.'

'How long did he live here with you?'

'Until he died. I was six,' Jamie said.

Stella levered off the lid of a wooden crate using a flathead screwdriver. It was full of unopened seed packets. She picked one up at random. A pretty watercolour of a pea plant on the front and the price '1d' on the back. 'I don't think your grandfather threw anything away,' she said.

'Look.' Jamie held up a microscope, his face lit up. 'I wonder if this was his. Or Dad's.'

'Older, I think. Could be your great-grandfather's.' She was about to add 'or grandmother's' out of an automatic loyalty to her gender, but she stopped. How likely was that when you were talking about the early nineteenth century? And she didn't believe in whitewashing the past. You had to look it in the eye and, hopefully, learn from it. Otherwise, what was the point?

'You ought to get that valued,' Stella said. 'For the insurance.' She had been reading about the increased interest in old medical and scientific equipment. Jamie wasn't the only person keen on the polymaths of the past. Sotheby's had recently sold a cabinet full of glass eyes for twenty-five thousand, and an ebony-handled surgical saw had gone for six grand.

There was a large mahogany sideboard pushed against the rafters. It was ornately carved and stunningly ugly. Now that she'd moved the packaging from around it, she began searching the drawers and cupboards systematically.

'You're really into this, aren't you?' Jamie said, and Stella straightened up, startled. He was closer than she expected, and she could have put out a hand and touched the middle of his chest.

'I'd love to find something which relates to the papers,' Stella said, meaning Jessie's letters but not wanting to admit it out loud. She was obsessed. If anyone would understand obsession it would be Jamie, but he was so private about his family that she didn't want to alarm him, either.

'I love that you're doing this with me,' he said. 'I don't know if I've told you how much I appreciate it.'

'You're welcome,' Stella said. She wanted to say something flirty about him demonstrating his appreciation last night, but she suddenly felt too embarrassed. She couldn't manage flirty. It just wasn't in her nature.

Jamie was staring and Stella wondered what he was thinking. It was the intense look he got when he was listening to a science podcast or trying to work something out.

'Christ,' he said, 'I can't stop thinking about you.'

'Oh.' Stella swallowed. She could feel her heart fluttering and, without meaning to, her hand found its familiar place on her chest, pressing, feeling.

'Are you all right?' In one step, his body was filling her vision, his hands on her shoulder.

'Fine,' Stella said. 'Just—'

And then he kissed her and her heart beat hard and fast, but with a steady rhythm that made her feel like an athlete finishing a race, rather than a fish gasping for air on the deck of a ship. And then she wasn't thinking about her heartbeat at all and she was just kissing Jamie, her mind and body alive.

He broke the kiss long enough to look at the floor. 'I don't know if those floorboards will give you splinters.'

'I could go on top,' Stella said, laughing. 'But we're supposed to be researching, you know.'

Jamie made a mock-offended face. 'You're supposed to be so overcome with lust that you forget everything else.'

'How about we finish looking up here and then get overcome with lust when we're downstairs near a bed.'

'Practical as well as beautiful,' Jamie said. 'A winning combination.' He kissed her again for good measure and then let her go.

In the sideboard there were some boxes of vintage Meccano in pristine condition and several mismatched glasses and dishes. One of the drawers had linen napkins and another newspaper cuttings. Stella looked at a couple but they seemed to be random 'funny' stories and not the sort of thing she imagined the Munros collecting at all. The image of Jamie's great-great-grandfather, gazing sternly from his portrait, flashed across her mind. Perhaps he was a riot after a glass of sherry? She took the pile out of the drawer and put it into a folder to go through.

'Hello,' Jamie said, his voice slightly muffled. He was buried deep in a pile of bulging canvas sacks with drawstring tops, the posh equivalent of storing stuff in bin liners. He shuffled backwards out from the pile dragging a leather bag. It was dark brown and a bit bigger than a modern duffel.

'Kit bag?' Stella said, thinking of the wars, even as her brain told her that it was the wrong shape for one.

Jamie pulled the top open, revealing ingenious layers, with a variety of instruments nestled in felted compartments. 'Medical bag,' Stella said. She had an overwhelming urge to take the bag and run with it somewhere private; at the same time, she felt lightheaded and almost frightened.

Jamie held up a pair of callipers. Stella felt in the bottom of the bag and found a smooth rectangular box. Inside were a variety of scalpels. She shut the box and put it back.

'Did you know your grandfather was a doctor?'

'He wasn't,' Jamie said. 'This must be older.'

There were initials burned onto the side of the bag, in the bottom right-hand corner. 'J.W.L.'

'Definitely not your grandfather's dad, then,' Stella said. She traced the letters with her fingertips.

'I guess not,' Jamie said.

'Where did your family come from before Arisaig?' Stella said, unable to stop looking at the bag and its contents, no matter how queasy it made her feel.

'I don't know,' Jamie said. 'We've been here forever.'

'Not according to the folk I've spoken to. They say you're relatively new.' Stella touched a finger to a glass bottle with a length of rubber tube protruding from the stopper. 'And where did the money come from originally? To build this place?'

Jamie shrugged. 'I haven't the faintest idea. Slavery or something equally awful, I imagine.'

'Have you never wondered?'

'When I was wee I just accepted what we had. You know how it is, you think your family is just normal. And when I was older, I never felt part of this family. It never felt like my inheritance or destiny or anything like that so I didn't really think about it. I was just thinking about getting away from here, and once I did, I've been very happy not to think about it.'

'What about now? What's changed?'

Jamie put the callipers back into their place in the bag. 'I don't know. I've been so focused over the last few years, so sure of what I'm doing and what I want. Now I just feel a bit . . .' He broke off, looking embarrassed. 'I don't know.'

'Adrift?' Stella said.

He looked at her gratefully. 'Exactly.'

They took the bag downstairs and placed it on the dining table. It looked comfortable there, among the antique furniture. If Stella ignored Jamie's iPhone lying next to it, she could imagine she was back in time, waiting to see the doctor. She felt a rush of gratitude that she was not, in fact, about to submit to some leeches or whatever the hell those callipers had been used for.

'Water?' Jamie seemed distracted and Stella didn't want to step away from the bag. There was something magnetic there, something drawing her close. She opened it, gazing at the rows of instruments and lifting out the boxes and bottles from the base. It had an ingenious design, with the trays suspended above each other and a delicate cantilever system to move them over one another for easy access.

She ran one finger over the compartments and the edges of the bag. One of the trays had a small rectangular box, in a dark blue velvet, perfectly fitted to the tray. It was difficult to lever it out, but Stella managed to get her fingernails around the sides. The fuzzy surface of the box was at odds with the glass and metal utilitarian equipment. It was like a jewellery case, and Stella wondered if it had been placed in the bag by accident and she would find a necklace or brooch.

There was a buzzing in her ears and she realised that her vision had darkened at the edges and her heart was pounding. She lifted the hinged lid of the box and found four glass vials nestled in.

She stepped away from the bag and took deep breaths until her pulse calmed.

'Are you okay?' Jamie returned with two glasses of water, startling Stella out of her thoughts. The bag seemed much larger than it had a moment ago.

'Hmm?'

'Stella?'

'Who is J.W.L.?'

Jamie put the water down and turned the bag towards the light. Stella had to stop herself from batting his hands away. 'Is it definitely an "L"?'

'Lockhart,' Stella said quietly. 'Jessie's husband was a doctor named James Lockhart.'

Jamie looked at Stella as if she had grown a second head. 'You think this bag is James Lockhart's?'

'Why not?' Stella said. 'Jessie Lockhart's letters are in your family archive. Why not James's bag?'

'I suppose.' Jamie frowned. 'I just thought the letters were a bizarre mistake. Misfiled somewhere along the line.'

Since setting eyes on the bag, Stella's mind had been racing and one possibility seemed larger, more real than all the others. 'What if James Lockhart is your great-great-great-grandfather, James Munro?'

Jamie's frown deepened. 'Why would you think that?'

'He could have changed his name.'

'I think you know more about my family than I do,' Jamie said, shaking his head. 'But why would he have changed his name?'

'I don't know. A scandal of some kind? He was very combative with James Young Simpson and the medical establishment in Edinburgh. Maybe he got on the wrong side of someone important.'

'Mebbe.' Jamie traced the letters on the bag.

'How are you getting on with the journals?'

'Most of them are more recent, but I do have one of James Munro's. His name is on it and the dates are right, but there's not much in the way of personal detail,' Jamie said. 'It's all numbers and diagrams.'

Stella wanted to push Jamie's hand away from the bag. She didn't know why, but she felt even him looking at it was wrong. Her heart was thumping and, as she gazed at the bag, it got faster.

'Tea?' Mercifully, Jamie was walking in the direction of the kitchen door.

'Brilliant,' Stella followed him, and as soon as she was away from the bag, she felt her pulse slow to normal. She realised that Jamie had been speaking for some time and she hadn't heard a word. 'I'm sorry,' she said. 'Miles away.' The image of the scuffed leather bag sitting on the polished wood of the table just kept jumping into her mind. It seemed important and Stella didn't know why. She didn't know why she felt so frightened.

Jamie hit the switch on the kettle and got one of his disgusting green smoothies out of the fridge. 'I was asking if you would you like to have dinner with me tonight?'

'Are you cooking again?' Stella said, struggling to pull herself into the conversation.

'Could do. Or we could skip the food part and get straight to the red wine and sex.'

Well, that did the trick. He was refreshingly upfront, and it felt wonderful to be wanted. 'Why don't we go out tonight? We could go to the hotel restaurant.'

'I didn't realise you had a thing for doing it in public,' Jamie said.

'I'm being serious. I think it would be good for us to get out for a while, get away from the research.' And away from that bag.

He pulled a face. 'You know I don't—'

'I know,' Stella said, as gently as she could. She didn't want to be disappointed and wasn't even sure why she was pushing him. It was his life, he could live it the way he wanted. More to the point, there was no reason for him to make any kind of effort, and if she pushed him, she would just push him away. Maybe that was what she wanted, to hasten the end of the fling or whatever this was, before it could do any real damage.

'All right,' he said. 'Challenge accepted.'

It was a Saturday, but Stella hoped the hotel wouldn't be too busy. The boys were always in the bar on a Friday and, after all, none of them had that much money. Jamie opened the door for her, but she told him to choose a table, figuring that he would know where he would feel most comfortable. Stella went to the bar to get a gin and tonic and a glass of water.

The noise level in the room dropped, like a scene from an old western. The girl serving wasn't from the village and she seemed oblivious, but people were whispering and casting glances into the corner Jamie had chosen. Stella risked a look, too, and saw Jamie's stony expression.

Her stomach dipped. This had been a bad idea. She squared her shoulders and took their drinks to the table.

She sat side-on, wanting to be able to see what Jamie could see and not have her back to the room, hoping that if people knew she could see them, they wouldn't openly glare at Jamie. Stella had thought that she had built up good will in the village, that she had made real friends. Surely that would buy Jamie a bit of decency?

'Are you sure you don't want a proper drink?'

'I'm driving,' Jamie said.

'You don't have to, we can walk. Or you can have this.' Stella pointed to her untouched glass. 'I told you I'm happy to drive.'

Jamie shook his head and picked up his water.

'I want you to relax.'

He smiled tightly. 'I said I would take you for dinner, I never promised to relax.'

'This is true,' Stella said. She asked him about San Francisco, trying to get him talking and take his mind off being out of his comfort zone.

After fifteen minutes or so, Jamie stood up. 'Let's go.'

'What?'

'To the restaurant,' Jamie said. 'It's time.'

Relieved that he wasn't marching out, Stella followed Jamie across the hallway to the restaurant. She had glanced through the doorway but never been into the room. It was a good size with pleasant, light decor and modern wooden tables and chairs. The waitress who greeted them was smiley and she chatted as she seated them, asking if they were on holiday. Stella wondered if she was new or if she only ever worked on the restaurant side.

She was leading them to a table at one side of the room, but when they arrived Jamie didn't sit down. 'May we sit in the window, instead?'

'Um. I don't know, they might be booked.' She glanced over to the area Jamie was indicating. 'And they're tables for four people.'

'When I booked I asked for the best table. This is not the best table.'

'We don't really have a best—' she began.

'No.' Jamie held up a hand to stop her speaking. 'You mean you're not aware of the optimum positions for the tables and their relative merits. Which is a sign that you're not very experienced or very observant or particularly good at your job.'

'Jamie,' Stella said, trying to telegraph through the medium of glare that he should stop being an arse. To the girl, she said, 'I'm sorry.'

'No, it's okay. I'm sure it's fine for you to sit in the window.' She led the way to a large table and Jamie sat down.

As soon as the girl had left to fetch menus, Stella leaned forward. 'Why so rude?'

'I wasn't rude,' Jamie said. 'I was firm.'

'You told her she wasn't good at her job.'

'That was honesty. You're too nice.'

'I prefer my food not to come with a spittle garnish,' Stella said. 'And I don't like unprovoked attacks on people who earn minimum wage doing a difficult job.'

'It's hardly difficult.'

'It is when dealing with people like you,' Stella said. She paused while the girl brought their menus and resumed once she was out of earshot. 'Besides, how the hell would you know? I doubt you've ever waited tables or collected glasses in a pub.'

He looked around, and for a moment Stella thought he was going to get up and leave. Instead, he blew out a sigh. 'Fair point.' He flipped open the menu and began reading, not looking up.

Stella opened her own menu and tried to relax. When the waitress came back, looking nervous, she ordered hot-smoked salmon with new potatoes. Jamie asked for the same and a side salad, but not before interrogating the waitress on the origin of the fish, the vegetables provided and salad dressing options. Before the waitress could escape, Stella asked for a glass of red wine.

'Merlot or Cab Sauv?'

'Merlot, please.'

'What is the Merlot?' Jamie said.

'Um—'

'Never mind,' Jamie said, not smiling. 'I'll have some water.'

'I can find out . . .' the girl began.

'Just water will do, thanks.'

Stella sat back in her seat and regarded Jamie. It was as if the previous few weeks hadn't happened and she was back with the prickly, closed-off man she had first met. As the silence between them lengthened, Stella began to wonder why he had bothered to take her out at all. She opened her mouth to tell Jamie they should leave, that she had no interest in having dinner with him anymore, when she heard her name being called. She turned to see Stewart and a woman she didn't recognise.

'Hello, you,' she said, making to stand up.

'We won't disturb you,' he said, glancing at Jamie and then doing a double take. 'Bloody hell,' Stewart said. 'It's you.'

'You're not disturbing us,' Stella said at the same time as Stewart said, 'Long time no see,' staring at Jamie as if he'd seen a ghost.

Jamie stood up and held out a hand. 'Good to see you. Would you like to join us?'

Stewart paused and Stella held her breath, unsure whether he was going to take Jamie's hand or not. Eventually, he did, shaking it quickly and introducing his friend. 'This is Rebecca. We've got a table booked. Mebbe see you for a drink after, though. If you're still around.'

Stewart nodded to Stella and walked on, taking a table by the back wall of the room.

'Wow. So how long is it since you saw Stewart?'

'Long time,' Jamie said.

The waitress was back with their meals, and she placed Jamie's down without looking at him and departed hastily. Stella didn't blame the girl.

'We'll see them for a drink, though. You two can catch up properly.'

'I don't know the guy,' Jamie said. 'You don't catch up with someone you last saw playing tig.'

Stella unfolded the cloth napkin. 'I thought you came home to find your roots.'

'My family, yes. I don't know why you're so keen on me getting to know the whole village.'

'And I don't know why you're so resistant,' Stella said.

'Can we please talk about something else?' Jamie made a visible effort to lighten the mood. 'This is supposed to be a romantic evening.'

'Is that right?' Stella wasn't about to let the subject go that easily.

'Yes.' Jamie reached a hand across the table and caught her wrist, rubbing his thumb along the tender underside. 'And I want to talk about you.'

'I think we should talk about your book. I was reading an interview with the oldest person in Scotland, I thought you'd be interested.'

'I am interested. In Stella Jackson. Why has she fallen in love with this rain-soaked corner of Britain, not that I'm not grateful. What does she want, what can I do to make her happy . . . ?'

He was being charming. Ben had been charming and it had all been a lie. Making her happy had actually meant keeping her quiet while he got what he wanted and she wasted her time. She forced Ben from her mind and concentrated on Jessie Galant. 'Her name was Jessie, just like our Jessie, and she lived to one hundred and nine. She said the secret to her long life was staying away from men.'

Jamie released her hand and sat back, smiling. 'Well, I should be golden, then. I'm not much for the gents.'

'Ah, but I think it's different for men. Wasn't there that study that showed that married men lived longer than unmarried?'

He shook his head. 'I'm not much for marriage, either, I'm afraid.'

The jokey tone of the conversation took a sudden and unexpected dip. Stella blinked. It was ridiculous to be upset by a throwaway comment from a man she had known for a few weeks. Pain that Stella had been expecting for days drove in on a bus and sideswiped her.

'What?' Jamie stopped smiling. 'Christ. What did I say?'

'Nothing.' Stella shook her head. She was not going to cry in front of Jamie. Not in this restaurant. 'Sorry,' she said. 'Bit of a sore spot.'

He frowned. 'I don't—'

'Ben,' Stella said. May as well get it over with. 'We were engaged but he broke it off. He decided he wasn't for marriage, either. More accurately, he wasn't up for marriage with me. He met somebody else.'

'Oh,' Jamie said, visibly regrouping. 'I'm sorry.'

Stella took a healthy slug of her Merlot. 'We bought a house together, too. That's actually trickier to sort out than a broken engagement.' Stella mimed taking off a ring. 'That was pretty easy. Tears, removal of heirloom ring, fling ring back at boy. Done.'

'Was he unfaithful?' Jamie's face was stony.

'I don't know,' Stella said. 'Probably. The thing is' – she took another sip of her wine, fortifying herself – 'we weren't very compatible in the bedroom. We were best friends, really, and we had an agreement. If he'd just been honest and told me he wanted to have the physical stuff elsewhere, then we could have made it work.'

'You would have got married?' Jamie frowned.

'He loved me,' Stella said, certain it was true. 'He loved me very much and I loved him and we both thought it could work. We were lying to ourselves, and he realised it first.'

'You're being very reasonable.'

'I'm a very reasonable person.' Stella drained the last of her wine and looked in her bag for a tissue to blow her nose.

Jamie shook his head. 'I'd be furious.'

Stella blinked. 'Why angry?'

'How long were you together?'

'Six years. We got together in my last term of university. Before I had to drop out with my health issues.'

'And were you, um, compatible to start with?'

Stella shrugged. 'We met at an LGBT club and I assumed he wasn't interested in my gender. But we started going out and it was brilliant. We clicked. Stayed up all night talking, all those clichés.' Stella picked up her empty wine glass and then put it down again. She would be a mess if she carried on drinking at the same speed. 'And by the time I realised the sex side wasn't going to kick off, I was in love. And he always said it wasn't important to him, that it was just something he didn't crave.'

'I don't know what to say,' Jamie said.

'And I was fine with that. I might have known that we weren't perfectly matched in the bedroom, but we were best friends and he was going to give me what I wanted.'

'What did you want?'

'More clichés, I'm afraid. A home of my own. Children.' She smiled to show she knew she was pathetic, that she was laughing at herself. 'I told you I wasn't very interesting.'

'But why did you need him? You had a job, right? And there's always—'

'Don't say "sperm bank". I didn't just want a baby, I wanted the whole experience. Two parents. Two children. I wanted to be a mother, but in a certain way. And with a certain person. Ben has brilliant genes. We would have made excellent children together. He is nice-looking and healthy and intelligent.'

'That's a bit cold,' Jamie said.

'Why? What's wrong with being logical about this kind of thing? It's important enough, surely? I think it's good sense. And I did love him.' Stella said the words without thinking but she wasn't lying. The past tense felt true. 'I knew what I wanted and I felt as if I didn't have time to look for something better. I mean, I loved him and he loved me and we were a brilliant team. He was my best friend. Yeah, maybe there was some perfect other person who fancied me as well as all the rest, but what if . . .' Stella stopped herself from saying 'what if I died before I met them?' That was way too dramatic. Jamie was still her employer, as well as her . . . something else, whatever that turned out to be. And he was a perfectionist control-freak employer, at that. He didn't want to hear about her less-rational side.

'But why settle so young? I mean, if you were knocking on forty or something and your biological clock was getting loud, maybe—'

'I've always been very aware of how lucky I am to be alive, that's all.'

'Yeah, I feel that, too. Doesn't make me want a marriage of convenience, though.' Jamie was frowning at her, like he was trying to solve a puzzle. 'I mean, you're only twenty-five.'

'Twenty-six. And my parents were told I wouldn't see eight,' Stella said. 'The younger I have children, the more chance I have of seeing them safely into adulthood. I mean, I'll probably be fine, but I might not be. And I wanted to tip the odds in my favour.' Stella's throat had tightened and she looked away.

'I don't know what to say to that,' Jamie said.

'Tick tock,' Stella said. She pushed her plate away, pretty certain she wasn't going to eat anything else now. The wine was sloshing in her stomach and her eyes felt tight. She wanted to curl up under her duvet and sob. She knew she was out of practice with dating, but this was ridiculous. Tell the man you want babies and marriage. The international playboy who probably doesn't even believe in monogamy. *Good move, Stells.*

'I don't understand,' Jamie was saying. He actually looked worried. 'You're okay, aren't you? Did Alek find something?'

'I'm fine,' Stella said, wondering how many times she'd used those words. She summoned a smile. 'It's just a feeling I've always had, that I don't have much time.'

'Tick tock,' Jamie said, understanding on his face. 'You know, a very wise woman told me something once. "Feelings lie."'

Stella was trying to formulate an answer, something which would explain that she understood how to deal with illogical anxiety, but what about worry which was based in fact?

'Do you still feel that way?'

'About what?'

'Kids. Your life.'

'Yes,' Stella said. 'But I know I can't force it to happen. I didn't think I'd ever say this, but I'm glad that Ben called things off. It would have been a mistake.'

'Well, that sounds healthy. Do you mean it?'

'Almost,' Stella said. 'Right now. Might feel differently tomorrow. Or in an hour.'

Their waitress ran past, calling out before she reached her destination, 'Stewart! Alarm's gone!'

Moments later, Stewart rushed past. Stella reached out to grab his arm. 'What's wrong?'

'Lifeboat,' Stewart said and carried on walking.

The other diners were craning their necks, and an agitated murmur went around the room.

The waitress was back, delivering drinks to the next table. Stella turned in her chair. 'Excuse me? Do you know what's happened?'

The girl looked around and, seeing that everyone in the room was listening, raised her voice. 'Lifeboat call. Fishing boat radioed in an engine problem and then they lost contact. Hopefully it's just a false alarm.'

Stella turned back to Jamie.

'How could it be a false alarm?' Jamie had pushed his plate away, too.

'If the communication is broken, but the boat and crew are fine, I guess.'

'And if it isn't?'

'Then the lifeboat crew will do their job.'

'I didn't know Stewart did that,' Jamie said.

'And Doug,' Stella said. 'It's all volunteers from the area. They train and everything and then, when the alarm goes, they go out and risk their lives to save whoever is in trouble. It's properly heroic.'

Jamie asked the waitress for the bill. He went over to Stewart's table, where Rebecca was poking morosely at a salad. 'I'm sorry your evening has been ruined,' he said, gesturing to the empty place opposite and Stewart's barely touched food. 'May I get your bill? As a thank you to Stewart for the service he provides the community?'

Rebecca looked up at Jamie and smiled. 'Thanks. That's really nice of you.'

The waitress was back, with a sheet of tinfoil and a plastic tub. 'I'll get this parcelled up for Stewart for later. For when he gets back.' She laid a hand lightly on Rebecca's shoulder and then got busy wrapping.

Jamie came back to the table and sat down. 'How long are they usually out?'

Stella shrugged. 'I don't know.' She was trying not to think about Stewart clinging to the handrail on the boat as it bounced across the waves. Worse yet was the thought of somebody in the water, feeling the freezing pull as they hoped rescue came in time.

'Is there anything we can do?' Jamie said. 'Anything we're supposed to do?'

'I don't know,' Stella said. They went through to the bar and Stella saw Doug, looking unusually serious.

'Did you hear?' he said, putting his pint down and wiping his mouth.

'Stewart just left,' Stella said. 'I wonder how long he'll be.'

'I'm not on call,' Doug said, indicating his pint. 'I should be out there but I'm not on call so I've had a few and I can't go.'

'You are allowed to be off-duty, Doug,' Stella said gently.

'Aye, but even when Stew isn't on call, he's safe to go out, like.'

'Stewart doesn't drink,' Stella said to Jamie.

Doug nodded. 'If I was the same, I could be out there. I should be with the crew.'

'And you will be the next time the alarm goes and you're on call,' Jamie said.

Doug's eyes narrowed. 'What would you know about it?'

'Hey,' Stella said. 'Don't be—'

'Nothing,' Jamie said, staring right back at Doug.

Doug nodded as if satisfied and took a long pull of his pint.

'I hope it's a false alarm,' Stella said. 'Maybe they'll all be back soon.'

'It was just offshore. Alarm from a small fishing vessel near the rocks. Shouldn't be too long.' Doug crossed himself and reached over and rapped on the wooden table with his knuckles. 'Touch wood.'

'Shall we wait here? Or will Stewart go home?'

Doug's eyes widened a little as he looked at Stella. After a moment, he said, 'There's a call list. For when the boys get home. I can add you if you like.'

'Yes, please,' Stella said. She turned to Jamie. 'I can give my mobile, if you prefer, but the reception isn't very good.'

'No, landline is fine,' Jamie said, and he reeled off the number as Doug wrote it down.

Stella put her hand on Doug's arm but then realised she didn't know what to say. She smiled weakly and Doug nodded. He patted her hand. 'Stewart will be all right. He's been out on the boat loads of times.'

'I'm sorry about tonight,' Jamie said as they walked to the car.

'It's hardly your fault,' Stella said, thinking about the lifeboat out on the black water.

'I was really tense,' Jamie said. 'Kept thinking I was going to panic. And I wasn't showing my best side, which is annoying.'

Stella looked at him, and saw that he was watching her intently. 'Why?'

'Because I really want to show you my best side.'

Stella reached out and squeezed his hand. 'Apology accepted.'

He unlocked the car and held the passenger door open for Stella. The rain had eased, but the wind was bitterly cold and so strong that she felt it could lift her off her feet at any moment. She ducked gratefully into the car.

Jamie paused before starting the engine, staring out of the windscreen for a moment. 'I wonder who went out when my dad's boat got into trouble. Do you think the lifeboat tried to save them?'

'Most likely,' Stella said. 'Unless the alarm wasn't sounded for some reason. Do you want to know?'

'Yes,' Jamie said. 'I really do.'

'I can look into it. I bet the lifeboat folk keep a log. The crew who went out might even still be around.'

Back at the house, lights were blazing from several windows and Stella felt Jamie tense next to her. He went ahead, calling out: 'Esmé?'

Tabitha and Angus came rushing out, their frantic barking combining with the roaring wind.

Stella got the dogs inside and shut the door.

'Hello, children,' Nathan said, appearing from the kitchen with a sandwich in one hand and a glass of single malt in the other. 'I was wondering when you'd be back, I've been so bored.' His shrewd eyes were fixed on Jamie, but then he looked very deliberately at Stella. 'Working late, aren't we?'

'Not working,' Jamie said. 'How was Glasgow?'

Nathan made a see-saw motion with one hand. 'Up and down.'

'I bet,' Jamie said. He turned to Stella. 'Do you want anything to drink?'

'No, thanks,' Stella said. 'I'll leave you to catch up.'

She hadn't taken more than two steps before she felt Jamie's arm around her waist. 'Hang on.'

Nathan smirked and Stella wanted to throw something at him.

'I'll see you tomorrow, yeah?' Jamie said. 'Stella and I are on a date.'

'I think the mood might be somewhat broken,' Stella said.

'You're not going to sleep now, though, right?' Jamie said. 'Let's stay up together until we get the call.'

'The call?' Nathan said, looking interested.

'Lifeboat went out,' Jamie said. 'We're waiting to hear that it's back safely.'

Stella liked the 'we' in that sentence. It was nice to be a 'we' again, if only for one night. She went into the kitchen and put the kettle on for tea and Jamie followed, getting mugs from the cupboard and milk from the fridge. 'Will we hear the phone?'

'Definitely,' Jamie said. 'But I've a spare phone that I can plug in upstairs. There's a socket in my bedroom.'

Stella carried two mugs of tea upstairs and she and Jamie sat on top of the duvet on his bed, pillows piled against the headboard, and played cards to pass the time. They didn't talk about the lifeboat and Stella was glad. She felt like she was in suspended animation, just waiting to hear that Stewart and the rest were back safely.

After a couple of hands of rummy, Jamie said, 'I've been thinking about Ben.'

'You've been thinking about my ex-fiancé?'

'Yes.' Jamie put his cards down and took her hand. 'I'm sorry if I upset you.'

'You didn't,' Stella said.

'But just because you two weren't compatible, doesn't mean you're not going to have that. Have it all. I mean, look at us. Definite chemistry there.'

Stella smiled to soften her words. 'Bit of the opposite issue there, though. I don't suppose you're looking for marriage and babies.'

He frowned. 'That's a bit—'

'It's none of my business,' Stella said quickly. 'I just don't think it's as easy as you think to find the perfect relationship.'

'I don't think it's easy. I just think that it is going to happen for you, that you don't need to worry.'

Stella wanted to ask why, on what evidence, but she knew he was just being nice.

'There's something that I ought to tell you, though.'

Stella forced herself to look at him. He was going to say that last night had been a mistake. That he liked her but not in that way. That they should just be friends.

'I don't usually have exclusive relationships. I mean, this one is exclusive at the moment, but—'

'You are barely leaving the house,' Stella finished.

'Yes. I believe in being honest and I don't want you to have any illusions about me and relationships. I don't believe in monogamy,' Jamie said, not meeting her eye.

'You don't think it exists?' Stella kept her voice neutral. This was exactly what she deserved for telling the man that she wanted marriage and babies. She ought to be grateful he was still speaking to her.

'For some people, I guess,' Jamie was saying. 'Just not for me. And not for most people if they were really honest.' He picked up his wine glass and took a fortifying sip. 'Marriage is a social construct. Historically it had to do with the transfer or acquisition of assets, the control of power. Now it's still useful to cement family units for child-rearing and asset-sharing. I mean, lots of my friends in the Bay couldn't make their rent on their own so it's a flatmate or a partner, and a partner is often preferable.'

Stella kept quiet, thinking about the mortgage back in London.

'So I think people make a compromise. They choose security or power or money or comfort, whatever, and are willing to trade their sexual and romantic freedom for those things.'

'What about love?'

'Ah, well. I think love fades. I've been in love dozens of times but it never lasts. Soon there are doubts and annoyances and I can't help thinking about what I'm missing out on and wondering if that girl or that girl would be a better match.'

'You haven't been in love,' Stella said decisively.

Jamie smiled. 'You have no idea how many women have said that to me. I don't agree. I just think I'm too rational to fall for the promise of an all-conquering emotion. Emotions are fickle. They change. They can be changed by a good meal or a long fast or a good fuck.'

'Surface feelings change,' Stella said, ignoring the blush she could feel in her cheeks. 'There are deeper ones. Ones which aren't so easily moved.'

He shrugged. 'I don't agree.'

'You're just like a child,' Stella said.

Jamie raised his eyebrows. 'How so?'

'Monogamy is for grown-ups. It's for truly rational people who understand that you cannot have a deep and meaningful bond with another human without it.'

'With respect, that's a little naive. There are successful polygamous relationships. Some good friends of mine have been together for two years, and there are three in the relationship.'

'Well, maybe, but I think that is the exception rather than the rule for a good reason. A monogamous partnership is about trust and about being a team. I want to be on a team where two people back each other every time. The rules of that team can be individually tailored to suit the people involved, but there have to be rules and the team has to be special. Nobody else allowed.'

'Well, that does sound nice. In theory—'

Stella cut across him. 'Do you know what I think when you say that you don't believe in monogamy? I think you are a greedy person with no self-control who has the childish belief that you can play with all the toys in the shop at once, but are also continually dissatisfied that you can physically only hold two at any time. I think you are always looking over to the next shelf, the next aisle, wondering what you are missing out on, and so a polygamous relationship or playing the field or whatever is going to suit you the best. It doesn't mean that you aren't flawed. Or that you aren't missing out on a truly profound, loving relationship.'

'You could be right,' Jamie said. He wasn't smiling any longer. 'I do wonder whether I'm missing out.' He looked physically pained and Stella realised that he truly meant it. The idea of missing out on a good experience or, worse still, the ultimate experience, was horrifying to him.

'It must be exhausting being you,' Stella said, with feeling.

'It really is,' Jamie said, but then he broke into a grin.

Stella was about to ask him how he could be so cheerful when the phone rang. Stella dived across the bed to pick it up and a female voice she didn't recognise said, 'Crew is back safely, no problems.'

'Oh, that's wonderful,' Stella said, feeling the tension rush from her body. 'Thank you for letting us know.'

After relaying the news to Jamie and sharing a relieved smile, Stella got up from the bed to go to her own room.

'Wait. You're leaving?'

'I thought you just gave me the break-up speech,' Stella said, keeping her voice light.

'No,' Jamie said, frowning. 'I gave you the honesty speech. So that we can start things out right.'

Stella knew there was no point starting anything at all with a man who didn't believe in love or monogamy. He couldn't give her any of the things she wanted. Then again, she had chosen Ben for exactly that reason, and look how that had turned out.

'I have no idea what the future holds and I don't want to make any promises except that I will be honest. I have no interest in anybody else right now and no plans to go looking. I really like you and we're at the brilliant beginning where all I want to do is rip your clothes off. If you feel the same way, I vote we enjoy it while it lasts and not worry about the other stuff until we have to.'

Well, that sounded good in theory. Until you're sat on the bathroom floor sobbing, with your heart ripped out of your chest.

'I know you're still recovering from your break-up and this is probably just a rebound thing, but I'm okay with that.'

'I bet,' Stella said, with more heat than she intended.

'But I hope it's more than that,' he said.

'Okay.' Stella stood still, halfway to the door. Unable to move to either the safety of the hall or towards Jamie and the massive unknown he represented.

He stood up and crossed the room, putting a hand on the curve of her jaw and tilting her face to his. 'Are you going to take a risk?'

Stella put her hand on his cheek, feeling the scrape of his stubble and feeling the kick of desire in her stomach. She thought about saying yes, but then went on tiptoe to kiss him instead. She pressed herself against him and felt his arms tighten in response.

The kiss deepened, opening a black hole of mindless sensation and need, and she let herself fall into it.

CHAPTER SEVENTEEN

1st November, 1848

My dearest Mary,

Mr Simpson refused to visit. Apparently Mr Lockhart had been very rude to him on previous occasions and had written scurrilous articles. I had no idea and feel quite embarrassed. Worse still, my husband has decreed that I must dress in old clothes and go to Mr Simpson's house alone, presenting myself as a different person in the hope that he will see me. I know that Mr Lockhart is desperate for a view into the interior world of Mr Simpson and of the way he practices obstetrics, but what he thinks I will be able to reveal by being examined is beyond my ken.

To prepare for the role, he has bade me be counselled in the ways of the underclass by my maid, and has showed me anatomical illustrations from which I may never recover. I am feart J.Y.S. will see through my disguise and become angry. I am feart that he will not and that I must submit to his treatment when I have never been tended to by any other than our dear Dr Laird or my own husband. I wish with all my heart that I was not a married lady but a girl again. At home in Haddington, picking blaeberries with you and paddling in the burn.

I will stop writing now and continue another day, when I hope to have better news. I will wait before sending this letter, as I do not wish to worry you but, more truthfully still, Mr Lockhart believes I write too often and I fear he will stop me from sending two messages instead of one.

Mary,

I have seen the great man. I must not refer to him that way in front of my husband, but I may tell you how kind and comforting he was. He says that everything is progressing perfectly well and that he felt no abnormalities or cause for alarm when he examined me. I almost gave myself away by asking after my uterus, not a word commonly used, but managed to cough instead. He said for me to send word when my time was near and not to go to the hospital unless absolutely necessary. He said that if I keep a clean home, I am better off there. I will be sent to the hospital by my husband, I know. Although he won't be able to guarantee that it is J.Y.S. who attends me.

I know that I must not let fancy take hold, but I feel terror when I awake and when I lie alone at night. The babe moves but I am frightened it will never draw breath. I feel a horrible foreboding and no amount of prayer helps. Mr Lockhart gives me nerve medicine but it does not help my mood. I must try harder to think of pleasant things.

Your loving Jessie

Dearest Mary,

Good news! I am to be allowed to deliver at home. My husband seems to have given up his idea to spy upon Mr Simpson and has a new light in his eyes. He looks five years younger! He believes that he has a new way to prevent childbed fever and wants me to be the guinea pig. I have told him that if it will help his research, I am willing. In truth, I am feart, but if the experiment is a success, it could save thousands of lives. Imagine that, Mary! Thousands of women alive because of one little experiment. I know that the achievement would be Mr Lockhart's, but it is nice to think that I would have played a small part. Besides, Mr Lockhart assures me that I would be in no danger and that he would never let any harm befall his 'little dove'. How can I refuse?

After the babe is born, Mr Lockhart will prescribe an ointment for the afflicted areas and I am to get up as soon as possible. Mr Lockhart believes that the reason there are so many cases of childbed fever is because women are forced to remain in the childbed for so long. He says it is the common factor (other than the birth, of course, and he cannot very well remove that from the equation) . . .

Stella looked up from the letter. It was the last one in the bundle and it stopped abruptly as if Jessie had finished writing and had never had the chance to finish. She had barricaded herself in her office to get some work done, knowing that if she saw Jamie she would be distracted.

The cardboard archive box which had held the bundles of letters had a slew of photographs in the bottom, and a few oddments such as a tarnished medal with threadbare ribbon and a ticket stub from a dry cleaners in Livingston, dated 1962.

Jamie had abandoned James Munro's journal, saying something about looking closer to home. Stella knew the lifeboat had sent his mind back to his parents and she hoped that he found something of comfort. He had barely been out of his teens when the accident had happened, and away at university. It must have had an enormous effect, but at that age you kind of accepted that the grown-ups knew what they were doing. It made sense that being back at Munro House had stirred up memories, but Stella feared there was nothing good for him to find. She wished he would stay focused further in the past, where his ancestors seemed to have been inventors and experimenters, and anything personal was too far removed to have any emotional impact.

Stella began putting things away in the box, laying the journal on top of the photographs; then, knowing she didn't have anything else to do, she took it out again and began leafing through. Jamie was right. It was all diagrams and lists of numbers. The name in the front was James Munro and then a squiggly signature, repeated a few times, as if he had been practising it.

The binding was soft with age and a few pages were loose. Stella took them out and smoothed them down, tucking them back into the book as best she could. As she did so, she realised that one of the pages was a different colour and thickness to the others. It was another letter:

Mary,

I am very weak now, and the light hurts my eyes. I cannot get a breath and can hardly remember the wee girl who went blaeberry picking with you. I know I had my baby as my stomach is no longer full and swollen. I feel the loss like an empty room, but a room which was once beloved and warm and now sits cold and unused. I think I had a baby girl. Mr Lockhart will not speak to me of it. He will not speak to me. I know this letter will not be sent and that you will not read it. He will read it. And then he will place a cloth over my face and hold it there until I sleep. Maybe this time I will sleep and not wake up. I am swimming deep underwater and I cannot see the surface. I cannae rise.

The writing was so small it was difficult to read. Jessie had filled every available space on the paper, as if there were a shortage, or she felt it was her very last piece.

Dear Mr Wood,
As you can see from the enclosed, written in Jessie's hand, your daughter is unwell. She has become confused and violent and I am forced to treat her with calming tinctures for her own comfort and safety. I did not send this letter at first as I thought to protect you and your family from the horrors of her condition. I only relay it now to demonstrate that Jessie is receiving only the very best care that money can buy. Rest assured, I will do anything to make my precious wife well again. As her husband, this is my responsibility and one I will not shirk. I ask that you respect our privacy at this difficult time and I will send word the very moment there is improvement. I understand that you are anxious to see your daughter, but I must insist that you do not visit as you suggested. Jessie is at a very delicate stage in her treatment and any upset to her routine could be disastrous.
Yours, J. W. Lockhart

Jamie knocked on the door and walked in. 'Coffee?' he said, and then, seeing Stella's face, 'What's wrong?'

'She had the baby,' Stella said. 'But she was very ill after. I don't think she survived. James Lockhart wrote to her father, anyway, and that's the last letter. If she had survived there would be more, wouldn't there?'

Jamie reached out and touched her hand. 'Mebbe they were lost.'

Stella wanted to cry. 'I don't know why I'm so upset. It all happened so long ago. I don't even know the woman,' she added unnecessarily. Of course she didn't know Jessie. But she felt as if she did. Jessie had been brave, had been determined to help her husband with his research, to do something good in the world even though she was a woman and had limited options.

Stella felt her breath catch, the familiar hitch as she tried to fill her lungs.

'Do you want me to check the journals? I can let you know if Jessie is mentioned again. Or her child.'

Stella nodded, not trusting herself to speak. The paper felt thin and soft in her fingers, as if it might disintegrate at any moment.

And then what would be left of Jessie Lockhart?

Nothing at all.

'At least she had a baby,' Jamie said. 'Perhaps they survived. Perhaps she lived on in that way.' The words sounded awkward, forced, but Stella appreciated the effort. He hovered awkwardly, clearly uncertain, and then headed for the door. 'I'll get you some tea.'

'No. I'm fine. Thanks.' Stella just wanted to be alone.

She wondered if Jessie really had been out of her mind. The cramped writing certainly looked like the hand of a disturbed person, and it was a world away from the gentle slopes of the early letters. There were more ink stains than usual, too, as if Jessie hadn't had blotting paper or a good surface to lean on. She had likely written it in bed, of course, but perhaps her husband had refused to provide her with the tools she needed. Stella felt a spurt of anger on Jessie's behalf. She couldn't help thinking that her husband had probably discouraged her from writing at all. As she looked, Stella felt the handwriting looked less and less disordered and more intense.

A word – 'help' – jumped from what Stella had thought was a large ink splatter. The word was at right angles to the rest of the sentence, and Stella turned the paper to read it better. At once, the marks between the lines, which she had taken as mistakes or nonsense words in among the cramped sentences, appeared as legible writing. Tiny, yes, and sometimes skew-whiff, winding crossways between the horizontal lines, but readable. Stella fetched the magnifying glass Jamie had been using and used it to follow the lines as best she could.

Help me. I am trapped here. He will not let me up. I hear my baby cry but I cannae see. I am feart we will not see each other again. Find my baby. Tell her that her mama loved her.

Stella felt her skin trying to crawl from her body. She thought of Jessie frightened and helpless. Sick and in pain and wishing for her family. She realised that she was holding her breath and forced herself to stop. She would make tea after all, or take a walk. Anything to disperse this nervous energy.

On her way, she passed Jamie's office and his door was open. He was sat in front of his computer, more still than she had ever seen him, and the sight made her pause. 'Jamie?'

He looked around, his expression bleak.

'What's wrong?' Stella stepped into the room, wanting to put her arms around him.

'Did you know that you can look up criminal trials online?'

Stella took another step closer. 'No, why—'

'I found James Lockhart,' Jamie said, and Stella felt a jolt in her chest. 'He was put on trial for the murder of his wife, Jessie.'

'Jesus Christ,' Stella said, feeling weak.

'He wasn't found guilty. It was recorded as "not proven", but I guess the trial ruined his reputation. He disappeared from Edinburgh soon after it was over.' His mouth twisted. 'There was a very helpful piece in *The Scotsman* all about the scandal.'

Stella felt her legs buckle, and she sank to the floor to sit cross-legged before she fell down.

Jamie was up immediately and by her side. 'What is it?'

Stella swallowed hard. 'Your great-great-great-grandfather maybe murdered his wife. Don't you find that upsetting?'

'Yes, of course.' His voice was tight.

'I don't understand why Jessie's letters are in your family's archive, though. Surely those would be with Mary. Passed down through her branch of the family.' Stella felt strange, like she was standing on the edge of a cliff. She closed her eyes and could see water boiling below, a swirling vortex. What was it called in Scotland? A corrie?

'Put your head down.' Jamie's hand was on the back of her neck, pushing gently.

Stella obliged and felt her mind clear, the crashing waves receding.

'James Lockhart left Edinburgh in disgrace in 1849, the same year that James Munro arrived in Arisaig carrying a medical bag with J.W.L. stamped on the side and a bundle of letters from Jessie Lockhart.'

'Don't,' Stella said. 'I feel sick.'

Jamie sat on the floor and put his head very gently against Stella's. 'I guess he collected the letters from Mary when he took the baby to her. He did a swap.' Jamie's voice was very quiet, thoughtful. 'That's what I would do in his situation. After the trial he didn't want any evidence of his wife's state of mind to be circulated, opening up questions or being used against him. He offered Mary the care of her sister's child in return for the letters and her keeping quiet. Or mebbe he did it before the trial, to stop the letters coming to light during it. Mebbe before he was arrested, if he knew it was going to happen.'

Stella was only half listening. Her hand was on her chest and her heart stuttering. 'You think the baby survived?'

'I hope so,' he said. 'And if so, leaving it with Jessie's sister or some other family makes sense. James Munro didn't arrive at Arisaig with a baby. At least, not as far as we know.' Jamie was peering at her, concerned. 'Okay?'

'Fine,' Stella lied. The revelations had been too much, too sudden, and her mind was only just beginning to catch up. However, one piece of information floated to the top: Jamie Munro was descended from the man who killed Jessie Lockhart.

'I've got to go,' Stella said. 'I need fresh air.'

'I'll come,' Jamie said, reaching for his jacket.

'No,' Stella said, the word coming out more strongly than she intended. 'I just need a bit of time on my own.'

Stella left the dogs in the house, feeling guilty. She walked briskly up the road, trying to ignore the biting cold. The lights of the Arisaig Inn were too inviting to resist and Stella opened the door to the welcome warmth and the sound of voices.

It was past the lunchtime rush and Stella got herself a small red wine and a seat next to the wood burner. She pulled her mobile out of her pocket and checked for a signal. Mercifully, one bar was showing and she began composing a text to Caitlin, striving for the right words to convey a casual-but-urgent invitation to the pub. Caitlin would know what to do. Even when they were both clueless teenagers, Caitlin had always known the right thing to do in any given situation. And if there was nothing that could be done, Caitlin had always known exactly what to say to make Stella feel better. Whether it was bad news from the hospital or Joshua bloody Cooper telling her that he had only gone to the cinema with her on her seventeenth birthday because he had felt sorry for the 'sick girl', Caitlin had always managed to make it okay, make the pain manageable. Stella took a calming sip of wine before pressing 'send', but was interrupted when a woman slid into the seat opposite and held out a hand. 'You're Stella, right?'

'Yes,' Stella said, surprised into putting her phone down and shaking the woman's hand.

'Aileen McCartney. Can I get you a drink?'

'I'm fine, thanks,' Stella said, trying to work out if she'd met the woman before. She looked vaguely familiar, but in a place like this you tended to see the same faces.

'I wanted to have a wee chat about your job.'

'I'm sorry—' Stella began, but the woman cut across her.

'You work for Jamie Munro, right?'

'Yes, but—'

Aileen's face suddenly fell into a sympathetic expression. She put a hand on Stella's arm. 'I was so sorry to hear about Esmé. Is she back at the house yet?'

'No,' Stella said. 'She's staying with her sister for a while.'

'Recuperating?' Aileen said. She had a soft Glaswegian accent and eerily perfect make-up. Her nails were smooth ovals, shiny with pale-blue gel polish. The colour was oddly disturbing, but Stella couldn't work out why. Then it came to her – they reminded her of her own fingertips when she had oxygen deprivation. Sexy.

'Having a holiday,' Stella said.

'The police haven't closed the case against Mr Munro yet, have they?'

'What?' Unease spread through Stella. 'I'm sorry, how do you know Esmé?'

'It is a bit suspicious. Are there a lot of dangerous substances left lying around the house?'

'I beg your pardon?' Stella said.

'You are perfectly placed to give your side of the story. Or Mr Munro's side, if you prefer. He could really use a friend right about now. You could be that friend.'

'Which paper are you from?' Stella said flatly.

'*Record*,' Aileen said. 'Jamie Munro is a Scottish success story; we've got no interest in dragging his name through the mud. If you agreed to talk about what it's like to work with him, his daily routine, things like that, it would show his human side. Offset things, provide balance.'

'Balance for what?'

Aileen narrowed her eyes. '*He's still a suspect, you know.*'

'No comment,' Stella said.

'There is money to be made here,' Aileen said.

'I'm not interested, thanks.'

Why had she added 'thanks'? Bloody British politeness.

The woman leaned forward and tucked her business card into Stella's jacket pocket. 'Just in case,' she said. 'Times change.' And then she actually winked.

As soon as the journalist had left the bar, Stella got up and followed her to make sure she was leaving. She stood underneath the porch canopy at the main entrance and watched Aileen get into a silver car. She started the engine, but didn't pull away. Instead she hauled a bag across from the back seat and began looking through it.

The thick mist that everybody called 'smirr' had rolled in from the sea loch, and Stella felt her clothes soaking through with the freezing damp. The phone signal was strongest outside, so she tensed against the cold and, with one eye on Aileen, called Caitlin. 'Did you give my name to a journalist from the *Record*?'

'No,' Caitlin said quickly. ''Course not.'

Aileen was tapping quickly with both thumbs into her smartphone. Stella wondered how long she was going to wait in her car, and whether she would go back into the pub and try to find other people to speak to about Jamie. 'How did they know where to find me? Or what I looked like?'

'She could have asked anyone,' Caitlin said. 'Everyone talks around here. Anybody could have pointed you out.'

Stella closed her eyes. 'How did you know she was female?'

Silence. Then: 'Sorry, Stells. I'm really sorry.'

'I don't understand,' Stella managed. 'Why?'

There was another pause. 'Rob suggested it.' Caitlin's voice was very quiet. 'You know money is tight and Rob doesn't think much of Jamie—'

Something hit Stella. Her thoughts began to whirl. 'Is this why you were so keen for me to come and stay. To go for this job? So that I could feed you stories to sell?'

There was another silence and Stella felt her world tilt.

'I wanted to tell you,' Caitlin began, but Stella stabbed the button to cut the call. She switched her phone off for good measure, her fingers numb and clumsy from the cold. She pushed the phone into her jeans pocket and bounced on the balls of her feet. A sudden rush of energy made her want to move, but the journalist, Aileen, was still sat in her car. Stella hesitated for a split second longer and then crossed the car park and rapped on the window. Aileen jumped a little, which gave Stella a moment of satisfaction. The electric window whirred as it opened. Aileen looked up, her expression pleased. 'You want to chat?'

'Not for any amount of money,' Stella said. 'Although I do have one thing to say.' She leaned down, bringing her face close to the other woman's. 'Back off.'

Stella straightened and walked back to the pub.

Inside, the sudden burst of energy drained away and she sank into her seat, feeling shaky. Her half-full glass of red wine was still on the table and she took a long sip.

'All right, hen?' Stewart ambled across the room. He put a bowl full of ice cream on the table in front of him. There were at least three scoops, with whipped cream and little cubes of fudge sprinkled over the top. Whoever thought being teetotal was healthy clearly hadn't met Stewart.

'Not really,' Stella said, blinking back tears. 'Did you see that woman just now?'

'Blonde one with the daft shoes?'

'Yes. Please don't talk to her about me. Or Jamie.'

He frowned. 'I wouldn't.' He stopped. 'What do you mean?'

'Sorry. I know,' Stella said. 'She might offer you money, though.'

'Journalist?' he said, understanding dawning.

Stella nodded.

'Well, I won't, but I cannae vouch for everyone. Times are—'

'Tough,' Stella interrupted, thinking angrily of Caitlin. 'I know.'

'You want some of this?' Stewart said, pushing the bowl towards her.

Stella put her hand on his arm. 'Thank you.'

Stewart's ears went pink. 'It's only pudding, hen.'

CHAPTER EIGHTEEN

Stella was hoping for a quiet morning and some more time to think things through before she saw Jamie. She was still reeling from the revelation that the Munro curse went back a very long way.

She knew it wasn't helpful to think of it in that way, but bad news seemed to have stalked the family for a long time, and Jamie's ancestor had been in such dark trouble that he had changed his name to try to escape it. It was a revelation that had kept her in the pub yesterday after the journalist had left. She felt sad, too, about Jessie. That her bravery had amounted to nothing. She had been stoic in the face of fear and pain and she had still died.

It didn't matter how brave you were. It didn't matter whether you wailed and cried or smiled nicely, your body did not care. You could do everything right and take every precaution and your body might still betray you.

While Ben and Rob and Caitlin were happily living their student lives, going to lectures and pub crawls, writing essays late into the night and holding fancy dress parties to celebrate the end of every set of exams, Stella had found it increasingly difficult to make the trip from her parent's house into university. Her head felt fuzzy and the facts she so desperately craved seemed to pass through her mind, finding no purchase. She began to fall asleep while studying. And then on the train, during lectures, and at the family dinner table, waking with a start to see her parents exchanging worried glances. It had been so gradual that she couldn't pinpoint exactly when 'a bit tired and breathless' had become exhaustion. When the strange, stuttering beat in her chest had become a constant companion, and the dizzy spells no longer only came when she walked upstairs.

Lying on the bed in the warm, darkened room of the cardiac radiologist, with the whooshing sounds of the equipment and the jelly spread across her chest, Stella hadn't felt frightened. Having survived heart surgery as a baby and having had her congenital heart defects miraculously fixed, there could not be anything else wrong. Fate could not be that cruel.

Of course, fate had nothing to do with it and Stella's heart did not know or care what she was feeling. A valve that had worked extra hard while it was still growing had simply not formed quite as it should. It was flapping when it should have been firmly closed, weakly waving a distress signal. That knowledge was a few hours away then, though; it was something that Stella would discover in the bright light of her consultant's office. As Stella lay in the dark and listened to the strange underwater Doppler sounds of her systole and diastole as the ultrasound probe pressed insistently against her ribcage, she passed the time by silently thanking her heart for beating, and hoping, hoping, hoping.

'Are you all right?' Jamie's voice cut through her thoughts.

Stella had been making coffee, but now she realised that she had been stood holding the packet and staring out of the window above the sink.

'Fine,' Stella said.

Jamie looked as if he wanted to ask something else and Stella spoke quickly to head off the possibility. 'How are you doing?'

He held up a hand, flat, and tilted it from side to side. 'I want to know more about my parents' accident.'

'Right.' Stella couldn't look at him directly. Truthfully, she didn't want to think about his father, not after everything she had heard in the village. But she didn't blame him for turning his attention from James Lockhart.

'Will you help me?' Jamie sounded so lost that Stella found her resolve to stay away from him, away from the Munro family, dissipate like mist. It wasn't his fault, after all. You couldn't help what you were born with.

❦

Stewart was meeting them at the lifeboat station and they parked in the centre and walked down to the harbour. After the off-season quiet of Arisaig, Mallaig was full of hustle and bustle. Stella found herself thinking it was busy and laughed inside; the old Stella had been used to the crowds of London, would have thought Mallaig was a dead village.

The sky was a solid slab of grey cloud and the wind coming off the sea was bitterly cold. It ruffled their waterproof jackets like it was trying to find a way in, and Stella pulled on a knitted hat and put her hood up for good measure.

'You look like an Eskimo,' Jamie said.

'Inuit,' Stella corrected automatically, and Jamie's smile grew wider.

'Cute and clever. You are the complete package, right enough.'

Stella wasn't sure if he was laughing at her or with her, but she smiled anyway, glad that he seemed in good spirits. He definitely seemed more comfortable with leaving the estate, had driven out in his monster four-by-four to walk through Glen Beasdale just the day before, but he still avoided populated places.

He seemed determined not to talk about the purpose of their trip and he kept up a running commentary of jokes and bits of local information. 'That's where the CalMac ferry comes in. We should go over to the islands sometime. You would love them.'

The RNLI station office was above a shop selling souvenirs and second-hand books in aid of the charity. It hit Stella how precarious the lifeboat service was. Not only was it run by volunteers who risked their lives every time they went out on the boat, but it was funded by donations.

Stewart had told them to ring the bell on the door next to the entrance to the shop, so that's what they did. Moments later he opened the door, a paper bag with grease spots in one hand.

'Come away in,' Stewart said. The stairs were narrow and covered in thin industrial carpet that was peeling away from the edges. Attempts had been made on a couple of the steps to stick it back down with black tape.

The office contained an ancient-looking computer with a bulky monitor, a tall metal filing cabinet and piles of paperwork. Jamie had gone quiet and Stella chatted to Stewart, thanking him for helping them out.

'We keep a log of all call-outs,' Stewart said, sitting in front of the computer and bringing the screen to life. 'But I'm not sure if they had moved to the computer system at that time. What was the year?'

'2008,' Stella said when Jamie didn't answer.

'Aye, should be here, then.' Stewart tapped the keys and then said, 'Got it.'

He stood up and gestured to the chair, but Jamie waved at Stella, indicating that she should take the seat. Stella sat down, conscious of Jamie standing behind her, and read the words on the screen. There was the date, the time of the call-out and a link to the report.

Stella clicked on it and then scanned the information. She had both hoped and feared the report, wondering how much detail would be recorded and how traumatic it might be. In the end, it was just the bare facts. The time the call came in. The time of the lifeboat launch. The time the mission was declared over. The time the boat returned to the station.

Stella looked at Jamie. 'Does that help?'

He shook his head, his face tight.

'Is that an unusual length of time?' Jamie asked, his voice very quiet. 'They were out for four hours.'

'It's a wee while,' Stewart said. 'But normal in a search scenario.'

'Are there guidelines on how long to look before calling off a search?'

'Oh, aye,' Stewart said. 'I've never done one myself, but they can go on for days. Different call-outs. And other agencies get involved, too.'

'Why did they stop looking? It doesn't seem long enough.'

'Mebbe the coastguards took over. The lifeboat is an emergency service.'

'You mean they weren't looking for survivors anymore?'

Stewart looked uncomfortable. 'People don't last that long in the water. Not as a rule.'

'And that's them lost?' Jamie said. 'Forever.'

Stewart studied his Danish pastry for a moment, then he said, 'They usually wash up eventually.'

'My God,' Stella said.

'My folks didn't though,' Jamie said. He sounded perfectly calm. 'That's unusual then?'

'I don't know,' Stewart said. 'Debris gets caught in the tides around the islands, but not everything. Some things slip through and end up out in the ocean.'

Jamie nodded. 'I suppose there will be a list of unidentified remains somewhere. Where would that be?'

'Coroner?' Stewart said. 'But if your folks had washed up, they wouldn't have stayed unidentified.'

'How so?'

'DNA,' Stewart said. 'Dental records. Clothing scraps.'

'What if they'd been in the water a long time. Years.'

'Well, then.' Stewart shrugged. 'I'm no expert.'

Jamie closed his eyes. 'I hoped this would tell me why they went out.'

'How do you mean?'

'She hated the water,' Jamie said, his eyes still closed. 'My mother would never have gone out in the boat. Especially not in bad weather.'

'It might have sprung up. Unexpected.' Stewart pointed at a print-out on the top of a pile of papers. 'The forecasts are good, like, but we can all get surprised sometimes.'

'Is there a record of the crew on the first call-out?' Jamie said. 'Mebbe if I could speak to someone who was there.'

Stewart nodded. 'I'll check.'

Stella stood up and Stewart took the chair again. She wandered around the room, looking at the tide tables and the thank-you letters that were stuck next to the nautical navigation chart for Mallaig Harbour.

'Rob Baird,' Stewart said. 'Well, he's definitely still about.' Stewart was smiling, pleased to have a positive result. 'I had no idea he had been out on that run. Must've been still at school.'

'Is that legal?' Stella said, imaging a teenager out on the freezing cold sea, the waves high.

'Seventeen for the boat crew, as long as they have parental permission. Young is good. It's bloody hard work.'

'Rob Baird,' Jamie said. 'I had no idea.'

Stella felt the sinking of her heart as she anticipated his next question.

'Do you think he'll talk to me about it?'

'I don't know,' Stella said. 'He's not your biggest fan.'

Stewart finished the last flakes of his pastry and screwed up the paper bag, throwing it across the room so that it bounced off the wall and into the bin. 'I'll talk to him, if you like?'

'Thank you,' Stella said.

Jamie nodded, still looking preoccupied. 'Can I have a printout of that?' He indicated the screen with the list of timings from his parents' accident.

'Sure . . .' Stewart began tapping at the keys again.

They left the harbour buildings with a single sheet of paper folded into a square, and a source who certainly wasn't going to be in the mood to be helpful. Worse, Stella was worried that Rob might be harsh, and give painful details just to hurt Jamie.

She was shocked at that thought and she examined it in her own mind, turning it over. Did she really think Rob would do that? Maybe. He was full of surprises, after all.

Jamie was quiet, too. He held Stella's hand, but seemed very distant. They had been raking up the past for the last few weeks but this, his parents' accident, seemed fresh in comparison, like it had only happened a month or two ago. Stella tried to imagine what it must have been like to lose both of his parents in one go like that. And in such sudden, shocking circumstances. Jamie had said that he had been away at school and then university and that they hadn't been very close, but still. Then it hit her.

Jamie was missing the most obvious source of information. 'Have you asked Esmé about the accident?'

He didn't answer her right away and Stella squeezed his hand.

'She wasn't there,' he said. 'She was at the house.'

'I know, but she might have some insight on the background. Why they went out that day—'

He stopped walking. 'You're right.' When he looked at her, his face was drawn, his mouth an unhappy line. 'I don't know why I didn't think of it before, why I've never thought to ask her . . .' He trailed off.

'Maybe you didn't really want to hear the answer,' Stella said. 'Maybe you weren't ready.'

Jamie nodded. 'I am now,' he said.

Stella walked up the path to Caitlin's house and rang the bell before she could chicken out. She was angry with her, but it was a feeling that was mixed with sadness and loss. When Caitlin opened the door she was pale and tired and Stella felt her emotions twist again. Caitlin looked so awkward, she wanted to reach out and hug her.

'I'm sorry,' Caitlin said, her voice cracking.

'Can I come in?' Stella said.

'Of course.' Caitlin moved aside. Her bump had grown so much in the past couple of weeks and Stella found she couldn't stop staring at it.

They went through to the kitchen and Caitlin stood next to the worktop, looking uncertain.

'Sit down,' Stella said. 'For God's sake.'

'I'm sorry,' Caitlin said. 'It was Rob's idea, but I shouldn't have gone along with it.'

Stella had known Rob for as long as she had known Caitlin. They hadn't had the same closeness, but they had spent countless nights out in clubs and pubs and sitting around the living room of his student house, not to mention meals and parties and holidays in the years since.

'How could you?' Stella said. 'Both of you? I thought we were friends.'

'We are,' Caitlin said. Tears spilled over and she wiped them away with the heel of her hand. 'I've just been so worried about money. And Rob said that Jamie was bad news. It would get you away from him, too.'

'But you guys sent me up there,' Stella said. 'If he's so terrible—'

'I know,' Caitlin said. 'But that was supposed to last a week. Tops. You were supposed to come back with stories of what a gigantic prick he was and we would laugh about it and that would be that.'

'And you'd sell a story, too. Bonus.'

'Yes.' Caitlin looked down.

'And pictures, too?' Stella suddenly realised who had been lurking out in the garden with a camera.

Caitlin nodded. She glanced up and Stella saw the misery on her face. It was genuine and she felt more of the anger slip away. She looked into her friend's eyes and a question formed in her mind, a question that hurt to articulate. 'Why didn't you just tell me the plan? Why lie?'

'I wanted to,' Caitlin said. 'I swear. But Rob said you would never do it.'

'Is that supposed to be flattering? That you thought I was too nice to spy for you or something?' Stella was surprised at how harsh she sounded. The waves of emotion just kept on coming. She felt betrayed and that realisation was like a stone in her stomach.

Caitlin straightened her shoulders. 'We didn't think you would take the risk.'

'What?'

'I didn't think there was a risk,' Caitlin said quickly. 'I don't believe all the gossip.'

'About Jamie?'

Caitlin nodded. 'You know. That he's reckless. Some kind of mad scientist doing wacky experiments. And then there's what they say about the house and its goings-on.'

Stella closed her eyes.

'I know it's stupid, just a silly story, but Rob is a real local and I think he half believes in it. He thought that if we told you that we wanted you to spy from inside the cursed estate, you would run a mile.' She smiled weakly. 'I mean, it's true. You are very cautious.'

'No,' Stella said. 'You don't get to make this about me.'

The wind had gotten up and was rattling the window. In the sudden silence of the kitchen the noise seemed to swell. The light dimmed and Stella sat down at the table, suddenly exhausted.

'Do you want some tea?' Caitlin said. 'Or something stronger?'

Stella shook her head. 'You should sit down too before you keel over.'

Caitlin pulled out the other chair and sank onto it. One hand was on the bottom of her bump, rubbing as if there was a pain. Stella was determined not to ask her about it, determined not to feel sympathy.

'Rob has always had it in for Jamie. Whenever he talked about home he made little comments about the family but I didn't realise how serious he was until we moved here. He's not alone, either,' she said, looking at Stella. 'You really can't trust him.'

'You're not really in a position to throw stones,' Stella said. 'And you don't know him.'

'Rob says his dad was really bad.'

'Jamie's not his father,' Stella said.

'No, I know that. But—'

'I'm not here to talk about Jamie,' Stella said. 'Although I do want Rob to answer some questions. About his parents' accident.'

'Rob's parents?'

'No. Jamie's. They drowned in a boat accident ten years ago and Rob was on the lifeboat that went to the scene.'

Caitlin's eyes opened wide. 'Seriously?'

'He never told you?'

'No,' Caitlin said. 'I can't imagine that. I suppose if they had the call out but didn't know whose boat it was, who was out there . . . That must have been a shock when they got there.'

'He wouldn't have gone out?'

'I don't know,' Caitlin said. 'They all take the duty really seriously. Maybe he would have. Just, the way he talks about the Munro family—' Caitlin broke off, as if frightened of what she was about to say.

A horrible thought occurred. 'Did Rob have something to do with Esmé getting sick?'

'No!' Caitlin said, too quickly.

Stella sat back. 'Oh my God. What did he do?'

'Nothing,' Caitlin said. 'He wouldn't.'

'You're not sure, are you?' Stella said.

It hit her then just how much resentment and anger Rob was carrying.

It didn't make sense. Not after all this time. He had never really spoken about Arisaig when they had been at uni, not to Stella, anyway. And he'd certainly never revealed any blood vendettas. 'What on earth happened with Rob and Jamie? Something when they were kids?'

Caitlin took a deep breath. 'He won't talk about it.'

'Never?'

Caitlin pressed her lips together.

'Not even when he was drunk?'

'He said that Mr Munro was a bastard. Hit his wife, apparently.'

'Yeah, I heard about that. Awful.'

'And Rob really liked Jamie's mum. People said she was stuck up, but Rob always said she was a nice woman. That she didn't deserve to be married to an unfaithful bastard like James Munro.'

'Who else would know about the accident? What about Rob's mum? Where did you say she moved to?'

Caitlin looked uncomfortable. 'Lewis. To be near Rob's gran. Gave us this cottage and bought a house in Stornoway. She might regret it now that this one is on the way' – she patted her bump – 'but we are very grateful for the place to live.'

'Right.' Stella stood up. 'Let's go.'

'To Lewis? Now?'

Stella didn't know when she had got so impulsive. She just had the feeling that a face-to-face chat would be more productive than one over the phone.

'I don't think Rob would like that,' Caitlin said. 'It feels sneaky. Talking to his mum about him. And it's a long way. Not a day trip.'

'Fine,' Stella said, pacing the floor. 'We'll phone, then. Do you use Skype? Then we could see her face, too.'

Caitlin didn't say anything for a moment. 'You're not going to let this go, are you?'

Stella stopped pacing and looked at Caitlin. 'What aren't you telling me?'

Caitlin stood up. 'Rob is going to kill me. This is private. You mustn't tell another soul.'

Stella hesitated. 'I might have to tell Jamie. If it involves his family.'

Caitlin blew out a breath of air. 'Fuck. Okay. But I'm only doing this because you are my friend. And I let you down and I want to make it up to you. I want you to know how sorry I am. If you hear this and you decide to tell him, then I won't blame you, but I would prefer you kept it to yourself. Rob will be furious if he finds out I told you.'

'I won't tell him where I heard it.'

Caitlin shook her head. 'I didn't know any of this when I invited you here or encouraged you to work at the estate. Rob only told me after Esmé got sick.'

'What did he tell you?'

'That his mum had been on the receiving end of Mr Munro's attentions. And that she hadn't been willing.'

'Oh, Jesus,' Stella said.

'I mean, maybe she said that when her husband found out so that he wouldn't leave her or whatever, I don't know. But when Rob was a teenager, his dad got drunk and told him that Mr Munro wasn't just a bastard who was quick with his fists, but that he had assaulted Rob's mother.'

'Did they report it?'

'No way,' Caitlin said. 'It was different, then. You kept quiet about that sort of thing. There would have been questions about why Rob's mum had been alone with Mr Munro, and Mr Munro knew the local police and the paper. They wouldn't have stood a chance. There were already rumours that they were having an affair.'

'But still, they didn't even try?'

Caitlin looked out of the window. 'You know the estate used to encompass the village. Back in the day. I mean, the village was even smaller then, and bits of land got sold off over the years. By the time

Jamie's parents owned the place, they still had most of this side, including this road.'

'They owned all the houses along the road into the village?'

'These three cottages and the detached place along the way.'

Her words sunk in. 'The Munros owned Rob's parents' house?'

'Until Rob was sixteen or so, yes. They paid Mr Munro rent on it, until one day when they didn't.'

'What do you mean?'

'Jamie's dad gave Rob and his mum this house. Rob's dad had left a couple of years before. After the incident.'

'Why would Mr Munro do that?' Stella said, the answer dawning upon her as she spoke. 'To keep them quiet?'

Caitlin nodded. 'I think so. Or because he felt guilty.'

Stella walked back down to the house, wondering how to deliver the information to Jamie. He was already reeling from the discovery that his ancestor had, most likely, been guilty of murder. Or, at the very least, manslaughter. Now she was the bearer of more bad news.

The father, who he had always hated and feared, was as big a bastard as he had always thought.

CHAPTER NINETEEN

Back at the house, Stella had gone through the post. There was an envelope with a local postmark that she gave to Jamie to open straight away. 'It's from the library in Mallaig,' he said. 'They've heard back from Surgeons' Hall in Edinburgh. Apparently some of my grandfather's heirlooms, including Lockhart's medical patents, ended up there.'

'We should go,' Stella said, not really expecting Jamie to agree. To her amazement he had nodded. 'I've been stuck here too long. A change of pace would be good.'

The high-ceilinged entrance led into a grand room with white pillars and a high mezzanine which ran around the perimeter. A glass case with a grotesquely inflated skull reared up on Stella's right. She looked away quickly but on the other side was a display of early dentistry equipment. There was a low hum of an air conditioner but Stella wasn't sure if that noise was actually inside her head, her blood buzzing gently with a sudden rush of adrenaline and nausea. Up on the mezzanine were rows of shelves, stacked with glass specimen jars, and at the end, two skeletons with grotesquely malformed bones hung, like permanent Halloween decorations. Jamie was looking around with utter fascination and Stella couldn't bear his avid expression. 'I need to sit down,' she said.

A man she had not noticed was by her side. 'Through here,' he said, leading her quickly to the end of the room and through an unmarked door. This led to a vast dark space, with a heavily corniced and gilded ceiling and elaborately painted wood panelling. Banquet chairs were lined up against the wall and Stella sank into the nearest one, putting her head between her knees and taking deep breaths.

'Is she all right?' She heard Jamie's voice from far away.

'It affects some people like this,' the man said. 'It's not uncommon.'

Stella could feel the dizziness pass and she sat up cautiously. The man from the museum had a neat pink shirt with a cashmere vest over the top and a bow tie. In a line-up she would have picked him out as the museum curator in an instant. 'Take as long as you need,' he said, his voice kind.

'Do you need a drink of water?' Jamie knelt down by her chair and reached out a hand as if he were going to touch her face. Stella, aware of feeling sweaty, moved away. 'I'm fine. You go and ask your questions.'

He cupped her cheek and leaned closer, searching her face as if looking for secrets, clues. She relaxed into his touch and managed a smile. 'I promise I'm fine,' she said.

'If you're sure.' Jamie straightened up. 'Join us when you're ready.'

The room had busts of medical men dotted around the edge and a plaque with a Latin inscription fixed above the tall windows at one end. A sign on the back of the door explained that this was the room in which undergraduates had sat examinations, and Stella couldn't imagine being able to perform in such an overwrought environment. When her hearing had returned to normal and she was no longer looking at the world from within a black tunnel, Stella stood up carefully and went to find Jamie and the curator.

They were at the bottom of a flight of stairs. The steps were roped off, but the curator moved it aside for them to pass, clipping it back into place behind them. He was in full flow, telling Jamie about a recent discovery of an anatomist's drawing which had been found in an attic in Kirkcaldy and bequeathed to the museum.

She assumed that Jamie was too engrossed in the topic to notice her return, but he reached out and took her hand, squeezing it gently. Stella was glad of the reassurance when they reached the top of the stairs. In front stretched out rows of white shelves, almost to the ceiling, and each one was packed with jars of unmentionable and horrifying samples in shades of bone-white, yellow and grey. Nothing was gory in the usual sense; there was no bright-red blood or pink flesh. Instead the room was a study of how the human body reacted to being suspended in formaldehyde for years. Familiar flesh made alien.

Stella read the label of the nearest jar: *Tumour of the face, 1867.* A bulbous shape, mottled grey and pale yellow, hung in the liquid. The hairs on the back of Stella's neck lifted. Some primeval part of her brain knew what her senses were denying: that this was a part of a human being. This strange swollen thing had been cut from a body. It had once functioned as part of a living, breathing person. Most likely, it had once killed a living, breathing person.

'I'll let you look around,' the curator said.

'Is there an index?' Stella said, tearing her eyes from the cancerous growth.

'What is it you want to see?'

'I wondered whether you had the names of the people?'

'The surgeons?'

'No. The patients.'

'The samples were often recorded as anonymous. They are displayed here in accordance with the Scottish Human Tissue Act of 2006 and we treat the specimens with the utmost respect. These people advanced our understanding of the human body and helped with vital medical research.'

Stella recognised an oft-quoted speech when she heard it. 'So, are any of the specimens identified?'

'We have a pocket book made from Burke's skin downstairs.'

'Grim,' Jamie said. 'I saw that.'

'There are a few other convicted criminals. The hangman was a popular source of cadavers before the 1832 Anatomy Act. There would be a rush to claim the body, with relatives fighting the doctors to cut it down and carry it off. Actual fights . . .' The curator shook his head. 'It's hard to imagine now.'

On the contrary, Stella found it all too easy. She thought of Jessie and her horror at the bodies being brought into her house in the dead of night. Even after the Anatomy Act, some of those might have been cut from the noose, dug up from a grave, or maybe even worse.

'No index, though.'

'Not of names, no.'

Jamie turned to Stella. 'If we knew for sure what she died from, we could search under disease or abnormality.' He looked at the curator. 'What about the donors? If people made a bequest to the museum? You had a record of my grandfather's donation, for example.'

He smiled. 'Certainly, we keep those records. How accurate they are as we look further back is hard to say.'

'The museum didn't always keep records?' Stella said.

'Not necessarily complete ones.' The curator spread his hands. 'Again, it depends on the provenance of some of the samples.'

'Could you look?'

'Of course.'

'Lockhart,' Jamie said. 'James Lockhart. Or Jessie Lockhart. His first wife.'

'Please feel free to look around while you wait.'

'They are very helpful,' Stella said. 'And it's nice of them to let us up here.' She was making small talk to distract herself from the specimens, which seemed to be growing in size the longer she spent on the mezzanine. Truthfully, she wasn't at all sure that 'nice' was the word.

'Great-granddad Munro made a generous donation, I guess it buys goodwill.'

They moved slowly along the aisle, Jamie peering with great interest at the samples. Stella let go of his hand and moved quickly past when they reached a section of larger jars. A swift glance had told her everything she needed to know and didn't need to see up close: human foetuses floating in preserving fluid. Swallowing down a fresh wave of nausea she began moving down the middle passageway, not looking left or right, just thinking to walk to the staircase at the end, down the steps and out into the bland reception area of the museum and wait for Jamie there. She was almost at the end when a bolt of electricity ran down her spine and along her limbs. It was exactly as if someone had touched a live wire to her neck and lit up her central nervous system. Stock-still and barely breathing, Stella waited for the familiar stuttering in her heart. It didn't come, and she could feel her pulse steady and true.

As if controlled by some invisible force, Stella felt herself turning to the left. The row of shelves in front of her contained yet more jars. Lines and lines of dead flesh and bone and skin. She didn't want to see any more. Felt she would never be able to remove the image of a carefully dissected head, the nerves floating free in the liquid like strands of hair or the fine tentacles of a sea creature. Stella was walking forward. She did not intend to do so but could not stop. It was as if the air behind her had become solid and was pushing her onward.

Once she had reached the jar she was meant to see, she knew it instantly. It was the split-second knowledge that came with the heavy ring of truth. Labelled *Heart with anterior hole in chamber*, it didn't have Jessie's name, of course, but Stella felt certain. The faded paper was handwritten in a delicate sloping hand: *Female, 1849* and a reference code, *E344*.

Poor Jessie. Stella wondered if Lockhart had dissected his wife's body. Or sold it to one of his anatomist friends. She reached out her fingers to touch the surface of the jar and felt Jamie join her. 'You found her,' he said.

Stella nodded, her throat suddenly tight. 'She had a hole in the heart. Like me.'

Jamie's arms were around her, holding her steady. 'I'm sorry,' he said.

'If she had been born now, she would have had that repaired. She would have been fine.'

'Do you think, mebbe, that he didn't kill her after all?'

Stella turned in Jamie's arms so that she faced him and put her hands on his cheeks, holding his face so that she could look into his eyes. 'Maybe not. Jessie definitely wouldn't have enjoyed a long life, whatever James did.'

Tension eased out of Jamie's shoulders.

There were footsteps and the curator appeared. 'E344,' he said. 'Donated by Dr J. Lockhart. It should be somewhere in this section . . .' He trailed off. 'Oh. It's right there.'

'Thank you,' Jamie said.

'Take all the time you need,' the curator said, walking discreetly away.

'I don't want to finish *Living Well Forever*,' Jamie said. He was addressing the shelf, as if embarrassed.

'You don't have to,' Stella said. 'It's your life and your work. You don't owe anybody.'

'I think I would like to write about James Lockhart and Jessie. It's not the story I was hoping to find, but the way I feel right now, it just seems like the right thing to do.' He looked at her. 'Nathan is not going to be pleased. It's not a commercial idea.'

Stella smiled at him. 'I would love that,' she said. 'If it wasn't for people like this' – she indicated the room – 'I wouldn't have had a life at all.'

His arm tightened around her and they stood for a moment longer, paying their respects.

The line between human remains and scientific samples had never felt so blurred. Stella looked at Jessie's heart and felt the answering beat of her own.

∽

Coming back from one night in Edinburgh felt like coming home. Stella went to unlock the front door while Jamie carried their bags, but she couldn't find her key.

'Here,' Jamie said, dumping the bags on the steps and taking his own from his pocket.

Inside, Stella went into her office to check for anything urgent, and Jamie went to find Nathan and tell him to pull the publishing contract and pay back the advance.

She was ploughing through some admin when she heard the door. Looking up, she found Jamie lounging in the doorway. 'Tea break?' He was smiling, looking more relaxed than she had ever seen him.

'Okay,' Stella stood up. 'I'll put the kettle on.'

He put a hand on her waist as she went to pass him. He was very close and she turned to face him, putting a hand onto his chest and tipping her head back to look into his eyes.

'Or a different kind of break?' he said. Enquiring, inviting.

She kissed him, her breath coming quickly as his hands tightened on her. When they broke apart for a moment, she opened her eyes and saw him staring at her. His pupils dilated, clear need written over his face, and she felt beautiful and desirable and powerful. 'We should probably have some exercise,' she said, smiling. 'It's very important to take regular screen breaks.'

'I prescribe twenty minutes of vigorous physical activity,' he said, leading her towards the stairs.

'Twenty minutes?'

'Minimum effective dosage,' he said.

'Let's go crazy,' Stella said. 'Try for thirty.'

He smiled down at her, stopping to kiss her again, as if he couldn't wait until they were in the bedroom. 'Whatever you say.'

❧

The next morning, Jamie and Stella were sitting up in Jamie's bed, chatting about the new book and planning a proper research trip to Edinburgh, when they heard the dogs go wild downstairs.

Jamie was dressed first and he went ahead, Stella following.

Tabitha and Angus were barking like they were possessed, and Angus was running up and down the staircase between the front door and the landing, as if trying to physically patrol two places at the same time. Jamie glanced at Stella, frowning. 'I didn't hear the bell,' he said, walking swiftly to the hallway.

Esmé stood in the doorway, water dripping off her raincoat and onto the tiles. The dogs launched themselves at her, but she made them sit before she patted their heads and stroked their ears. 'Aren't you going to offer to get my bags?'

'Of course,' Jamie moved forwards, kissing Esmé on the cheek as he passed. 'It's good to see you.'

'Have you been spoiling them?' Esmé fixed Stella with a terrifying look. 'Tabitha's put on weight.'

'How are you feeling?' Stella said. 'Do you have the all-clear?'

Esmé snorted. 'Lot of fuss about nothing.' She led the way into the kitchen and Stella put the kettle on to boil, while Esmé rinsed out the teapot and opened the fridge and then the cupboards, assessing the damage from her time away. She flipped the lid of the breadbin and tutted. 'I'll have to get baking.'

'I can do that,' Stella said. 'If you're not up to it . . .' She trailed off when she saw Esmé's expression. And so she added, 'That would be great. I've missed your cakes.'

Esmé made a noise that sounded like 'humph' but she didn't look entirely displeased. She disappeared into the larder and came out with a cake tin. It was newer than the rest of Esmé's collection and Stella, who hadn't ventured into the larder even in the last couple of weeks, considering it Esmé's domain, didn't recognise it. It was pale pink with cutesy drawings of cupcakes, and Esmé eased the lid off and peered inside. 'Don't know if this has kept all right,' she said. 'We could have a slice with our tea and find out.'

Stella was fetching the plates when Esmé said something that stopped her cold.

'Need to get this tin back, anyway. Caitlin will be needing it.'

'Caitlin?'

'Aye, Caitlin Baird.' She nodded. 'Your pal.'

'This cake was given to you by Caitlin?' Stella felt that she had to be absolutely sure of all the facts.

'Well, her husband brought it round, but I assume Caitlin did the baking. Although,' Esmé said, 'you can't be sure these days. Could have been his own work.'

'Was this the cake you were bringing through when you were taken ill?'

Esmé nodded. 'What's wrong? You've gone awfy pale.'

'Did you eat any?'

'A wee slice,' Esmé said. 'Bit dry for my taste, but waste not want not.'

Stella didn't have time to decide whether to confront Rob or not. He called her mobile as she was on her way up to the cottage to visit Caitlin. 'Speak of the devil,' she said, answering. 'I was just thinking about you.'

'Nice things, I hope,' Rob said, sounding strained. 'Can you meet me at the pub at half twelve?'

'Aren't you at work?'

'Lunch break. I won't have long.'

A public place seemed like a good idea. Stella wasn't exactly frightened of Rob, but there was no sense in taking unnecessary chances. Besides, she didn't want to upset Caitlin. Not in her condition.

It was a bright and frosty day and the walk into Arisaig, with the sunlight on the whitewashed houses, was at its very best. After the crowds and petrol fumes of Edinburgh, Stella could feel her body relaxing back into the pace and beauty of the Highlands. As odd as it was, with everything that was going on, her soul seemed to respond to the scenery and she felt strangely calm. As she took the narrow road along the water and saw a pair of black guillemots diving into the sea loch, she knew she never wanted to leave. Which meant that she had to think like a local. Handle Rob carefully and keep things quiet. For Caitlin's sake as well as Jamie's.

The pub was reasonably full with the lunchtime crowd, but Stella didn't feel hungry. She asked for orange juice, but when Rob came back from the bar he put a glass of wine in front of Stella. She pushed it away.

'Thanks for meeting me.' Rob's gaze was moving all around the room, as if he couldn't bear to look at Stella.

'What is this about? Is it Caitlin?'

'No, she's fine,' Rob said, finally glancing at her. 'She's doing well.'

He looked pale and there was a sheen of sweat on his forehead.

'You don't look well,' Stella said, the words coming automatically. 'Are you sick?'

'Bit of a cold. And I'm not sleeping well.'

Stella was trying to hold on to the sense of calm she had felt outside, but instead, an instinctive revulsion was forcing her to lean back in her chair. In that moment Rob seemed like a stranger to her and she could not believe that he had been her friend and protector for so many years. 'It's horrible to be ill, isn't it?' Stella said, watching his face. 'Like poor Esmé.'

Rob winced and Stella was glad. She hoped he felt terrible. She was certain that Rob had put vitamins into a cake and delivered it to Munro House. Presumably he had hoped to hurt Jamie, but really he hadn't cared who had gotten sick. She didn't believe for a moment that he had intended to seriously hurt anyone, just that he had wanted to add some fuel to the rumours of 'dangerous experiments'. But it had been reckless and selfish.

'I need you to get out of that house,' Rob said, spitting a little as he spoke. He wiped the back of his hand across his mouth.

'What?'

'Go back to London.'

'No,' Stella said. 'I like it here.' An image of her and Jamie entwined beneath his bedsheets jumped into her mind and she felt herself blush.

'Fuck,' Rob said, sitting back. 'What is it with that family?'

'It's my job,' Stella said, keeping her voice reasonable. 'And I love it here, I want to stay.'

Rob looked at her for a moment, breathing heavily. Then he dug in his pocket and produced a set of keys. Stella recognised them instantly. 'Where did you find those?' Jamie would pretty much kill her if she had dropped them somewhere.

'I took them,' Rob said, his red eyes narrowing. 'I needed to get inside and I didn't think you would lend them to me.'

'You broke into Munro House?' Stella felt the first rush of fear. It was probably a bit late, but she had known Rob for so long, and he had always been such a caring presence. He had made some bad decisions recently, hadn't been in his right mind, but still. He taught primary school children, after all, wore one of those knitted vest things over his shirts when he went to work.

'I went into the house while you and Jamie were on your romantic mini-break.' Rob was openly sneering.

'How do you even know—'

'He has keys,' Rob interrupted. 'To the cottages that used to belong to the estate. He has keys to my house.'

'That's what this is about? You think Jamie has been in your house?'

'Not him. His dad. A long time ago. I need you to tell me everything Jamie has ever said about my family.'

'You manipulated me into working for Jamie Munro,' Stella said, ice in her heart. 'You lied to me. And now you want me to betray my boss for you, violate a legal agreement and my own ethics.' Stella had been going to add 'and you poisoned Esmé' but something stopped her. The same instinct that was telling her she ought to get far away from this man.

'I think he's covering something up.'

Rob reached out and put his hand over Stella's on the table. It was sweaty and Stella forced herself not to move immediately. She wanted nothing more than to leave, to take deep breaths in the fresh air, but she had to find out what Rob was talking about first. 'I know you don't like Jamie, but he hasn't done anything wrong—'

'Mebbe not him,' Rob gripped her hand, 'but he is hiding something.'

'What?' Stella pulled her hand out from underneath Rob's and crossed her arms. 'You are going to have to do better than vague accusations.'

Rob looked around as if he expected to be overheard, then he spoke quietly. 'James Munro senior was in the habit of taking what he wanted and who he wanted. By the time I was fourteen, Mum and Dad were arguing all the time. Dad got drunk one time and told me Mum had been busy up at the big house. That was why things were so bad between them. He said it was an affair but she said she couldn't help it, that Munro forced things.'

'Jesus,' Stella said. 'That's really bad, but—'

Rob carried on. He wasn't looking at Stella, just staring at the table as if seeing the past played out on its surface. 'My dad left us not long after that. I never heard from him again. Neither of us did. It was pretty rough for those years. Mum really struggled to keep us going. I got a Saturday job, but there was never quite enough cash.'

'And you blame Jamie's dad for your parents breaking up.'

Rob looked at her then. She expected sadness, but there was just blazing fury. 'You don't get it. The night that Dad got really steaming and told me that stuff. That's the last time I saw him.'

'You haven't been in touch?'

Rob shook his head slowly. 'I was angry with him for leaving. And Mum didn't want to talk about it so we didn't. And then I left, went to university. I got out of this place and got myself a career. I put it all behind me.'

'I'm sorry,' Stella said. 'You never talked about your parents. I had no idea—'

'See, I always thought he had passed out on the couch that night. I was off out myself the next night. I got blootered with Doug and stayed at his. Didn't go home till the weekend and by then he had gone. Left us. I always thought it was because he believed Munro, and not Mum, and that telling me about it just brought it up for him. Last straw, like.'

'You think he thought your mum had an affair, that it wasn't assault.'

'Aye. But now I'm not so sure he just left.' Rob rolled his shoulders. 'I mean, I never heard from the man again. For a while I was so angry with him for leaving and with Mum for sleeping with that rich bastard that I didn't think it through. Then I was really fucking angry with Munro. Maybe Mum had been telling the truth and he forced things, mebbe not. Either way he fucked things up for my parents.'

Rob was staring at the table as he spoke, his fingers picking and tearing the label on his beer bottle. 'I thought I'd put it all behind me, moved on, but moving back here just brought it all up. It's like it's just been waiting for me. Thing is, I've been thinking about those first few days. We were both in shock, me and Mum, and then she didn't want to talk about it anymore. I thought she was embarrassed. I mean, everyone around here seemed to know she'd had a thing with Munro and she felt judged.'

'The downside of a small community,' Stella said.

'I know that when she came back from work that day she found a note. I never saw it and I don't know what it said. Mum just told me he had said sorry. His duffel bag was gone with clothes, his toothbrush, his razor and a few clothes. He had taken the library book he was halfway through and his passport. Thing is' – Rob was staring intently at Stella now, like he was willing her to understand the significance of his words – 'he didn't take his star medal.'

'I don't—'

'He loved that bloody thing. Used to bore me senseless with the story about how his granddad had brought it back from the war. Now that I think about it, I cannae believe that he would leave without taking it.'

'Maybe he didn't mean to leave for good, maybe he thought he would cool off and come home and that's why.' As Stella spoke she felt a prickling sensation. She remembered packing her own overnight bag, no clear intention of how long she would be away and half-mad with grief and betrayal.

She had still picked up her glass inkwell.

CHAPTER TWENTY

Stella wanted to go for a long walk to clear her head, but she went straight back to the house. She had no idea whether she was going to tell Jamie about Rob's suspicions, but she was hoping that instinct would kick in and tell her what to do for the best.

Jamie and Nathan were in the living room, tumblers of whisky in hand. Nathan had clearly not been out of bed long, as his hair was messy and he was wearing a dressing gown made of a navy shiny material which looked suspiciously like silk. He could have happily auditioned for the part of 'international playboy' in a low-budget film.

'Join us,' Nathan said, his eyes shining. 'We're toasting the end of Jamie Munro's career as a *New York Times* bestselling author.'

'Ach, give it a rest,' Jamie said. After spending time with Rob and his sniffing, Jamie looked even healthier than usual in comparison. His skin positively glowed and his eyes were bright and clear.

'I mean it.' Nathan tipped his glass towards Jamie. 'You must be the first person to ever mail back a quarter-mill advance and for such an insane reason.'

Stella opened her mouth to say something supportive of Jamie and his business decisions, but the dogs began barking wildly and then the ancient doorbell clanged.

'I'll go,' she said, standing up.

Stella called for the dogs to be quiet. She was expecting the slimy journalist from the *Record* or an out-of-season tourist hoping for a hotel. Somebody she could get rid of quickly and then, hopefully, get Jamie alone to talk about what Rob had said. There was so much on her mind that it took Stella a moment to place the man standing on the steps.

Ben was looking around the courtyard and seemed to have to drag his gaze back to her. 'I can see why you stayed,' he said.

Stella was trying to adjust to the sight of him. He looked both the same and utterly unfamiliar. 'What are you doing here?'

He smiled easily. 'You don't call, you don't write—'

'We broke up,' Stella said, as if explaining something to a child. 'That's generally what happens.'

'I want to talk to you. I wanted to see you.'

'I think I made my feelings pretty clear.'

'Don't be dramatic,' Ben said. He walked up the steps and past Stella, as if he belonged. That old confidence. How had she found it so reassuring? Within seconds, Ben was surrounded by the dogs and they were barking again, loudly.

'Shush,' Stella said sharply. 'Come here.' She didn't really expect them to obey her commands, she wasn't Esmé after all, but they stopped barking and stopped circling Ben.

Tabitha pushed her nose into Stella's hand and Angus sat right in front of her, as if guarding her from the intruder.

'You can't be here,' Stella said. 'Please leave.'

'Stella . . .' Ben took a step towards her but Angus began growling, deep in his throat, and Ben stepped back.

'I made a mistake.'

Stella felt a sound like wind whistling in her ears. She resisted the urge to shake her head to dislodge it. She put a hand to her chest, instinctively. Her heartbeat was steady.

'Please,' Ben said. His eyes were on her hand, and she knew that he knew what she was doing. She dropped her arm, feeling naked. Would anybody ever know her as well as Ben?

'I don't think you did,' Stella forced herself to say. It was true, but that didn't make it less painful to admit.

'No,' Ben said. 'We're good together.'

'We were.' Stella patted Tabitha's head for comfort.

'Could be again.'

'I don't think so.' Stella tried to smile. 'I think we should have stayed friends in the first place. Best friends.'

'That's what successful marriages are built on. Friendship.'

Stella could feel emotions coming back. Ben's face was so dear to her and she knew that if she stepped forward and let him hold her, she would breathe in his smell and feel like she was home. He had always meant safety.

'Hello.' Jamie stepped from the living room. 'Who are you?'

'This is Ben,' Stella said.

'Oh.' Jamie hesitated, and then held out a hand. 'Jamie Munro.'

Ben didn't shake it and, after a moment, Jamie dropped his hand. 'Right, then. Do you two need a moment?'

'No,' Stella said at the same time as Ben said, 'Yes.'

'She's the boss,' Jamie said, 'which means you have to leave, pal.'

He crossed the hall and opened the front door wide, gesturing for Ben to walk through it.

The moment was broken by the sight of Nathan in his silk robe. 'Hello, children,' he said. 'I see we have company.'

'Ben was just leaving,' Stella said.

Nathan gave him a lascivious look up and down. 'Shame.'

'You're drunk,' Stella said. Nathan was flushed and his eyes were shining in an unnatural way. 'You should go and lie down.'

'How many men live here?' Ben said, looking annoyed.

'Loads,' Jamie said easily. 'And we're all big fans of Stella here.'

'He's kidding,' Stella said.

'No, he's not,' Nathan said, and tipped the remains of his whisky into his mouth.

'Shush,' Stella said, feeling bad for Ben and suddenly very happy.

'I've come all this way,' Ben said, looking so lost that Stella felt the sudden urge to put her arms around him, comfort him. Habit, she supposed.

'Come on, I'll walk you out to your car.'

'I didn't drive,' Ben said. 'I got a taxi.'

'That must have cost a lot,' Jamie said, and Stella gave him a look.

'I don't care about the money.' Ben was staring at Stella.

'You can get the train back,' she said. 'I'll drop you at the station.'

'It takes over five hours to Glasgow,' he said. 'That's why I paid for the taxi.'

She passed Jamie and led Ben outside. 'Why didn't you drive?'

'I thought we would be going back together, in your car.' For the first time, Ben sounded uncertain.

Stella unlocked the boot and put his bag inside. Then she got into the car and waited for Ben, who seemed to be struggling with the failure of his grand plan.

Finally, he got into the passenger seat.

'Please . . .' He tried to take Stella's hand. 'Let's go somewhere and talk.'

'I'm sorry you made an unnecessary trip,' Stella said, checking the mirrors and avoiding Ben's gaze.

'Did you hear me in there?' Ben was starting to sound more annoyed than anything else. 'I think we should get back together.'

'What does Laura think about that?' The words popped out and then Stella realised something: she actually didn't care.

Ben looked uncomfortable for a second. 'That was a mistake. Infatuation. But it's passed now. I know I hurt you and I'm sorry—'

'No,' Stella said. 'It's okay. You were right. I wish you could have been honest with me, but it's done now. And it's for the best.'

Stella drove to the station in Arisaig but didn't feel she could just abandon Ben. She waited while he checked the times. 'There's nothing this afternoon.'

'Nothing?'

'Well, there's one from Fort William, but I don't think we can make it in time. I should probably stay here tonight.' He looked hopeful and calculating at the same time, and Stella felt her heart harden.

'I'll get you there,' Stella said.

It was an hour's drive to Fort William and Stella tried to keep the conversation on practical matters. It wasn't easy, but as Ben talked about the new start they could have together, the more certain Stella became. She didn't know when it had happened, but her feelings had changed and she knew the change was permanent. She was proud of how reasonable she was being. How calm.

Outside the station at Fort William, Ben tried one last time. 'Come home with me,' he said. 'Please.'

'I'm staying here,' Stella said. She passed him his bag. 'Safe journey.'

'You're his employee, you know?' Ben said, his sadness turning to anger. 'I know you're desperate for a home and a family, but you're his servant, not his wife.'

Stella swallowed.

'Come back with me and we can live in our house again,' Ben said, his tone conciliatory. 'We can get married right away, have a baby as soon as possible. I will do whatever you want. You can have it all.'

It was the word 'baby' that broke her. Stella felt white-hot rage, like a bolt of electricity. Her scalp actually tingled. 'A baby?'

'Yes,' Ben said eagerly. 'I know how important that is to you. I'm willing to—'

'You said that before. When you proposed. Do you remember?'

'What?' Ben frowned. 'I know we talked about the future—'

'You said that you had reconsidered and that you were willing to start a family.' Stella was running out of air, her voice getting thin. She forced herself to stop, to take a breath. 'You said we could try for a baby.'

'I did.' Ben nodded. 'And I'm saying the same thing now. Nothing has changed. We can start again—'

'When did you decide to have a vasectomy?'

Ben stopped speaking. 'What?'

'A vasectomy. Without telling me. When did you book the appointment? How long after we got engaged? Or was it when you started sleeping with Laura?'

'How do you know about that?' Ben put a hand on her arm. 'It was ages ago. I've changed my mind—'

'Ages ago,' Stella said, letting the anger fuel her, make her strong. 'After my valve operation or before? Our deal. It was never really true, was it?'

Ben looked down, his shoulders slumped. Stella waited, not saying anything. She had no desire to make this easier for him.

'I didn't know what was going to happen with you.' Ben was speaking to the floor. 'Everything was so uncertain.'

'You mean you didn't think I would live long enough for it to be a problem. You regretted the deal when you realised you might have to follow through.'

He looked up. Misery on his face and something else. Guilt. 'I didn't know that when I proposed. I didn't know how I was going to feel. I was so happy that you were well and you were so happy that you could really think about children and I didn't want to disappoint you. I'm not a complete bastard.'

'I know,' Stella said. She remembered those heightened few weeks, the mix of excitement and terror. Feeling so ill, every step exhausting and simple things such as stairs suddenly out of the question. Her life narrowed down to breathing and sleeping and trying to gather the energy to eat. And then the operation and the miraculous recovery. The joy of feeling well, of having her whole world unfold like a map.

Stella realised something: she hadn't properly come down from the rush, hadn't fully adjusted to her new situation. Ben had been by her side through the post-op weeks. He had cooked her meals and cleaned the house and taken her to her check-ups. He had loved her as he had always done and he had tried to give her what she had always wanted. Maybe he hadn't felt able to look her in the eye and tell her that he had preferred their relationship when it had a best-before date. And, honestly, she could sympathise a little with that. He wasn't a monster.

'You should go,' she said finally, getting back into her car and pulling away from the drop-off area. She didn't look back.

He wasn't a monster, but he wasn't what she wanted, either.

It took Stella over an hour to get back to Munro House, having been stuck behind a tractor with no place to overtake safely. She drove carefully, as always, but was impatient to see Jamie.

Rob had seemed so certain in the pub that it had begun to infect Stella's thoughts. What if Jamie's dad had killed Rob's father? From all she had heard about James Munro, she could imagine a fight getting physical.

All it would take is a push and an awkward fall. A temple cracking on a coffee table or a misjudged punch to the head. Accidents were all too common, the human body more fragile than most people realised.

Jamie's car was in the driveway but the house was quiet when Stella walked through the front door. The dogs were absent, and since Esmé was nowhere to be seen, Stella assumed that they were out for a reunion session with the plastic ball-thrower. In the office, Stella found a cold cup of green tea on Jamie's desk and the window half-open. The flesh on her arms rose in goose pimples, but Stella didn't think it was just from the cool air rushing through the room, ruffling the loose pages on the desk.

Something was wrong.

She went through the rest of the house, calling Jamie's name. Nathan was fast asleep in one of the bedrooms and she woke him up long enough to glean that he smelled like a distillery and he hadn't seen Jamie since Stella had left with Ben.

Stella looked out of the window in her bedroom, scanning the gardens for Jamie, hoping to see his figure loping through the trees at the edge of the grounds or crossing the lower lawn, the dogs jumping around him.

The landline rang and Stella ran downstairs to answer it, taking the stairs so fast she was in danger of going head over feet. 'Yes?'

'Rob's gone out in the boat,' Caitlin said.

'What?'

'He's taken the dinghy out.' Caitlin sounded terrified.

Stella couldn't work out, in that paralysed moment, why Caitlin sounded so upset. She settled on the basics. 'Rob has a dinghy?' Absurdly, Stella was picturing a small inflatable, the kind of thing you sat on to float around in the shallows on a hot summer day.

Caitlin blew out a fast, exasperated sigh. 'Everyone has a boat. Or knows someone who has one. He and Bark bought the dinghy together a couple of years back, but he hardly uses it. But he didn't come home from work and he didn't tell me he was going out. He always lets me know where he's heading, it's basic safety procedure.'

Stella was still scrambling to understand why Caitlin sounded so terrified. 'Maybe he just forgot to tell you, maybe he's told the boys or he's out with Stewart or Doug—'

'I called and he hasn't spoken to either of them. It's not a good day to be out; the sky is black over the water.' A pause. 'Is Jamie there?'

Stella went cold. Caitlin's voice had become suddenly and artificially casual.

'No,' Stella said. 'Why?'

'Do you know where he is?'

Stella shook her head, even though Caitlin couldn't see her. 'He isn't home,' Stella said. 'Do you think—' She broke off, unable to finish the sentence.

Caitlin said, very quietly, 'Shit.'

'Why would Jamie go out with him?'

'If Jamie asked about his parents, maybe Rob offered to show him where the boat went down. Maybe he's doing a nice thing.'

'Rob ground up vitamins and put them into a fruit cake which he delivered to the house.'

'No,' Caitlin said. 'He wouldn't go that far. Besides, anybody could have eaten that cake. Rob wouldn't want to hurt Esmé. Or you.'

'He encouraged me to move into the main house,' Stella said.

There was a silence on the line, one that confirmed Stella's suspicions. 'Bloody hell, Caitlin,' she said. She had thought that her stomach could not fall any lower, but she had been wrong.

'He said that you needed a push. That you would never get close enough to get the dirt on Jamie if you weren't forced together.'

Stella got off the phone as soon as possible, feeling that Caitlin was too deeply in denial about Rob's instability to be helpful. She also worried about upsetting her too much, with the vague feeling that you weren't supposed to stress a pregnant woman. Caitlin had betrayed their friendship, but Stella still loved her. She certainly didn't wish her any harm.

She rang Stewart and he said he would come and pick her up right away. He drove them to the harbour front in the village and spoke reasonably about why they shouldn't alert the coastguard or the lifeboat. 'The emergency services are stretched thin,' he said. 'If we call them out from Mallaig and there's a life-threatening situation elsewhere, it could be pretty serious.'

Stewart's usually smiling and open face was sombre and Stella got his meaning. If they tied up the lifeboat and someone else needed it, they would be responsible for the loss of life that could ensue.

'I can take you out, though,' Stewart said. 'We can go for a wee cruise, see if we can spot them. Put your mind at rest, like.'

'You have a boat?'

'One I can borrow, no bother. Aye.'

'Thank you,' Stella said, even as the terror gripped her. She had learned to swim, of course, even though she hated the water.

She had forced herself through the levels until she could swim strongly in a current, dive down to the bottom of the pool to retrieve thrown objects, and rescue a dummy while fully clothed. It wasn't about enjoyment or mastering the skill, it had been another grim exercise in risk avoidance. She hadn't kept it up, though. Despite her best intentions, she avoided water and reasoned to herself that as long as she never put herself in any water-based situations, it didn't matter that she was out of practice.

Sitting in the back of the small fishing boat and tying the straps of the yellow life jacket Stewart had just handed to her, Stella tried not to think about all the things that could go wrong. The conditions were fine for a trip. Stewart was a trained member of the lifeboat crew and an experienced sailor. There was no need to panic. He had calmly explained that they would navigate from the moorings across the sea loch and then cruise around the small isles, Eigg and Rùm.

'Munro's yacht went down between the isles, but they have quite a head start. We'll probably meet them on their way back.'

Stella hoped he was right. Anything that would shorten this trip would be a blessing. The boat sat much lower in the water than she had expected and, seen from her new vantage point, the water seemed dangerously close, as if only the smallest swell would wash over the side.

Stella shifted her view to the distance, but it didn't help with her nerves. 'Is that a storm?' Stella pointed at the bank of black clouds amassing on the horizon.

'Nah, just a wee shower,' Stewart said. 'I've checked the forecast, hen, and we're all clear to go.'

'Great,' Stella said.

Stewart paused in the act of unwinding the rope which tethered the craft. He peered into Stella's face. 'Are you sure you want do this? I can go out and have look on my own, if you like?'

'No,' Stella said. 'I want to come. I need to do something.' And it was Jamie. Funny, strong, vulnerable Jamie. Out there somewhere on those rolling waves with a man who hated his guts and a pit of guilt eating away at his insides. She couldn't explain why, couldn't find the words to tell Stewart why it felt so important and so urgent, but she had to look for him. Couldn't leave him to face this alone.

When the motor kicked in and boat began moving, Stella gripped the side for a few seconds, but it actually felt all right. She could do this. They moved into the channel that led out of the harbour, Stewart pointing out boats which belonged to vast extended family. 'See that one?'

Stella followed his pointing arm to a neat red tug with the name *Bonnie Jean* painted on the side. 'My uncle renamed it to get out of trouble with my auntie Jean.'

'Did it work?' Stella said, grateful to Stewart for trying to distract her.

'No idea,' Stewart said. 'They're still in the same hoose, though, so mebbe.'

And then, before Stella had gotten used to the idea of being in the boat, on the water, they were out of the confines of the marina and heading across the loch to the south channel. In great volume and from the low vantage point of the boat, the water seemed more like a solid mass, the sharp edges of the waves black and shining. Stella stopped watching the movement, closing her eyes to relieve the sudden nausea, although that seemed to make it worse.

Stewart threaded the boat through the gap between the promontory and the islet of Luinga Mhor, and within minutes the land fell away and they were out on open sea. Immediately the boat began dipping up and down, and the waves alongside looked threateningly choppy.

Stella resisted the urge to ask Stewart, yet again, if this was safe. He was doing her a huge favour and it was rude to question his judgement. A tiny thought pushed forward: she should keep him on side, in case he had to dive into the water to save her.

The wind seemed to have picked up, too, and it was far colder than Stella had imagined. Her cheeks already felt frozen and they had only been out for five minutes. Stewart didn't seem affected by the cold and he moved around the boat as comfortably as if he were in the bar. He leaned in and cupped his hands, protecting his speech from the wind which was now slapping angrily against the side of the boat. 'We'll go as far as Rùm. Okay?'

'Yes,' Stella said, nodding for good measure. Stewart fetched an insulated flask from his rucksack and poured them both tea in small enamel mugs. The tea was stewed with milk already mixed in and lots of sugar, but it tasted amazing. Despite her thermal gloves, Stella could no longer feel her fingers, and she had no idea how Stewart was managing with no gloves at all. When she asked him, he said that he needed dexterity and that he ran hot. He put his hand on her cheek and she was amazed at the warmth in his skin, had to resist the urge to hold his hand in place, use it as a makeshift hot-water bottle.

They saw a vessel in the distance and Stella squinted, trying to see if it was the right shape. Stewart called back that it was too big. Stella was surprised but then she realised that the grey water and the waves and the dark sky were all conspiring to alter her perceptions. The vessel resolved itself into the clear outline of a fishing trawler.

'Over there!' Stewart shouted over his shoulder, both hands occupied with the controls at the stern. Stella looked around wildly, seeing nothing but the massive dark waves and the ever-present plumes of sea spray, eruptions from the deep.

'Where?' she shouted back, her words battling against the noise of the wind, which was now truly terrifying. The black clouds were closer and the boat was rising much higher before crashing back down onto the water. Stella had never been on a roller coaster – the safety statistics were horrifying – but this was as she had always imagined it would feel. Only about a hundred times worse. She doubled over, suddenly convinced that she was going to be sick.

Stewart had her arm and was shouting into her ear again: 'Over the side.'

She twisted her body and aimed as best she could, tasting vomit in the back of her throat, gagging with it. She took a breath of salty air and forced herself to look at the horizon, some trick for sea sickness that she had read somewhere. Amazingly, the nausea receded a little, but she clung to the edge of the boat, her head hanging and her body shuddering with tremors that mirrored the vibrating, bucking, shuddering boat. All at once, dying didn't seem so frightening. It would mean, at least, an end to feeling this sick.

The flat profile of Eigg was closer than Stella had expected and she could see bright-yellow kayaks nestled against the rocks. To her right was the taller, bigger and altogether more dramatic prospect of Rùm. The Cuillin of Rùm, a volcanic ridge of peaks with Scandinavian names Stella half remembered Jamie telling her – Askival and Trollaval – split the sky. On the map the islands looked small, but as they drew closer, Stewart steering them around Eigg and into the Sound of Rùm, they loomed dramatically, the grey stone unforgiving and craggy and the black water set alight with dancing sparkles where the sun was reflected. Stella had never experienced anything like it. She was in an alien environment, and the familiar shapes of the small isles that she had spent the past few weeks gazing upon from Munro House now seemed utterly new.

The sun burst from behind the clouds and transformed the scenery all over again. The black water turned navy blue and the slopes stretching above the grey basalt columns turned rich brown. There was bright white foam where the waves were breaking on the rocks, and the sound of the birds wheeling high above suddenly sounded hopeful and holiday-like, rather than a terrifying omen. Despite her fear of the water and her worry for Jamie, Stella felt the thrill of excitement. She felt grateful for this experience, for this different view. The adrenaline rush had set her heart racing, but for once she was so preoccupied by other concerns that she forgot to be frightened by it.

Stewart shut off the engine and steered the boat using an oar. He let them float towards the shore of Rùm. 'Use the binos, see if you can spot them.'

Stella unpacked the binoculars and, with her back wedged firmly against the side of the boat and her arms tucked against her sides to keep them steady, she searched the water and the base of the cliffs and the piles of rocks that marked the shoreline.

Stewart started the motor and guided the boat between the islands. A white boat that looked huge in comparison to their small craft and had *Highland Wildlife* painted on its hull, cruised past them. There were only a handful of tourists on board, dressed in rain ponchos and loaded with cameras and binoculars. Its wake caused big waves, one of which even slopped over the side. Stella called out in alarm, but Stewart just smiled. 'Not to fret,' he said.

Stella tried to take comfort from the sight of another boat, but the weather changed again as they navigated to the north side of Rùm and the sky was signalling a clear change. The long, rugged shape of Skye rose out of the sea to the left, and the sun disappeared once more and a strong south-westerly blasted them as they rounded the island. Stella was trying to use the binoculars to scan the shoreline, but looking through them as the boat rose and fell was making her feel sick again.

'There,' Stewart shouted.

Stella put the binoculars back to her eyes. A flash of orange which resolved into the shape of a rigid-framed inflatable, rising and falling with the waves. It looked as if it was quite close, but Stella knew that distance was hard to judge out here on the water and she had no experience, no way to work out whether they were metres or miles away.

Stewart used the motor to move towards the inflatable and it seemed to take a long time, the craft not seeming to get any closer. The black clouds were flinging rain now, which joined with the sea spray making the entire world wet and grey. 'I can't see them,' Stella shouted.

Stewart had stopped the engine and he stood next to Stella, taking the binoculars for a few moments. 'Visibility is getting worse. We should head back.'

'They were just there,' Stella said.

'They've probably turned back or gone around to the nearest landing. Rob knows not to stay out when it's like this.'

'He hates Jamie,' Stella said, finally voicing her true fear. 'I think he might hurt him.'

Stewart didn't contradict her immediately, which made the cold pit in Stella's stomach widen. It made her babble, the words coming out in a rush as she leaned close to Stewart. 'I know he's your friend, but the way he's been acting about Jamie . . .'

'I know,' Stewart said, putting an arm around Stella and squeezing. 'Something's up with him, right enough. We'll keep looking.'

He went back to the controls and used the motor to pilot the boat closer to Rùm. The volcanic cliffs emerged from the mist, looking more forbidding the closer they got. The upper part of the island was shrouded and Stella could imagine those cliffs climbing upwards forever.

Stewart was gripping the tiller, his face tense. 'Cross-currents,' he said. 'Gonnae spin us.'

At that moment, the orange inflatable appeared on their right. There were two figures standing and Stella leaned forwards, trying desperately to get a better view. The figures were merged, as if they were hugging, and Stella felt a surge of relief before the reality of the situation hit her. The figures were not hugging. They were fighting. Grappling, stumbling. Stella recognised Jamie's coat before she got a clear look at his face, and she shouted his name. The figures didn't turn, didn't stop.

Time slowed but Stella knew that they would not reach the dinghy in time. As the craft dipped low on one side, Stella saw Rob power forwards, clearly aiming to push Jamie over the edge and into the sea.

Stella was shouting as loudly as she could, thinking that if Rob knew he had an audience, he would stop.

She could hear a whistle blasting and they were still moving closer and closer. The men were a similar height and Jamie had breadth and muscle on his side, but Rob had momentum and madness. Stella saw Jamie's body bent backwards and Rob trying to pull away as gravity did the rest of the job, but Jamie was holding onto Rob, trying to stop himself from falling, and their bodies twisted together.

Rob lost his footing and both men went over the side and into the black water.

A sudden swell tipped the boat and Stella stumbled, reaching for the edge to stop herself from falling, too. Stewart stopped blowing on his whistle and grabbed the radio, sending a distress call even as he manoeuvred the boat alongside the inflatable.

'Get the lifebuoy,' Stewart shouted, and Stella began fumbling with the cords which lashed the ring into place. He was leaning down over the side of the boat, arms outstretched, and Stella saw a pale oval – a human face – appear and then disappear a metre or so away from the boat's side.

'Fuck, fuck, fuck,' Stewart was chanting. Stella pushed the lifesaver into his arms and he stood up, wound the end of the rope around his arm and then threw it into the water, shouting as he did so. His words were whipped away by the wind and Stella didn't think Jamie would hear.

He was appearing and disappearing in the swell, the freezing water probably slowing his heart and muscles. How long could a person last in water that cold? Minutes? She tried not to think about the dark fathoms and the wrecks littering the seabed. A shape appeared near to the orange inflatable and Stella hoped it was Rob grabbing onto the side.

Stewart had switched off the engine and the boat was drifting. 'The rocks—' Stella began, but then Jamie broke the surface near to the lifebuoy and threw an arm over the ring. Stewart was hauling it towards the side. 'Ladder!' he shouted, and Stella unhooked the emergency steps and unfolded them over the side just as Jamie, towed by the lifebuoy, came alongside. She moved out of the way so that Stewart could lean over. He was trying to grab hold of Jamie's arm, help him to the bottom of the ladder. Stella sat down and wrapped her arms around Stewart's legs, anchoring him to the boat.

It seemed to be taking forever and, from her position on the floor, Stella couldn't see what was going on, only hear Stewart's shouts of encouragement and the wind howling.

Then, his eyes shut and skin white, Jamie's head and body appeared at the top of the ladder, hauled up by Stewart with impressive strength. Seconds later, the rest of his body tumbled onto the deck, Stewart falling with him in an ungainly heap.

Stella had let go of Stewart at the last moment and thrown herself clear, but she still caught a face full of icy water and wet jacket.

She dived across to Jamie, pushing aside the wet hair which was plastered over his face. He was breathing. He was alive. Stella tried to roll him into an approximation of the recovery position but his body was heavy with the water and stone cold. He began shivering violently and Stella tried to remember if that was a good sign. She pulled his wet gloves off and held his hands in her own, trying to warm them.

Stewart scrambled to his feet and back to the controls. They were fighting the current and the back of the boat swung out to the side so that they were moving diagonally. 'Blanket,' Stewart called, pointing at the supply locker. 'Try to get his coat off.'

That was when Stella realised she had been chanting Jamie's name. 'It's okay,' she said. 'I've got you.'

He opened his eyes, seemed to focus.

'Can you take this off?' Stella was trying to tug the sleeve of his jacket and he tried to help, moving slowly as if he were still underwater. She stumbled to the supply locker and fetched the emergency blanket, wrapping it around Jamie as best she could. 'Rob . . .' Jamie said.

'It's okay,' Stella said. 'You're okay.'

She stood up, struggling to keep her balance on the bucking boat. The waves were bigger, threatening to break over the side. She squinted through the spray, hoping to see Rob climbing aboard the inflatable. Instead, she saw a flag of orange a moment before it disappeared under a wave. The dinghy had sunk. 'Got to go,' Stewart shouted, and Stella clung to the side as the boat swung around in the swell.

Stella scanned the waves for any sign of Rob, but all she could see was water, like black ink, heaving and rolling. The whole sea seemed alive, like a gigantic creature which wanted to throw them from the boat and devour them whole.

This was their last chance to spot Rob, they were moving further and further from the place he had gone overboard. Stella was torn between looking for a figure she didn't think could still be alive and tending to the man on the deck.

She cast one final look at the water and threw herself down next to Jamie. 'Hey.' She reached for his hand, squeezing it gently. 'How are you doing?'

'Stella,' he said, opening his eyes. He was still shaking but the silver thermal blanket seemed to be helping. His fingers were purple and there were dark shadows underneath his eyes, but he already seemed stronger and more focused. More Jamie-like.

'You came,' Jamie said, wonder in his voice.

'Of course I did, you stupid bastard,' Stella kissed his frozen cheek, pressing her face against his.

She wrapped her arms around him and the silver blanket, pressing herself against him to transfer body heat. She was shaking, too, and the deck was cold and hard, but the relief was flooding through her body, making her feel invincible and strong.

They had found Jamie. They were bringing him home.

❧

Back on dry land, Stewart drove them to the hospital. 'No sense in tying up an ambo,' he said. He produced dry coats from the boot and piled them on top of Jamie on the back seat and, with the car heater blasting, took them carefully to hospital.

Once Jamie had been checked over and pronounced fit enough to go home, Stewart drove them back to Munro House. He gave Stella his phone while he was driving and asked her to read any text messages that came through. They were almost back to Arisaig when one came through from Doug. *No sign of Rob. CG out. Still looking.*

'CG?' Jamie said.

'Coastguard,' Stewart said, his eyes firmly on the road ahead.

There was a silence in which nobody pointed out that it had been three hours since Rob went into the water. It was no longer a rescue mission.

'Do you want coffee?' Stella offered hospitality because she found that she couldn't find the right words to convey her feelings. How did you say 'thank you for saving a life?' The life of the man she loved with every atom of her being, every beat of her fragile heart.

'I'll head off,' Stewart said. 'You two get some rest.'

'How can I repay you?' Jamie said, offering his hand for Stewart to shake.

Stella stiffened, willing Jamie not to offer money to Stewart and offend him. 'It was kind of you to come looking,' Jamie was saying, 'and bloody useful, as it happened.'

That was taking stoic understatement to a new level, Stella thought.

'I will never be able to thank you enough,' Stella said, feeling her eyes fill up.

Stewart looked away, his cheeks flushing. 'Nae bother, hen.' To Jamie he said, 'Buy me a pint. And make sure you tell folk where you're going next time.'

'You don't drink,' Stella said, pulling Stewart into a tight hug.

'Sticky toffee pudding, then,' Stewart said, dropping a quick kiss onto the crown of her head. 'With extra cream.'

She waved to Stewart from the door, closed it and turned to face Jamie. He was wearing the dry clothes they had given him at the hospital and one of Stewart's spare coats. She had meant to tell him to get changed into something comfortable, but all her worry morphed into sudden fury. 'How could you go off like that? With Rob! Without leaving details with anyone.'

She couldn't say the words she really meant. *You nearly died. Rob tried to kill you. I almost lost you.*

Jamie enveloped her in a hug. Stella stood stiffly in his arms, unable to relax.

'I'm sorry I frightened you.' He spoke into the top of her head.

Esmé appeared on the stairs. 'I thought I heard you,' she said, her voice as dry as always. 'Glad you're back safely.'

'I'm fine,' Jamie said and Stella stepped away, suddenly aware that she was about to start sobbing.

She left Esmé and Jamie and went into the kitchen and made tea, blinking rapidly and taking deep breaths. If she started crying, she felt as if she wouldn't stop. The adrenaline had ebbed away, and every muscle in her body ached and her limbs were heavy. Every so often, a little jolt of electric fear would spark, as if her mind hadn't quite accepted that she was no longer on a boat in a storm. As if she could not quite accept that she was home, safe, and that Jamie was in the living room chatting to Esmé.

Stella put her hand to her chest, expecting to feel her heart racing, but it wasn't. Then it hit her; she hadn't felt her heart while on the boat, either. She had been too worried to feel faint. And apart from the sea-sickness, she had felt perfectly strong throughout. The thought stopped her in her tracks and she hesitated, one hand on the handle of the kettle.

Esmé came into the kitchen and got a chopping board out. 'I'm making soup,' she said. 'It seems like the right thing to do.'

Her appearance released Stella and she finished making the tea. She patted Esmé's shoulder and put a mug of tea on the worktop next to a growing pile of chopped carrots. Then she carried through two mugs of tea and found Jamie sat in the living room, warming himself by the wood burner.

Stella put the tea carefully down on a side table before asking, in as calm and measured a tone as she could manage: 'What the hell were you doing?'

'I wanted to see where it happened.'

'Why?' Stella couldn't imagine what seeing a stretch of water could do.

'He said it would help me understand, that I had to see it.'

'That doesn't make sense,' Stella said. 'You must have known he was—' Stella had been going to say 'dangerous'. Her old friend. The man who was now at the bottom of the dark, cold water. She swallowed hard.

'I wanted to know about my dad. He said he'd talk to me but only if I went with him.' Jamie put his head in his hands, pushing up his still-damp hair into little wings. 'It was stupid,' he said, the words muffled.

'Did it help?' Stella said, sitting next to him on the sofa. At the hospital, Jamie had told her that Rob had shown her the place his dad's boat had gone down, and when he was turned away, looking out to sea and trying to have a moment of contemplation, that was when Rob had first pushed him, trying to catch him off guard.

'Mebbe.' Jamie was looking into the flames of the wood burner. 'Hearing about it in situ certainly made it more real.'

'Was it not real before?'

He shook his head. 'I had been away at school for years, this place was always just a holiday spot. Somewhere temporary. And we weren't a close family. I was sad when it happened, of course, but I never felt I had been sad enough. I mean, they were my parents. I should have been devastated.'

'But you weren't?'

'I didn't think so. With hindsight it's when I got really busy, though. Really focused.'

'Is it when you started experimenting with your own health?'

'Yeah.' Jamie looked at her. 'I didn't connect the two at the time. I really didn't.'

'Grief is weird.' Stella thought about how her grief had sent her north, to this place. To Jamie.

'I think it's time I spoke to Esmé. Properly.' He straightened his shoulders.

There was a light knock on the door and Esmé appeared, carrying her tea, Tabitha following her like a shadow. She sat on the armchair facing the sofa and Tabitha laid her head on her lap. 'What?' Esmé said, looking from face to face. 'What's wrong?'

'I'll leave you to it,' Stella said, not wanting to intrude.

Jamie caught her hand. 'Stay. Please.' To Esmé he said, 'I want to talk about the accident.'

Esmé put down her mug. 'What do you want to know?'

'Why did Mum go out on the boat with Dad? She hated the water.'

Esmé pursed her lips. 'I don't know.'

Jamie looked down for a moment. Then he said quietly, 'I think you do.'

'What good will it do? Raking over old ground never turns up anything worth the trouble.'

'Do you remember when I stole pennies from your purse and you skelped me?'

'Aye,' Esmé said, looking wary.

'You said that I had to set a good example, that I was privileged and that meant I had to be more hard-working, more moral, more honest than anybody else. Why did you say that?'

'You were a wee toerag, I was just trying to bring you in line.'

Jamie didn't say anything, he just looked into Esmé's face until she looked down, sighing. 'Fine,' she said. 'Your dad made your mum go out on the boat that day. He told her that it was the least she could do after everything.'

'After everything? What did he mean?'

Esmé's lips went thin. She shook her head.

'Please,' Jamie said. 'I just want the truth.'

'Your mum was stepping out with another man.' Esmé spoke quietly.

'What?'

'He deserved it, to be fair. Wasn't exactly a choirboy himself.'

'I heard that he was violent.'

Esmé nodded. 'He could be.'

'Did he hit Mum?'

Stella's heart contracted at the misery in Jamie's voice.

'No!' Esmé said. 'Well. Mebbe once. I can't be sure. They did get physical when they fought, sometimes. Smashed plates and that kind of thing. I don't think he ever struck her, but it's not like I was with them for every minute of every day.' Esmé shook her head, thinking. 'Your mum had a terrific temper of her own and they used to really go for it. I'm surprised you don't remember.'

'I remember Dad shouting. Things crashing. I assumed it was more him than her.'

'Aye, well. There's never any excuse for raising a hand to a woman, right enough, but I don't think he did. She scratched his face plenty of times, sore provoked him. Sometimes they would wrestle, like a couple of kids. That often turned into something else, though.' Esmé went pink. 'It was no way to behave out of the bedroom.'

'What about her wearing shades to hide the bruises?' Stella hadn't meant to speak, but the words were out.

'Where did you get that?' Esmé said, surprised. She shook her head. 'She wore sunglasses when she'd had too much to drink. Which was quite often.'

Stella felt her heart lift. It was still awful, of course, but not as simple or horrifying as the image of mother and son being terrorised by a monstrous father.

She peered at Jamie, trying to gauge how he was feeling. His face was serious, and he was intently focused on Esmé. He looked the way he did when he was trying to understand the data in a meta-study on increasing human growth hormone, or the chemical reactions brought on by ketosis.

'So he was angry about her affair?'

'I suppose,' Esmé said. 'He was angry about everything at that time. He wasn't a very happy man, you know.' She pursed her lips. 'He wasn't very discreet, caused no end of bother for different folk. Just didn't seem to care.'

Jamie nodded. 'Why do you think he wanted her to go with him?'

'I've thought about it over the years, gone over every detail, and I honestly don't know. I swear I'm not keeping anything from you,' Esmé said. 'I think they just got like that. They couldn't stand each other, but they couldn't stand to be apart, either. They were joined and no matter how much they pulled, something stuck them in place.'

'I don't remember that,' Jamie said. 'I remember them in different parts of the house. Sitting in the audience at my school events, but not speaking to each other. I always thought they had grown indifferent to each other.'

'Never that,' Esmé said. 'When your mum was running around with Fraser Baird it was only to get back at your dad.'

'Fraser Baird?' Stella said.

Esmé nodded. 'Your friend's father. He left his wife and son, probably for the best, although no doubt it didn't seem like it at the time.'

'You didn't say anything.'

'It's nobody's business,' Esmé said. 'Why should I?'

'Did Fraser come to the house?' Stella said. Jamie looked at her in surprise, but she carried on. 'Did he and James fight?'

Esmé's eyes slid to the left. 'I don't think so.'

'Fraser left his wife and his son and was never heard from again.' Stella watched Esmé carefully. 'Rob started to wonder whether he ever really left Arisaig.'

Jamie looked at Stella with wide eyes. 'What are you saying?'

'There's a reason Rob hates your family,' Stella said, 'and it's not just that they were all playing creepy seventies wife-swap.'

Over the next week, Esmé kept mostly to her room. Coming into the kitchen only when it was empty to make vats of soup, bake bread and scones, and to leave roast dinners warming in the oven.

Stella saw it was a way to take care of Jamie without having to speak to him, and while part of her wanted to lock Esmé and Jamie in a room until they had talked everything through properly and openly, she recognised that they had maintained a close and loving relationship for many years, and so perhaps the situation didn't need her meddling. Besides which, Esmé was still mostly terrifying.

Stella and Jamie spent hours together in her office. Jamie sat at the computer transcribing while Stella read him Jessie Lockhart's letters and they discussed the book that would come from them.

'I don't want to just write about the court case, the scandal,' Jamie said, 'I want to show the human side to the experiments. And the good that can come from them, even if the people suffered. Even if they didn't make it through themselves.'

There was no news of Rob and, after two days, the coastguard called off the search. Rob's remains would wash up eventually, perhaps on a distant shore where nobody knew him, or perhaps as close as Mallaig or Oban.

Stella spoke to Stewart for an update on Caitlin, uncertain as to whether she would want a visit. She felt as if she ought to offer to help arrange his funeral and all the things a friend should, but she felt awkward as well as inexplicably guilty. 'Survivor's guilt,' Stewart said. 'You're still in shock.'

On the Friday, the doorbell rang, sending the dogs into fits of excitement. Stella shushed them and was pleased when they obeyed. Caitlin was stood on the steps, a vision of glowing health at odds with her tragic expression.

Stella didn't think, she just stepped forward and wrapped her arms around Caitlin, hugging her as tightly as she could with the enormous shape of her pregnancy pushing between them. 'I'm so sorry,' Stella whispered into her ear. 'I'm so sorry for your loss.'

They were both crying, the cold stinging the salt water on Stella's cheeks, when Esmé's voice cut through the sniffing and nose-blowing. 'Come in if you're coming, you're letting the heat out.'

'Is that okay?' Caitlin said, worry etched across her face.

Stella took her hand. 'Of course. You are always welcome here.'

Inside, Stella helped Caitlin take off her boots and Esmé led them into the kitchen. 'I've a lemon loaf cooling and we've fruit tea if you're off the proper stuff.'

Tabitha pressed against Caitlin, laying her head in her lap as soon as she sat down.

Jamie walked in saying, 'Can I smell cake?' but he stopped speaking when he saw Caitlin.

After a beat he bent down and gave Caitlin a brief shoulder-hug. 'I'm so sorry. How are you holding up?'

Caitlin shook her head, unable to speak.

'Is there anything we can do?' Stella said. 'Do you need help arranging anything?'

'I wasn't sure . . .' Caitlin began. 'I don't know how to say sorry.' She took a shuddering breath and then spoke in a rush. 'Esmé, that fruit cake that Rob brought. I swear I didn't know, but I should have realised how bad things were. And, Jamie, I'm sorry. I did know that Rob wanted to get in here, to dig up dirt—'

'Words,' Esmé said dismissively. 'You can make it up to me over time. I want to see that bairn when it arrives, for starters. Don't know when I'm going to get grandchildren of my own.' She looked significantly at Jamie as she said this and Stella winced, but he just grinned back at her.

'But what he did,' Caitlin said. 'What he tried to do. I can't—'

'It's not your fault, hen,' Jamie said.

'You really didn't know about the vitamins in the cake?' Stella said, needing to see Caitlin's face when she answered.

'No,' Caitlin said immediately. She looked sick. 'When I think what could have happened. Any of you could have . . .'

'Died,' Stella said. 'It's hard to wrap my mind around. I mean, Rob . . . I can't really believe it, it seems so extreme.'

'I know,' Caitlin said, her eyes filling with tears again.

Esmé was banging the cups around, clearly uncomfortable with the emotions on display.

'When are you due?' Esmé said, putting tea in front of Caitlin and signalling a change of subject with firm determination. She and Caitlin began to discuss the wobbly science of due dates.

Jamie grabbed a green smoothie from the fridge and went back to work, and Stella leaned back in her chair and enjoyed the warmth of the tea and Angus lying across her feet.

She closed her eyes while she listened to Caitlin and Esmé talking about baby equipment and the local maternity ward and wondered how, given everything that had happened, it was possible to feel so safe and so happy.

Once Caitlin had gone home and Esmé was in the kitchen, doing yet more baking, Jamie put his head around the door. 'Fancy a walk?'

The rain had stopped and there was a gleam of winter sunshine illuminating the clouds, so Stella nodded. Outside, the cold took her breath away, but within a few moments she had warmed up and was glad to be out in the salt-edged air. She felt strong and steady and grateful all at once.

Jamie and Stella walked along the shore in silence. It didn't feel awkward, more like a mutual agreement not to start talking yet. They passed the cliff overhang at the edge of the bay with the makeshift stone hearth and the blackened ground of a hundred campfires, and made their way over the rocks until they began to get bigger and more jagged and they were using their hands to steady themselves. Stella climbed the rock she had sat on all those weeks ago. She couldn't believe it had only been weeks; it felt like years.

Jamie took another route and got to the top before her. At once, he was above her, holding out a hand.

Settled on the flat surface, facing across the water, Stella pulled in great lungfuls of the cool air. The sea and the sky stretched out forever with no boundary, wide open. Stella tilted her face to feel the touch of the sun on her face.

Jamie finally spoke. 'Nathan has gone home. He's not too thrilled with me right now.'

Stella shot an amused glance at him. 'That's what you want to talk about?'

Jamie shrugged and so Stella told him about the postcard Nathan had left on her desk.

It had a picture of a Highland cow on one side, to which Nathan had drawn a speech bubble with the words 'my bad'. Stella got the impression that he didn't often apologise, so she took it as a sign of acceptance. The emailed John Lewis voucher helped, too.

'I don't like Ben,' Jamie said abruptly.

'You don't have to like him,' Stella said. She had been waiting for Jamie to say something about Ben's visit, knowing that the subsequent events had overshadowed it but also feeling worried that it didn't seem to have registered on his radar. And then she'd worried about what that said about his feelings for her.

'You said it was over.'

'It is,' Stella said.

Jamie didn't look at her and Stella could see the muscle in his cheek tense. He had let his stubble grow out again until it was thick, almost a beard. His skin was red from the cold wind and she wanted to reach out a hand and cup his cheek.

'Why did he come here?' He stopped, shook his head. 'I guess my real question is how you feel about him coming here.'

'You know when you brush your teeth and you think your teeth are really clean and then you floss and you find all these bits?' Stella didn't know why this image had popped into her mind and she wished it

321

hadn't, but she ploughed on. 'It's like that. I thought he was all cleaned out, but there are just some last little bits left. To spit out.'

'I use a water pick,' Jamie said.

'I know.'

'Blasts everything in one go.'

'Yeah, well. You're efficient. Do you want a medal?'

The quickest of smiles and then his jaw tightened again. 'I just want to know.'

'I've told you. What else can I say?'

'Do you still love him?'

'No.' The word came quickly. Stella looked across the sea to the islands, remembering this view, this place, and the mobile phone in her hand. She had wanted to throw it out into the water then. She had let Ben go at that moment, but it had taken these weeks and all that had happened since for the process to complete. You couldn't just blast a person from your life in one go.

'I know he'll always be important to you.'

'Who knows,' Stella said. 'Time is strange. I always thought time was running out, but I feel like I've had more of it in the past few months than I've had in the previous ten years. I don't know anything about the word "always" or how I will feel in a year or next month.' This wasn't sounding as reassuring as she had planned. 'I just know how I feel today, right now.'

Jamie looked at her then, his eyes on Stella's. Pale green-blue and fringed with golden eyelashes. The chicken pox scar above his left eyebrow and the lines which creased the corners of his eyes. 'You don't have to tell me,' he said.

'I want to be with you,' Stella said. 'I would like to stay here, but I'll go where you go. If you want me to.'

'I do,' Jamie said.

'Good.'

He put an arm around her shoulder and she moved close, leaning against him and wishing they didn't have so many layers of clothes, that she could feel more of his body against hers.

'I don't just want you, though,' Jamie said, squinting as the winter sun moved from behind a cloud and pierced the water with silver spikes.

Stella's heart seemed to pause in the middle of a beat, the systole waiting for the answering release of the diastole.

'I love you. There's a difference.'

ACKNOWLEDGMENTS

When I'm working on a book it seems impossible that it will ever be done and, despite my best intentions, I forget to make a note of all the people I will need to thank on this page. Which is to say a pre-emptive 'sorry' to the folk I will undoubtedly forget to name. I hope you know that my gratitude is not dimmed by my poor organisational skills.

Books are never easy, but this one refused to come together for what felt like a very long time. Huge thanks to Agent Fabulous, Sallyanne Sweeney, for helping me to shape my ideas and for encouraging me to stick with it, and to Sammia Hamer at Lake Union for her patience and enthusiasm. Thank you to Victoria and the rest of the Lake Union team for all your help in bringing this book into the world. I am a very lucky author.

To my brilliant bookish friends on Twitter and Facebook – thank you for keeping me company when I am taking a 'quick' writing break – and extra hugs to Keris Stainton and Clodagh Murphy for writerly support.

I don't intend to list all of the books and sources I used while researching the historical strand of this novel, but I must mention *Simpson the Obstetrician* by Myrtle Simpson, which helped to give me a good flavour of the fine Edinburgh doctor James Young Simpson.

My heartfelt gratitude goes to all who work in medicine and health-care, and those who dedicate their lives to medical research, with a special mention for the cardiac department at the Heath Hospital, Cardiff. Like Stella, I would not be alive today if it were not for their efforts.

Thank you to all my friends and family for being understanding, supportive and loving, especially when I have been stressed and distracted. Emma, thank you so much for your positivity and kindness; Lucy, for letting me whinge and for plying me with wine; and Cath, for being my partner-in-crime for almost thirty years. Blimey!

A massive thank you to my wonderful children, Holly and James, for their loving support and for inspiring me with their hard work and brilliance.

And finally, as always, thank you to my Dave for everything; this book would not exist without you. I am grateful every single day for your love and support. I love you more.

ABOUT THE AUTHOR

Sarah Painter writes novels which sometimes have historical elements or touches of magic, but always have an emotional core. Her debut novel, *The Language of Spells*, became a Kindle bestseller and was followed by a sequel, *The Secrets of Ghosts*. Her last book, *In the Light of What We See,* was also a bestseller and a Kindle First pick. Sarah lives in rural Scotland with her children, husband, and a grey tabby called Zelda Kitzgerald. She drinks too much tea, loves the work of Joss Whedon, and is the proud owner of a writing shed.

Printed in Great Britain
by Amazon

21303136R00192